To ‌

THE DEVIL'S
CROWN

Time to adjust
Your crown.

Mon ♡

Time to adjust

THE DEVIL'S CROWN

A DARK ROMANCE

International Bestselling Author
MONICA JAMES

Cover Design: Perfect Pear Creative Covers
Cover Model: Philippe Leblond
Photographer: Ren Saliba
Editing: Editing 4 Indies
Formatting: E.M. Tippetts Book Designs

Follow me on:

authormonicajames.com

OTHER BOOKS BY
MONICA JAMES

ALL THE PRETTY THINGS TRILOGY

Bad Saint

Fallen Saint

Forever My Saint

The Devil's Crown - Part One (Spin-Off)

THE MONSTERS WITHIN DUET

Bullseye

Blowback

STANDALONE

Mr. Write

Chase the Butterflies

AUTHOR'S NOTE

CONTENT WARNING: *THE DEVIL'S CROWN* is divided into two parts. It's a spin-off, but I recommend you read **ALL THE PRETTY THINGS TRILOGY** before starting this book. Part Two will release shortly after Part One. This is a continuing story, therefore, not all questions will be answered in Part One. If you don't like cliff-hangers, you best turn back now.

THE DEVIL'S CROWN is a DARK ROMANCE containing mature themes that might make some readers uncomfortable. It includes strong violence, possible triggers, and some dark and disturbing scenes.

This twisted tale is not intended for the fainthearted. So, if you're game…welcome to the madness.

God save your soul.

DEDICATION

This is for my ангел's who begged for more.
Alek loves it when you beg…

CHAPTER ONE

I hope it's just as pretty where you are...
W x

Looking out the tinted window of my black SUV, I thumb over the corner of the tattered postcard. "I wish it was... дорогая."

Speaking that name almost feels blasphemous as I haven't allowed myself to think of her often. But beneath this expensive suit, this cold-blooded stare, lies a broken man, something I never considered myself capable of.

I've endured the consequences of the many choices I've made throughout my life. But when *she* made a choice, when she chose the better man and ripped out my heart, those consequences weren't so easily accepted.

Someone who was meant to be my prisoner, in turn, made me hers.

As I focus on the postcard's picturesque landscape, it seems Willow and Saint are lost in paradise. The postmark says it was sent from somewhere off the coast of Italy, but I know Saint—he doesn't leave tracks.

That bastard was a thorn in my side, but now that he's gone, I realize what he was, and that was a friend. In light of our circumstances, I understand how ridiculous that sounds, but I respected him, and in his own way, I think he respected me.

But none of that matters because they're in the past.

Eighteen months have passed, and although it feels like only yesterday when I laid my eyes on a woman who set my entire world on fire, it's not.

Things have changed.

I have changed.

I carefully fold the postcard in half as the worn crease threatens to tear if I don't handle it with care. This is the only thing I have left of Willow, and unlike when she was with me, I will keep it safe.

A tap on my window reminds me that I am obsessing over a postcard like a lovestruck дурак. Quickly placing it into my inner jacket pocket, I open the door and greet Pavel. He's the closest thing I have to a friend even though I know when he looks at me, he's reminded of everything I've done.

"Ready?" Pavel asks, scoping out our surroundings.

This deserted neighborhood is no stranger to illegal dealings, which is why I chose this location. A tortured scream and a gunshot ringing out in the dead of night aren't uncommon occurrences.

Once upon a time, I ruled this city, but now, I'm forced to hide in the shadows. My past has made me hated by all. The good, the bad, and the in-betweens all want me dead. I've been labeled a traitor, and that's because I am.

I happily sacrificed the lives of my "friends" because their spilled blood granted her freedom. Everyone can hate me, and I don't care. I only seek forgiveness from one person. But it'll never come.

Pushing such sentiments aside, I focus on the task at hand and what's important—violence and vengeance.

My Glocks sit snugly in my shoulder holster as I'm now the one responsible for taking out the trash. But honestly, I like it. It's the only time I feel like I'm in control once again. Stepping from the SUV, I button my suit jacket and reach into my pocket for a Cuban cigar. This calls for a celebration, after all.

I was knocked from my throne, and I won't lie, I don't like sitting at the bottom of the food chain, especially when the new "king" of this town is a worthless son of a bitch.

Cupping my cigar, I light it slowly, savoring the tobacco hit. It's the simple things in life that give me great pleasure—a neat scotch, a good Cuban, and slitting my half-brother's throat.

That night, eighteen months ago, we all lost something. Lives were lost as was love. As I can't do anything to rectify the deaths of Ingrid, Zoey, and Sara, I live with their deaths on my conscience every single day.

But the only way I can ensure their deaths aren't in vain is to find Serg Ivanov and deliver him the same fate. I killed his father, my stepfather, and I plan on doing the same thing to him. Twirling my pinkie ring, the one which once belonged to Boris Ivanov, gives me great pleasure knowing that tonight brings me one step closer to achieving this.

Pavel and I commence a casual stroll toward the abandoned warehouse. Even if someone is watching, no one will dare get involved. Pavel reaches for his gun the moment we enter through the back door. I, however, continue smoking my cigar. It's all about the simple pleasures, remember?

It's a warm night, and the sun has just set. There is an electrical pulse thrumming. It's an evening when magic can happen, and what I see before me only accentuates the feeling.

A string of incoherent mumbles fills the air, and even though I can't make out what he's saying, it's safe to assume Viktor Belov is one unhappy boy. I mean, he *is* tied to a chair in the middle of a rat-infested warehouse.

Stopping several feet away, I peer down at him, continuing to puff on my cigar leisurely. The calmer I am, the more irate he becomes. See, I told you I'm a simple man.

As Viktor is Serg's right-hand man, I plan to take his right hand as punishment. Pavel's patience is wearing thin, however, and he storms over to Viktor, ripping out his gag.

Viktor moves his jaw from side to side. "скотина!"

I reply by blowing out a ring of smoke high in the air.

"You are nothing." He spits, wishing me to know what he thinks of me. All this does is cement my decision to cut out his tongue. "I'm not telling you anything. You may as well kill me now."

As he continues to ramble, I look down at my Rolex. At

this rate, I'm going to be late, so I decide to get this show on the road. With my cigar between my lips, I reach into my shoulder holster and am overwhelmed by a shiver when I come into contact with the cool metal.

"Hello, Viktor. How's your mother?" I ask casually, producing my gun.

Viktor isn't surprised I'm carrying, but rather, that I'm asking how his dear old mother is. "If you're trying to blackmail me into talking, then you'll need to try another tactic, Мудак!"

Tsking him, I take a draw of my cigar with my left hand. My right is busy with my gun trained on him. "You kiss your mother with that mouth? I must pay her a visit and inform her of your insolence. I fear she'd be most disappointed."

He scoffs, incredulous, but when I rattle off her address, he realizes I'm not playing.

"So this will go one of two ways. You tell me where that piece of shit is, and I kill you. Or you tell me where that piece of shit is, and I kill you. The choice is yours," I offer with a smirk because there isn't a choice.

His fate is decided. And I'm fine with that.

He struggles against his restraints, grunting in anger. "Your brother—"

"Half-brother," I correct, curling my lip in disgust.

"He is the new king of this town. You are a joke."

Oh, this waste of space is really testing my time and now, my patience. "We're going to have to agree to disagree because he wishes he were a king. He's merely a scared little boy, hiding behind his mother's skirt."

His mother, Zoya—who is sadly also mine—is the reason he was able to infiltrate my empire and ensure it came crashing to the ground. So it goes without saying that she must also pay for her crimes. She made her choice—we all did—and now, it's time we deal with the aftermath.

Viktor isn't going to talk, but that's okay. We all have our weaknesses. And I plan to exploit his. "Your loyalty to a bottom-feeder will get you and your family killed."

He bursts into laughter. "Please, you'd be doing me a favor. I'd pay you to kill my свинья of a wife. And I doubt those kids are even mine. So if this is your grand plan, you lose—again. The feared Aleksei Popov is nothing but yesterday's news."

Pavel yawns beside me.

Tsking Viktor, I decide to put an end to his theatrics because I have someplace to be. "You know what separates me from Serg? I earned my place by adapting to my environment. That's what a victorious leader does.

"I ensured I knew every single thing about my enemies because when the time came, I would use this for my gain. Like right now."

Walking toward Viktor, I smoke my cigar casually. "It appears you've been a very busy boy, going back and forth between your wife and mistress. I don't know how you can keep up."

I take great pleasure in seeing him pale.

"Why don't you just divorce her?" I ask. Even though I know the answer, I just want to see him squirm.

Before he has a chance to reply, I tap my forehead as if I'm struck with an epiphany. "Maybe it's because your beloved is married herself? What do you think would happen if her husband knew the son he loves so much is actually yours?"

Viktor stops struggling. We all have a price. And I've just found his.

"You bastard," he snarls while I shrug offhandedly.

"Just like your son."

"You wouldn't hurt them," he says, but the small quiver to his tone reveals his doubt.

"You're right, I wouldn't," I reply with a nod. "All you need to do is tell me what I want."

"I tell you that, and you kill me anyway!" he yells, spittle coating his chin. "I'm fucked either way."

Desperation reveals a man's true colors. If he cowers in the face of fear, then you know if you prod hard enough, he'll eventually budge. Viktor is the perfect example of this.

"Yes, your fate is already decided. But for once in your miserable existence, you can do something right and save someone's life; not take it away."

I know Viktor's secrets. He wasn't selected by Serg for his physical prowess. He's a cold-blooded killer, and no one is off-limits. This isn't an excuse as to why I will feel nothing for ending him. He's a bad man. But I suppose, so am I.

When Viktor shakes his head firmly, sealing his lips shut, I decide he needs a little encouragement. Taking one last pull of my cigar, I savor the hit as I hate to waste it, but...

Without hesitation, I press the scalding end into Viktor's cheek, appreciating his cries for mercy and the smell of burning flesh. He seems to forget he's tied to a chair as he desperately struggles to pull away.

"Where is Serg?" I ask calmly, forcing the cigar deeper into his cheek. His flesh bubbles under the heat, and a small part of me yells that he's had enough. I realize that part only exists because of Willow. What would she say if she were here?

But she's not. She made her choice. And I've made mine.

Being vulnerable is for the weak; something I will never be again. I am where I am because I tried this humanity suit on for size, but guess what? It doesn't fit. I'd much rather this suit of armor because its impenetrable walls protect me from this disgusting thing they call love.

"Okay! He, he…" Viktor's spluttering reminds me of the task at hand as I'd forgotten I currently had a burning ember pressed to his cheek. "He moves around a lot. He knows being at one location will get him killed."

I decide to remove the cigar before there isn't any flesh left to burn.

Viktor whimpers in relief when I toss it to the ground, but that is short-lived when I press the muzzle of my gun to his temple. "He has to have a base. I want to know where that is. I also want to know where Raul is."

Raul is Chow's son—the double-crossing asshole I killed because he was selling his product to both Serg and me. Since I'm out of the game, there is no competition, so people have no choice but to do business with a bottom-feeder like Serg. But that's about to change. Just as he did to me, I'm going to bring down his empire and claim back what is rightfully mine.

If this were most, they'd be thankful they were still alive. But not me. All I feel is this burning desire to make those who took from me pay. Me being alive highlights the error of my ways. I was too soft, too blinded by something that will never be mine—and that's a happily ever after.

I hate to disappoint you, but if you're looking for a story with a hero, then you best turn back now. This is the point of no return.

Once upon a time, I thought that maybe I could do this thing, this living a "normal" life. The devil lay dormant for a while, humoring me because he knew we were cut from the same cloth, and sooner or later, I would need to feed the darkness inside me. Mayhem, power, and control are what course through my veins and what made me a victorious leader.

And now, I want my fucking crown back.

"пожалуйста," Viktor begs, eyes wide. "Let me go. You'll never see me again."

"Stop begging," I spit in disgust. "It's quite unbecoming." It seems Viktor needs an incentive to loosen his tongue.

Pavel reaches into his jacket pocket and produces a remote control. Viktor's eyes widen. It's the type of remote you'd see in a movie to make the high power explosives go *BOOM*. Pavel is known for his love of explosives, so Viktor knows what this is.

"You have three seconds, three *fucking* seconds to tell me what I want. Otherwise, you'll be scraping what's left of your loved ones off the walls." This isn't a threat. It's a promise. "Tell me why this city is dealing with this lowlife. He is a nobody. How has he gained the trust of all?"

He was able to worm his way into my kingdom on the merit of my mother. But unless she's fucking half of Russia, there is a reason he has climbed the food chain and is sitting pretty on top of it. He is where I was, and I need to know how he got there. I didn't become the most powerful, most feared man in Russia overnight. But Serg has, and there is a reason for it.

When Viktor remains mute, my last tether snaps. "Pavel," I order with a flick of my chin.

Viktor shakes his head wildly. "Okay! Okay!" he shrieks, his eyes begging Pavel not to push the button. "If I tell you, promise me you'll look after my family."

"Which one?" I ask, unmoved.

He understands this for the simple transaction it is. He tells me what I want, and I kill him quickly in return. "He is… making a name off you."

I blink once, stunned, but I keep my emotion hidden. "What?"

"He has gained the respect of all because he neutered the feared Aleksei Popov. You are nothing because of him. You may as well have died with your friends."

And there it is, the truth, glaring me in the face.

Serg has piggybacked his way to the top using my name while I'm forced to hide in the shadows as nothing but a leper.

I'm not totally ruined, thanks to Pavel and his connections. It seems he has allies all over the world who trust his knowledge in stolen ammunition and high power explosives. I am now his lackey, as he is the one calling the shots. But a trusted man in this business is hard to find, so we need one another.

"долбоёб!" I curse, angered that this little prick is still breathing. "I am going to take great pleasure in seeing him bleed."

Inhaling, I center myself.

"Where is he?" This is his final chance to speak. If he doesn't, I will cut out his tongue and feed it to him.

Viktor hangs his head in defeat. "He's hiding out in a small farming village with your mother. The coordinates are..."

As he rattles off the location, I raise my face toward the ceiling and take a moment to savor this. I haven't felt a victory in so long. This is just one step closer to regaining my life.

Once Viktor has given Pavel the directions to find my beloved family, I meet his eyes and see nothing but fear reflected in them. I suddenly begin to grapple with my conscience. He has given me what I wanted, so really, there is no need to kill him.

"I gave you what you wanted," Viktor pleads, in tune with my thoughts. "Let me go. Please don't kill me."

But letting him go shows weakness. He won't appreciate my leniency. It will just confirm what everyone thinks of me. Aleksei Popov lost his nerve all because he fell in love. And I did. I fell deeply and irrevocably in love, and it's because of this that I cock my gun and pull the trigger without remorse.

Blood and brain matter coat my face and white shirt, but I stand tall, calmly examining the mess I've made. A trickle of blood oozes from Viktor's mouth as his chin sags to his chest. There is no doubt he's dead.

Pavel steps forward, but I grip his forearm. "This is my mess. I'll take care of it."

A lifetime ago, I had an army at my disposal who would have been more than happy to clean up after me. But it turns out, I don't mind getting my hands dirty. So I suppose Viktor is right. On the night my friends died, I died too.

I was once feared, respected among this land for being ruthless and cruel. But they haven't seen anything yet. Love hurts, and now, it's my turn to hurt love.

Viktor is buried in a shallow grave with no marker left to commemorate his resting place.

I brought a change of clothes, knowing I couldn't go to the orphanage covered in blood. Looking at my reflection in the visor mirror, I hardly recognize myself. My brown hair has grown longer. I can now tie it back if I want, and I quite like it this way. My stubble is heavy. The usual steel blue color of my eyes is now permanently bloodshot thanks to sleep evading me most nights.

Straightening my tie, I know that regardless of this fancy suit, Mother Superior will see through the smoke and mirrors. She always does.

Stepping from my SUV, I do a quick sweep of the orphanage grounds. This is my safe place in more ways than one. But I can never be too sure, which is why I'm carrying two guns beneath this jacket.

Locking my vehicle, I sprint toward the back door. I'm late thanks to Viktor. But the moment I step into the orphanage, I suppress those thoughts because it seems almost blasphemous to think about him in this place of worship.

"You're late," Sister Margaret whispers, ushering me

inside quickly.

"I know, sorry," I apologize, thankful she was able to sneak me in through the back door. "Has Mother Superior noticed?"

Sister Margaret looks down her nose at me. Of course, she has. Nothing slips past her. "Come."

We scurry down the hallway toward the dining hall where tonight's celebrations are being held. Thankfully, the beautifully decorated room is packed full of guests, so no one notices me as I snare a glass of grape juice from a waiter's tray and blend in with the crowd.

"This wouldn't be possible without the efforts of many," Mother Superior says from the temporary stage at the front of the room. She seems to scan the room until her attention lands on me. "Our angels don't do it for recognition; they do it because they have a good heart."

I throw back my drink, not wanting acknowledgment. If only she knew where I was an hour ago, she wouldn't be so quick to sing my praises. I robbed four children of their father tonight, and I don't feel a thing.

But I smile, nonetheless.

"Thank you for coming tonight. It means so much to us. Our children are a gift from God, so let us celebrate life and love." Mother Superior's speech is received well as the room applauds her loudly. But she's not interested in praise. She's here because these kids are her life.

Mother Superior is the glue that holds this orphanage together. Yes, I may be behind the money that has helped keep this place afloat over the years, but she has made the orphanage a home for the children and also for me.

God knows she should have thrown me out when I came to her, seeking refuge. But she didn't. If it weren't for her, I don't think I'd be standing here today. She saved Willow and me. And for that, I will be indebted to her for the rest of my life.

"Nice of you to arrive," she says softly, interrupting my thoughts.

"You know I don't like these sorts of things," I reply lightly. What I speak of is this fancy event the orphanage has thrown to attract new investors and hopefully potential people who want to adopt.

The orphanage is at full capacity, but Mother Superior would never turn a child away. I give her what I can. A job Pavel organized was able to help with the vital facelift this place needed, but my funds are running low.

In the past, money wasn't an issue, but now, it is. I live in a shack in the mountains. I tell myself it's because I want to live off the grid to evade my enemies, but honestly, it's all I can afford. I was once surrounded by wealth and riches, but now, I barely have five thousand dollars to my name.

My suit, this Rolex, the Cuban cigars, everything I own, it's all stolen from the men I've killed. To play the part of king, one must dress like royalty. I now understand the saying beggars can't be choosers all too well.

"I know. But you are the reason the orphanage has undergone such changes. You're the reason these children—"

But I hush her gently. "*You* are the reason, Mother Superior. I won't hear of anything else."

She purses her lips, knowing not to argue.

It pains me that she must throw such an event. I hate that it seems she's almost groveling to the rich assholes to throw her a fucking bone. I was once rich. I'm still an asshole, but at least I gave to this place without Mother Superior having to beg.

I know what it's like to be hungry, to be unwanted and have nowhere to call home. If only I had a Mother Superior in my life when I was younger, things may have turned out differently for me. This place is special to me because I can relate to every single child in here.

Clenching my jaw, I realize this is merely temporary. Once I find my half-brother and murder his traitorous ass, the natural order will be restored. Until then, both Mother Superior and I are at the mercy of others.

"Ski! Ski!" screams a lively voice before my leg is ensnared by two small hands.

Peering down, I can't stop my smile. It feels foreign because it's genuine. "Why aren't you in bed?" I playfully scold Irina in Russian.

She responds by poking out her tongue.

Irina has been here for five months. She was left at the orphanage gates with nothing but the rags that hung off her emaciated frame. She was riddled with lice and so malnourished that the doctors originally thought she was four. Upon further examination, they guessed she was somewhere closer to seven.

Her vocabulary is almost nonexistent, so Mother Superior knows almost nothing about Irina. These circumstances have made Irina one of the unfavorable children among potential adopters. She's been returned countless times like some dog at a pound by the do-gooders who thought they could "fix" a troubled child. But they soon realized they weren't cut out for the hard work.

Insufferable quitters.

Irina speaks to no one, bar me. I don't know why, but the moment we met, she took a shining to me. I dare not tell Mother Superior my theory that I probably remind her of the company her family may have kept.

Regardless of the reason, I don't care. Seeing her freckled face and blonde pigtails thaws whatever is left of my deadened heart. Just as I'm about to pry her from my leg and give her a hug, a spark of fire unexpectedly tackles me from behind.

I realize where that fire comes from when I hear a soft voice I've not heard before. It's American. "Irina, how did you get away so fast? I'm so sorry, Mother Superior. I thought she was asleep."

With Irina still attached to my leg, I turn slowly, desperate to seek out the voice of the stranger. However, nothing can prepare me for what I see.

A sister I've not seen before stands a few feet away, wringing her hands in front of her. The habit conceals her hair, but the few strands which have slipped free reveal a deep brown color. Her olive skin and full pink lips seem to emphasize the bright hazel of her eyes.

For the first time in a long time, I'm moved. I don't know how to explain it, but I don't feel so…numb. The sister quickly averts her eyes when I continue to stare at her.

"Aleksei, this is Sister Arabella. She just transferred here from America," Mother Superior reveals.

I simply nod, willing this beautiful woman to meet my eyes again. She is bashful, as her cheeks turn a subtle pink. I've not experienced such innocence since…since I met another American beauty. However, the large silver cross around Sister Arabella's neck is a reminder that she too belongs to someone else—someone else I can never compete with.

Remembering where I am, I clear my throat and stamp down the emotion that has no right being there. "Lovely to meet you, Sister Arabella."

She works her pouty bottom lip before slowly looking up at me from under her long dark lashes. "It's an honor to meet you, Mr. Popov."

I'm surprised she knows who I am. That surprise must show because she quickly explains. "I worked at an orphanage in Savannah. I read all about the recent developments here at the orphanage, so when the opportunity arose to do an exchange, I jumped at the chance. Mother Superior told me you're to thank for a lot of the changes." Her soft voice is smooth like a neat scotch and contains the same burn.

I know I'm staring at her again, but I can't stop. She is absolutely beautiful.

Even though the tunic conceals her body, I can still see that her curves are in all the right places, and I like it. I suddenly wonder what she would look like without it. She looks young, maybe late twenties. An old man like me, almost double her age, could be her father.

Thankfully, Irina is the reminder I need as her sharp little teeth sink into my leg. "Ski! Choo-choo," she demands, not appreciating being ignored.

I completely forgot she was still attached to my leg, which makes me feel like an utter bastard but also, a fool. Here I am, visually undressing a sister with a small child clinging to an appendage. There is so much wrong with this picture.

This woman made a solemn vow and belongs to God. But why does that make her all the more desirable? Her sinful looks are only intensified thanks to her habit. It's given me a peek, but I want so much more.

I know once this life is done with, I'm headed for one place and one place only. But I need to remove myself from this situation because I will not disrespect Mother Superior this way.

"Mother Superior likes to exaggerate," I reply with a smirk, finally finding my voice. "It was nice to meet you, Sister Arabella, but I think it's time I read this little цветочек her bedtime story. Oh, and please, call me Alek."

I go to turn, but Sister Arabella quickly extends her hand. I notice it tremble slightly. To the untrained eye, it would go undetected, but to survive in this world, one must pay close attention to uncover if one is friend or foe.

I have a feeling Sister Arabella will be both.

Not wanting to embarrass her, I slip my hand into hers, but the moment I do, an electrical charge pulses throughout my entire body. I'm the one who's now embarrassed because I can't prevent the low hum that escapes me.

Those magnificent eyes instantly dart to my mouth before her tongue shoots out and quickly sweeps along her bottom lip.

The action catches me by complete surprise because no, it can't be. There is no way. But the small intake of breath and the sweet pink to her cheeks betray her. She felt it too.

Jerking back her hand, she seeks the crucifix hanging from her rosary belt. She clutches it in her palm, eyes downcast, and all I can do is stare at her like an idiot because her innocence and her shame have increased my desire to corrupt her all the more.

I begin to wonder things I shouldn't—the length of her dark hair, the taste of her golden skin, the fullness of her breasts, and if that sweet pussy tastes anything like the dark fruity floral scent I'm currently basking in.

I recognize that smell. Sister Arabella may have given herself to God and renounced the pleasures in life, but it seems her love for expensive perfume is one vice she couldn't sacrifice.

She wears a hint of Hypnotic Poison by Dior—how very appropriate. To the untrained nose, one may mistake the fragrance as nothing but Sister Arabella's natural scent. But to me, it spells H-E-L-L.

Nevertheless, I welcome the burn.

Lifting Irina into my arms, I nod to Mother Superior. I need to get out of here because I refuse to disrespect her in her house. Sister Arabella still won't look at me, but that's okay. Her being a submissive just confirms how utterly screwed I am.

My intentions were good, but who am I kidding? I will always be a sinner.

Walking out of the room and down the hallway toward Irina's room, I suddenly realize that I have no qualms about breaking Sister Arabella's vow. I don't care that she is off-limits because a hunger, a fire has awoken inside me. I want Sister Arabella—in all ways, any way I can. I know what this means, but I already have a date with the devil. It's time I adjusted my crown.

This city will again be mine as I need a kingdom for my queen. The ruthless passion I once wore like a well-tailored suit wraps its hands around my throat, squeezing life into me. I was limping through life without direction, but that has changed.

I found my purpose.

Kill my half-brother.

And ensure there is only one god Sister Arabella will worship before on her knees. And that's me.

A-fucking-men.

CHAPTER TWO

We have to move fast.

Serg will miss Viktor and know something is amiss if he doesn't hear from him, which is why Pavel and I are stalking his house or, more accurately, his shack. The small village is about two hours out of the city. I'm surprised my mother would agree to stay here because it's a dump.

It gives me great pleasure to know they're hiding out here. The power Serg has is temporary, and he knows it. He's running scared, and I intend for everyone to know I'm back. No one neutered me.

It's game on, little brother.

Cracking my neck from side to side, I nurse my fourth or maybe fifth cup of coffee as I haven't been to sleep yet. Once I read Irina her favorite Thomas the Tank Engine story twice, I tucked her in and exited through the back door as quietly as I entered.

Every bone in my body was demanding I seek out Sister Arabella for one last glance, but I can't rush this. I meant it when I said I wouldn't disrespect Mother Superior in her home. But I'm faced with a conundrum. Before Willow, I was accustomed to getting everything I wanted. It was as simple as snapping my fingers, and it was mine.

Looking back now, I see how arrogant and ungracious I was. I thought Willow would be like all the others, but she challenged me, and I didn't realize how much I liked it until I met her. She was my equal on so many levels.

Sister Arabella is another challenge altogether, but the same fire begins to burn as it once did.

It excites me. The chase. The utter wickedness to it. I wouldn't pursue this if I didn't think she felt something too. I don't know what this *something* is, but I can't ignore it.

Now, however, I can't ignore the fact that Pavel and I have been watching this house for what seems like hours. It's evident from the lack of activity inside that the place is empty.

Looking at my watch, I see that it's after three a.m. I doubt Serg is out doing business. Yes, it's the witching hour, but most criminals need their beauty sleep, and operating under the guise of daylight is less suspicious if they get caught.

A cloud of doubt floats over me. Was he tipped off?

Anger courses through me, and I pitch my coffee cup into the bushes next to me. "Fuck this," I curse, storming over to my SUV.

Pavel knows better than to follow.

Reaching into the trunk, I seize two gas cans. One was for Serg. The other for Zoya. It's a shame for them to go to waste.

Yes, I would have preferred to douse the house *and* them with gasoline, but I am done standing around.

"Aleksei!" Pavel scolds when I blow our cover and storm toward the shack. His warning falls on deaf ears.

I almost rip the rusted gate off its hinges when I shove it open. I'm focused on the door, expecting it to open any moment and be confronted with an arsenal, but it doesn't. Charging up the front steps, I kick it open, slamming it into the wall with a thud.

If anyone is inside, I've just made a grand entrance, and it's their turn to make themselves known. But all I hear are my labored breaths echoing in this empty space.

It's dark, but the full moon allows me to see that the interior is just as shitty as the exterior. The weathered walls are a faded lime color, and the floor is missing a few boards. The furniture is sparse, but what is here is old and barely standing.

With gas cans in hand, I climb the creaky stairs cautiously, listening for any sounds. When I reach the door at the end of the hallway, I push it open and peer inside. There is a single bed in the middle of the room, the blankets tossed to the side as if someone jumped out of it in a hurry.

The minimal possessions have me guessing Serg slept here. The cupboard has no doors, so I'm able to see the bare coat hangers. My suspicion continues to mount. There is no way they stayed here without any belongings.

They were definitely tipped off.

Rage swarms me, and I kick the bed frame, it spinning and slamming into the wall. Opening the gas can, I pour gas around the room, ensuring to douse this place good and proper. Even if Serg had anything hidden, he would have taken it by now. This place is just an empty shell.

I'm too late. Again.

With a snarl, I storm from the room, going from bedroom to bedroom and drenching everything with gas. I'm blinded by sheer fury. When I get to the last room, my ragged breathing and thumping heart are deafening, but I will myself to calm down.

This room isn't as bare as the others, and that's because it belongs to my mother.

The double bed has been made in haste, but it shows that even in light of fleeing in the dead of night, Zoya can't help but be a perfectionist. No surprise to why she stuck with Serg. He was the perfect son, after all.

Me? I was a disappointment who killed her only shot at happiness. And I mean that literally. She loved that vermin, Boris Ivanov, which is one of the many reasons I killed him. Any therapist would tell you my rage comes from the unresolved issues I have toward Zoya. All these supressed feelings and all that.

But in reality, I just hate freeloaders.

Zoya could have gotten a job when my father died, but instead, she thought she could win the love of any suitor who had enough zeros in his bank account by welcoming him into her bed. Most disposed of her when they grew bored until she met Boris.

One year was all she needed to forget about the so-called love of her life.

They married, and when she got pregnant with Serg, it

seemed she was about to live her happily ever after. She was so close.

Dropping one of the empty cans on the floor with a thud, I walk over to the foot of the bed and slump onto the end of it. I place the other can beside my feet and take a moment to look around the bedroom.

It's been so long since I've been in the vicinity of my mother that she almost feels like a mythical creature. Closing my eyes, I inhale deeply, pushing past the spilled gas from my hands and clothes and focusing on her sweet floral scent lingering in the air. I associate it with my childhood—a time before Boris and Serg existed.

My father was a driven man and worked his ass off to provide for us. My childhood is divided into halves—before and after him.

Before he died, I was happy. I didn't appreciate that happiness until he dropped dead of a heart attack. He did his best to give us everything, but times were tough, and when he died, we went from living comfortably to barely surviving.

After he died, my mother revealed what a weakling she truly was. She bed-hopped, uncaring her son who lost his father was witness to her immoralities as she never bothered to close her bedroom door. All she cared about was herself, and when she found Boris, she thought she'd found her meal ticket out of hell.

He was a cruel asshole, but it didn't bother her. All that mattered was he was rich. When they married, he saw me as nothing but a nuisance, a tie to Zoya's past—a tie he wanted to sever. He punished me for everything, and Zoya stood by and said nothing. She watched him beat me with his belt night after night for merely being alive.

When she fell pregnant, and with a son nonetheless, Boris's punishments became harsher. He didn't just want to punish me; he wanted me dead. And most times, I wished that I were. He beat me until I was unconscious. Then he would throw scalding or freezing water over me to wake me, only to repeat the punishment again and again.

He robbed me of food as a power trip. He wanted me to know that the food I ate was because of him. In the end, I would rather starve than break bread with him, so I began stealing to survive, and this was where I found solace in three other kids who were just like me.

Borya, Oscar, Astra, and I were thick as thieves in every sense of the word. We understood one another because our parents were carbon copies of the other. It made sense for that friendship to extend into adulthood. Yes, they were immoral and bad, bad people, but so was I.

But when you don't have anyone in this world, you take what you can because our friendship was on an equal playing field. That was, until they hurt the only person I ever loved. Our friendship meant nothing because my дорогая changed everything.

I interlace my fingers between my splayed legs, unbelieving this is how my life turned out. My pinkie ring catches the moonlight, the one which once belonged to Boris, the one I cut from his finger when he was still alive. I was thirteen when I ended his miserable life. He didn't suffer enough, but knowing what his death would do to my mother and her son canceled out any regret when I slit his throat.

Zoya never forgave me for my sins, but that's okay. I never forgave her for hers.

I learned how to survive on my own, and the streets became my training ground. All I had was my street smarts and my three friends. Now, I have none of that. Things have changed, and I must start from scratch.

Turning my chin, I see something shiny on the dresser. I clench my jaw as my entire body contorts in fury. It seems they left something behind, but this was done with intent. This is their way of announcing they're three steps ahead of me—again.

Standing slowly, I walk toward the dresser, eyes focused on the ruby necklace. The jewel itself isn't what has captured me, but the meaning behind it. This necklace belonged to my grandmother, my father's mother. Zoya knew how much it meant to me, so she gave it to Astra. That's the kind of person my mother is.

Astra was wearing this the day I shot her dead. Serg must have stolen it from her corpse before he fled into the dead of night like the coward he is. And here it is. A clear fuck you.

Seizing the necklace off the dresser, I clench it so hard, it cuts into the skin of my palm. But I welcome the sting as I envision it's Serg's neck I am squeezing tight. Zoya will also suffer the same fate because she made her choice when she sided with this asshole.

History is repeating itself because just as she tried to fill my father's shoes with Boris, she is trying to fill my shoes with Serg. They can have one another.

Placing the necklace in my pocket, I don't hesitate and begin dousing the room with gas. It gives me great satisfaction to soak Zoya's sanctuary, and when I reach into my pocket for a pack of matches, that satisfaction turns to utter joy.

Striking the tip, I flick it onto the bed, mesmerized as the floral bedspread goes up in flames. The heat from the flames thaws out the chill to my bones, but I won't be whole until I find my mother and do to her what she did to me.

I may be standing here, breathing and functioning with a beating heart, but I'm dead inside.

The flames lick at the walls, setting them alight quickly. With one last look, I exit the room and repeat the same action in Serg's bedroom. I then robotically pour the remaining gas down the hallway and stairs.

Standing at the bottom of the staircase, I light the pack of matches and stare into the flames. Yes, I failed—once again—but they know I'm onto them. Therefore, they know I won't stop until I find them. They'll be running for the rest of their lives, looking over their shoulders, and for now, that will do.

Tossing the packet of matches onto the stairs, I turn and walk out the front door. The fire crackles loudly, a small victory for me because I will burn every house in this city until I find them.

Pavel waits for me by his truck, smoking casually. This is just another day at the office for him.

Adam was my supplier after I killed Chow, but he is nowhere to be found. I don't know if that is by choice or if Raul found him and made him pay for having dealings with his father's killer. With every corner I turn, it seems I'm faced with another hurdle more complex than the one before it.

I rub over the postcard in my pocket. It's ridiculous that such a thing can provide me comfort, but дорогая has that effect on me. She always has.

Sighing, I jump into my SUV and bid farewell to Pavel. I am so done with this day, week, month, year. I plan on going home and attempting to sleep. There are no pit stops close by, so I turn up the radio and roll down the window, hoping the loud music and fresh air will keep me awake.

I stick to the backroads even though I'm the only idiot on the road at this time of the night. I don't mind the quiet because it gives me time to think. I need a new game plan. I thought I was one step closer to getting back my life.

Well, at least a semi balance between then and now.

I did learn a lesson from my life before. I will never exploit another human the way I did Zoey, Willow, and the hundreds of other women in my past. I thought controlling another person would somehow give me more power—that it would help me regain what I lost in my youth, and that it would fill this void in my life—but it never did.

Each woman I broke, just broke whatever shred of humanity I clung to.

So yes, I want my old life back, but there are some aspects I'm glad burned to the ground. This life isn't for everyone, but it's the only life I know. I feel most comfortable here; it's where I feel alive.

Static crackles over the radio, hinting I'm in a remote part of the countryside. Briefly peering down to change the station, I take my eyes off the road for a moment, but it's a second too long.

When I return my attention back to the gravel road, I see that I'm no longer the only one out here because standing yards away is a woman in white. Instantly, I swerve to avoid hitting her and slam on the brakes so I don't crash into the tree in front of me.

Jarring forward, I catch my breath before turning over my shoulder to ensure I actually saw what I did.

I did.

The woman is indeed frozen to the same spot, untroubled I almost ran her over. Something is very wrong with this entire situation. I need to put the SUV into reverse and forget I saw this stranger. This isn't my problem. I have enough of my own.

But when she continues to stand there motionless, I groan. This newfound conscience has caused me nothing but trouble, and I'm sure this time is no different. Nonetheless, I unbuckle my seat belt and open the door.

Her back is to me, but I can see she is in a white slip dress. It appears she just got out of bed. But her dirty feet and legs contradict this. I walk toward her cautiously, unsure what I'm about to see. She is awfully thin, and on closer inspection, I see that her filthy dress is torn.

"девушка, ты в порядке?" I ask if she's okay in Russian as I'm presuming she's from around here. However, she doesn't reply.

Her long golden brown hair hangs around her downturned face, and even though it's quite mild, she is shivering. I decide to address her in English. "Miss, can you hear me? What happened?"

I can't help but compare her to a scared animal, cowering and trembling on the spot. Something awful has happened to her. I recognize this look. Aren't I responsible for inflicting the same pain on many?

"May I help you?" I ask, not wanting to startle her any further. But she continues standing there immobile. I stop when I'm a few feet away.

We're in the middle of nowhere, and I haven't passed a house for miles. Where did she come from? And why is she out here in nothing but her sleepwear?

"Can I call someone?" The more questions I ask, the harder her gaunt frame trembles. I don't know what to do.

"My name is Aleksei Popov. I won't hurt you. Will you let me help you?" I don't know what she needs, but I at least have to offer.

I understand she's hurt and scared, but her silence isn't helping, so I decide to gently reach out and assure her that I'm no threat. As I step forward, the rustle of leaves beneath my shoes indicates my intentions, and the woman spins around swiftly.

I sigh in relief, but that is short-lived when I see what she has clenched in her right hand.

My headlights catch the glimmer of silver from the large butcher knife she holds. I slowly raise my hands in surrender, eyeing her and the blade cautiously.

"I'm not going to hurt you," I assure her once again. But it doesn't make a difference.

Her frightened blue eyes dart between me and the clearing in the trees. She wants to make a run for it, and if I was wise,

I would let her go, but I know if she runs, I will chase her. She reminds me of a time when the hunt excited me.

But I'm not that person anymore. I remind myself of the pep talk some two minutes ago.

If that's true, however, then why is my heart galloping wildly within my chest?

The front of her slip is torn, which has the left side of the material hanging quite low. It allows me to see her chest rising and falling rapidly. A silver locket hangs from her neck. Her pale skin is covered in mud. Her snarled hair has twigs and leaves tangled in the strands. It's hard to tell, but I'd guess she's in her mid-twenties.

Her disheveled state points to the fact she's someone's captive, but she's gotten away. And when she shakily raises the knife at me, it's clear she intends to continue on her way.

She opens her mouth, but a winded wheeze is in place of where her words should be. She licks her cracked lips twice before she finally speaks. "Give me your k-keys."

I stare at her, stunned that someone so frightened can sound so fierce. I wasn't expecting that. The excitement inside me continues to build because that fierceness, those blue eyes, and that American accent remind me of someone else who, ironically, was in the same position as this mystery woman.

"I said give me your keys!" she shouts, waving the knife my way, interrupting my trip down memory lane.

"They're in the SUV," I reply calmly, gesturing over my shoulder. "You want them, go get them."

A tiny whimper escapes her, betraying her bravado. She clearly wasn't expecting that response as she isn't the one currently being held at knifepoint. But I will not cower. I was only trying to help her, and this is how she thanks me. I should force her onto her knees for her insolence.

Shaking such thoughts aside, I focus on the situation at hand because that scratch, that darkness begins to rear its evil head, and I want to punish it with pain. I'm past this. But when the woman trembles, I realize that no, I'm not.

I'm still the messed-up asshole who loves to push the boundaries of pleasure and pain.

*Run, little rabbit...*I silently dare her, wanting nothing more than the chase.

The air turns thick, and the hunter becomes prey.

She looks over my shoulder, and I can see it in her eyes—it's time to run. The dirt kicks up as her feet dig into the ground, and she takes off into a sprint. Inhaling deeply, I give her a three second head start before chasing after her.

Each step I take breathes new life into me, and I am charged in ways I thought were dead. Doing bad, vile things makes me feel alive. I see that now. I really am a fucked-up bastard. But I can deal with this self-discovery later because no way is this woman taking off with my vehicle.

Yes, I do want to help her because I won't leave her here. But I can't resist eliciting some fear when I do.

She is fast, and I can see her shoulders sag in relief when she opens the driver's door. But that's as far as she gets. I come up behind her, slamming her body against the SUV. She fights me like a wild cat, thrashing and screaming madly.

"Calm down," I order, wrapping my arms around her. Her arms are locked by her sides, but that doesn't stop her from attempting to break free.

"Let me go!" she bellows, struggling against me. I only tighten my hold, causing the knife to drop to the ground.

"I will once you tell me who did this to you. I'm only trying to help you."

"Screw you! I don't need your help. I got away from him. And I will get away from you."

"Him? Who?" I ask, leaning back when she tries to break my nose with the back of her head. "Stop fighting."

This only encourages her to fight harder.

"Tell me who you got away from," I order, focusing on what's important.

"Why would I tell you anything? I know who you are. You look exactly like *him*," she spits.

Her confession leaves me all the more intrigued. "How do you know me?"

"Let me go!" She continues to thrash about, and I'll give her credit, she's putting up a good fight. But I'm growing weary of her defiance.

"You can come willingly or not. It's up to you," I offer, picking her up and carrying her toward the passenger door. I must find out how she knows me.

She kicks her feet, screaming, and the sick bastard inside me hopes she only screams louder. In my excitement, I underestimate her, and she wiggles loose. The moment she's free, she takes off into the woods.

"блять!" I curse, following in hot pursuit.

She hasn't gotten far, but she is fast and ducks and weaves, throwing me off track. The full moon goes into hiding, forcing me to use my sharpened predatory senses. They've laid dormant for so long, but it troubles me how easily it is to step back into these well-loved shoes.

Her labored breaths fuel mine, and when she stumbles over a fallen tree, I jump forward and tackle her to the ground. She thrashes wildly, clawing at my face and my shoulders, but I pin her down with my body, prohibiting her from moving. Her subtle body beneath mine does things it shouldn't.

"Stop fighting! How do you know me?" I demand, inches from her face.

She rears up and attempts to bite me, but I jerk back with a snarl. "Try that again. I dare you, малышка."

My threat has the desired effect as she stops writhing. However, what she does next changes the course of everything. "You don't scare me. I've met men like you before. But you, Serg, and the thousands of other men out there are nothing but cowards!"

"What did you say?"

When she squirms, my patience has run out, so I cup her chin, forcing her head backward. She is fucking terrified, and I'm scaring her. But I can't stop. Her fear feeds me, and I want more.

"Serg who?" I snarl, locking our eyes to ensure she knows I'm done playing.

I don't know what it is, but she must be able to read the sudden seriousness to my question because the fight in her dies. Her heaving chest is pressed to mine as she exclaims, "Serg." She wheezes. "The fucking king of this town! Serg Ivanov! But I showed him. I showed him," she repeats, but all

I can hear on repeat is my half-brother's name.

I thought Serg and Zoya were tipped off, but it seems I was wrong. This woman is the reason my family fled into the dead of night, terrified and I need to know why. She has suddenly become more valuable than I ever imagined.

And she realizes it too.

"No," she begs, peering up at me, petrified. "I made a mistake. I-I don't know you."

But it's too late.

However, her admission has me faltering for a mere second, which is all she needs. Somehow, she maneuvers her small body and draws her knee upward. I instantly see stars.

A winded breath leaves me as I try to breathe past the pain of being kneed in the groin. She takes this opportunity to shove me off her and jump up. She takes off into a dead sprint—again.

Even though my body protests in utter pain, I come to an unsteady stand and begin to stumble after her. She has a head start, and I'm injured, but I persevere. She cannot get away.

She turns over her shoulder, terrified when she sees me following. Her inattention is now her error because before I have a chance to warn her, she slams straight into a tree, knocking herself unconscious.

Hobbling toward her twisted body lying in a heap on the ground, I sigh, ashamed of my brutal ways. Maybe I'm not a heartless bastard after all? But when I formulate what I have planned for her, I realize that no, I'm not—I'm worse.

"I'm sorry."

Dropping to a squat, I lift her into my arms. I brush the

hair from her sweaty cheeks, not proud of my actions. Once this is over with, I'll go to church and ask for absolution, but there aren't enough Hail Marys to save my soul.

CHAPTER THREE

This is far from my finest hour.

I promised I wouldn't hold another person hostage, but that oath got shot to hell the moment I put an unconscious woman into my SUV, drove her to my home, and tied her to my bed.

There wasn't another option, I reason with myself. She has information I need, and she was hysterical, so I had to subdue her. This newfound morality is nothing but a nuisance, and I much preferred it when I didn't feel. I can deal with my scruples later because when the woman begins to stir, I sit forward, anxious for her to finally wake.

I'm sitting at the foot of the bed with intent. Like a king takes his place at the head of a table, I want to set the same precedence for my mystery woman. She didn't cower when most would have, which shows me she is spirited and won't break easily.

The challenge has me reaching for my scotch and sipping it leisurely.

When her eyes flutter open, she slowly takes in her surroundings. Confusion turns to fear and then to anger when her gaze falls on me. I simply lean back in my armchair, ankle crossed over my knee as I savor my drink.

She looks overhead at the rope restraining her wrists, tugging fruitlessly. "Untie me," she hoarsely demands.

In response, I swirl the scotch around in my glass, ignoring her.

I hear her wet her lips because I know she is parched, which is why I've decided to taunt her with something she can have, if she gives me what I want. This doesn't have to be difficult. I'd much prefer if it weren't.

But when a sardonic cackle fills the room, I realize there is only one way this is headed.

"Oh, wow. *This* is where you live? *Now* I understand why you're the joke of this town."

Every part of me demands I punish her for her insolence, but I keep my cool.

Lifting the glass to my lips, I take a slow sip, watching her over the rim. She lifts her neck, watching me closely. She was expecting a heated response, which is why she gets nothing in return.

She knows a lot about me, which is good. It means she's very valuable to me. "Would you like to shower? Maybe something to eat? Drink?"

The surprise is clear on her face. She just insulted me, and in return, I've offered hospitality. But this is all a part of the game. No question, Serg kept her locked up like some animal, hoping to break her this way. But she is someone who doesn't respond to such threats.

She has balls.

There are many ways to break a person. Serg clearly failed. But it'll be different with me.

"No, thank you," she snarls, eyeing me something wicked.

"Suit yourself," I reply with a carefree shrug as I toss back the remaining scotch. Coming to a stand, I stretch my arms overhead, something else I have deprived her of.

"Where are you going?" she demands when I turn my back, making it clear I won't tolerate her contempt. "You can't keep me tied to this bed."

With a grin, I spin around leisurely and commence a slow swagger toward her. She doesn't back down. Yes, I know she has nowhere to go as she's tied to the bed, but she doesn't cower. She keeps my gaze, daring my next move.

Seeing her bound, challenging me, stirs something riotous inside me. I can't help but compare her looks and her attitude to Willow. I know I shouldn't, but the similarities are uncanny.

Coming to stop by the bedside, I peer down at her blankly. She speaks to me this way because she isn't afraid of me. That needs to change.

"I can do what I want, малышка. I'm not the one tied to that bed, am I?" When she clenches her jaw, I continue. "So, how about we start again? I'm Aleksei Popov." I extend my hand, but retract it with a sarcastic smirk. "And you are?"

The room is heavy with hostility. If she were free, I have

no doubt she'd tear me limb from limb. However, she must be able to read my resolve because she does something wonderful—she submits.

"Renata Myers. I don't want to play twenty questions," she says, deciding to reveal why she's here in hopes this will be over with quickly. "I was backpacking around Europe with friends. We weren't supposed to come to Russia, but my friends insisted we visited The Red Square. They said it would be fun and that I would love it here. But they aren't the ones tied to this fucking bed, are they?" She tugs at the restraints, angered.

"I met Serg in a bar. I was drunk and fell for his charms."

It's a hard pill to swallow as this story is reflective of how I lured Zoey into my web. The apple doesn't fall far from the tree it seems. But I am *nothing* like that piece of shit. I'm not.

"He bought me a drink, and the next thing I knew, I was chained to a radiator in some shithole."

"What did he want with you?" I ask. It may seem like a foolish question, but I don't think he wanted a sex slave.

She blows strands of matted hair from her cheeks. "He said he wanted an"—she wets her lips, appearing to weigh up her next words—"дорогая of his own."

A hiss escapes me because I was not expecting this response.

Her pronunciation is awful, but I know what she's trying to say.

That son of a bitch. He loathes me, yet he wants to be me. No wonder he chose Renata. Her similarities to Willow are no coincidence. The fact disgusts me for so many different reasons.

"So he spoke of me?" I ask, focusing on what's important. I need to know everything. She is the closest thing I have to Serg.

She scoffs. "Spoke of you? That's all I heard. How you were nothing. How he was now king because he burned your empire to the ground. And how you were going to pay for killing his father."

Clenching my fists, I will myself to calm down because I need Renata on my side. "How long did he hold you hostage?"

She averts her eyes, as if embarrassed to reveal the truth. I realize that's because she sees her trust in him as nothing but stupidity on her part. She is incredibly proud. She's also spirited; far more courageous than most men I've fought alongside in battle.

"Three months," she shares, shaking her head. "The entire time, I thought he was going to...rape me. But he never touched me like that. He punished me, yes. He whipped me, had me begging on my knees, but things never crossed that line. I never understood why."

Nausea rolls in my belly because she may as well be reading a page out of my handbook. This is how I commanded Saint to break the faceless women I used for my entertainment all because I could. I've always had a way with people. And no matter their reservations, they always bowed to my commands in the end.

All but Willow.

"I figured it was because he didn't want his mom to see what a sick asshole he really is. But she knew what he was doing, yet she did nothing. I was like a brand-new puppy. She allowed him to play with me, and when he grew bored and forgot I existed, I got into trouble for making a mess.

"They left me for three fucking days without food or water. When I couldn't hold my bladder, Zoya punished me for soiling myself." She quickly wipes her cheek against her upper arm to brush away her tears.

"She is just as cruel as he is."

Renata is right. Zoya cares for no one but herself.

"Do you know anything about Serg's dealings?" Most would console someone after what they just heard. But I won't insult either of us.

"Bits and pieces," she confesses. "I overheard your name mentioned. A lot. Everyone seemed in awe of Serg because he brought you down. I don't know what happened, but Serg made sure everyone was aware of what he did to you."

"And what did he do?" I take a seat beside her, barely reining in my temper.

This is the first time I've been close to her. She has full lips, beautiful blue eyes, and once the muck is washed from her hair, the color will be a vibrant golden brown. I have the urge to brush the locks from her cheeks so I can see her better, but I don't.

"He claimed you were weak and taking everything from you was easy. You'd grown soft because you fell in love. You were nothing now. A forgotten name on no one's lips. He was now feared and respected. He was the mafia kingpin of Russia.

"I found it hard to believe, but when I heard the way people spoke to him, like they would do anything to please him, I realized it was true."

No matter how many times I hear this, it doesn't lessen the need to stab my half-brother in the jugular.

"Did you hear anything about who he's in business with?"

When her lower lip trembles, I wonder what's caused her suit of armor to crack. This is the first sign of weakness she's shown. "Yes. He is the reason I was able to get away."

"He?" I question, unsure where this is headed.

Her vulnerability is gone as soon as it appeared, and in its place is the fierce fighter that she is. "Untie me and I will tell you everything."

Shaking my head, I level her with a cold stare. "It doesn't work that way, малышка. Trust me when I say you are merely a means to an end. Just tell me what I want to know, and it'll all be over.

"I have no need to hold you prisoner. Once I have the information I need, you are free to leave. I will even drive you to the airport myself. But if you choose to be difficult"—I hover forward, inches from her face—"I will show you what true cruelty looks like. Serg wants to be me. But he has no idea what I've done or what I will do if you don't tell me what I want to hear.

"Serg chose you for whatever reason, but you're nothing to me. Remember that. You don't have an ace up your sleeve. So tell me what I *fucking* want to know before I lose my temper."

The demons roar to life, demanding violence, but I subdue them—for now.

Her chest rises and falls quickly, her sweet breath filling the small space between us. Her cheeks flush, and instead of fear, I smell…arousal. She is…turned on by dominance? Is this why Serg chose her? Was she the perfect puppet for him to control?

Unable to help myself, I languidly sweep my gaze over her flustered features, across the swell of her breasts and down her trembling body. Even though she's filthy, it's clear she's beautiful. I have the sudden urge to see what she looks like scrubbed clean.

However, I tamp down any curiosity because it has no right being there.

"Raul," she finally confesses, adding another layer to this already fucked-up tale. "He is the one who helped me escape. He was the one who was supposed to meet me, but he didn't. I thought he was different, but I was wrong."

Pulling back, I suddenly need to put some distance between us.

I now understand her comment back in the woods when she said all men are cowards. Raul left her. The hurt in her voice betrays her. She clearly thought she meant something to Raul, which means they formed some sort of relationship during her captivity.

I thought Serg and Zoya fled because of me, but I was wrong. They fled because of Renata.

If Raul would jeopardize his relationship with Serg over her, she is someone he cherishes, which means she is very valuable to me. I don't know why Raul didn't show up when he was supposed to, but the fact he helped Renata escape knowing full well what that meant for his partnership with Serg means he cares for her. And I plan to exploit that.

Maybe he got cold feet? Or maybe he realized the damage

it would do to his business? Whatever the reason, she is the bargaining chip I need.

"Do you know where he is?" I ask, keeping my space.

She shakes her head. "No." My heart drops, that is, before she adds, "But I know where both will be."

I arch a brow. She has my attention.

"On the seventh of every month, they do their exchange. Drugs for money. Money for drugs. I can take you. You just have to untie me."

Renata has come to realize how important she is. I need her; therefore, she does have an ace up her sleeve. She has the whole fucking deck.

"How do you know where they meet?" I question as I doubt Serg took her along for a drive.

She licks her lips slowly, deliberately. "My ankle was chained to that radiator. Sometimes my wrists. But my mouth never was."

I blink once, caught off guard by her frankness.

"It's survival of the fittest. And that's the reason I'm here and not buried in a shallow grave."

So she seduced Raul in hopes he'd set her free. And it worked.

Running my fingers pensively over my three-day growth, I ask, "And what happens if I agree? If you show me where they meet, what happens then?"

Renata's lips lift into a slanted grin. "Then both those assholes pay for leaving me for dead."

She is a woman scorned. I believe her feelings for Raul were real, but it doesn't seem she forgives easily. As for Serg, she just wants her revenge.

And just like that, foes have become friends as we want the same thing.

"Raul unlocked my chain, and I was to escape when everyone went to sleep. I did what he said. But when I finally broke free and waited for him outside, he wasn't there. I don't care what the reason was. He left me when he promised he wouldn't.

"I promise to tell you everything I know if you promise to let me inflict the same pain they imposed on me when you find them."

Pondering over her request, I find it's really a no-brainer. She's the missing link I need. And just like that, she became my lifeline.

"How can I trust you?"

She smells her victory. "You can't. But neither can I."

And she's right.

I'm just another man who would use her to get what I want, and I've told her that. But we're stronger working together. We may not like it, but we're all that we have.

She knows too much to be lying, and I recognize the look of revenge sparking behind her blue eyes. Whether she is a blessing or a curse, I've yet to decide. But when I reach into the bedside table and grab my knife, I can't deny that seeing this fierce woman tied to my bed leaves me feeling incredibly blessed.

Renata's throat dips as she swallows deeply. I'm the one now holding the knife.

Leaning forward, I cut through the rope at her wrists.

Once it severs and her arms sag in relief, I slowly lock eyes with her, daring her to make a move. She draws her arms down, rubbing over her red wrists with a pained expression.

I repeat the same action on the rope binding her ankles. This will be the real test. Once the rope snaps free, I brace for impact. She's now free.

Adrenaline courses through me as the hunter is desperate for another chase. But my inner strategist hopes she just does as she's told because I'm tired and want to at least catch an hour of sleep.

"Can I shower…please?" she asks, surprising me.

She too must realize the seventh is three weeks away, meaning we have to play nice for twenty-one days. A lifetime in this circumstance.

Peering up at her, I weigh my response. For this to work, she has to trust me. She doesn't have to like me, and it's better if she doesn't, but trust and respect are the two factors we need. Once upon a time, I would have led with fear. However, Renata doesn't scare easily.

"The bathroom is there." I point at the closed door near the tiny kitchen.

I remain sitting on the bed, not accommodating her as she slowly shuffles into a sitting position before swinging her legs and placing her bare feet on the floor. This action has us sitting side by side.

I expect her to stand, eager to get away from me, but she doesn't. She turns her cheek to look at me. It's the first time she's done so, so openly. She doesn't shy away from the way she scans over my face and down my body.

I know I have a way with women and men. That's not me being arrogant. I've been told by many that I'm handsome, and yes, that helps, but it's the confidence I've had my entire life that seems to be my superpower.

I could sell ice to an Eskimo. If she were an Eskimo woman, well…

And it's because of this experience I've had that I can recognize the telltale signs when a woman is interested. Usually, her pupils dilate, she subtly touches her hair, and her body is always turned toward you.

It's not rocket science. It's simply about reading her body language. And right now, Renata is an open book.

When I meet her curious gaze, she quickly averts her eyes—another sign.

The fact she finds me attractive is surprising. I don't dwell on it, though, and gesture with my chin that if she wants to use the bathroom, she better do so now. She gets the hint and quickly stands. She's unsteady on her feet as she commences a slow shuffle.

When she opens the bathroom door, I state, "You have ten minutes. Not a second more."

Her shoulders rise in anger, but she doesn't bite back. She slams the door shut.

Smirking, I stand and walk over to the freezer to retrieve a bottle of vodka. Unscrewing the cap, I take a large swig, needing a drink after tonight. I have no idea how the next twenty-one days will play out. I can't watch Renata 24/7, so I'm trusting that her vengeance is enough of a reason to behave.

My lodging has barely enough room for me, and now that

I have a houseguest, I wonder how this will work. I could be a gentleman and take the couch, but that's not likely as I'm double its size. The best-case scenario for the both of us would be for Renata to find somewhere else to stay.

But where?

My mind drifts to the orphanage and, more specifically, to Sister Arabella. An ache builds low just thinking of her. I definitely didn't see her coming, but I suppose the events of this entire night have caught me off guard.

I could ask Mother Superior to offer sanctuary to Renata, but I can't see Renata co-existing with, well, anyone. She is on the defense, and I understand why, but I'm not a damn shrink. I can barely stand my own company most of the time, so having her here disturbs whatever peace I have.

The shower switches off, hinting she's done. Looking at the clock on the wall, I see she has listened. She has two and a half minutes left.

"I need something to wear," she shouts to be heard through the closed door.

Sighing, I take one last swig of vodka before walking to my dresser. Opening the drawer, I grab a T-shirt and a pair of sweats. She'll be swimming in them, but considering what she was wearing, I don't think she'll mind.

"I'll leave them outside the door," I instruct.

"No, I don't want you seeing me. I'll open the door, and you can slip them through the crack."

I raise my eyes to the ceiling because she is testing my patience. "Don't flatter yourself, принцесса. You don't have anything I haven't seen before."

"Yeah, and that's the reason I don't want you seeing me," she counters quickly.

Gritting my teeth, I knock on the door with my knuckle. "Your highness."

The door opens just wide enough for me to slip my arm through. Jesus, I didn't take her for the shy type. But nonetheless, I carelessly place my hand through the gap, not realizing what I've done until it's too late.

A sharp sting slashes up my arm, and when I try to yank away, it only drives the blade in deeper. I try to push the door open, but Renata has a strong hold on it. She uses all her body strength, attempting to close the door with my arm still in it.

At this rate, if she doesn't break my arm, she'll slice it off with the small scissors she must have found in the medicine cabinet. This is my fault for letting my guard down, and when I think back to her show and dance in the bedroom, I realize what she was doing. She was laying on the charm to play me, knowing I'd lower my guard and underestimate her.

But this is the last time.

When she digs the blade in deeper, I allow my arm to go lax and stop fighting. Renata's hold on my wrist wavers, which is all I need. I use my shoulder to shove open the door, catching her unaware. The moment I burst through, I charge toward her, smacking her trembling hand away, which sends the scissors flying across the bathroom.

She realizes how this will end, and it's the ultimate standoff. She can surrender, or she can fight. But I've come to learn that Renata will never submit. It's time that changed. I've broken countless women, so what's one more?

I promised I wouldn't do that again, but if Renata doesn't learn the rules, well, it's either her head or mine. I haven't come this far for someone with a nice ass to mess up my plans. And it's only now do I realize that that ass is bare.

Renata is standing feet away, completely naked. Her cheeks are flushed, and her chest is rising and falling steadily, drawing attention to her pert breasts. My blood stains her hands. As much as I want to kill her, I can't deny she's a complete vision.

She does nothing to cover her nakedness. Instead, she stands proudly, daring me to do my best. Her golden brown hair is lighter than I thought, reminding me of a bright summer's morning. She's no longer coated in dirt, revealing her skin to be fair and covered in freckles. She is slender, but I don't mistake her for a wallflower.

I've fallen for her charms once before. It won't happen again. And she knows it.

The moment I charge her, she tries to make a run for it, but it simply spurs me on. Snickering, I pick her up and throw her over my shoulder.

"Motherfucker! Let me go!" she screams, squirming madly. I only tighten my hold. When she doesn't stop wriggling, I slap her on the ass—hard.

A stunned gasp escapes her.

Her surprise, coupled with the act of punishing her breaks down the small shred of humanity I was desperately clinging to. Who was I fooling? This is who I am. I wanted to lead with compassion and kindness, traits I didn't realize I had until I met Willow, but I can't do it anymore.

All that's gotten me is living in squalor as the laughing stock of this town.

But no more.

I charge through the room and toss Renata onto the bed. Before she has a chance to move, I dive on top of her, pinning her to the mattress with my body. She fights, kicking and screaming, but it simply feeds the depravity within me.

Reaching for the cable ties in the bedside dresser, I yank her arms above her head, securing them tightly to the headboard. When I look down at her with a smirk, she spits in my face. I only smile harder.

She tries to buck me off, but I subdue her by locking my legs around hers. This aligns us in the most delicious of ways. The dominance turns me on. The fight in her suddenly dies, and her blue eyes widen.

She shared with me that she wasn't raped, and I would never, *never* do that to a woman, but that doesn't mean I don't know how to tease, turning hate into lust. No matter how badly she wants to hate me, by the end of this, she'll want to fuck me more.

"I tried to be nice," I say, inches from her face, gripping her chin softly between my fingers. "But if you're going to misbehave and act like an animal, you can stay chained up like one."

Rising slowly, I stand next to the bed, sweeping my gaze down her body. She is flushed all over, and I can't stop my eyes from lingering on her bare breasts. She tries her best to cover her modesty by crossing her legs, but I've seen it all.

She's scared. I can smell it all over her. So, it seems she

does have a weakness.

When I continue looking at her without a word, her fight turns to fear. "You can't leave me tied here."

Cocking my head to the side, I ponder her statement. "On the contrary, малышка. You're a guest in my home, and as they say, my house, my rules. You've been most ungrateful. I think you need some time to think about what you've done."

Yes, my tone is belittling, but this is what I must do.

"I could have left you out there, but I didn't. I took you in, and you repay me by cutting me." My comment has me removing my gold cuff links before unbuttoning my shirt slowly.

Renata's eyes follow the movement of my fingers as she licks her dry lips.

"I should punish you for such disobedience. You may not know this, but breaking people, breaking women like you …" I add, unfastening the last button. My shirt falls open, revealing a sliver of my tanned chest. "It's my specialty. Do you want to know why?"

She nods, her eyes scanning down my naked flesh.

"Because I always get what I want. And I know what I want from you." Slipping off my shirt, I press it over the gash on my arm.

"What do you want from me?" she asks, but her tone has subdued.

"Well, clearly, I want information you have."

"And?" she prompts. She is a clever girl.

Smirking, I deliberately skim down her trembling body. "I haven't figured that out yet. Three weeks is a very long time, малышка."

"What does that mean?" Our conversation has simmered, just as I knew it would. I wish it wasn't this easy, but sometimes, it is.

"Little girl," I reply. "However"—I lick my top lip—"I can see you're not so little."

Instantly, her skin deepens to a deep pink hue.

"If you'll excuse me, I need to shower and clean up the mess you made." I go to turn, but stop, returning my attention to her.

She is sprawled out naked on my bed, and although most would leave her this way to demean her, attempting to break her, I do the complete opposite. Reaching for a woolen throw off the sofa, I gently place it over her, concealing her modesty.

She peers up at me from under her lashes, surprise clear on her face. "Why would you do that?"

Shrugging, I reply calmly, "Because I thought you might be cold."

Without another word, I grab a change of clothes and enter the bathroom, closing the door behind me.

Walking to the sink, I grip the porcelain and stare at my reflection in the small mirror. Renata will break. I don't know when, but she will.

The game plan has been put into motion because each woman is different. Some break with kindness. Others cruelty.

But when you take away someone's basic rights and then hand them back to them, they soon forget the malice you caused. They know they need you to survive. When they have so little... Like with Renata, she doesn't even own a pair of shoes, so when you give them something small, they appreciate it because they see you as a need to survive.

I could have left Renata naked, but to conquer someone, you need to read them, you need to be inside their minds. So covering her, after I cruelly stole away her freedom, will leave her wondering if maybe I'm not such a bad guy after all.

Turning on the cold water, I splash water over my face and smile. Little does she know, she's right. I'm not a bad guy...I'm worse.

CHAPTER FOUR

Renata was still sleeping when I slipped out this morning. When I emerged from the shower last night, she had managed to twist her body away from me. She is clearly disgusted by me, but she is most likely more sickened with herself for thinking I was anything but a monster. She has a lot to learn.

I slept a couple of hours on the tiny couch, but there is no way that can be a permanent arrangement for the next three weeks.

Exhaustion must have finally overcome her because she didn't stir when I dressed, made myself some coffee, and took out the trash. I decided to let her sleep because honestly, I need some time to think, which is why I'm here.

Yes, I've accepted the fact I'm prepared to do whatever it takes to get what I want. But I know to do that, I'll have to be creative. Renata is a challenge. She won't make it easy for me, but she will break. The methods I'll use, well, that's why I'm sitting in the chapel in the orphanage, hands clasped as I seek absolution from my Creator.

I don't know why I feel the need to pray. He gave up on me long ago. But being here in the quiet is one of the only times I'm at peace. The confessional booth is a place I have steered clear of for years. Actually, confessing my sins aloud seems rather ridiculous because where would I start?

However, knowing what I'll face over the next three weeks, I conclude my prayer with a sign of the cross and come to a stand. No one is here, which gives me a false sense of security as I walk toward the small wooden booth.

Pushing the red curtain aside, I look into the small confines, wondering if this is supposed to resemble what being inside a prison cell is like to deter one from sinning. Not really sure what the right protocol is, I contort my body and take a seat.

I wait. And wait.

Is this a sign that He has closed the door on me for good?

Just as I'm about to get up and forget this nonsense, the small door slides open. The privacy screen doesn't allow me to see anything other than a figure behind it. I wait for some sort of prompt, but I don't get anything, so I decide to start.

"Bless me, Father, for I have sinned. It's been…" I pause, unsure when my last confession was. "It's been a very long time since my last confession. Forgive me." I wait for him to speak, but all I'm confronted with is silence.

I know someone is behind the partition because I can see their outline. I can hear their breathing. Father Anton and

Father Mateo are the orphanage priests. Usually, I'm the one excusing myself from a conversation, but I guess this is hardly the time to make small talk.

Clearing my throat, I interlace my fingers and hang my head low. "I have done many bad things in my life. I've lost count of how many. It never bothered me, though. It was just a part of me. Of who I was. Until I met a woman who changed that.

"Her name is Willow. She taught me true kindness and strength. She saw something in me that not many people have. She's gone now, but that's okay because she's happy. That's all I ever wanted for her. I still think about her when I shouldn't. She belongs to another.

"But I sometimes wish she belonged to me," I confess. "Does that make me a bad man, Father?"

Silence.

Peering up, I try to make out any distinguishing features through the thick mesh, wondering who I'm speaking to. But all I see is a silhouette.

"No," says a deep voice, one I don't recognize. Maybe Father has a cold.

His reassurance is all I need to continue.

"I fear what I must do will change that. Most people are disposable to me. I know that isn't a very nice thing to say, but it's the truth. From a very young age, I learned that you must depend on only yourself to survive. And what I am forced to do is an example of this.

"I must exploit another human being for my gain." Sighing, I reveal the real reason I'm here. "And I'm okay with that."

I'm waiting for judgment. But I don't get it.

"Why?" Father asks. His voice still puzzles me, but it seems this purge has clouded my better judgment.

"Why am I okay with exploiting another?" When he doesn't reply, I assume that's what he's asking. "Because I was vulnerable once. And it left me where I am. I won't make the same mistake again."

And that is why I'm here.

I'm not seeking absolution. But confessing my sins has me accepting what I must do. And therefore, who I am.

A weight isn't lifted from my shoulders, and I don't feel a reprieve for acknowledging the wickedness within. I merely needed this as one would unburden their troubles to a friend with a supportive ear. I don't have one of those, so this was my sounding board in a sense.

"Thank you, Father."

I wait for instructions to repent, but once again, I'm greeted with silence. I suddenly wonder if maybe he's recognized me and instantly regret my overshare. Mother Superior knows I am far from an angel, but the Father has just heard me confess something that would tarnish her opinion of me.

I shouldn't be here.

Without thought, I quickly exit the booth, not looking back as I march briskly down the aisle and out the door. Thankfully, the hallway is empty. I sigh in relief, but that's short-lived because when I reach into my pocket for my SUV keys, I realize they're not there.

"Goddammit," I curse under my breath, flinching and silently apologizing to the man whose name I just took in vain.

Turning back around, I decide to do this fast because the longer I'm here, the more chance I have of being seen. There is no easy way to do this, so I push open the chapel door with intent to be in and out, but who I see exiting the confessional booth has me stopping dead in my tracks.

We lock eyes, both catching the other unaware.

When Sister Arabella averts her gaze, expressing her guilt, I realize the reason Father's voice sounded off was because it wasn't Father I was purging to—it was Sister Arabella.

It takes a lot to shock me these days. But now is one of those days.

Sister Arabella stands sheepishly, wringing her small hands in front of her. I wish this was some mistake, but it's not. She's heard my dark and deepest secrets, and now, I must decide what to do.

"Sister Arabella," I start, my voice echoing on the walls.

The moment I speak, she lifts her chin to meet my eyes. She appears utterly mortified by her actions.

"Mr. P-Popov—" she stutters, shaking her head as if angered at herself.

"I told you to call me Alek," I firmly state, as we are way past formalities. She chose to listen to my confession, breaking a sacred vow, and I need to know why.

"Alek," she says softly. My name sounds like utter wickedness rolling off her tongue. "I am so very sorry. I shouldn't have listened to something sacred between you and your God."

I'm thankful she hasn't lied.

"Why did you?" I ask, folding my arms, intrigued.

She works her plump bottom lip, appearing at a loss for words. "I-I don't know. I was just—"

"Just what?" I need to count my blessings that Sister Arabella seems to be more horrified of her actions than what she just heard and turn around and leave. But I find myself doing the complete opposite.

I commence a slow walk down the aisle toward her.

Our gazes are locked, and she's watching me with nothing but fascination. "I asked you a question, Sister," I coolly say, my measured steps echoing loudly.

She doesn't reply. She merely stands still, watching me closely. When I'm a few feet away, I come to a stop. Her perfume fills the space between us. Now that we're alone, I'm able to examine her openly. And I don't hide that fact.

Although her habit conceals a lot, I can see she has spectacular breasts hidden beneath it. As I noticed last night, she isn't wafer thin. She is voluptuous, curvy in all the right places. I can only imagine she'd look like a goddess beneath that robe.

Her eyes are piercing and a contrast against her chocolate-colored hair, golden skin, and pink lips; she is the epitome of a femme fatale. Everything tightens in my body as I desperately try to keep my hands to myself.

"Alek," she gently reprimands when I continue studying her without apology.

But if she wants me to stop, she needs to answer my question.

"Please don't tell Mother Superior," she pleads, troubled.

"I would never," I reply, transfixed by the tremble of her

supple lips. "I suppose I could say the same thing to you."

I'm just as guilty as she is.

Yes, what is confessed would normally never be repeated, but seeing as I confessed to Sister Arabella, she can tell whoever she wants.

"I would *never* tell her," she replies, breathlessly. Her response to me stirs my interest. "I promise."

"Do I make you nervous, Sister?" I ask, rubbing over my chin, curious.

She licks her lips twice. "Yes."

And one simple word has doomed us both.

"Why is that?"

The hollow of her throat dips as she swallows deeply. "I don't know," she replies once again, disappointing me.

Clucking my tongue, I unhurriedly lean down so our faces are inches apart. "I think you do. I think secretly," I lick my top lip, whispering, "you're a little wicked, Sister."

A gasp leaves her before she places a trembling hand over her mouth.

"I should g-go."

She turns abruptly, making it two steps before I spin her around and push her up against the wall. Her breasts press into me as they rise and fall with her quickened breaths.

"Answer me," I gently command, combing over her features. She is scared, but she is also… awakened.

"Please, let me go," she appeals, but it's weak. If she really wants to flee, all she has to do is push past me.

So I do the complete opposite. I align our bodies, pressing us chest to chest. The feel of her supple curves fires a shot of adrenaline straight through me. I can't suppress the low hum that slips free.

"I will. All you have to do is answer me," I promise, before laying my theories on the line. "You listened to my confession; you wear this expensive perfume—" I dip low, inches from her skin, and inhale.

A stunned whimper tumbles from her parted lips when I reveal I'm in on her little secret.

"All because beneath this habit lies a not so good girl. Am I right, Sister?" I ask, meeting her eyes once again.

Calling her sister just adds to the utter depravity happening before me.

"No, you are not right," she replies with bite. We both know she's lying. "You know *nothing* about me."

"Well, enlighten me then." I smirk, enjoying the sudden change in her demeanor.

My smugness stirs a side to the sweet sister that just has me falling deeper and deeper down the rabbit hole.

"I'm not one of those human beings you plan on exploiting," she snaps, throwing my confession back at me. "Whatever you choose to do is between you and God, but I don't plan on being brought into your mess."

"Well, if you didn't feel the need to eavesdrop, then we wouldn't be having this conversation, would we?"

She opens but soon closes her mouth as her argument is void. Her feistiness turns me on. I'm invading her personal space, and I have no intention of removing myself from it.

At any moment, anyone could walk in and see me in a very compromising position with the sister. But that's half the fun.

The thought of being caught makes this even more immoral. And when Sister Arabella stands on her toes, bringing us to eye level, I embrace the wickedness with both hands.

"Good luck to her," she says, attempting to push me away, which tips me over the edge.

"How do you know it's a woman?" I ask. Slamming my body into hers, I pin her to the wall once again.

She squirms, which allows me to feel every delicious inch of her ripple beneath me. "I don't, but I can imagine most women would permit you to exploit them without complaint."

"Why would you imagine that?" The harder she struggles, the more I want to rip her apart.

"Don't insult me," she replies, and by all that's holy, she rolls her eyes.

Sister Arabella is spirited, sinful, and utterly sexy; I am so done for.

"You're right. I won't insult you." I place my hands on either side of her head, caging her in. "It *is* a woman, and right now, she is tied to my bed. Naked."

Sister Arabella stops struggling. She can't hide her shock at my admission.

"I plan on breaking her because she has something I need."

"How could you be so cruel?" she asks appalled, never breaking eye contact with me.

Snickering, I remove a hand from the wall and give in to temptation and thumb over her pouty bottom lip. "Who said anything about being cruel, Sister?"

Her sweetness lingers on my thumb, so I place it into my

mouth, sucking gently. I taste raspberries. I want more. She watches me closely, blushing profusely.

"There are many ways to break a person," I reveal calmly once I'm done tasting her. "My methods are always effective because they may not know it at the time, but they want me to. They fight me in the beginning, but deep down, they want me to win."

I'm telling the sister this because I want her to know what's coming her way. She's a challenge, one I won't back down from. She is so completely off-limits, which just makes me want her all the more. If she submits to me, this conquest will be my greatest one of all.

"Maybe you haven't met your match yet?" she poses, which merely baits me.

"Maybe you're right, which is why I will continue doing what I do until I find her."

"And what happens when you do?" She gasps when I shift my hips, allowing her to feel my arousal pressed against her.

"I'm not sure. I doubt she exists, but I suppose all I can do is…pray for a miracle. But I think I fell out of favor with Him long ago."

"He forgives," she declares passionately, appearing to need to say the words aloud for her sake as well as mine. "No matter your sins, He would never turn his back on his flock."

"Oh, is that right?" I decide to test this theory out as I wrap my fingers around her waist. "Would he be so forgiving if I lifted your skirt and buried myself between your thighs? I bet you taste like sweetened honey."

Her eyes widen, and her mouth parts in utter surprise.

"Aleksei—" She plants her hand over mine, begging me not to do it. Her warm flesh only excites me further.

"What do you think, Sister Arabella? Do you think your Lord would forgive me if I forced you onto your knees and fed you my cock here, in His home? In this place of worship."

My filthy words have her quivering all over. "Please, please don't," she pleads breathlessly, clutching onto my hand.

Her plea falls on deaf ears. "What about if I bent you over His altar and spanked that glorious ass? What do you think He'd say then?"

She whimpers, her beautiful eyes filling with tears as she turns her cheek. She can't look at me. I'm disgusting. The sight is my undoing.

"I didn't think so. Forgiveness isn't intended for a man like me."

Before she has a chance to speak, I step back, letting her go. She sags forward, confused and relieved yet also disappointed. Her attention drops to the front of my slacks. I don't hide what our encounter has done to me. I want her to know this response is because of her.

"Good day, Sister Arabella."

She blinks once, puzzled. "I-I—"

"Unless you plan on taking off that habit, Sister, we're done."

Her confusion sparks to anger as she strikes out and slaps my cheek. "How dare you."

Cupping my cheek, I grin. "How dare I indeed."

She stands before me, seething, but this was the only way I could show her who she's dealing with. She listened to my confession because she's interested in me, and I need it to stop. If she doesn't, then I will have no qualms about destroying her because that's what I do.

This was her lesson. She may think she doesn't want me to break her, but she's wrong. And I don't want that for her. I want her to be the strong one and stay away because I can't. And the only way I can do that is for her to see what an asshole I really am.

I want her, and that's the problem. I can't have her. I thought I was okay with breaking her vow, but I'm not. Every part of me demands I stop being a занудный and give her what we clearly both want, but I tamp down that voice.

I can't do that to her. I won't.

"No wonder she belongs to another," she utters, speaking of Willow. "No one would ever choose you." She pushes past me, her scent lingering as a reminder of all that I've done.

When I hear the sacristy door slam shut, I know that I'm alone. Mission accomplished. Turning around, I focus on the large crucifix. There is no point in seeking absolution after what I just did.

Sister Arabella is right. No one *would* choose me. Zoey thought she did, but in reality, she was a naïve, lovestruck fool with a weak mind. She was easy to manipulate into thinking she loved me. She may have believed her feelings to be real, but they were there because I broke who she was and molded her into who I wanted her to be.

Walking numbly toward the confessional booth, I duck my head into the curtain and see my keys on the floor. Cursing, I reach for them and wonder if this was a sign from God. If so, then He has a sick sense of humor indeed.

I stopped in at a thrift store on the way home to buy Renata some clothes and other essentials.

I still have no idea what I'm supposed to do with her. But I do know I can't keep her naked for the next three weeks. Opening the front door, I brace for anything because she has proven to be unpredictable.

Thankfully, she is still tied to the bed.

She twists her body, eyeing the door. When she sees me, a look of relief washes over her, but it's gone a moment later.

Without a word, I place the bag of groceries I bought onto the kitchen counter and begin unpacking them. Renata must be hungry and thirsty, and although she is tied to my bed, that doesn't mean she's a prisoner—well, not in the conventional sense of the word. So once I set some ground rules, I will allow her to eat and bathe.

Once I'm done, I reach for the bag of clothes.

"Renata," I commence, walking toward the bed. "For this to work, I'm going to lay down some rules."

She narrows her eyes but allows me to continue without interruption.

"I don't want to keep you tied to my bed. Quite frankly, it's an inconvenience to us both. But if you continue to run, I will be forced to keep you bound. I've bought you some clothes," I explain, placing the bag onto the end of the bed.

"We both want the same thing. To see Serg dead. And for

that to happen, we have to work together. Do you really think you can achieve that on your own?" I pose, standing by the bedside and looking down at her.

When she doesn't reply, it seems my message isn't being heard.

Inhaling, I take a seat beside her. Instantly, she recoils, attempting to shrink away from me. But she's got nowhere to go.

The blanket has slipped low, revealing the top of her luscious breasts. I make no secret that I'm examining her closely. She squirms, clearly not liking being subjected this way.

"I asked you a question," I calmly say, leaning forward and brushing over the restraints at her wrists. The skin is raw. "This doesn't have to be hard on you, малышка. You won't win. Obey me and the next three weeks will be easy.

"Defy me and I promise you"—I continue tracing a path down her arms and over the top of her breasts—"you won't like the outcome. Or maybe you will."

She whimpers, attempting to shift away from my touch, but it's weak. Her flushed skin tells me otherwise.

Backward and forward, I stroke along her skin, teasing and testing how far I can push. The blanket is thin and allows me to see her nipples pebble beneath the material. She may hate me, but her body doesn't. But the truth is, after being subjected to nothing but violence and cruelty for so long, any sort of kindness would stir a positive response.

Breaking her may be easier than I thought. "So, what do you say? I untie you, then you can shower while I make us something to eat. I bought you some clothes." I gesture with my chin toward the bag.

She doesn't want to make it easy for me, but I know I've won this battle. "Fine," she begrudgingly replies.

With a smile, I stroke along her skin one final time before reaching into my pocket and producing my switchblade. She doesn't falter.

Leaning forward, I cut through the cable ties binding her. When they snap free, Renata lowers her arms with a relieved sigh. She locks eyes with me, and I can see her debating whether she should run. But in the end, she won't.

Standing, I pocket my knife before turning and walking into the kitchen. I may not have eyes on her, but I listen intently as the rustle of the plastic bag hints she's interested in what's inside. Her uneven footsteps toward the bathroom please me beyond words.

However, when I hear the creak of the door, I pause from hunting through the refrigerator. "Leave the door open," I order.

All I get in return is a huff, but the door stays ajar.

I grant her privacy by ensuring I keep my back turned as I prepare lunch for us. Having no idea what she likes, I decide to make a Borscht soup. This is one of the only happy memories I have of my mother. She perfected this recipe because it was my father's favorite.

As I go about chopping what's needed, my thoughts focus on Zoya. Renata's interactions with her leave me curious. I almost want to know more about her than I do Serg. She's the reason for all of this. I often wonder why she turned her back on me.

Even before I killed Boris, she despised me. She said I was the spitting image of my father, a fact I thought she would like, but when he died, it seemed her love for him did too. But Zoya only loves one person, and that's herself.

Footsteps sounding against the kitchen floor drag my mind from the past—a place I cannot afford to be. Turning over my shoulder, I see Renata freshly showered and wearing the blue summer dress I bought her.

I also purchased other supplies like toiletries. I have firsthand knowledge of what a captive needs. I was the one who supplied Saint with all the essentials when he kidnapped Willow. A heavy feeling sinks in the pit of my stomach when I think how history seems to be repeating itself.

"Can I please have a glass of water?"

Renata's manners have me nodding before returning to preparing our meal.

I'm aware of her lithe movements as she pads across the kitchen and toward the sink. She reaches for a mug in the dish rack and turns on the water. She gulps down four helpings before wiping her mouth with the back of her hand.

"Is that Borscht?" she asks, peering at the food on the counter.

"Yes." I'm impressed she knows what it is. However, what she says next has me wishing I'd chosen another meal.

"Your mother used to make that for me. She said it was your favorite."

I grip the knife handle tight, breathing steadily to calm myself down. "My mother is full of shit," I snap, slicing through the beetroot in anger. "I wouldn't believe a word she told you."

Renata is quiet, pensive even. "She said you fell in love. Is that true?"

For this to work, we have to gain one another's trust. This is the last topic I want to broach, but I suppose it's a starting point. "Yes. I did."

"Hmm," she says as if finding it hard to believe. "Your mother said she was your weakness. That you sacrificed everyone for her."

I don't reply. But that doesn't deter Renata.

"They're looking for her."

Her admission has me turning my cheek to look at her. "What?"

"The woman. They're looking for her."

My stomach drops and bile rises. "They'll never find her. She is with someone who'd move heaven and earth to protect her."

"Saint?" she questions.

Renata is the inside man I need. Her knowledge will help me defeat my enemies. "Yes, Saint. He once worked for me."

She nods, mulling over what I revealed. "Where are they now?"

Renata has random pieces of a puzzle that she has no idea what the picture is of. She's trying to make sense of this. "I don't know," I reply truthfully. "And it's better that way."

If Serg ever found out their whereabouts, he would use them both as bait.

"I don't understand any of this," she confesses, running a

hand down her face. "Why did he choose me?"

With a sigh, I reveal, "Because you look like her, like… Willow. My дорогая."

Renata's mouth parts in horror. "Oh, my god. Serg wanted his own…pet?"

I flinch, but she's right. This is what Willow was supposed to be. A plaything. But she turned out to be so much more.

"Willow was so much more to me than a pet. But essentially, yes."

Renata takes a moment to process what I've just shared. "How did you protect her? You kept her safe when you had nothing."

"I had help from some friends." Some of whom are now dead.

"Serg said you didn't have any of those left. You killed them all."

"He's right," I counter sharply.

Renata is inquisitive, but this is the last thing I want to be discussing. She senses my bad temper over this topic. "Sorry, I just…you were all he talked about. Actually meeting you is kind of surreal. He has no idea where you are, and it really pissed him off.

"He doesn't know who your allies are. Whoever you have on your side is loyal, and he hates that."

"Allies?" I shake my head with a sad grin. "I don't have very many of them anymore. I am merely a shadow of who I once was."

Renata shrugs, leaning against the counter. "If that were true, then why is he so desperate to find you? Why is he trying to be you?"

As I continue chopping the vegetables for our meal, I realize Renata has given me food for thought. I never saw it that way. He is making a name off me because he is nothing. I may now be poor and everyone's enemy, but it seems I still have social standing. It gives me hope that when I find Serg and kill him, I can claim back what's mine without any pushback.

"Raul told me Serg is living in your shadow," she reveals. "That he wishes he was you. He doesn't respect him. I think that's the reason he had no issues going behind Serg's back."

Renata's overshare is my gain. I don't know why she feels compelled to tell me this, but whatever the reason, I don't question it. "Raul doesn't respect me either," I explain. "That's what happens when you murder someone's father."

Renata doesn't seem surprised by this fact, which means Raul told her. "He wants you dead, yes, but in regards to who he respects more..." She pauses and shrugs, leaving her comment open for discussion.

My cell rings, interrupting a conversation that has given me a lot to think about. Wiping my hands on a tea towel, I reach into my pocket and see the caller is Pavel.

This isn't a social call. When Pavel calls, it's usually because he has work. I answer, keeping it brief as I know Renata is listening.

Pavel has a job lined up. A family I know well is looking to buy three hundred semi-automatics rifles, hand guns, and grenades. They want them tonight.

"Are you in?" Pavel asks when I don't give him an answer.

This is a big job, and a lot of money is at stake if I say no. But I have a problem, and that's Renata. What am I supposed to do with her?

"Yes," I finally reply.

He gives me directions and a time, and then the line goes dead.

With a sigh, I slip my cell back into my pocket.

Renata is watching me closely as she plays with the locket around her neck. She knows something is amiss. I want to believe she won't run if I leave her, but I know she will. We may be speaking civilly, but I don't mistake this for anything other than another ploy of hers.

"So, respect," I commence, referring to our conversation before Pavel called as I turn to look at her. "I will respect you as long as you do the same."

She nods quickly, too quickly, setting off alarm bells. I thought I had more time, but the test starts now.

"Good," I commend, folding my arms across my chest. "I feel I've been more than respectful toward you." Before she has a chance to scoff, I continue. "I brought you here when I could have left you in the woods. I allowed you to shower. I covered your modesty. And now, I am preparing us a meal."

She slowly backs away from me, unsure where I'm going with this.

"As I see it, it's now your turn to reciprocate."

"How?"

She is nervous. Good.

Without hesitation, I order, "Kneel."

She scoffs as if I'm joking. But when I deadpan her, she

soon realizes I am not.

"What the hell? No!" she exclaims, shaking her head.

Chuckling, I counter, "Bless you for thinking this is optional."

She moves further away, her eyes never leaving mine. "I am not *fucking* kneeling. I'm done being someone's prisoner."

Clucking my tongue, I remain rigid, allowing her to think she has a head start. "Who said anything about being a prisoner? This is a sign of respect. I bowed to you, not in the literal sense, and now, I want you to bow to me."

"Why?" she asks, her voice cracking. She looks rather lovely in her blue dress. After my encounter with Sister Arabella earlier today, I can't deny I have a lot of steam I need to blow off. But not like this.

"Because this will show me that you'll do what you're told." I know she'd rather cut off her arm than submit again, but she's coming to learn obeying me makes things easier. She's hungry, tired, and the fight in her is simmering.

I expect her to reach for the door handle and try to make a run for it, but she doesn't. This is hardly her surrendering completely, but it's progress. With a scowl, she drops to her knees slowly. If looks could kill, I'd be a smoldering pile of ashes, but I take it because what I see is utterly exquisite.

I've forgotten the euphoria experienced with submission, especially when a stubborn, beautiful woman like Renata submits. I take my time, examining the sight before me, and suddenly, I wish I had another beside Renata.

Sister Arabella is also stubborn and fiery. I know I promised to leave her be, but one can fantasize.

It's been so long since I've been with a woman. Something which was at my disposal whenever I wanted it is now a distant memory. But Renata presented this way has me wondering if she just may, in fact, break me.

"Now what?" she asks, licking her lips nervously.

Walking over to her leisurely, I savor the way she anticipates my next move, and I can't deny it excites me. The leader I once was is basking in the power. I think back to seeing her naked. I know what lies beneath that flimsy dress.

Standing before her, I gently cup her chin and run my thumb along her bottom lip. "How old are you, малышка?"

Her lip quivers with my touch. "Twenty-five," she replies, attempting to conceal the nervousness to her tone.

"You're merely a child," I say, shaking my head. "I'm almost double your age. An old man compared to you."

She doesn't reply. But she doesn't need to speak. The way she responds to my touch speaks volumes.

Seeing her this way has memories of Willow smashing into me. The resemblance is uncanny. I am fond of Renata because of this. Usually, I wouldn't lower my guard as I have with her, but looking into those blue eyes has me melting under their stare.

Running my thumb along the column of her throat, I watch the way her body grows lax. Beneath her tough exterior, she wants to submit. The thought of spending the next three weeks with her suddenly doesn't seem so bad.

But I need to focus.

This prejudice is only because of Willow. I need to remember why she's here.

Circling over her pulse, I run my finger along the thin chain at her neck. Opening the locket, I see there is a photo of a dog inside. No mother? Sister? Boyfriend?

I remove my hand, watching the way she sags forward, appearing to be under a spell. This is dangerous ground we both tread. "Once we finish eating, I need to take care of some business. Can I trust you to stay here unsupervised?"

My voice seems to snap her from her stupor as she fumbles to close the locket. "Yes. We want the same thing," she says. "Besides, I don't know where I am. To get my revenge, I have to work with you. You're the lesser of two evils."

I examine her closely to see if I can detect any cracks on the surface. I have to trust she is telling me the truth. We're not there yet, but unless I tie her up again, I have to listen to my gut. "If you run," I commence, cupping her chin and arching her head backward, "I will find you. And when I do, I won't be so tolerant. Understood?"

She nods slowly.

Releasing her, I go back to preparing our meal. I wonder if I've made the right choice. The smart thing to do would be to tie her up. But this is a test. To gain her trust, I have to reciprocate with trust. This won't work otherwise.

However, as Renata stays on her knees, watching me prepare us a meal, I realize if this works, then I'm surely screwed.

CHAPTER
FIVE

I pull my SUV up by the curb. Pavel waits for me in his van by the mansion gates. This transaction isn't operating under the guise of darkness. The Macrillo family has most of Russia on their payroll. No one would dare to double-cross them.

We had a mutual respect for one another when I was top dog. We stayed out of each other's business because while my specialty was drugs, the Macrillo family dealt in weaponry. We coexisted because we were never a threat or competition to one another.

But now, that respect is no longer.

Pavel reaches out of his window and presses the intercom, announcing our arrival. A moment later, the gates swing open. Nostalgia sweeps over me when the impressive white mansion comes into full view. The manicured grounds are immaculate, a must for any upstanding household to have. It's the first thing a visitor sees. First impressions last.

I follow Pavel up the driveway and toward the house. Once we've parked, Pavel exits his van and opens the side door. I'm here to help him unload his goods because three hundred pieces of heavy artillery is exactly that—heavy.

Slipping on my sunglasses, I open my door and commence unloading the duffel bags from Pavel's van. It's a nice change not having to look over our shoulders. The Macrillo family doesn't want trouble. They just want their arsenal.

In total, there are four bags. Pavel and I carry two each toward the marbled entrance. We don't have a chance to ring the bell before the front doors open, and we're greeted by Santino Macrillo—the head of the family.

"*Ciao*," he says with a smile.

Santino was born in Sicily, where the Macrillo family name had no standing. But that soon changed when Santino realized he was destined for great things. He annihilated all his competitors, and once he had taken over Italy, he decided Russia was next on the agenda when he met his now wife, Mila.

Santino has four boys—all of whom have taken after their father.

In short, you don't fuck with this family.

"Hello, Santo," Pavel says casually as though he's greeting an old friend. But people like Santino don't have friends.

I guess that's where we differed.

Santino looks my way. I'm accustomed to the looks of pity on the faces of my former equals. They see me as nothing but pathetic. That it would have been better if I had died that night in the field. But Santino is different.

I don't see pity. I see interest.

"*Ciao*, Santo. *Come stai*?" I ask how he is in his native tongue.

"I am good, my old friend. And you?"

"Living the dream," I reply with sarcasm, taking off my glasses.

Santo laughs as he welcomes us into his home.

I've been here once before when one of Santo's sons, Lorenzo, got engaged. It was a grand affair, but nothing less was expected. The foyer itself is about twice the size of my home.

We don't say a word and follow Santo as he leads us through the hallways and into his office. Everything is decorated in gold. This space is to once again display Santo's wealth. Like anyone would forget. And when I notice him continuing to look at me, I begin to wonder why I'm really here.

"Place everything there," he instructs, gesturing to the bar. We do as he says.

He opens the bottom drawer of his wooden desk and tosses a black duffel onto the polished surface. "You can count it," he casually offers.

Pavel shakes his head as he reaches for the bag. "No need."

That's how business operates with men like Santo and Pavel. Their word is enough. If they were to ever go back on their word, then many would pay with their heads.

Pavel shoulders the duffel, hinting it's time to leave. However, Santo walks over to the bar and reaches for a bottle of scotch. "Aleksei, will you have a drink with me?"

The offer isn't extended to Pavel. Only me.

"Of course," I agree. Pavel nods his farewell to me. There is a man standing at the door, waiting to escort Pavel outside.

When he's gone, Santo gestures for me to close the door as he pours us our drinks. I do as he asks.

This is Santo's domain, and I will respect him and whatever is headed my way. He offers me the crystal glass. I accept, cherishing the feel of good crystal in my hand because it's been a while.

"I have a proposition for you, Aleksei," Santo commences, not bothering to sugarcoat why I'm here.

I drink my scotch, waiting for him to continue.

"You were here when my eldest Lorenzo got engaged, weren't you?"

"Yes, I was. It was a joyous occasion," I reply with a nod.

"That it was. His wife is a wonderful woman. Did you know three of my sons are now married?"

"I did." I have no idea where he is going with this, but I soon find out.

"My youngest, Francesco, he was to be married in three months' time. To a…foreigner," he reveals with a disapproving scoff. "I told him she was not right for him. But my Frank, he is stubborn, just like his papa."

"I suppose one cannot help who they fall in love with."

Santo sips his drink, appearing to mull over my words. "This is true. I can't blame him. She is an absolute beauty."

"The dangerous ones usually are," I say from experience.

Santo laughs, understanding my personal response. He soon turns serious however. "She promised me she loved him and understood what becoming a part of this family meant. But she lied, Aleksei."

I finish my drink, needing a moment to process what he's just disclosed.

"She broke Frank's heart when she decided she no longer wanted to marry him. She betrayed this family. And for that, she must pay."

This poor woman is living on borrowed time. No one betrays the Macrillo family and lives to tell the tale.

"Loyalty is hard to come by, Santo. Believe me, I know this firsthand," I share as he knows of my story. He knows what was done to me and what I did, which is why we're having this conversation.

He knows what I did to my best friends. He knows I had no qualms about killing them.

"Yes, you, my friend, have experienced a similar betrayal. I hate to see you this way. Your place is rightfully on top, but it was stolen from you...which is why I want to help you."

He gestures to fill up my empty glass, but I wave him off. He has something I want. And I have something he wants—I just don't know what that is yet.

"Serg is a parasite. Quite frankly, he is a disgrace to our world. I want him gone as he has caused nothing but problems for me and many of my colleagues."

I keep my emotion under key because I still don't know what Santo wants.

"I will find your brother and deliver him to you, and once you're back where you belong, I will help you stay there. It won't be easy. Alliances have divided, and as it stands, no one wants to do business with you. But I can change that. I will ensure your name is once again feared and respected."

He is offering me everything I desire on a silver platter. But what's the catch?

"In return, I ask that you find that whore who betrayed this family and bring her to me. I would do it myself, but Frank, the sentimental fool, still loves her. I need this to be discreet. No one in the family can know of this, which is why I've come to you, old friend.

"This needs to be an outside job. If Frank were to ever find out, he'd never forgive me."

Piece by piece, I come to understand my role.

Santo could do this himself, but the Macrillos are a tightknit family, so Frank would eventually find out. This needs to be done by an outsider.

The prospect of Santo delivering Serg to me is most appealing. I already have a date with destiny in three weeks, thanks to Renata, but his help is imperative. I need "friends" now more than ever.

Thinking over my options, I decide that whether Santo delivers me Serg or Renata does, the result is the same. Serg will pay with his life. If I find this woman before the meeting with Serg and Raul is to take place, then I will still have a date with Raul three weeks from now.

He must also pay for siding with the wrong brother.

As I see it, I can't lose. Santo is someone I need on my side. And you don't say no to Santo.

"Of course, I don't expect you to do this without payment. Would a hundred thousand dollars be enough?"

And that's the bounty Santo has on this woman's head.

I think of what that money could do for me and for the orphanage. But agreeing means I'm condemning an innocent woman to death. I promised I wouldn't do that again, but is the life of a stranger more important than mine? Of that of the orphaned children?

God forgive me.

"Make it a hundred and fifty and we've got a deal."

Santo smirks, enjoying the challenge. "Excellent. I will compile all the information I have on her. Give me a couple of days? I need to be cautious."

Nodding, I understand his concerns. His sons are involved in all aspects of his business. He needs to ensure no one uncovers his plans.

The conversation is over, so I don't prolong the inevitable. "Very well. Call me when you're ready."

Santo is absolutely pleased to do business with me. And why wouldn't he? He knows I won't stop until I find her. What he's offering is everything I've fought for these past eighteen months.

"Oh, Aleksei," he adds, walking toward his desk. "Be careful. Her beauty has blinded many."

I sense hurt in his comment. Could it be Santo was the one blinded? This is personal—but just not the way I thought.

Whatever the reason, it's not my concern. I have a job to do. And that's what this woman is—a job.

"Not to worry, Santo. I won't make that mistake again."

Santo nods, opening the drawer. He places five stacks of hundred-dollar bills onto the desk. This is my down payment—merely pocket change for a man like him. He then places the money into a black plastic bag and pushes it toward me.

We're done. For now.

Without anything further to say, I accept his offering and leave. Following Santo's bodyguard, who waits outside the door, I exit through the front door and walk to my SUV calmly. Tossing the bag onto the passenger seat, I get behind the wheel and commence my drive toward the open gates.

I drive impassively for minutes until I come to a stop at a red light. Peering over at the bag, I feel my stomach fill with dread. To get what I want, I need to sacrifice the life of yet another innocent human being. But that's the life I live.

Sighing, I dial the cell I gave to Renata. It once belonged to a man I killed. She picks up on the third ring. "Hello, малышка," I say, using the nickname which has stuck.

"Hi," she replies. Before I ask, she opens the oven door. It whines loudly, and I smile. This is to show me she has obeyed me and has stayed at home.

I didn't tie her up, so it was a gamble. I'm glad she listened.

"I have to drop in and see someone. Can I get you anything while I'm out?"

Silence.

I acknowledge playing civil is a strange concept, but I think she is coming to see I'm not the enemy here.

"Can you get some orange juice? You have a lot of vodka, but nothing to mix it with."

Scoffing, I playfully shake my head at her audacity. "That's because you don't mix vodka with anything. But very well.

Anything else?"

"No. Thank you," she adds before hanging up.

That was progress. For starters, she hasn't run, so that's definitely a plus. However, remembering the way Renata looked on her knees when she was submitting to me has me wondering what's ahead for us. I can't imagine it's anything good.

I drive to the orphanage as I want to give Mother Superior twenty thousand dollars. It'll help her immensely as I know times are tough. Once I get more money, I'll ensure she gets at least half.

The prospect of seeing Sister Arabella again stirs a passion deep in my loins. I know I promised to stay away from her, but I can't help the excitement I feel. After our last encounter, she most likely will not want to be in the same room as me, but just seeing her from afar is more than enough.

I realize I have two very different women in my life. Both interest me for varied reasons. Over the past eighteen months, no one has caught my eye, but that's because I wasn't looking. I'm still not, but I can't deny that Renata and Sister Arabella have awoken something inside me.

Like night and day, both have one thing in common.

They're both trouble.

The kids are playing happily behind the gates, and when they see my SUV, they run toward the steel fence, looping their small fingers through the links. They're happy here, but most are looking for their forever home.

They want a family to call their own.

I park my car and grab the plastic bag. When I exit, I

wave to the children as they scream out their hellos. Sister Yali lightly shoos them away from the fence. I walk up the front stairs, smiling at Sister Robin as I sign in at reception.

"Is Mother Superior in?"

"Yes. Should I page her?"

"It's okay. If I don't say hello to Irina first, she'll ensure I read her favorite story three times instead of the standard two times." Sister Robin grins and buzzes me through the security door.

With my bag in hand, I walk down the hallway. A sense of peace always falls over me when I walk these halls. It's changed quite a lot since the refurb, but I still remember like it was yesterday when Willow, Saint, and Zoey were here.

It's a strange memory to have—it's bittersweet, I suppose you can say. Although we were fighting for our lives, it was a time when I felt I wasn't alone. Zoey emerged a phoenix, and the sight was truly beautiful. I squashed that fire in her all because I was a selfish asshole who got off on power and control.

Sara and Ingrid also suffered. I wonder what life Sara and Max would have lived if her life hadn't been cut tragically short. Max has long gone, the memory of seeing me too brutal to deal with. I reminded him of his lover's death. I wish I could go too.

But I can't. Living with this on my conscience is punishment for what I've done.

"Aleksei," Mother Superior says, almost bumping into me as she exits the library. "What a lovely surprise."

She looks beyond exhausted, which is why I decide to

give her thirty thousand instead of twenty. "May I speak with you in your office?"

She peers down at the plastic bag in my hand, then walks down the hallway. I follow, certain she knows the contents of the bag. Once inside her office, I close the door behind me before taking a seat.

She sits behind her desk, steepling her fingers, waiting for me to speak. In this circumstance, actions speak a lot louder than words.

Digging into the bag, I retrieve three piles of money and place them neatly on her desk. "There is thirty thousand dollars here," I start before she can object. "This isn't negotiable. Take it."

"Aleksei," she says, shaking her head. She never asks where the money comes from because she knows I would never lie to her. She'd rather not know because, in this case, doesn't the greater good win out?

"Please, Mother Superior. You need this, now more than ever. The orphanage is struggling. I know you'd rather I—"

But she doesn't allow me to finish. "I wouldn't rather anything, my child. Your generosity is just too much. I know you seek penance for all that you've done, but He sees everything. We're not perfect. Even the Lord himself made mistakes."

All that I've done and all that I plan to do are hardly comparable to the Lord's minor misdemeanors.

"You're a good man, Aleksei."

"That all depends on who you speak to." I push the stacks of money toward her, not wanting praise. "I will have more soon. And then no more begging to the rich ass—"

Mother Superior purses her lips, interrupting my curse.

"You know what I mean," I settle on saying. "I don't want you to struggle. The kids deserve this. You deserve this."

Mother Superior has always grappled with accepting money. She isn't stupid. She knows it's dirty. But most money is. Whether one threw someone under the bus to get the promotion or lied to get extra shifts, we do what's necessary to survive.

And if Mother Superior doesn't accept this money, it'll make surviving here at full capacity very difficult.

She eventually concedes, leaning forward and drawing the money toward her. She opens the desk drawer and places it inside. "Thank you. This orphanage would be nothing without you."

I appreciate her kindness, but it does nothing to erase the horrible things I've done.

"I better go see Irina." When Mother Superior toys with the large cross around her neck, I arch a brow. "What's the matter?"

"I didn't want to say anything, but Sister Arabella found cuts on her legs."

"On whose legs?" I don't understand what she's saying, so she clarifies.

"Irina. We believe she is self-harming. Sister Arabella found a paring knife she stole from the kitchen under her pillow."

"She's *seven* years old." I voice my horror, my disbelief aloud.

"I know, Aleksei. I didn't want to worry you."

Running a hand through my hair, I exhale, sickened. It's too late. I *am* worried. "What can I do?"

"Just being here for her does more than you know. She needs stability. A family who won't return her because she is hard work."

In no way is Mother Superior trying to drop a hint, but we both know that if my life was completely different, I would adopt Irina without a second thought. But truth be told, I would never do that to her. What do I know about raising a child?

I would screw her up more than she already is.

"I sometimes wish life was different for us all, Mother Superior."

She nods in understanding.

Needing to see Irina, I stand and bid farewell to Mother Superior.

What I just heard makes me feel sickened beyond words. I can't shift this heavy weight in the pit of my stomach. I want to find Irina's family and murder them with my bare hands. Needing a moment to calm down before I seek Irina out, I shove open the door leading to the gardens. Thankfully, I'm alone.

Tossing the bag across the lawn, I begin to pace, interlacing my fingers behind my neck, unsure what to do with this emotion inside me. Before Willow, I was so detached from my feelings. It was easier this way. I want to go back there because I don't know how to deal with, with…*this*.

Midpace, someone gently grips my elbow, but I don't see

their touch as gentle. It's an attack, and I spring into action, ready to take down whoever is before me. I'm blinded by the rage currently animating me. I don't know what I'm doing until I'm basking in a dark fruity floral scent.

"Al-Aleksei?" Her soft voice washes away the anger, and I realize what I've done.

I have Sister Arabella pinned to the brick wall with my forearm pressed over her throat. I don't even remember doing this.

"What's wrong?" she gasps as I feel her swallow beneath my grip. Instantly, I release the hold on her throat, but I don't let her go. I enjoy the feel of her pressed against me as I cage her in by placing my hands on either side of her head.

"What's *right*, Sister? That's the better question here," I counter, looking deeply into her expressive eyes. "I am so… *fucking* angry. The urge to hurt someone is almost unbearable. Before I knew I had a conscience, life was so much easier. I did what I wanted, when I wanted."

She allows me this purge. Yet another confession, it seems.

"I did *who* I wanted. But now, I'm a prisoner to this thing called life. My manacles are invisible because I'm a prisoner to caring when quite frankly, I wish I didn't."

"What has made you so upset?"

Bless her for caring because after our last encounter, she shouldn't be trying to console me. But that's the type of woman she is.

"How can a seven-year-old even think about self-harming? This should be the best time of her life. But instead, she's been returned countless times like some dog at a shelter,"

I share, not needing to clarify who I speak of.

Her face expresses her sadness. "I understand. It's not fair, it really isn't. But He—"

"Oh, fuck Him!" I snarl, not wanting to hear about God's plan. What exactly is His plan for Irina if He believes this is the right path a seven-year-old should be on?

Sister Arabella flinches as I've just insulted her Almighty, but He can go to hell as far as I'm concerned. "Alek, please calm down. Irina is safe here. She has friends. She has you."

"Me?" I question, shaking my head with an angry, lopsided smirk. "And what good am I to her, Sister? I read her a story every so often, ask her how she's been, but then I go back to my life, leaving her here, wondering when I will be back."

My anger won't subside. My body vibrates with it. Sister Arabella can feel the rage pulsating through me. She should push me away, but she doesn't.

"What can I do?" she asks, reaching up slowly and wrapping her cold fingers around my wrist. "Let me help you."

"Be careful what you ask. You may not like the answer," I warn, the touch of her dancing with my demons. "Why do you care? Why can't you seem to leave me alone?"

She licks her lips but doesn't back down. Surely, she knows I want her the way I shouldn't.

"Tell me what you want," she softly says, her breaths quickening.

Once again, Sister Arabella has shocked me.

After our encounter in the chapel, it seems she wants more. "I want these...feelings to go away. Usually, I would find solace in a woman or two and lose myself to the Utopia of being connected in the most primeval way there is. But I don't want that now."

"Why not?" she dares to ask, and like the desperate man I am, I submit.

Lowering my lips to her ear, I savor her sweet scent as I confess, "Because I want you, Sister. All ways. Any way I can get you."

The gasp that escapes her feeds me. I want her on all fours while I lift her habit and spank that magnificent ass. I want her bound while I fuck her brutally, and the only thing she wears is the crucifix around her neck, swaying between her beautiful breasts.

"What do you think about that? Still want to help?"

Slowly pulling away, I ensure our lips are mere inches apart. I could close the distance and give in to temptation, but I don't. The chase, the game of cat and mouse is what I want for now. But what she says next throws me on my ass.

"I give you a blowjob or allow you to…fuck me, and what then?" Those filthy words spilling from her ruby lips leaves me speechless. "You may feel better for a small fraction of time, but the pain will always return. These are quick fixes, Alek. You need to find the root of the problem and deal with it.

"I think it's time you stopped running. Don't you think? Face your problems or, rather, *problem*." How can she read me so well? But more importantly, why does she care?

She speaks of Willow, and she's right. I can't get over her. I don't know how. She was the first person in my entire life who actually cared about me, really cared. She came back for me when no one, *no one* else ever did, and I wanted her. I still *want* her, but she doesn't want me.

I'm truly happy for her and Saint, but that doesn't lessen my pain. She is everywhere I look. And I don't know how to make it stop.

"You know nothing of my problems, *Sister*," I bark, my walls standing firmly in place.

"Then tell me," she counters, squeezing my wrist. "Because all I see is a desperate, lonely man begging for help."

In other words, she sees me as weak and pathetic, things I promised myself I would never be again.

"We're done," I state, still invading her personal space. I knew Sister Arabella would be dangerous, but I just never anticipated how much.

"Alek, it's okay to be vulnerable. You're a good person. I know that you are. I just want to be your friend."

Snarling, I push away, hating that she can read me so clearly. "Enough! You can't give me what I need, so I will find it elsewhere. And trust me when I say you don't want to be my friend. They all die."

"Why are you so cruel?" she asks, looking at me like I'm a puzzle she desperately wants to decipher.

"Because that's all I know to be." She watches me as I retrieve the bag and make my way toward the door. I don't look back. I won't make the same mistake again.

As I'm charging through the hallway, blinded by my rage, I bump into Sister Margaret. "Oh, excuse me, Sister," I say, gripping her biceps to stop her from falling.

"That's okay, Alek. The Lord does work in mysterious ways."

I smile, tamping down my need to express what I think of *her* Lord, and His ways as I let her go.

"I wanted to speak to you about Mother Superior's birthday. We know she doesn't want anything, but it's her seventieth birthday. A milestone. Don't tell her I told you her age," she adds nervously.

"I wouldn't dream of it," I reply lightly.

She sighs, thankful. "We were thinking of organizing something here. A dinner maybe? What do you think? You're her closest confidant."

"I think she will hate every second of it, which is why I think it's a marvelous idea. You only turn"—she pales while I chuckle—"twenty-one once."

Sister Margaret's lips lift into a grin. "That's what we thought. The sisters and I are putting some money together to—"

But I shake my head. "You will do nothing of the sort. Here." Offering her the bag, I place my hand over hers to stop her from looking inside. "This should cover everything. Please put what's left into the orphanage fund."

"Oh, Aleksei, you are most generous. Thank you so much."

"Good day, Sister," I say, not wanting praise. She wouldn't be so grateful if she knew what I was doing minutes ago.

I'm too worked up to see Irina, so I'll come back tomorrow. Now, I have to get away from the one place which provided comfort.

But nothing lasts forever.

I forgot the damn orange juice, but Renata didn't seem to mind. I was surprised to see her sitting on the sofa, watching TV. I half thought she'd have run by now. Without a word, I opened the freezer, grabbed the bottle of vodka, and then picked up two glasses.

That was three hours ago.

The vodka has helped loosen Renata up. She is sitting cross-legged on the sofa watching some American TV show, which is utterly ridiculous. She sips her drink, talking aloud to the characters as if they can hear her. Her slurred words hint that she's drunk.

If only I was that lucky. No matter how much I drink, it only seems to sober me up.

My phone sounds. It's a text from Pavel informing me that he'll drop off the money he owes me tomorrow. I don't know how much Santo gave him, but seeing as I gave fifty grand to the orphanage today, I'll settle for anything.

I answer, letting him know I want to run something by him tomorrow. He replies with a thumbs-up. Seems so harmless in light of what I want to discuss.

I have a lot of money coming to me soon, which will help with my grand plan of climbing my way back to the top. At least one thing is working in my favor.

I'm so restless. I desperately need to burn off this stagnant weight pressing down on my chest. I could go for a run. I thought the vodka would help, but it hasn't. I really miss my piano at times such as these. It was the one thing that calmed the roaring demons within.

I don't understand why Sister Arabella won't back down. Her tenacity reminds me of Willow. When she looked at me, it was evident she was desperately trying to work me out. I notice the same look in the Sister's eyes.

She cares, and I don't know how to feel about that.

Without a word, I stand, aware of Renata watching me. "Where're you going?"

"Outside for a smoke," I reply, snatching the gold cigar case from the coffee table. I can't remember who I stole this from.

"Can I come?"

I don't sense any malice in her request, so I nod.

She stands unsteadily, giggling when she realizes she's drunk. Her carefree nature must be a nice thing to have. She follows me outside, her bare feet sounding lightly on the floor. When we step out onto the small balcony, I open the case, offering her a thin Cuban.

She looks down at it, working her bottom lip, but eventually reaches for one. She watches in interest as I cut into the cap with my blade before holding the lighter flame to the foot of the cigar, rotating it a few times. Once it's warm, I light it and inhale.

Lighting a cigar distinguishes the men from the boys.

I pass Renata the lighter, but it's clear she has no idea what to do, so I puff on my cigar, then pass it to her. She accepts with a shy smile. When she inhales deeply, I wait for the coughing to commence.

"Oh god, that's strong," she wheezes, thumping her chest. But I'm impressed when she doesn't allow that to deter her.

Lighting my own cigar, I lean against the railing, savoring the tobacco hit. I look out into the vast nothingness, angered my half-brother is still breathing the same air as I.

"Where did you go today?"

I don't want to make conversation; however, she is nothing but persistent. "Just had some business to take care of."

"What sort of business?" she asks. She's curious, which is natural, but I don't plan on sharing my life events with her like discussing the weather.

"Are you always this nosy?" I counter, not making eye contact with her.

"Yes," she replies, not deterred by my frankness. "I just figured if we're stuck with one another for the next few weeks, maybe we can talk instead of sitting in silence."

"Or maybe not," I disagree lightly, blowing a ring of smoke.

"How are you going to do it?" she questions, ignoring me. "I can tell you where to find them, but will you ambush them? You can't expect to do this on your own. You have allies, right?"

"Let me worry about that." I'm not sure how much more straightforward I can be.

"What happens when they're…?" She leaves the sentence unfinished, suggesting she isn't ready for what I have planned for Serg, Raul, and whoever else is against me.

Pavel is smart. He has achieved all he has and stayed alive

because he works alone. He is discreet, and he doesn't mess in matters that don't involve him. Not many people know we're allies, which is why I have an advantage over Serg.

I plan on reenacting that fated night, seeing as my half-brother and my "friends" felt sentimental by using the grounds of where my house once stood as their meetup spot. But this time, I'll be victorious. There will be no survivors because if you're not with me, you're against me. And lucky for me, Pavel is with me. He has all the ammunition and explosives I need. I may not have manpower, but I have dynamite and high-powered guns.

It's not foolproof, but no plan ever is. My need for vengeance will ensure I don't fail.

I just need to be within the same space as Serg. I've been chasing a ghost, but thanks to Renata, that's going to change.

"When we both get our revenge, I'll ensure your safe return back home."

"Oh." I can hear the surprise in her tone. "How are you going to do that? Serg made it seem like you didn't have any pull. But he was wrong?"

"You should know by now that he is full of shit," I reply, turning my cheek to look at her. "I may not be where I once was, but it's only a matter of time."

"You're going to make sure your mom pays as well, aren't you?"

Renata is a smart woman. "Yes. As I see it, she and I have unfinished business."

When a smile tugs at her lips, I realize this fact pleases her. Zoya's impending death has that effect on people.

"Well, I want to help. Any way I can."

"You can tell me where this alleged meeting is to take place," I counter quickly as she still hasn't shared the details.

I don't blame her. It's her only bargaining chip. We may be able to play civil, but we're a long way away from trusting one another.

"Nice try. If this whole thing has taught me anything," she says, taking a long pull of her cigar. "It's don't trust handsome men."

The moment the words spill free, she bites her upper lip, as if trying to hold back what she just shared. But it's too late. I heard it.

I don't know how to respond to her admission. The last time she flirted, I ended up stabbed. But I don't sense any deception this time.

"Sorry, I'm drunk." She backtracks quickly, pinching the bridge of her nose in embarrassment. "I don't know what I'm saying."

"Don't worry about it." I brush it off because I honestly don't want to deal with any more awkwardness.

She nods, and I think we're good, but she catches me completely unaware when she leans across and kisses me.

At first, I wonder if maybe I am drunk, but when her soft, warm lips part mine, nudging me to reciprocate, I realize this is really happening. My mouth moves against hers, savoring this close connection with another being because it's been so long.

Turning my body, I wrap my fingers around the back of her neck, drawing her closer to me. She stands on her toes to accommodate my sudden need to consume her whole. Flashes of what I want to do to her spark to life, and a carnal need to push her beyond pleasure so she's straddling pain overtakes me, and I pick her up, slamming her ass onto the balcony railing.

We continue to kiss. She threads her fingers through my hair while I dominate her lips and body, never giving her a chance to breathe. She doesn't fight me. She surrenders, which only awakens the sleeping lion within.

When she begins to unfasten the buttons on my shirt, the line we're about to cross becomes clear. Yes, I'm old enough to be her father, but we're two consenting adults. And right now, she feels so good, and I can think of nothing else.

However, when she murmurs my name, something else inside me rouses. Sister Arabella's scent and the curves of her body slam into me, and I realize that's because no matter how good this feels, it's secondary to what I want.

Renata isn't who I want. Sister Arabella is.

She is completely off-limits, which is a part of the reason I want her. But doing this with Renata will only complicate things, and I don't need any more complications. I need her, but not in this way.

"малышка, no," I say from around her lips before pulling away.

Her bubble soon pops when her eyes flicker open. Her red puffy lips are like waving a flag in front of a bull, but I'm doing the right thing. I need to stop this before it crosses the point of no return.

"No?" she questions. "It didn't feel like no a few seconds ago."

Her temper surfaces, which is another reason I had to stop things. She is unpredictable, and there is too much riding on this to give in to temptation. I brought this on myself. It appears my methods are still effective.

"I'm sorry. I can't." I let her go, allowing her to jump down from the railing when she realizes I'm serious. She folds her arms across her chest, clearly angry.

Yes, no one likes being rejected, but there seems to be something more to her response. I don't know what that is, but it unsettles me.

"That can never happen again," I state firmly, wanting to shut this down immediately.

She flinches, but soon conceals her hurt. "Okay, whatever." She tosses her cigar over the balcony, then brushes past me and goes back inside.

Sighing, I turn back around to look out over the balcony. Smoking what's left of my cigar, I begin to wonder if there is more to Renata than she is letting on. I don't know anything about her, which is a very dangerous thing.

She submitted easier than I thought. But she seems to have a way of making me lower my guard. I don't even realize it until it's too late. And I know why that is.

She holds more resemblance to Willow than I thought possible. But I must never forget that Renata isn't Willow. I can't make that mistake ever again.

CHAPTER SIX

A banging on the door wakes me.

Rubbing my eyes, I see that I fell asleep on the deck chair outside. It seems I'd rather sleep out here than inside as memories from last night surface.

Groaning, I come to a stand, shielding the morning sun from my eyes as the banging continues. Renata is sprawled out on my bed on her stomach with her dress pulled up, exposing her ass. Ignoring the sight, I walk toward the front door.

When I open it and see Pavel, I quickly close it behind me, but he's seen enough.

"Who's the girl?" he asks, eyes narrowed.

"She is my ticket to Serg."

He folds his arms, indicating he's listening.

I detail our encounter, and just who she is and how I intend to work with her to finally get my revenge. Once I'm done, I wait for him to speak. Pavel has mastered his poker face, so I don't bother attempting to decipher what he's thinking.

"Are you sure she is who she says she is?"

Shaking my head, I reply, "No. She could be Mother Theresa for all I know, but she knows a lot. She knows personal things that only someone who had firsthand contact with Serg would know. She also knows about Raul."

Pavel whistles, impressed. "Let me do some background work on her and see what I can find. In the meantime, don't let that пизда distract you."

It seems he saw her ass as well.

"Here is your cut from the job. What did Santo want?" Pavel passes me a black duffel.

I nod my gratitude, accepting it. "He wants me to find someone who betrayed the family and bring them to him."

"Why can't he do that himself? He has more pull than anyone in this town."

"It's his youngest son's ex-fiancée," I explain. Pavel frowns, already expressing his empathy for the woman.

"You do this, and you know you won't be able to get out of that family," he warns.

"If I didn't know any better, I'd say you were worried about me," I taunt with a grin.

He doesn't appreciate my jibe and digs into his jacket pocket, producing some mail. No one knows I'm here, which is why my mail has been directed to Pavel's mom's house. The place holds bittersweet memories as I associate it with my old life, and that's cemented by who lies buried behind the barn.

Sara, Zoey, and a memorial for Ingrid lay under a large tree, marking their final resting place. We couldn't lay them to rest legally, so burying them at the last place we were all together made sense.

I was only permitted on Pavel's mom, Larisa's, property for the burial. Once it was done, she showed me the door with her shotgun in hand, in case I misunderstood her. I didn't. I was grateful she allowed me to put Sara, Zoey, and Ingrid to rest.

Flicking through the letters, I stop when I see a postcard. This time, it's from Mexico. I don't need to turn it over to know who it's from. Only one person would bother writing to me.

"Be careful." Pavel doesn't need to clarify. He saw me with Willow. He saw firsthand how I happily sacrificed everything for her.

Running a hand through my snarled hair, I nod. "Let me know if you find anything on the малышка. Say hi to your mom from me."

Pavel scoffs playfully, then turns around and walks toward his car.

Once he's gone, I open the door to see Renata is thankfully still sleeping. Not wanting to wake her, I quietly walk through the house and into the bathroom. Closing the door softly, I walk over to the claw bathtub that takes up way too much space.

However, this isn't here for decorative purposes.

Carefully placing the postcard onto the edge of the sink, I quietly move the bathtub over and roll back the mat. I unlock the small trapdoor I cut into the old floorboards and reach inside. The safe I bolted and then cemented into the ground is the safest place for my money.

I can't deposit it into a bank. And hiding it anywhere within these thin walls is out of the question. So the only sensible solution was to deadbolt it into the ground, then pour concrete around it, ensuring no one could dig it up.

Entering the code, I open the safe and commence placing the large stacks of cash into it, forty thousand dollars in total. Once it's all loaded in, I lock the safe and carefully place everything back in place. Just as I am rearranging the bathtub, the bathroom door opens.

Quickly stuffing the duffel into a drawer, I dart over to the toilet and flush it, faking doing up my fly.

Renata pauses when she sees me. Her blushing cheeks reveal she remembered everything that happened last night. "Sorry, I didn't realize you were in here."

"It's fine. I'm done." When I stuff the postcard into my pocket, Renata arches a brow. She's seen it, but she can never know who sent it. The less people know of Willow, the safer she'll be. "I'll leave you to it."

She steps out of the doorway so I can push past her. It seems she can't stand the touch of me after last night.

Good.

Closing the door behind me, I exhale slowly, as that was a close call. I will never get used to this houseguest nonsense, but I do need to be more careful on all accounts when it comes to Renata.

Needing to put some space between us, I toss all my dirty clothes into a bag and decide to do some laundry. I leave a note for Renata, once again putting my trust in her that she won't run.

Where I'm headed is about twenty minutes away, but I still drive. I won't take the risk of walking anywhere; it's the reason I'm still alive. Willow's postcard burns a hole in my pocket, but I decide to read it later, so I place it into the glove compartment before heading to Lia's.

The "laundromat" isn't your conventional storefront. It's in a ninety-one-year-old's backyard. Her name is Lia. She has eighteen grandchildren and ten great grandchildren, but I haven't met any of them. She lives alone. She does my laundry, and in return, I buy her groceries and pay her well for her silence and her ability to get the bloodstains out of my whites.

Oleg is the local farmer I get all my produce from. Keeping hidden means sticking to the shadows and steering clear of the mainstream. When I pull into his driveway, he waddles into his house, emerging moments later with a boxful of food.

Eggs, fresh meat, produce, and milk are all derived from his land. This is as organic as one can get. Leaving the motor running, I meet Oleg and take the box from him. Peering inside, I see he has once again packed enough food to feed a small army.

"Are you trying to fatten me up?" I tease in Russian, digging into my pocket for my wallet. I give him three hundred dollars, which is probably far more than any reasonable person would pay for groceries. But this also buys his silence.

He places the money into the top pocket of his shirt. "A hungry man is an angry man," he replies in Russian.

I don't argue because he has a point.

Placing everything into my SUV, I bid Oleg farewell and head for Lia's. A part of me doesn't mind living off the grid like this. I'm accustomed to riches, but living simply does have its benefits. When you're on top of the food chain, everything is handed to you.

But now, everything I earn, everything I have is a direct result of my doing.

Once upon a time, if I wanted my suit cleaned, I'd send someone to do it. Or I'd simply call my tailor and have him make me a new one. But those occurrences are a thing of the past. Now, nothing gets done unless I have a hand in it.

Back to the basics, I suppose you could say, and when I pull into Lia's long driveway, this is as simple as one can get. Lia lives on an old wheat farm. The earth has long dried up and produces nothing of value, but this is her home.

I park my SUV round back, seeing her scrub a floral dress down the washboard. Everything is washed by hand. If this were anyone else, I would offer to buy them a washing machine, but I wouldn't insult Lia that way.

Grabbing my clothes, I announce my arrival loudly because although Lia's hearing is superb, her eyesight failed her long ago. She stops her scrubbing, smiling when she hears me greet her.

"Здравствуйте." I kiss both her cheeks as I say hello. "I've come from Oleg's," I inform her in Russian as she doesn't speak a word of English. As I attempt to unpack my clothes from the bag, she slaps my hand away.

I take the hint and leave, grabbing the groceries. Going inside, I unpack the meat and put it in the fridge.

Oleg packed extra, knowing I would give what I don't need to Lia. In this community, we look out for our neighbors but mind our own business. That's how I've been able to remain hidden here for so long.

Lia hums along to a Russian song over the radio like she always does, always appearing most happy when busy. I wonder where her family is. It's awfully sad knowing she is here by herself most of the time, but she never complains.

But this generation never does. They push on through because that's how they were raised. Their strength is admirable, and I can only wish to be like Lia when or if I get to her age.

Once I've put the groceries away, I tidy up because her house is a mess. I doubt anyone has been by to visit her in days. Once the toilet is cleaned, I remake her bed and do a quick sweep of the house. As I sweep down the hallway, I catch my reflection in the window.

In secondhand trousers and a creased blue shirt that served as my pajamas, I don't recognize myself, but that's common these days. I once took pride in my appearance, and I still do, just not in the same way. My beard is long, as is my hair. The impeccably groomed and noble Aleksei Popov is no more.

I wish Willow could meet this version of me. I wish for a lot of things.

Thinking of her has me finishing up the sweeping and deciding to read the postcard while I wait for my laundry to dry. As I place the broom back into the closet, I notice something is out of place.

It's silent.

Lia's humming no longer floats through the air. It's deadly quiet.

I'm unarmed as I've never felt the need to carry anything when coming here. But now I realize that decision will cost me dearly. Looking out the window, I can't see anything out of place. But as I sneak down the hallway and into the kitchen, I see that that's no longer the case.

My wet clothes are strewn on the grass by the silver bucket, and Lia's chair is knocked over. Lia is nowhere to be seen.

Reaching for a knife out of the top drawer, I open the back door and scope out my surroundings, but it's too late.

"You gonna cook us dinner, старик? Drop it."

The unmistakable feel of the cool metal pressed to my temple has me doing what this lowlife says. The knife clatters to the ground while I search the yard for Lia.

"Where is she?" I order calmly, turning my cheek to look at who holds me at gunpoint. I don't recognize him, but he's barely out of diapers. How dare he hold a gun to my head?

"Why? She your girlfriend?" he mocks in broken English, laughing.

"Take whatever you want. Just don't hurt the woman."

He scoffs, moving the gun from my temple to the middle of my forehead. "I don't need your permission. We *will* take what we want, and what we want is you."

I am unmoved by his threat. "Get in line, мудак. Hurry up then."

I'll go anywhere with them and figure it out once I am away from here and Lia. However, when I hear a muffled scream, it's evident I'm too late.

Lia is dragged out from behind the house by a boy who

holds her against his chest, forearm pressed over her throat. She struggles against him, but he's young and strong. Just who are these assholes?

"Are you okay?" I ask her in Russian, thankful I can't see any cuts or bruises on her. "I'm so sorry to drag you into this. Forgive me." The sight breaks my heart.

"There is nothing to forgive, my son." She is furious these brats are here, disrespecting her in her own home.

"Let her go," I demand, eyeing the asshole who has a tight hold on her.

He laughs, tightening the hold around her neck.

"We have no interest in her," reveals the boy with the gun trained on me. "But you, we have a lot of interest in you."

"Stop talking then, идиот. Let's go."

The boy doesn't appreciate me belittling him, and as punishment, he pistol whips me.

Grunting under the impact, I rein in my temper because I can kill him later. Now, I just need them away from Lia. But Lia must have clued onto what happened because before I can stop her, she manages to twist out of her attacker's hold and stomps on his foot.

He whines, jumping on the spot, while she blindly races away from him.

"Turn around and run left!" I scream out to her, but it's too late.

When the boy next to me aims his gun at her, I shoulder him with force, and he tumbles to the ground. A wave of relief falls over me, but it's short-lived when a deafening boom shatters the world around me.

Frantically scanning the yard, what I see has me rubbing my eyes in disbelief. But no matter how many times I look away, the image of Lia's twisted, bloody body will forever be burned in my mind. With fire burning through my veins, I pick up the discarded gun near me, charge over to the stunned мудак who shot Lia and shoot him straight between the eyes.

He drops to the grass with a thud, dead even before he hit the ground. But it's not enough. I kick him in the ribs, in the stomach, wanting to expunge his measly existence from this universe.

"мудак!" I cry over and over, wishing to resuscitate him so I can kill him again.

"You motherfucker!" screams the boy who still stands. "You killed my brother!"

"Don't worry, you'll be joining him soon enough." Blinded by my rage, I'm switched off to everything around me, which would have cost me my life if not for someone who just saved my ass.

Another gunshot rings out, echoing in the usual peaceful neighborhood. Frantically turning over my shoulder, I see the boy drop to his knees as he clutches the gaping wound across his chest. It does nothing to ease the need to rip someone apart.

Spinning to look at who inflicted the gunshot wound, I do a double take, certain I'm hallucinating. But I'm not. Standing feet away is Renata, holding a smoking gun in her trembling hand.

When we lock eyes, she seems to realize what she's just done and tears well in her eyes. "He was going to hurt you," she says numbly, as if trying to justify her actions.

But there is no need. She did the right thing.

"Yes, малышка, he was. It's okay. Shh." I walk over to her slowly, not wanting to startle her more than she already is. I extend my hand, a silent command she give me the gun. On closer inspection, I see that it's my gun.

She gives it to me, eyes glued to the carnage before her.

Tucking it into the small of my back, I walk back over to the boy who is minutes away from bleeding out. "Who sent you?" I order, peering down at him as he gasps for air.

When he doesn't reply, I stomp down onto his kneecap, breaking it.

His howls feed my depravity, and I drop to a squat. "I can end this for you. Just tell me—"

The offer to end his suffering is enough to loosen his tongue. "No one sent us," he pants, eyes wide. "We live down the road, and we heard you come here. Word on the street is that Serg has a quarter-million-dollar bounty on your head."

Scoffing at their stupidity, I am insulted my half-brother thinks so little of me with that stingy reward.

This fool and his brother are or, rather, were wannabe gangsters. Every kid knows who Serg is, just as they knew who I was. He is renown among the younger generation; their *king* who sells his product to anyone as long as they have enough money.

He is an amateur and utterly disgusting. And now two kids are paying with their lives for worshiping a bogus god.

"We were going to take you to Serg. We don't know where he is, but we were going to write a letter—"

I don't allow him to finish. I've heard more than enough. This waste of space is breathing air when Lia lies dead.

Retrieving the gun from the small of my back, I place the muzzle to his temple, and just as he begs for mercy, I pull the trigger. He and his brother are where they belong—in hell, where my kin will soon join them.

Covered in blood and matter, I come to a slow stand, spitting on the boy I just killed. His vigilante, naïve ways killed an innocent person who didn't deserve to die. Raising my bloodied fists to the heavens, I scream in downright fury, wanting to kill the God Sister Arabella has so much faith in.

It doesn't make me feel any better, but nothing ever will.

Turning around, I walk toward Lia's body with nothing but regret and guilt in my heart. Another innocent person is dead because of me. Death and pain are all that follow me.

I'm mildly aware of Renata staring at me, but I can't deal with her now. Now, I have to bury the dead.

"Wait for me in the SUV," I order, exhausted beyond words. She knows better than to fight me this time.

"Wh-what happens now?"

"Now"—I sigh, eyes never leaving Lia—"we leave. We can't stay here any longer."

If these two idiots were able to find me, then it's only a matter of time before someone else does. Serg won't need to hunt me down when he has his own personal flock more than happy to do the job for him. And with that sort of money as bounty, it'll only encourage more and more budding vigilantes.

It was fun while it lasted, but playtime is over.

Renata doesn't say a word.

She watched nervously as I packed my belongings into two bags. I ordered her to wait in the SUV, which thankfully didn't end in an argument as I stuffed my money, passport, and other possessions from the safe into the duffel.

Once I was packed, I locked the door on my once home, unsure when I would return.

I am once again on the run with no fixed address. And like last time, there is only one place I can go.

When the orphanage comes into view, Renata shuffles in her seat. I understand she's apprehensive about this. Her life is once again about to change. But I couldn't leave her behind. Not only does she have the information I need, but she also saved my ass back at Lia's.

She said she followed me. She found an old bike I'd forgotten about behind my house and rode around until she saw my vehicle. Only one road led from my house, so it didn't take her long. She found my gun in the dresser.

She is resilient and smart. Normally, I would punish her for disobeying me, but if she hadn't defied me, then I would probably be dead.

Lia is buried under her favorite tree. I did the best I could, but it will never be enough. The two assholes, I cut into pieces and fed them to Lia's pigs. They may as well be useful for something. Pavel will retrieve their car come nightfall.

Renata watched me do all this, which is why she hasn't said a word. She's seen who I really am. And no surprise, the sight isn't a pretty one.

I park my SUV around the back, thankful it's away from prying eyes. The walls are high, and no one is able to get back here unless they have the code to the gate. Nevertheless, I ensure the coast is clear before I gesture for Renata to exit the car.

I grab our things and wait for her to take everything in. She takes in every corner, working her bottom lip nervously. She escaped one prison only to be locked in another. But it's only temporary. Once she tells me where that meeting is to take place, she is free to go.

Sister Yali greets us at the back door. She doesn't waste a moment. "I'll show the girl to her room. Mother Superior wishes to see you in her office."

Renata shakes her head, but I gently console her. "It's okay. You're safe here."

Sister Yali purses her lips. She doesn't conceal her disapproval of me as she takes Renata's bag. I hold on to mine however. I may have showered the blood off me, but she knows who I am. She knows what I did.

Renata eventually follows Sister Yali while I make my way to Mother Superior's office.

I called her, asking for sanctuary once again. She didn't ask questions and told me to come immediately. But I know I owe her some sort of explanation. I will not put this orphanage at risk. But I'm only here for a couple of weeks. As for Renata, I still haven't figured out what I'm going to tell Mother Superior.

I knock on her door even though it's open. She peers up at me from her desk, gesturing for me to enter.

She can smell the guilt all over me but doesn't say a word. Taking a seat, I drop my bags by my feet and clasp my hands together between my splayed legs. "Thank you for granting me sanctuary. Again. It's not for long. I—"

But she waves me off. "You can stay for as long as you'd like." She addresses me in Russian, which is never a good sign. "But how long can you live this life, Aleksei? I'm not naïve. I know something terrible must have happened for you to be back here."

Lowering my eyes, I can't face her. I'm ashamed for coming here. "Yes, Mother Superior. Something so heinous occurred, I can't even look at you."

"Did an innocent suffer?" she asks, not realizing the half of it.

"Yes," I reply softly, eyes still downcast.

"Was it your fault?"

After a pregnant pause, I answer. "Yes."

Silence.

She knew I was wicked, but I don't think she ever realized how much so.

"Aleksei, I don't believe you'd hurt an innocent with intent. They were hurt as an indirect result of you?"

It doesn't make a difference. It all leads to Lia being dead.

"It doesn't matter. I may not have ended her li—"

"Of course, it matters," she interrupts. "You're a good man."

I scoff because she has no idea what I've done. In my past,

I've directly hurt many innocents. "Thank you, but I don't want your praise. The girl, Renata. May she stay here too? It's only for a couple of weeks. After then, I'll ensure her safe passage back to America."

"Yes. She is welcome. As are you. Always."

Lifting my eyes, I bow in servitude. "Thank you, Mother Superior. We must ensure we keep doors and gates locked at all times. Security measures are imperative now more than ever. I'm sorry to drag you into my mess time and time again."

"You haven't dragged me into anything. It's my choice to have you here. Just as it was the first time I met you."

I remember the time well.

I needed a place to put my dirty money into, and no one asks questions when that place is an orphanage. But after a while, after being here and meeting Mother Superior, it became more than that. I could relate to every child in here, and even after all the despicable things I'd done, I always held a small shred of my humanity because of this place.

Mother Superior's life is this orphanage. She rarely ventures outside of these walls. She doesn't watch TV and only reads the paper occasionally. She doesn't know who the real Aleksei Popov is in a world that is not hers. But in her world, even though I am flawed, she loves me, nonetheless.

Coming to a stand, I pick up the duffel, my dirty money having no place in her home. "I will stay in the basement," I say as I know there are no rooms free.

She wants to argue because the basement is full of old furniture and supplies, but she knows it's an argument she won't win. "Renata may stay in Sister Julia's room. She's visiting her sick mother and won't be back for a few weeks."

"Thank you again, Mother Superior." Thanking her seems so mediocre in light of what she's doing for me. But she doesn't expect anything from me.

Leaving her to her paperwork, I make my way to the basement. Renata is in good hands with Sister Yali. Besides, I need some time alone. Once I clear my head, I will find Irina and let her know I'll be staying here for the next few weeks.

I plan to spend as much time with her as possible, hoping the urge to hurt herself will disappear.

Passing by reception to get the key for the basement, I tug on the front door twice, ensuring it's locked. The security here is top-notch—it has to be because of the curious children—but I'm paranoid. Once I have the key, I make my way toward the back of the orphanage.

It's the oldest part of the building, and although it saw some renovations, most of the original foundation stands. The plan is once I get enough money together, I'll knock it down and build more rooms for the kids. That isn't too far off now, thanks to Santo.

I have no idea how I'm going to pull this off, but I'll wait until he calls with the information. I have enough shit to deal with at the moment.

After I unlock the old iron door, I peer down the wooden spiral staircase. This basement encompasses every stereotype you can think of—dark, dank, and full of cobwebs. As I'm halfway down, I reach into my pocket for my cell and switch on the light.

Once I descend the bottom step, I stop and take a look

around my lodgings for the next couple of weeks as I switch on the lights. It's quite a large space, which is why it's filled with junk. Christmas decorations, boxes upon boxes of paperwork, old books, broken toys…this place is the junkyard where things go to die.

Pushing aside a statue of the Virgin Mary, which is missing an arm, I walk to the far corner of the room where there is a single bed. There are boxes piled high on top of it, so dumping my bags onto the floor, I stack them onto a table close by.

The bed has no linens or a pillow, but I'm sure I can find something down here as a substitute. Or maybe divine intervention is at play.

"Hello? Alek? It's me…Sister Arabella," she adds in case I've forgotten her voice. But how could I forget something so angelic wrapped in pure sin.

"Down here, Sister," I call out to her, toeing my duffel under the bed.

Her soft footsteps announce her arrival, but when she falters, it's clear she's seen the true state of this place. I turn to face her, admiring the graceful way she moves. It's probably a good thing I'm down here as I would never pollute her beauty by luring her down to this dungeon.

"Wow," she says, looking around the basement. "You're going to need a tetanus shot to stay down here."

"It's fine," I reply with a smile. "There's even a bathroom down here."

She has a pillow and some linens pressed to her chest. When she notices me looking at it, she shakes her head as if remembering why she's here.

"Mother Superior asked me to bring these down to you. But I think I should have brought down some cleaning supplies instead."

Unable to stop my chuckle, I extend my hand. "Thank you. And it's okay. I've slept in worse places. Trust me."

She doesn't reply as she passes me the supplies.

Dirt and god knows what else cover the mattress, so I swipe my hand over it, coughing when plumes of dust fill the air.

"Oh no, Alek—"

But I gently grip Sister Arabella's wrist as she tries to stop me from making the bed.

The moment we touch, my body responds how it usually does when she's around. But after today, I don't deserve any gratification, so I let her go.

She seems disappointed by my action. "I feel like we got off on the wrong foot," she reveals. "I really am sorry for what I did."

She speaks of eavesdropping on my deepest, darkest secrets. But she has nothing to apologize for. I've done far worse.

"You have nothing to be sorry for, Sister Arabella."

"Ella," she says, while I arch a brow, confused.

"Call me Ella," she clarifies with a small smile.

The name suits her perfectly, but for me to call her by her name feels too…personal. I'm trying to keep this as platonic as I can—especially since I'll be sleeping under the same roof as her—but she is clearly extending an olive branch. It would be rude of me to refuse.

"Okay then…Ella."

A timid smile spreads across those beautiful lips.

"How long is your exchange here?"

The question is innocent enough, but she suddenly seems nervous. It has me realizing I know nothing about her, which isn't like me.

"Mother Superior said I can stay for as long as I like."

"You don't have anyone back in Savannah missing you?" I ask as I commence making the bed.

"Not really. I'm an only child. My parents are divorced. It's only been me for a long while."

"How long ago did you take your vows?"

She clears her throat once, clearly uncomfortable discussing this. "A little over two years."

Her answers are short, and if I didn't know any better, I'd guess she was evading them for a reason. But what reason would that be?

"Did you always know you wanted to be a nun? Or did you have an epiphany one night?" I don't know what the proper term is, but to commit your entire life to this way of living requires dedication.

When Ella doesn't reply, I casually turn over my shoulder to look at her. She seems torn. It's a simple question, or maybe it's not. Maybe the reason is private. But that just makes me all the more curious.

"You were right," she reveals softly. I have to strain my hearing to catch what she says.

"I *am* a little wicked…which is why I'm here," she splutters out in a rushed breath. "I'm not proud of some of my choices, but I'm here to repent."

Well, well, I was right.

Her admission leaves me all the more intrigued. Just how wicked are we talking? So far, she hasn't backed down. She's shown me she's spirited, and I haven't intimidated her in the slightest. She can hold her own.

She divulged she's been on her own for a while, so she's independent, and possibly a loner as she had no qualms about traveling to the other side of the world.

"How old are you?"

"I'm twenty-eight."

This means she made her vows when she was twenty-six. Oh, what dirty secrets does she guard?

"You're still a baby." I'm not trying to be condescending, but compared to me, she is. "What could you possibly need to repent for?"

When she averts her eyes, it's evident she feels as though she has a lot to atone for. "I fell…in love," she confesses, taking my breath away. "When I shouldn't have."

"Why not?" I ask, totally under her spell.

"Because he was a very, *very* bad man. And loving him kick-started a chain reaction."

I don't bother giving her a clichéd line about not being able to help who you fall in love with. You may not be able to help your feelings, but when acting on them, you're in control of your actions. And it seems regardless of Ella's knowledge, it didn't make a difference.

Now I understand why I was so drawn to her and she to

me. We're both sinners. This won't end well.

Turning around to face her, the task of making my bed long forgotten, I don't hide the way I openly take her in. I am so desperate to take her habit off to see what's beneath because this garment is her mask. It hides away her true self.

But I see her. And I like who I see.

"What do you want from me, Ella?"

Formalities are long gone. We were only playing nice because of where we were, but down here, in the darkness, we can almost forget the outside world exists.

"I-I don't know," she replies, but I cluck my tongue.

With an unhurried stride, I close the distance between Ella and me. She stands her ground, but the rapid rise and fall of her chest hints at her nerves.

"Don't lie to me," I caution lightly.

Her tongue quickly darts out and sweeps across her lips. "I'm scared of what I want."

"Why?" I continue walking toward her.

"Because I shouldn't want it. I can't."

Her admission does nothing to stop me. "If you tell me to stop, I will."

The closer I get to her, the deeper I fall. To know this, whatever this is, is reciprocated, animates me and some of the monsters inside me ebb away.

"And that's the problem…I don't think that I can," she confesses, tears in her eyes.

The crucifix around her neck catches the dim lighting, but it's not enough to deter me. I know this is wrong, but I don't care. I tower over her, but in her presence, I am dwarfed by the power she has over me.

Cupping her cheek tenderly, I watch in awe as she leans into my touch, ashamed. This shouldn't be a moment of regret, it should be celebrated, but who Ella is, and who I am, our union will always be colored in shades of gray.

"Alek…" she whispers, laying the softest of kisses on my palm. She may as well have kissed every inch of my flesh because it feels the same. I'm animated with a fire, and I want to burn us both alive.

"Tell me to stop, Sister." I use her title with intent because once we cross this line, there will be no going back.

She peers up at me under those long lashes, slaying me. "It's Ella."

God save her soul.

Just as I lower my mouth to hers, I get my wish.

"Alek? Are you down here?" Renata's voice seems to be the voice of reason Ella needs. She jerks out of my hold, placing her trembling hand over her mouth.

"Ella—" I say with regret.

But she shakes her head. The moment is ruined.

When Renata bounces down the last step, she stops, appearing to strain her eyesight to adjust to the dimness. When she sees Ella and me, she cocks her head with interest.

Ella turns her attention to Renata. She does the same. She looks back and forth between us, before something falls over her. I know what that is.

"Ella, it's not—"

But she doesn't let me finish.

"Very well, if you have everything you need, I best be off.

Good day, Aleksei."

"Ella, wait." I grip her elbow, but she recoils, angered.

"Good day," she repeats, eyeing me heatedly.

"We're not done here," I warn, looking down at her doggedly.

"Oh, we are so done." She doesn't allow me to argue because she's racing past Renata and up the stairs before I have a chance to chase after her.

"блять!" I curse, fists clenched by my side.

Renata sheepishly walks toward me, unsure of what just happened. But I know exactly what happened. Ella saw Renata, jumping to conclusions. I have no idea what she knows about my situation, but it's apparent she wasn't aware I had a plus one staying with me.

"Sorry, did I interrupt?" she asks, ruefully. "I knocked."

"No, it's fine. Are you settled in?" Renata isn't to blame for any of this. My half-brother is.

"Yes. The sisters are really nice. Are you really staying down here?" She doesn't hide her horror at my lodgings.

"It's just temporary," I reply, turning around to finish making my bed.

"Thank you," Renata says after a few moments of silence, surprising me. "I realize I've been nothing but a brat. If it wasn't for you, I don't know where I'd be. I know I'm only here 'cause you need me, but regardless, you could have been cruel, like your brother, but you're not."

I don't want her gratitude, but I nod, nonetheless.

"To show my appreciation, I wanted to wash your SUV. Can I have the keys?"

"You don't have to do that," I state, my back still turned as I tuck the blanket into the mattress.

"I want to. Just let me do this for you, okay?"

The gates are locked. There is no way she can leave the grounds. But a bothersome voice questions her motives, and she knows it.

"You're kidding me? After everything, you still don't trust me?"

"I don't trust anyone. Don't take it personally." Regardless of my words, I dig into my pocket and toss her the keys.

She catches them, shocked. But she doesn't make a fuss.

My cell rings, and when I see that the caller is Santo, I gesture to Renata that I need to take it. She gets the hint and leaves without a word. Once she's out of earshot, I answer.

"Hello, Aleksei. Have I caught you at a bad time?" It appears our deal means I need to be at his beck and call.

"Not at all. To what do I owe this pleasure?"

"I just need a couple of more days to get everything organized. Sorry for the delay. It's hard to get five minutes alone in this house. The joys of being a big Italian family, I suppose."

He's trying to lighten the mood, but here's hoping he changes his mind. I need the money, but is the headache worth it? Being tied to the Macrillo family isn't a onetime only deal. I do this and succeed, and I will be linked to them forever.

But the influence Santo has over this town is why I'm doing this. I need all the allies I can get. With Santo on my side, no one will dare betray me again.

"No problem. Just let me know when you're ready. I'm

ready when you are." I know what this means. By agreeing, I'm ultimately putting an innocent woman to death.

"That's what I like to hear. I'll call you when I have everything."

"Okay."

Before I hang up, Santo casually shares, "Oh, I spoke to a realtor friend of mine. There is a house a couple of miles from where you once lived up for sale. I will email you the link for it. It's absolutely beautiful."

Anywhere near my old neighborhood would mean the house is worth a large amount of money, money I don't have. But this is all a part of Santo's ploy to ensure I don't back out of our deal.

"I understand your circumstances at the moment aren't ideal, which is why my friend is willing to help you out. He only requires a small down payment; one you'll have soon."

He means when I find the woman and collect my payment from him.

"He will take care of the rest."

For me to regain the position of power I was once in, I need a kingdom, a throne. I can hardly do that from the shack I now call home.

"Thank you, Santo. I won't forget it."

He clucks his tongue. "Don't mention it. That's what friends are for."

We are far from friends, but I'd rather call him that than my enemy.

He hangs up, sending the link as promised five minutes later. I slump onto the end of my bed, scrolling through the pictures of the two-million-dollar mansion which once belonged to Denka Orlov—a world famous pianist. I wonder if someone didn't like his rendition of Beethoven's "Symphony No. 9."

I didn't know him well. He kept to himself, and as far as I knew, he was clean. But his loss is my gain as the house is what I need to reestablish myself as the boss. I just need to forget that it's built on the blood spilled by others.

Looking at the painting of Jesus on the wall, I reach for the pillow and toss it at the painting. It clatters to the floor, no longer judging, no longer seeing what I'm prepared to do.

CHAPTER SEVEN

I wake with a start, unsure of where I am. Once I gather my bearings, though, I exhale because I'm safe.

Unable to go back to sleep, I decide to go for a run. I manage to rummage up an old pair of sneakers and some running shorts in a box of donated clothes, but I don't bother with a T-shirt. Since it's still dark outside, I'm quiet as I walk down the hallways and out a side door that leads to the sports field.

There are basketball courts, a tennis court, and a running track around the half-sized football field. They hold their annual events here—Easter egg hunts, Halloween hayrides, and Christmas parades. Mother Superior ensures no child misses out.

After some light stretching, I commence a jog around the field. I don't have any music, but I don't mind. I like the silence. I've always enjoyed working out. This may be modest compared to what I'm used to, but I'm still thankful to be outdoors without needing to look over my shoulder.

Irina was overjoyed to learn of what she called my extended sleepover. I promised to read to her as many times as she wanted because I want to try to help her any way I can. Maybe having a constant figure in her life will help. Thinking back to when I was a child, I remember that's all I wanted. Stability.

I may not know Irina's background, but I recognize a child of abuse and neglect. Sadly, I can relate.

Sweat covers my body as I continue to push myself harder and harder. I think about Santo's offer and how I've decided to contact his realtor friend. I need a home. I can't stay where I am now.

A new life is within reach. Everything is moments away from changing. I'll finally be where I belong, where I worked so hard to be.

I know things will be vastly different, but I'm ready for anything.

Or so I thought.

Lost in my thoughts, I don't notice I'm no longer alone until I hear the side gate open. Instantly on alert, I stop running, straining my eyes to see in the approaching dawn.

It's a woman, but her back is turned to me, so I can't see who it is. She places her gym bag onto the bleachers before drawing her leg up behind her into a stretch. She's in black yoga pants and a crop top. Her long brown hair is tied in a high ponytail, the curled ends touching the mid strap of her top.

Is this a sister out of habit? I suddenly feel impious for studying her longer than I should.

She stretches her neck, limbering up for what I'm assuming is a morning run. She hasn't seen me, and when I hear her humming softly, I realize that's because she's wearing earbuds. She's lost to the music and not aware of her surroundings.

The suspense is killing me, so I jog over, desperate to get a closer look at this woman with the unbelievable ass. She has what most would call an hourglass figure. She is curvy, toned, and I find myself drawn to her in a way I suddenly recognize.

Is this the work of the Lord Himself? But when she bends down to tie her shoelace, I realize it's the devil who's at play. Her tight crop top just emphasizes the fullness of her breasts.

I know who this is, but now, the question is, what am I supposed to do?

We hardly parted on good terms yesterday when she stormed from my room. But I can't sneak out of here without her seeing me because she stands near the exit. She is out of her habit, which I know for a sister is sacrilegious. She will be mortified.

But the temptation of seeing her this way wins out, so I wait for her to turn around.

She takes a drink of water from her bottle, then tightens the elastic around her hair before granting me my wish. And when she does, we both seem to share the same level of utter disbelief.

She just stares at me with those big hazel eyes, but without the habit, I can see her face without anything in the way. And what a sight that is.

I knew she was beautiful, but seeing her like this, I was not prepared for such beauty. The column of her neck is graceful, a silly thing to notice, but the only thing I've been able to see has been her face. Her habit has always covered everything else.

So now that I'm able to see it all, I can't stop looking. Everything pieced together makes the most spectacular picture.

My gaze drifts down her body, my fingers desperate to follow suit. Her skin is tanned. I wonder what her heritage is. Definitely European. I begin to wonder a lot of things because I want to know everything about her. I thought I was in trouble before.

Now, I'm in shark-infested waters without a life raft.

"Oh my god, Alek," she gasps, covering herself, but she doesn't turn around.

I expect her to avert her eyes, yet she does the complete opposite. She focuses on my body or, more accurately, my chest. I'm shirtless and perspiring from more than just the run. I like the way her eyes come to life before me.

I allow her to study me because it's only fair. The image of her body is forever singed into my very soul.

We are treading dangerous waters, but neither of us seems to care. This attraction continues to grow, and now that the veil has been lifted, I can't go back. I know what she looks like beneath that habit, and I want it.

Right now.

"Come here," I order, not mincing my words.

She backs up a step, but she's not going anywhere.

"Don't force me to order you to your knees."

Her gasp echoes out here in the silence, hinting it's only us. No one can interrupt us.

"Ella," I warn, seconds away from exploding. "Come. Here...now."

"No."

Her refusal excites me. I want her to defy me as the punishment will sting sweeter.

"You've got your hands full, it seems," she bites, referring to Renata. "She's the girl who was tied to your bed. Naked, I presume?"

"Oh, Sister, that shade of jealousy is quite becoming on you," I mock with a smirk.

She doesn't appreciate my candor.

"Don't flatter yourself. Jealousy would mean I care, and quite frankly, I don't anymore."

She's lying, lying to mask her envy.

"It seems you're prepared to break all your vows."

"I beg your pardon?"

She is angry. Good.

"Deceit. Envy. Depravity. You don't do things in halves." I want her to be aware of the fact I know her better than she thinks. I recognize these sins because I've committed them every single day.

"For you?" she taunts, tossing my words back at me. "You really think I'd jeopardize everything for a quick...fuck? Is that it?"

Oh, her mouth is so filthy.

Shaking my head, I coolly reply, "Who said anything

about it being quick?"

"An old man like you? I hardly think you'd have the stamina."

She's baiting me, and oh, how it's worked.

"I don't have daddy issues. I already have a Father I obey. He's the only one I get on my knees for."

That mouth. I want to punish it.

Yes, this is wrong, *very* wrong, and we both know what happens if we cross this line. But this isn't a choice of what I should or shouldn't do. This choice is the differential factor to what I should do and who I am.

I should walk away, but I won't. I want Sister Arabella, and I intend to have her in every humanly way possible.

When she continues to stand still, challenging me with her uncouth words, I curl my finger with a smirk. "You have three seconds. That's all I'm giving you before I come over there and make you regret disobeying me."

Ella's eyes widen.

"One—" I commence.

"Bite me."

"Two—" I interrupt as her wish is moments away from coming true.

Just when she opens her mouth and I think she's going to refuse, she charges over and slams her lips to mine. It takes me all of two seconds to catch up to speed before I'm dominating that delicious mouth.

She stands on her toes to meet my height, but my kisses are brutal, and she stumbles forward. I steady her by digging my fingers into her waist. Her skin is warm and instantly prickles in goose bumps when I touch her.

She keeps up with my kisses, her tongue matching my strokes as she mewls softly. The feel of her is indescribable, far better than I could have imagined. With all this flesh on display, I'm a desperate man and run my fingers up and down her back, wanting to touch it all.

When I come to a stop at the back of her neck, I grip it tightly and angle her head so I can dominate her mouth and her lips. She allows me to control her, moaning each time I bite her bottom lip lightly.

I unfasten the elastic around her hair, and when it tumbles around her face, I'm engulfed in her unique scent. Threading my fingers through the long strands, I pull hard, yanking her head back, our lips no longer joined. A stunned gasp escapes her puffy lips. She peers up at me wide-eyed, her chest rising and falling rapidly as she awaits my next move.

I bite over her chin before working my way down her throat. She has a cluster of beauty spots, so I kiss each one, liking the way her body yields to mine. I want to take my time with her, I really do, but I can't. I want her too much to savor my meal.

She softly places her palms against my chest, trailing her small fingers up and down my slick skin. She wants me as much as I do her, and that fact pleases me more than it should. She hums in approval when she traces over the ridges in my abdominals and gently tugs at the sparse hairs below my navel.

With one hand still threaded through her hair, I walk the other between us and rub over the front of her pants. She buckles into my palm, a winded cry slipping past her parted lips. She rotates her hips, encouraging me to continue.

The material of her pants is so thin that I can feel her heat. I can't wait to taste her sweetness on my tongue. I rub circles over her sex as we lock eyes. She doesn't look away. She stares back at me, allowing me to see her vulnerability as I work her body without mercy.

I know she wants me to touch her in the flesh, but she won't ask, and her stubbornness drives me even wilder. She won't succumb because that means she still has control. She hasn't submitted completely…but she will.

Removing my punishing grip from her hair, I walk us toward the bleachers, sitting and drawing her onto my lap. She straddles me, then slams her lips to mine. I tug at the straps of her crop top, and when I yank the material down and her breasts spring free, my erection nudges against her sex.

The feel of her breasts pressing against me has me breaking our kiss, only to take one tight nipple into my mouth. She loops her arms around my neck, arching her back, granting me permission to taste her. I cup the other breast, running my thumb over her nipple.

Tonguing over her areola, I ensure our eyes stay locked as I want her to see it all. I want her to revisit this moment when she's in her habit, remembering how good it felt to be this utterly wicked and…free.

She rocks her hips, biting her bottom lip each time she rubs over my erection. I haven't been with a woman in a very long time, but my stamina won't be an issue. This is about her and her satisfaction.

Cupping her perfect ass, I feel she isn't wearing any underwear. I need to see, feel her without anything in the way.

Pulling away from her breast, I lift her, switching positions with her so she's now sitting. Coming to a stand, I take a step back, needing to look at her. The curled strands of her hair cover her breasts, but her pert pink nipples peep through, adding to the perfection of this sight before me.

Her body is utterly wicked—curved, toned, strong.

She chews her lip, appearing embarrassed, but we're way past that.

"Take off your pants," I order, relishing the way her stomach ripples with her raspy breaths.

I can see her weighing my command.

"That wasn't me asking," I say, in case she thinks stopping is an option.

I know we're out here in the open, but there is no way I'm leaving here without her scent slathered all over my face.

Thankfully, she does as she's told and toes off her sneakers and socks, before lifting her hips and taking off her pants. The sight is utterly enchanting. She shyly crosses her legs, but I've seen her, and I'll never unsee the goddess before me.

She slips the crop top over her head so she sits before me totally naked.

"Боже мой, ты прекрасна."

Oh my god, you are beautiful.

She arches a brow, hinting she has no idea what I just said. Which is why I reverted to my native tongue. I don't want her knowing how absolutely smitten I am by her. I shouldn't feel this way, but it's not simply her looks that leave me a bumbling fool.

From the first moment we met, she has tried to understand me, to help me because she's seen the darkness inside me. She's seen it because it's inside her too.

And that depravity sings to mine.

Walking toward her, I do something I haven't done since Willow—I drop to my knees slowly. Her surprise is clear as she peers down at me, her flushed flesh adding to the need to consume every inch of her. Wrapping my fingers around her waist, I drag her forward so her ass rests on the edge of the bleacher bench and bury my face between her legs.

I don't take her into my mouth. I merely rub her pussy against my face, spreading her arousal all over me. She tastes and smells how I imagined—like honey.

With my fingers still fixed to her waist, I angle her hips, coaxing her to open up to me. She leans back on her hands, using the bench behind her for support as she spreads her legs. Her offering is too much.

"A gentleman would ask if you're sure…" I start, looking up at her.

She gasps, eyes wide. She is terrified, but I can smell her desire. Her yearning overtakes her morals.

"But I'm not a gentleman and don't ever mistake me for one. I have no qualms about breaking your solemn vow when I bring you to orgasm with my mouth and tongue."

Hardly graceful but I want inside her, and if I give her the option of saying no, she can change her mind. But this is happening—right now.

Lowering my mouth to her sex, I lick along her entrance in one long stroke. She whimpers, opening her legs wider to offer me more.

"о блядь!" I curse, every part of me demanding I make her mine. She is warm, so warm, and so wet.

She moans, bucking against me. "Oh, my God," she whimpers, shuddering. "Forgive me."

Never loosening my grip on her, I hold her prisoner with my hands, mouth, and tongue. Her bare sex is like fire on my tongue as I devour her without mercy. With Ella, this is effortless.

I want to please her, have her screaming out my name.

She reaches down, tugging on my hair as she forces my tongue deeper into her. I comply, humming when she bucks on my face as the moans slipping from her feed my soul. I tease her, purposely evading her swollen clitoris. I want her writhing uncontrollably when she comes.

Hooking my arms under her knees, I drag her forward, deepening the angle as she leans farther back. Her legs are thrown over my shoulders, and she grows lax as I add a finger to her pussy. The bleachers behind her prohibit her from leaning all the way back, but she uses her foot to hold me captive against her heat.

"Just like that," she gasps, rolling her hips as I give in and circle her clitoris with two fingers. I kiss my way from her sex to her inner thigh and bite her—hard.

She cups my cheek, running her fingers through my beard. The gesture is that of a lover's caress. This means more to me than just a casual fling.

Needing her all over me, I match the speed of my fingers to that of my tongue as I flick it in and out of her. She is slathered all over my face, and I never want to wash away her sweetness. I am addicted to her taste, to her pleasured whimpers because I elicited each one.

I spread her sex open with my fingers, sinking and twirling my tongue around and around. She shudders, gripping my hair as she rides my face. I reach up, cupping her breast, rolling my thumb over her nipple. I want to imprint myself on every part of her.

"Alek," she whimpers, her voice drenched in nothing but hunger. "I'm going to come."

I bite her clitoris and knead her breast, which seems to set her off because with a muted scream, her body shudders around me wildly. Her sweet arousal floods my mouth, and I am so rock hard, I'm terrified I'm going to come in my pants like a pubescent teen.

Her spasms match her untamed cries, and when I peer up and see her biting her fist to mute her screams, I growl in gratification. I want her mouth, so I tongue over her sex one last time before biting her inner thigh and then crawl up her body, slamming my lips against hers. She kisses me fiercely, gripping my hair desperately, the pain a shot of adrenaline.

She tastes herself on my lips and licks me without caution. I'm so desperate to bury my cock where my mouth was, but not here. When I take her, it won't be rushed. This was just a taste of what's to come.

The tremors continue to rock her body for minutes before eventually, her breathing slows, as do our kisses. The passion is replaced with something more. And that more is why I pull away, rubbing my nose against hers.

My labored breaths brush the hair from her flustered cheeks. I sweep the locks away, needing to see that beautiful face. She opens her eyes slowly, and I watch as what we just did sinks in. I wait for regret or self-hate, but I don't get it.

Instead, she reaches between us and begins to work over the bulge in my pants. But I grip her hand, stopping her.

"Not here," I hoarsely command.

She seems embarrassed that I don't want her to reciprocate, but I lift her chin with my pointer finger.

"It's not your hand or mouth I want wrapped around my cock."

Her already flustered cheeks blister a deep red, and she nods. "So, what happens now?"

And that's the question on both our lips.

"I suppose we both pray for forgiveness," I offer because once she leaves here, the outfit she will put on displays her pledge to God, the pledge which I just broke when she came on my tongue.

I'm not naïve. I know she'll need time.

My truth seems to remind her where we are, and that she's very naked. She quickly reaches for her discarded clothes and gently pushes me off her so she can get dressed. She does so, refusing to look at me. Guilt has now settled in.

"Don't regret what we did."

Once her sneakers are on, she combs her fingers through her hair, tying her hair into a messy bun. "I don't," she replies, and just when I think we're on an equal playing field, she hits a home run. "I just regret it was with you."

I stand dumbstruck, watching as she shoulders her bag

and walks away.

It was far easier for her to leave, so I assume she stuck true to one vow—her words aren't heavy with deceit. She meant them. And I don't know how I'm supposed to feel.

"Are you sure you don't want me to read you another story?" I ask Irina as she sits on my lap, flipping her favorite book to page one.

"No," she replies, stabbing her little finger to the picture of Thomas the Tank Engine. "This."

"Okay, цветочек."

She bounces happily, clapping her hands in excitement. I'm glad I'm able to make one person happy today.

I'm seething after my encounter with Ella. She tricked me at my own game. I thought there was something more, but it appears I don't know anything at all.

She's kept herself scarce, which is a blessing for both of us because I won't be held responsible for my actions if I see her. I can still taste her sweetness on my tongue, and I hate it. I hate that I allowed myself to get wrapped up in a fantasy.

I won't make that mistake again.

Just as I'm about to start reading, Renata enters the living room. She looks quite striking in a green dress with her hair curled around her shoulder. When she notices me staring at her, she blushes and averts her gaze.

"Ski!" Irina scolds, annoyed I'm not on page three by now.

She has every right to be mad.

Focusing on the story I know by heart, I start reading, laughing as Irina squeals in excitement. Renata takes a seat next to us on the large sofa but doesn't say a word.

Just as I'm about to turn the page, Irina's small fingers stop me. She turns to Renata, and says, "Уйди."

Renata has no idea Irina just told her to go away and just smiles and nods in response.

"Irina, that's not very nice," I reprimand in Russian. "Why do you want her to go away?"

Irina grumbles unhappily, but this part of her behavior needs to be curbed. She needs boundaries, and telling people to go away is one she needs to obey.

"Irina?" I press, but it backfires, and she jumps from my lap.

Before I can stop her, she rips the book from my hands and throws it at Renata's head. She thankfully dodges it but gasps in confusion.

"Hey!" I raise my voice, bending forward and gently grabbing her tiny arm. "Say sorry."

"No!" she screams, yanking from my hold. "Bad woman! Пожар."

I have no idea why she thinks Renata is a bad woman. I also have no idea what fire means in the context of her sentence. I don't have a chance to ask her why because she's running from the room in tears.

"Fuck," I curse, running a hand through my hair. I can't do anything right today.

"I'm so sorry," Renata apologizes, appearing mortified she

did something wrong. But she hasn't.

"It's not your fault. Irina acts out sometimes. She's hasn't had a very good start to life, but that doesn't excuse her behavior." Her shitty upbringing angers me beyond words.

"I can't blame her." I arch a brow, confused. "For wanting you all to herself," she confesses in a whisper.

I don't know what to say with her openly confessing something like this. Her mixed signals are confusing to say the least, but they're not reciprocated. I shouldn't have kissed her, and I understand that. But I've been up-front since that mistake.

Thankfully, I see Mother Superior walking down the hall and excuse myself. Renata doesn't hide her disappointment.

Mother Superior is distressed, which isn't like her. "What's wrong?" I ask, chasing after her.

She didn't even realize I was following. "Oh, Aleksei. Please forgive me. I was miles away."

"I could see," I reply, walking beside her. "What's the matter?"

She scans the hallway, ensuring we're alone. When we are, she softly reveals, "Some paperwork from my office has gone missing."

"Could you have misplaced it?" I question even though I know the answer.

"Not these documents. They're the orphanages finances, as well as a list of the benefactors over the years."

She doesn't need to spell it out. I've been the main benefactor. Is this a personal attack? But no one knows I'm here.

"No unexpected visitors have been by?"

She shakes her head. "No. I've checked the security tapes. And asked the Sisters. No one has been here without reason. I'm certain I had these files on my desk yesterday as I was logging your last generous contribution."

This is bad. We have a mole in our midst, but the question is, who?

"I hate when you get that look," Mother Superior says, side glancing me. "Do you think you could look in the basement in case I filed them away by accident? The box will be labeled in three-month increments for the first half of this year. There should be two boxes."

"Of course. I'll do it now."

Her urgency is apparent, and right now, I need to also get to the bottom of this. Mother Superior is meticulous with her paperwork, so I know someone is snooping.

"Can you check on Irina? She left quite unhappy with me."

"Yes, of course. There must be something in the water," she says, shaking her head. "Sister Arabella behaved quite strangely moments ago when it was her turn to go into the city to set up the soup kitchen for the destitute. She refused and was quite unhappy when I insisted she go."

I try not to let my guilt show as I'm sure her bad mood is because of me and what we did. "Did she go?"

Mother Superior shakes her head. "No. Maybe she's just having a bad day?" she offers as a plausible explanation.

But I know the truth.

"Yes, maybe," I reply, feeling horrible lying to Mother Superior. I bid her farewell and make my way to the basement, intent on finding something, anything. I want to help as it may lessen the guilt I feel for what I've done.

Once down here, I look at the stacks of cardboard boxes and exhale. This is going to take longer than I thought. There is no order to this madness, so I roll up my sleeves and get to work.

Everything and anything you can think of is stored in these boxes, except for what I'm looking for. Cracking my neck from side to side, I reach for the next box. It isn't labeled, so I flip open the lid, fanning the dust away.

As I flick through the documents, one piece of paper catches my eye. It's a letter from the Holy Mother of St. Michael's—an orphanage in Savannah.

The letter is short, but it's from the Holy Mother to Mother Superior, recommending Ella for the exchange program. The Holy Mother is clearly fond of Ella using adjectives such as kind, caring, and compassionate…which I discovered this morning is a load of shit. As did Mother Superior when Ella refused to feed the needy.

My mood is soured because of her. I just can't get the way she aloofly left out of my mind. She just broke her vows and didn't even seem concerned. This person the Holy Mother speaks of doesn't sound like the Ella who was yanking at my hair and riding my face.

Something seems off about this entire thing. I thought she'd be happy to spend a few hours out of the orphanage and away from me.

I decide to do a quick Google search, seeing as I have the information on hand. I can't hide my disappointment when the story checks out. St. Michael's has a Sister Arabella who is known for her charity work and a Holy Mother who sings her praises.

Maybe I just bring the worst out of people. It wouldn't be the first time.

When I hear someone's frantic footsteps coming down the stairs, I stop my riffling and look to see who it is. It's Sister Margaret.

Something is wrong.

"It's Irina." She doesn't need to say another word.

Pushing the boxes out of my way, I dart up the stairs two at a time with Sister Margaret following close behind. "We can't find her. We've looked everywhere. She's been gone for over an hour."

This is my fault.

I should have chased after her when she left distressed. I just didn't think. I was too busy being caught up in my own shit to think of someone else, and now Irina is missing because of my selfishness. I have to find her.

The orphanage is in a panic as the sisters race around, calling out for Irina. The kids look on, confused and scared because nothing like this has happened before. Sure, children have been unaccounted for, but it's been for a few minutes and not over an hour.

She could be anywhere.

"Irina!" I call out, racing down the hallway and out the door which leads to the sports field where I was in this morning.

The area doesn't allow much for hiding spots, but I frantically search every possible place she could hide behind.

She's not out here.

For the next thirty minutes, I search the orphanage from top to bottom, my calls for Irina becoming more and more frantic. But with each passing minute, I know Mother Superior will need to inform the authorities.

I can't be here when she does.

Half the payroll would be loyal to Serg as they were once to me, so I can't risk anyone knowing I'm here. Yes, most know I'm a benefactor at the orphanage, but they're not aware of how close my ties are with Mother Superior.

If anyone was to find out, they'd use her as collateral. Me being here is a danger to her, to everyone.

I decide to pack my things and let Renata know she can stay here. I cannot however.

As I make my way to the basement, the chapel door opens, and Ella exits. We lock eyes, and if circumstances were different, I would take great pleasure in making her squirm, but now, I just need to be gone.

I walk past her, not bothering to say a word. I suppose enough was said this morning. She's in her habit, hinting nothing is amiss with her faith—good for her.

As I continue walking, I hear footsteps pursue me. I don't bother slowing down and take the stairs down to the basement.

"Are you seriously ignoring me?" Ella asks, incredulous.

In response, I make a beeline for my bag, intent on packing my minimal belongings and getting out of here immediately. But Ella isn't interested in quiet time.

"Alek, look at me." Her voice displays a shred of

desperation, which confuses me. She made her feelings, or lack thereof, perfectly clear this morning.

But I humor us both.

"Whatever for? You didn't seem interested in me looking at you this morning." I turn around, expressionless. "I'm sick of the mind games. You have no idea who I am."

"Who are you?" Her anger has simmered.

"You don't want to know."

She arches a dark brow. "That's *all* I've wanted to know, so try me. I know underneath everything…you're a good man."

I shouldn't entertain her, but her leaving this morning was a blow to my ego, and it also hurt. It's time I showed her how much so. "I kneeled before you this morning. I think it's your turn to kneel before me."

Her mouth parts because she reads my mood. If she kneels, I will punish her because it's the only thing that will override this all-consuming anger inside me.

Pain gets me off—it always has—as does control, and the more it slips away from me, the more I want. The more I need. But with Ella and even Renata, they're the ones controlling me. It needs to stop.

At one time, I was ruthless and feared, and I need to be once again.

"Unless you plan on doing as I say, then leave." My words are impassive because I mean them.

She must be able to sense the gravity to my demands because with eyes locked on mine, she drops to her knees slowly.

What a sight. A sister in full habit about to worship

another god.

Taking my time, I walk toward her, stopping mere feet away. We don't break eye contact. She is challenging me, but she has no idea who she's defying.

"The woman I spoke of, Willow," I share, revealing who I was speaking of during confession. "I bought her. She was sold to me in a poker game."

Ella can't hide her surprise, but she asked for an insight into who I am. So, she's about to get it all.

"I organized her kidnapping. She was blindfolded, bound, and taken away on a yacht. Her kidnapper worked for me because he hoped to free his sister, Zoey, who was my... pet. She did everything, and I mean *everything*," I hum in remembrance of all the things Zoey did for me. "She wanted to please me because she believed she loved me.

"But I manipulated her into thinking that she did. As I did with the endless other women who were at my beck and call. But I grow bored very, very easily, which is why I wanted a new pet."

Ella can't hide her horror at the tale I'm sharing.

"Saint is the name of the man who was supposed to kidnap Willow and bring her to me. In exchange, I would free him and his sister. You see, everyone was my prisoner. They stayed not because they wanted to but because they had to."

Something passes over Ella, something which I was not expecting. Pity.

I clench my fists. I don't want her empathy. "Saint's instructions were to break her, teach her who was master. I wanted a docile little lamb."

She nervously licks her lips.

"I taught Saint everything he knew because I know how to manipulate anyone to get what I want. But Willow, my... дорогая, she was unlike anyone I have ever met before. Instead of me breaking her...she broke me," I confess with a bittersweet smile.

"It seems out of hatred grew love because Saint and Willow fought for what they wanted, and that was each other. I don't fail to see the irony in it. They fell in love. Regardless of what he'd done, she loved him. But me, she could never love me like that.

"Yes, she cared for me, but I wasn't her Prince Charming. And that's okay." I smirk viciously. "I much prefer to be the villain. They have all the fun."

"What happened to Zoey?" she asks, interrupting my trip down memory lane.

Leveling her with nothing but harshness, I declare, "She was murdered. As was Sara and Ingrid. Other women I exploited because I could."

Tears sting her eyes, and I savor each one. She cries tears I cannot for women who deserved so much more.

"Still want to know who I am?"

She clutches at the cross around her neck as if seeking forgiveness for breaking her vows with a monster.

"I killed my friends to save Willow. Friends I've known since I was a child. So the reason I'm telling you this is because"—I grip her chin between two fingers and force her head back to look up at me—"if you think you're special, that you can make me...feel anything at all, then you're wrong.

You're not special. You're just a conquest, one which was far too easy to surmount."

A tear trickles down her cheek. I sweep it away with my thumb before drawing it into my mouth. Her salty kiss is the brutal punch I needed. I close my eyes, tip my face to the ceiling, and savor the power I feel.

I've hurt her because she, she hurt me today. She walked away so easily when I couldn't.

"I let my guard down once...It won't happen again. Understood?" I ask, looking at her once I've basked in my glory.

She nods, her lower lip quivering.

"Good girl," I commend, patting her cheek. "Still think I'm a good man?"

Peering up at me from under those long lashes, she whispers a single word that smashes down my walls, "Yes."

And she means it.

After everything I just shared, I don't sense a hint of disgust. It's time I changed that. "Do you want me to show you how easy it was for me to break them?"

With a slow nod, Ella seals her fate forevermore.

"On all fours...Sister," I command, electricity sparking through me.

She does as I order.

I take a moment to appreciate the sight because this is a new one for me. I've broken many women before, but a sister? This is a first for us both.

Walking around her slowly, I tilt my head to the side, examining the way her body trembles uncontrollably.

Excitement. Fear. I can smell it radiating off her. I've missed this power.

Once I come to a stop behind her, I reach for the hem of her tunic and lift it slowly. Inch by inch, I uncover her shapely legs before her glorious ass comes into view. Her underwear are seconds away from being the only thing separating her tender skin from my punishment.

Unthreading my belt through the loops on my black pants, I wrap it around my fist and tug it tight. The anticipation is just as satisfying as the actual punishment, so I draw out the wait, wanting to see Ella squirming with need.

Shaped like a peach, her ass is soft and juicy and perfect to be whipped into submission.

The first strike lands seamlessly across both ass cheeks. I haven't lost my touch. Ella cries out, the impact jarring her forward, but she bounces back in position, wanting more.

I hit her again, harder this time, leaving a red lash across her hip. She surprises me when she slowly returns to her stance.

"Take them off," I order, my voice thick with yearning. The fact she wants this and is coming back for more is unlike anything I can describe.

With trembling fingers, she lowers her underwear.

I don't hesitate and whip her again. And again.

Her whimpers feed me, and sweat begins to gather on my brow. I bring down the belt again, and she buckles forward, whimpering. Red welts cover her ass.

"Enough?" I question, hopeful she says yes.

But she shakes her head.

Her body vibrates as she's quivering so hard. I doubt she'll be able to withstand more without any help. Usually, I would use her luscious locks as reins, but seeing as there are none at my disposal, I exercise what I can.

Reaching over her shoulder, I grip the cross around her neck and draw it toward me, using the long necklace as a lead as I whip her again and again. Her neck is arched backward, but the habit provides protection from the chain against her throat.

Her cries are fuel to me, and I shudder in utter ecstasy because she can take it, but better yet, she likes it. And when I gently kick her legs wider to expose her swollen sex, she announces just how much so.

"More," she demands, arching her back like a cat so I can see her needy center. My mouth was on that sweetness today. I can still taste her on my lips. My cock twitches at the memory, wanting more.

I swing the belt in a way that strikes her sex. I do this over and over. She wants to collapse forward, but the restraint around her throat prevents her from moving. The crucifix leaves an indent in my palm from where I'm gripping it so tightly. This is so blasphemous, and I love every second.

With one last lash of my belt, I drop it to the floor, breathless and covered in sweat. I release Ella, who sags forward, trembling with tiny cries.

Her body is a live wire. I know what she wants. And after giving me so much, it's time I returned the favor.

Dropping to my knees behind her, I wrap an arm around her waist and draw her backward, pressing her back against my chest. Her quivering body is on fire under the habit, and I feel just how much so when I lift the front of her tunic and sink two fingers into her pussy.

She cries out, shuddering around me as I stretch her wide. She feels unlike anything I've ever felt before, and I've felt a lot of women in my time. Her underwear are halfway down her thighs, but they're in the way, so with a sharp tug, I rip them off and toss them over my shoulder.

She opens her legs wide in approval, allowing me to work her more freely, moaning when I circle over her needy clitoris.

Her flesh is slick, ripe, and ready for the picking. "Твоя пизда прекрасна." I can't help the Russian which spills from me.

"Wh-what did you say?" she pants, contorting her body to move with mine.

"I said your...cunt is beautiful." It's crude, but it's the god's honest truth.

She whimpers, leaning her head back so we're pressed together tightly. This intimate act was supposed to be a form of punishment, but I suddenly feel like the one being chastened because she owns me.

Her strength, her courage feeds me, and I realize Ella is more to me than I want her to be.

She has the power to bring me to my knees, but I can't. Not again. I'm...afraid to give myself to another again, only to lose them. I won't survive it.

"Aleksei?" Sister Margaret calls out to me from the top of the stairs, suddenly breaking the spell Ella is under.

She squirms, frantically attempting to break free. But

she's not going anywhere.

With my fingers buried deep within her, I place my other hand over her mouth to mute her cries. "Yes, Sister Margaret?"

I don't invite her down, so I know she won't come down here. But Ella isn't privy to this fact. I continue sinking my fingers deep while simultaneously flicking over her center.

"We've found Irina."

Shit, Irina.

All thoughts of her were forgotten, which seems to happen a lot when Ella is around. I forget the outside world exists. I need this to stop. This will only end with more death. I can't touch anything without hurting it.

One way or another, I will hurt Ella. And I don't want that for her.

I pump my fingers fiercely, tightening the hold over Ella's mouth. I can feel she's close. The possibility of getting caught excites her. She places a hand over mine, coaxing me to go in deeper, harder.

"She's in your SUV. We need your keys, though, because she's locked herself in."

Relief is mixed with sadness. She sought out the comfort of my vehicle when I was the reason she was melancholy in the first place. This just confirms my belief. I destroy everything I touch.

"I will be out in just a moment, Sister. I just need to…er, finish something first." Ella's screams are muffled by my palm as she writhes against my fingers inside her.

"Okay then. I'll meet you outside."

Ella nips over the back of my fingers, the sharp sting of

her teeth pleasing me greatly. But this was to show her who I truly am. I've told her about the atrocities I've committed. Now it's time I showed her.

Just as I feel her spasm around my fingers, I withdraw my fingers from her sex.

She grunts out a frustrated and confused cry as she slumps forward. "Why, why did you stop?"

"Frustrated? Confused?" I question coolly, licking clean the fingers that were just inside her.

She nods shakily as she turns over her shoulder to look at me. Her flushed cheeks will be the death of me.

"Good, because that's how you make me feel." I let her go and come to a stand.

Her eyes narrow, and her lust soon turns to hate, but it's always been there. It's just as easy as flipping a switch, and I need that switch to stay on.

What I did was cruel and demeaning, but this cannot happen again. I need her to hate me because this is who I am.

The cruel, unfeeling monster who exploits for his own gain. She wanted something from me, but I refused her because I can. I give and take as I please, and so far, I've given too much. Denying her something she wanted will teach her never to ask anything of me again.

This is how I break people. I take and give. But with Ella, there will be no more giving.

She turns back around, refusing to look at me as I leave her on her knees and on the cusp of sin yet again. I grab the keys off the table and coolly walk into the bathroom to wash my hands. I refuse to look at my reflection in the mirror. I don't need to see my image to know what a bastard I am.

She's sitting on the end of the bed, face in hands, when I climb the stairs and leave her alone.

CHAPTER EIGHT

"The end." I close the book, but Irina's small fingers overlap mine, hinting we're not done. Unable to control my laughter, I give in. "Are you sure you don't want me to read you another story?"

She looks at me as though I've gone mad.

She isn't too far off the mark, however. It's been two days since I was swathed in Ella's sweetness, and it's been two days since she's said a word to me.

I don't blame her. I got what I wanted—her hating me. But that doesn't make it any easier to breathe.

My cell rings. It's Pavel. "Hello."

"Can you meet me today?"

"Why? You have a job?" I ask, rubbing Irina's cheek when she pouts.

"Not a job. But I have something I want to show you. Meet me at the usual place. It's Friday, just in case you forgot."

And he hangs up.

This is typical, paranoid Pavel. Never on the phone for longer than he has to be. Our usual place on a Friday, around this time, is a small laundromat which never ask questions when Pavel brings in his whites stained red because it's a business front for his money laundering.

He is a silent partner, so no one can ever trace any illegal dealings back to him. The manager doesn't question a thing. Working there means she has a steady wage, and no one dare mess with her while under the protection of Pavel.

"I have to go out for a little while. I'll be back soon."

Irina nods with a small frown as she draws the book to her chest.

"How about I bring you back some Medovik?"

Her eyes light up as she licks her lips happily. The honey cake bribe worked. I'll make sure I bring back the biggest one I can find.

Kissing her forehead, I make my way to the exit as I have my keys and wallet on me. As I turn the corner, I stop dead in my tracks as a head of flowing golden brown hair catches my eyes.

Дорогая?

However, when Renata turns around, my hope fades to disappointment.

"Where are you going?" she asks when she sees my SUV keys in hand.

Sister Yali leaves us to talk in private.

Clearing my throat and forgetting my nostalgia, I reply, "To meet a friend. I won't be long."

"Can I come with you?" She looks at me with those big blue eyes, and against my better judgment, I nod.

She smiles, again reminding me so much of Willow. "Thanks. I want…" she looks around, ensuring we're alone, before whispering, "to buy a birthday gift for Mother Superior. Sister Yali just told me about her surprise party."

I completely forgot about the party. There is no way I will be attending, but it might be nice for Renata to do something other than cook and clean. Since arriving here, she's ensured to pull her weight and help any way she can.

Mother Superior and the sisters don't expect her to do any of this, but I've hardly seen her. She's too busy in the kitchen or scrubbing the floors. I don't know if she needs to stay busy to help take her mind off things. She did shoot a man.

He deserved it, but I'm not sure that lessens the guilt.

I unlock the back door with the master key I have. Mother Superior has given me all access codes and a master key to the doors. She didn't explain why, but I know it's because she wants to give me an all-access pass in case I need to flee in the dead of night.

Once we're in my SUV, I turn on the radio to fill the uncomfortable silence and drive toward the exit. I punch in the code on the panel and wait for the gates to open. Usually, the Sisters don't bother locking this gate as the children can't get back here.

It's used for deliveries only. But now, security is tight. It has to be.

The laundromat is about a twenty-minute drive, which suddenly feels like two hours because I can't get over how much Renata looks like Willow. Now that she is safe, her walls have come down, and I can see the vibrant, carefree young woman she is.

She radiates, just how Willow once did.

"What?" And when she speaks, her American accent tricks me into believing that she could be.

But no one can be her.

Renata rubs over her nose, thinking I'm staring at her because she has something on her face. But what I'm staring at can't be rubbed away.

"Nothing," I reply, returning my attention back to the road. "How are you?"

When she doesn't answer, I wonder if she heard me. But when she giggles, I know that she has. "How do you think I am?"

She's right. Until those who took from her pay, she's merely filling in time.

"I'll make arrangements for your safe passage back home," I reveal, deciding to talk to Pavel about this today. If she delivers on her end of the agreement, then so will I.

"You can do that?" Her surprise in my competence is offending, but I can't blame her. Serg has tainted my name. But she will see what I'm capable of when I come face to face with my half-brother.

"I can do that," I confirm with a grin. "If you wanted to leave earlier, however, you could always tell me where they meet."

She scoffs. "I don't think so. Just because we're playing nice doesn't mean I trust you."

It was worth a shot.

She's a smart girl. As long as I need her, she knows she's safe. I'm sure she won't tell me a thing until I have her passport in hand. Her freedom in exchange for my kin's head. It's a fair trade.

"Mother Superior won't want any gifts," I say, deciding to change the subject.

"I know, but she's been so good to me. I want to get her something to show my gratitude."

It's a nice gesture, but Mother Superior doesn't work that way. I know this firsthand. But I humor Renata. "What are you thinking of getting her?"

She purses her lips as if thinking. "I don't know. A candle maybe?"

I can't stop my smirk because Mother Superior has enough candles in the chapel. But I won't ruin Renata's fun. "Sure. Whatever you think."

She senses my cynicism, and snaps, "Maybe a desk organizer then because God knows she needs it." It's out before she can retract it, and she knows it.

Turning to look at her, I ask, "How do you know what her desk looks like?"

Mother Superior's door is almost always locked. So I want to know how she knows this.

She tugs at her seat belt nervously. "I just do."

"That's not an answer."

She has seconds to reply before I pull over and force an answer from her, and she senses it.

"I went to see her, to seek advice," she reveals on a rushed breath.

"Advice on what?" I ask between clenched teeth.

She chooses to stay silent, which will not work in her favor.

"Renata, so help me God—"

"On my feelings for you!" she cries, glaring at me.

I open but soon close my mouth because I was not expecting that response. *Feelings?* What feelings? And she spoke to Mother Superior? I'm suddenly mortified.

"Happy?" she barks. Falling back in her seat, she folds her arms and turns her cheek to look out the window.

No, I'm not happy. I'm confused.

Thankfully, the laundromat comes into view, ending this very awkward conversation. Pavel is already here. I park my SUV, and Renata opens the door before I even have a chance to turn off the engine. The door to the laundromat opens, and Pavel looks at Renata and then at me. He is clearly unhappy she's here.

"Why is she here?" Pavel asks in Russian.

Locking my vehicle, I don't bother replying because I know Pavel won't appreciate the sentiment. He will call me out for being a damn fool.

Digging into my pocket for my wallet, I give Renata some money. "There is a bakery just around the corner. Can you ask for a Medovik? It's a honey cake," I explain. "And this should be enough for a birthday gift."

She snatches the money from my hand but then nods. "Keys?"

I eye her suspiciously.

"I'm sure you don't want me joining you and your *friend*."

She narrows her eyes when looking at Pavel. "Once I'm done, I'll wait for you in the SUV. I won't wait on the sidewalk like some dog, awaiting their master.

"Besides, it's not like I can go anywhere without you seeing me."

She's embarrassed by what she shared, and the only way she knows how to respond is to act out aggressively.

She's right. The SUV is parked in front of the laundromat. She wouldn't even get the key in the ignition before Pavel shot her dead, so I place my keys into her open palm.

"Thanks." She marches off, refusing to acknowledge Pavel.

This part of town is quiet with only a handful of shops run by families who don't want any trouble. She can't venture far, but Pavel doesn't hide his disapproval. He walks back into the laundromat, a silent gesture that I'm to follow.

I give Mariska, the manager, a wave, following Pavel out back into his small office. I close the door behind me. He sits at his desk, lips pinched. "You have learned nothing," he says, shaking his head.

Taking a seat in the torn leather chair, I turn my finger in the air, hinting if he has a point, then to make it.

"Is it because she looks like Willow? Is that why you're being so foolish?" So he sees the resemblance also.

Good, at least I know I'm not losing my mind.

"No, it's because she has information I need," I explain calmly, but Pavel doesn't buy it. "She gives me an upper hand. I've been searching for that son of a bitch for so long. I'm done looking. I just want this done."

"Are you sure about that?" Pavel asks.

Before I can ask what he means, he reaches into his desk drawer and produces an iPad. He slides it across the desk so I can see what's on the screen.

Reaching forward, I see that it's Renata's Instagram page.

Scrolling through the pictures, I see that her story checks out. The last picture she posted was taken in Moscow. It seems she was traveling with three girls, and they appear happy. Normal. No foul play that I can see.

A blonde girl with a bright smile seems to be Renata's best friend as they're in a lot of photos together, laughing and having fun.

Looking through the rest of her page, I see she worked in a bar back in Chicago. She had a white fluffy dog and a pissed off-looking cat. She is also one of those people who like to document every meal they've eaten.

I have no idea why Pavel is showing me this nonsense.

"Congratulations, you've learned how to use social media," I quip.

However, Pavel doesn't see the funny side.

Steepling his fingers in front of him, he asks, "How long did she say she was held captive?"

"Three months."

Pavel nods, gesturing with his head toward the iPad. "You don't find it strange that not one comment on her pictures asks where she is? If she's been missing for three months, wouldn't you think a parent, sibling, family member, friend, anyone would comment on her photos, asking where she was?"

I quickly scroll through her comments on the photos and see that Pavel is right. If she were missing, surely someone would reach out to her, asking where she was.

"She has an older sister. Scroll down to the bottom. They seem quite close. I can't imagine she'd be so quiet that her baby sister is missing. Unless—"

"Unless what?" I question, peering up from the iPad.

"Unless she's not missing at all."

"So what is she then?"

Pavel shrugs, and he seems genuinely baffled. "I don't know her, so I can't tell you that."

This is bad. "Did you find out anything else about her?"

He shakes his head. "Nothing that's of interest to you. She seems relatively boring. But Alek, something isn't right with her. What would Aleksei Popov, when he was king of this fucking city, do?"

Leaning back in my seat, I sigh. "I've been too lenient with her. It is because of her resemblance to Willow," I confess. "But she knows Serg. Of that I'm sure.

"I just don't know how. She has no contact with the outside world. I don't know what her motivations are."

"Well, it's time you found out," Pavel says sternly.

She knows barely anything about me. If she were sent by Serg to spy on me, he'd have come for me by now. Patience isn't a virtue of his.

I try to think like him. How are they connected? What would I do if I were him?

Her resemblance to Willow can't be a coincidence. But I don't understand what her connection to him can be. There are too many what-ifs.

"When do you meet with Santo?" Pavel asks, changing

conversational pace.

"I'm just waiting on his call. I guess even if I was having second thoughts about doing this, I don't have a choice now." I may need all the manpower on my side now, depending on just who Renata is.

Pavel nods. "I was just thinking that. Until you find out who she is, consider her an enemy, Aleksei. You remember what you used to do to your enemies?"

"Yes, мой друг. I don't need a reminder." He thinks I've lost my nerve. But not in this circumstance. If Renata is a mole, then she will be dealt with accordingly.

"Good. No matter our past, I hate to see you being made a fool of."

Leaning across his desk, I pass him the iPad. I've seen enough. "Not for much longer," I affirm, standing. "Whether Renata or Santo leads me to Serg, I will find him and Zoya, and they will pay, pay painfully for what they've done."

Pavel nods his approval. "Good. You need to make an example of them both. And you need that example to be very public. It's the only way you'll reclaim your status."

He's right.

And if Renata is a spy sent by Serg, then I will need to make an example out of her too.

"When that time comes, I hope you'll do me the honor of standing by my side."

I don't wait for an answer. That's not how Pavel and I operate. We say what we need, and then we're on our way.

I bid him and Mariska farewell as I leave the shop.

Renata is waiting in the SUV. When she sees me, she

turns her cheek to look out the window. Every action I now scrutinize in ways I didn't before, but I should have.

I don't hint that anything is amiss as I open the door. The box on her lap means she found the Medovik, and there is a gift bag by her feet. However, I don't say anything. Starting the engine, I drive back to the orphanage, strategizing how I'm going to approach this.

I have no idea what her objective is, but I intend to find out the moment we return. The question remains, what happens when I do? If she is working with that son of a bitch, she leaves me no choice.

Gripping the steering wheel, I realize I don't know if I can do it. The only message Serg will understand is her mutilated corpse, delivered on his doorstep in a box and wrapped with a red bow. I'll ensure she tells me everything and only then will I show mercy by delivering death.

My stomach turns in disgust, but Renata made her choice. And she chose the wrong side.

When the orphanage comes into view, the significance of what I'm prepared to do in a place that is holy isn't lost on me. I have disrespected the entire foundation of the orphanage. From consorting with Ella to now, having murderous thoughts, just reinforces the fact that I'm a bad man.

I drive through the gates and park the SUV. This doesn't have to happen. I can find another way. But when I think about what is at stake, I realize the answer is no, I can't. I need this to happen now.

Just as she opens the door, I gently grip her wrist. "Would you come to the basement with me? I want to talk to you about what's going on with us."

She blinks once, licking her glossy lips as she turns over her shoulder to look at me. This is the first time I've acknowledged an "us." But it's just not the way she thinks.

I can sense her suspicions and almost hope she'll say no. But I know she won't.

"Fine." She shrugs from my grip, exiting the vehicle with the box and gift bag in her hands.

We stand feet apart, not saying a word as we commence our walk toward the basement. It feels like a death march, and I suppose in some ways it is. When we get to the basement door, I unlock it and gesture for Renata to proceed first.

She doesn't see the significance in my action because when she's halfway down the staircase, I close and lock the door behind me. There is no way for her to escape.

Once we're down the stairs, she places the goods onto the table and turns to look at me, arms folded across her chest. "So what do you want to talk about?"

There is no way to sugarcoat this, and I will not take any pleasure in torturing her. So, I stand at the bottom of the staircase, prohibiting an exit.

"I want to know why you're here," I calmly start, watching her closely. I've come to learn Renata is an excellent liar, so I need to watch for any signs of deceit.

"What do you mean?" she asks, matching my cool composure. She doesn't sense any threat—yet.

Leveling her with a cold stare, I reply, "I mean, what's your connection to Serg?"

She opens her mouth, but I place my palm out, stopping

her. "Save your breath. I'm not interested in your lies. You have one chance and one chance only to tell me the truth."

When she snickers, I realize this is going to get messy. "I *am* telling you the truth. Now, get out of my way. I'm done with your paranoia."

She stalks forward, attempting to shove past me, but I stand firm.

I can see in the way her lower lip quivers and her pupils darken that she's frightened. But she doesn't back down.

"I'll scream," she threatens, eyeing me viciously.

With a smirk, I say, "Good. I like it when they scream."

She must be able to read my determination because she slowly backs up, frantically looking around the room for an exit. There isn't one.

I follow her slowly, never taking my eyes off her. She reaches for whatever she can find, throwing it at me. I dodge flying books, ornaments, and whatever else she can use as a weapon. Her reaction proves her guilt.

It angers and saddens me all in the same breath.

She bumps into an old cabinet, yelping in fear. "I don't know anything!" she cries as tears fill her eyes.

But she does.

"I wish I could believe you, малышка, but I don't. Which is why I'm going to hate what I have to do."

"What do you mean?" she asks, a tear spilling down her cheek.

"You know what I mean," I state with no emotion as I reach into my pocket and produce my knife.

Her eyes widen when she focuses on the blade. "Please

don't," she whimpers, shaking her head. "Serg kidnapped me. I'm telling you the truth!"

The cabinet prohibits her from moving, so I slowly walk toward her. She is frozen in fear. "I know that you're not," I calmly argue. "If that were true, then why doesn't your social media have one inkling supporting this claim?"

She grips the cabinet behind her so hard, her knuckles turn white.

"I'd think if your story was, in fact, true, then there would be at least one comment from your friends and family asking where you were. But it seems nothing is amiss. And that's because you're not actually missing, are you?"

She shakes her head, more tears now falling. "Please, no," she cries, which is the first time I've seen her cower in the face of fear.

Thus far, she's been nothing but strong, but now, she's frightened because she knows I've found out her secret. And now, I must deal with her accordingly.

"I'm sorry, малышка. I really am, but I cannot allow a spy to live."

My words incite a fire under her, and she attempts to make a run for it, but I lunge for her wrist, drawing her into my chest. She struggles madly, screaming at the top of her lungs. I place a hand over her mouth, ignoring the bile rising at what I'm about to do.

"Shh, shh," I coo into her ear, removing my hand from her mouth, only to bring the blade to her throat. "It can all be over with. All you have to do is tell me the truth."

She thrashes against me, but I have a tight hold on her.

Her heart thrashes wildly against my arm across her chest, as do her tears as they wet my hand when they tumble down her chin.

"Why did Serg send you?" I ask, pressing the blade over the dip of her throat. It would cut through her soft skin like a hot knife through butter. "Answer me!"

She trembles uncontrollably, sobbing and gagging, words escaping her. She's scared, which is why my methods are usually not this uncouth. Seduction is far more effective than fear.

When she doesn't reply, I realize I'll have to try another approach.

Walking us toward the bed, I toss her onto it, facedown. When she tries to get up, I press my body over hers, pinning her to the mattress. "Maybe I can get you to talk another way."

With the blade still pressed to her throat, I lift the hem of her dress and yank down her underwear. She squirms wildly, her cries muffled into the pillow as I restrain her with my weight. I feel sick to my stomach doing this, but I need her to talk.

I would never take from her without permission, but she doesn't know that. I need her paralyzed in fear. I need her to know that I'm done playing. Whoever she thinks I am, I'm far worse. I've brought her to her knees and tried to subdue her, but it hasn't worked.

So this is the last resort.

Twisting my body, I bring my hand down on her supple ass and spank her hard. There is no pleasure behind this, though. It's purely punishment to degrade and break her so she tells me the truth.

Her body jars up the bed from the force of my strokes, which I continue delivering until she gasps for air. "P-please s-stop," she begs, growing limp.

Her flesh is on fire beneath my hand. I know that I've won.

"Why are you here?" I repeat, revealing that is the only option when she tells me the truth.

With a guttural sob, the truth comes spilling from her. "Because he h-has my best friend. He k-kidnapped us both. He let me go but is holding her r-ransom. He made us call our families, saying that Olivia and I were fine and that we decided to extend our time abroad. He lets us 'check in' every so often so as not to rouse s-suspicion.

"If we didn't do what he said, he would threaten us with punishment or worse. We had no ch-choice. That's why my social media looks normal. No one knows we're m-missing."

This is far worse than I ever anticipated.

"My job was to seduce you into telling me everything and then relay everything back to Serg at the m-meeting."

"So there is no meeting between him and Raul?"

She shakes her head, weeping. "It was a trap. I was to bring you there, thinking you'd have the upper hand. But in reality, he would.

"He knew you were coming for him when he didn't hear from his friend. That's why he let me go. He knew my similarity toward the woman you love would tug at your heartstrings and you'd show me mercy."

That son of a bitch.

"I was to find out everything about your connections so

he could exploit them. His allies aren't allies anymore because their loyalty is still with you…and he hates it.

"But you clam up. I can't get anything out of you. I tried to seduce you, but your interest lies elsewhere, doesn't it?"

And she's right. On all accounts.

"So you and Raul?"

"All bullshit," she confirms softly. "But what I said about being tied to that radiator, I wasn't lying. It didn't matter that the rope burns were so bad that I could barely move; Serg still used me and Olivia for his pleasure day after day."

She said he never raped her. Was that a lie too?

I suddenly feel like I'm going to be sick.

Getting off her, I run a hand down my face, disgusted beyond belief by what she just shared.

Renata's raw ass stares up at me, confirming there is no redemption for me because I believe her. This tale makes more sense than her escaping with the help of Raul. And the reason I believe her is because I once hatched this exact plan.

Didn't I hold Zoey for "ransom" while I forced Saint to retrieve Willow for me? His reward—I would let Zoey go.

Love is a dangerous tool, especially if it falls into the hands of a villain because it almost always can be used as collateral. Just how it has now.

Serg has mimicked every single move of mine, and why wouldn't he? I've laid down the blueprints. This is my karma for Saint and Zoey.

"My friend is still with him. Please help me help her," she pleads, gripping the bedsheets in anger. "He is a monster. Please don't k-kill me. If I don't succeed, her blood will be on my hands."

I should, but I won't. This shows weakness, but I like to think of it as compassion. Besides, I still need her. She will still lead me to Serg.

Placing the knife into my pocket, I walk into the bathroom, wetting a hand towel with cool water. Renata is still lying on her stomach, sniffling when I reenter the room and sit on the bed beside her.

"And so am I," I state, referring to her comment about my half-brother as I gently apply the cloth to her behind.

She hisses, and I know it hurts. The imprint of the ring I wear on my pinkie is clearly visible on her skin.

She doesn't deny my claim, and why would she? I am a monster. "I will get your friend back," I affirm, tending to her wounds. "We will attend that meeting as planned. And I *will* have the upper hand, not him."

The details will need to be discussed with Pavel, but Serg has gone to this effort because he realizes his days on top are numbered. He will be the reason for his own demise. His carelessness, his cockiness will be the cause of his death.

And I will be there, looking on with a smile.

However, when I hear a voice behind me, that smile won't come for a long while.

"What...I...oh, god." Turning over my shoulder, I see Ella standing feet away, looking at a sight which could be misconstrued in a dozen ways. But considering her ass was raw down here just days ago, she has jumped to the most obvious conclusion.

"Ella—" I start, but she violently shakes her head, not

interested in anything I have to say.

She takes one last look at Renata on the bed before me, ass bared, before she turns on her heel and races up the stairs.

It seems a locked door doesn't mean anything to the curious sister.

Renata has witnessed it all. When I open my mouth, she nods toward the stairs. "Go. I want to be alone anyway."

Of course, she does.

Passing her the hand towel, I leave Renata alone and chase after Ella. I've hidden my valuables behind the far brick wall. The loose bricks were the perfect place to hide one's possessions. Just because Renata has shared the truth doesn't mean I trust her.

If anything, it just makes me more guarded around her.

I may have uncovered the truth with Renata, but at what cost? The look on Ella's face confirmed her utter disgust in finding me in a compromising position with another woman. No matter how hard I push her away, she comes back, twice as hard. I don't know what to do anymore.

I know Ella is repentant for her sins, so there is only one place she'll be. Opening the chapel door, I see her in the front pew, kneeling and praying to her God.

Closing and locking the door, I walk down the aisle slowly. She knows I'm coming because I don't mask my footsteps. I'm prepared for anything.

She doesn't turn around when I sit in the pew behind her. She continues praying with her rosary beads clutched firmly in her hands.

Looking up at the crucifix on the altar, I confess to my

god or, rather, goddess. "Please let me explain. It's not what it looked like."

She doesn't reply.

"Okay, I guess it was," I backtrack because those welts were there thanks to my hands. "But it wasn't because I wanted to…not like I did with you."

Her shoulders rise in anger. I'm suddenly tongue-tied, making no sense.

"Ella, please look at me."

"I don't want to look at you. You disgust me. But worst of all, I disgust myself more."

Fair enough.

"You have every right to hate me," I say, coming to kneel on the pew cushion and reaching into my pocket for the postcard. "You need to stay away from me. I hurt everything I touch."

Carefully unfolding the postcard from Willow, I realize due to the insanity over the past few days, I'd completely forgotten to read the one she just sent. This isn't like me. Maybe this is how letting go starts?

I trace over her handwriting with my fingertip, wondering what she'd say if she saw me now.

"Why did you come down to the basement? I assume you used the master key to let yourself in? Why? Why can't you stay away?" All I have are questions because I don't understand this pull between us.

She knows what I am. And I know who she is. Yet none of that seems to matter when we're together. It should, but it doesn't.

"You merely use and abuse people for your gain," she spits, eyes still focused on the altar. "I've tried to ignore you because Alek, you're a dishonorable, sinful man and...a killer."

I hang my head in shame.

"The things you've done to me, the things you've made me feel, I should be ashamed that the hands of a monster could feel so good. But I'm not...and that's the problem. If I don't seem to care about all the vile things you've done, then what does that say about me?"

Slowly lifting my chin, I measure my breaths because I don't know where she's going with this.

She turns over her shoulder, her attention riveted to the postcard in my hands. She knows who the sender is. "You're like this because of her. You've shut yourself off because you fell in love with someone who didn't want you. And for someone who is so accustomed to getting everything they wanted, she not only broke your heart, she broke your pride.

"You're cruel because of her."

I grit my teeth, my temper spiking when she speaks such things about Willow. "You know nothing about her," I warn, wanting to do horrible things to her for insulting my дорогая.

"That may be true, but I do know that you never want to be vulnerable ever again because that makes you human. That makes you susceptible to being hurt again."

Before I have a chance to condemn her for tainting Willow's name, she lunges for the postcard, yanking it from my hands. She slides across the pew and rushes toward the altar, using it as a barricade between us.

I chase after her, heart in my throat, but when she waves

the postcard in the air, I come to a sudden stop, glaring at her over the altar.

"A...fucking postcard elicits more of a response from you than when you robbed me of pleasure. That was cruel. Do you see how messed up that is, Alek?"

"Yes, I do," I say quickly, agreeing to anything she says. "Just give it back to me."

"This?" Ella smartly replies, waving it high in the air. "You made me feel like nothing but a whore. Do you know that? You take from me, but I can't say no. And I'm sick of being weak.

"I want to know why you do that. Why do you show compassion, only to then overshadow it with cruelness? I don't understand it."

"I don't either," I confess, looking at the postcard clutched tightly in her hand. It feels like she's squeezing my heart. "Don't you see? I need you to be the one who walks away because I can't do it. I need to leave you be, but I can't.

"And the last time I felt this way...people died. People left. I was left alone to pick up the pieces. I was weak. I can't be that ever again."

"Why did you do that to Renata?" she asks, appearing to gag on her name.

"Because she lied to me. And I don't like liars. Are you lying about anything, Sister?" I know Ella isn't an angel; as a nun at twenty-eight years old, there has to be a secret she guards for her to be here.

"No," she replies, her chest rising and falling with her labored breaths. She's lying. Her sisterhood isn't merely because she fell in love with the wrong man.

A sinner recognizes a fellow delinquent, and Ella is just as wicked as I am. I've met my match—in more ways than one.

"I don't believe you," I challenge with a grin.

"I don't care what you believe," she spits, cheeks reddening in anger.

The sister has a nasty temper. And when it rears its devilish head, I respond in ways I shouldn't.

"I believe you're jealous over what you saw. You wished it was your superb ass I was lashing."

She clenches her jaw.

"The truth hurts, doesn't it?" I taunt, enjoying this banter way too much.

Ella tongues her cheek, before she reveals just how much it can hurt. "It sure does, Aleksei." And with one smooth motion, she rips the postcard in half.

I simply stare at the postcard in her hands, ripped in half, like my heart. It wasn't merely a postcard to me. It was the meaning behind it; the fact that Willow, after everything I did to her, still cared enough to send me something to show she's thinking of me.

And now, it lays ruined in the devil's hands.

"Oh"—I tip my face to the ceiling, inhaling deeply—"you're so going to regret doing that."

Leveling Ella with nothing but a predatory glare, she knows it's game on—no holding back. I don't care that we're in a chapel or that Jesus Christ is looking down at me from his burdensome cross; I am going to bend her over His altar and fuck her until she's crying out for another god.

Me.

A startled whimper escapes her before she takes off toward the sacristy door but been there, done that. She isn't getting away this time.

Breaking into a sprint, I round the altar and tackle her before she has a chance to open the door. She thrashes wildly as I wrap my arms around her, securing her back to my front. Her scent is amplified tenfold, and my mouth salivates, wanting another taste of her.

"Tell me you don't want me," I goad against her cheek.

"I don't want you!" she cries out, fighting like a wildcat.

I cluck my tongue as I walk us toward the altar, lifting her off the ground when she continues to fight me. "You lie, Sister. I bet your pretty pink cunt can show me otherwise."

"You animal! Put me down!"

I do as she asks when I wedge her against the edge of the altar. She can't move because I am pressed up against her. "Bow," I order, pushing between her shoulder blades.

"Fuck you," she spits, exciting me further.

"Father Anton would have you saying ten Hail Marys for speaking such blasphemy in this place of worship," I quip, chuckling when she attempts to break free.

When she continues to struggle, I apply a little force, and she slumps forward, pressing her chest over the edge of the altar.

"Arms above your head."

She does as I command.

Lifting the hem of her tunic, I round her hip and don't bother with formalities. I bypass her underwear and sink two fingers inside her. We both hiss at the connection.

"Told you," I smugly say, when the walls of her wet sex suck my fingers into her sinful warmth.

She moans, clutching at the altar cloth as she rolls her hips.

She is primed and ready for my cock, and I don't think I can wait a moment longer. I need inside her, and I need it now.

But she surprises me when she pants, "I want to suck you. Let me. Please."

О Боже...

Who am I to deny such a beauty?

With one final circle of her clitoris, I remove my fingers, missing her warmth instantly. She sags forward with a grunt, gasping for air with her cheek pressed to the marble.

Stepping back, I wait for her to catch her breath before she rises slowly and turns around. Her gaze drops to the huge erection tenting the front of my trousers. Reaching for my belt, she draws me closer toward her and commences unbuckling it.

Once my belt is undone, she flicks open the button, lowers my zipper, and slips her hand into my boxer briefs. She isn't shy and grips my shaft, familiarizing herself with my girth. I dare not move in fear I'll come in her hand.

She begins to work my length, rubbing her thumb over the head of my cock. She does all this with her eyes locked on mine.

The feeling is beyond words because my body is aching for her, but this is her show. I allow her to use me. I want her to.

She chews her bottom lip, gauging what I like as she continues to stroke me up and down, up and down. I remain unmoving, but an inferno rages inside me. I want her so badly that I don't think I can stand a second more.

But when she removes her hand, only to drop to her knees before me, I focus on the magnificent sight of Ella in her full habit about to take my cock into her exquisite mouth. She lowers my pants and boxer briefs to free my straining cock.

Her eyes widen when she sees me in the flesh. I've been blessed by the gods as I am well endowed. That is one thing I can thank them for. However, make that two things because when Ella licks her lips before leaning forward and taking me into her warm mouth, I need to thank them for bringing her into my world.

A string of Russian leaves me as she takes me deep, not intimidated by my size. I peer down, the sight utterly wicked as she works my shaft with her supple pink mouth and tongue. I run my hand over her head scarf, wanting nothing more than to tug at her soft hair. But this will do because I don't think what we're doing could get any more sacrilegious.

She braces both palms against my upper thighs, arching her neck and bobbing her head so I slide down her throat with ease.

"ох блять. вот так. Work my cock."

She moans around me, gripping my legs. "You like when I speak filthy words to you in Russian, красавица?"

She nods, gagging on my cock as she takes me deeper.

"Then I will speak it whenever you wish," I promise, falling deeper under her spell.

She uses her tongue like a wicked tool, cupping it around the underside of my cock and dragging upward toward my head, where she suckles me like a lollipop. I am so lost to the feeling of her pleasuring me that I don't realize her suction begins to tighten around me until she uses her teeth to bite down.

It stings, and when she doesn't let go, I realize this was a trap, one I fell for.

"What are you planning on doing down there?" I coolly ask, peering at her.

She gazes up at me, those long lashes framing her brilliant eyes. She wants to speak, but her mouth is currently disposed.

"You shouldn't talk with your mouth full, pet." I gently stroke over her chin with my thumb.

She hasn't thought this through. Negotiating with my cock in her mouth was not a smart move on her behalf. But when she bites down harder, she reveals talking was never on the agenda.

The pain is excruciating, but I don't falter. I allow her to assert her dominance because it's about to be taken away. When she loosens her grip, I cup the back of her head and coax her deeper onto my length. She gags, slapping my legs because she's choking.

She's already displayed her ability to take me deep, which is why I know she can take it, so I continue to feed her my cock. "Relax your throat, красавица."

I stroke my fingers over her cheek, encouraging her to do as I say, and when she does, I hit the back of it. "That's it."

Tears leak from her eyes, but she takes me deeper,

humming around my length. Was her plan of attack to bite off my cock and run? But we both want this, and I am done fooling around.

Letting her go, she pulls back, gulping in mouthfuls of air. As much as I enjoy seeing her on her knees, I yank her up and slam my mouth over hers. Her mouth is wet and welcoming as she kisses me back fiercely. Standing on her toes, she threads her hands through my hair and tugs—hard.

We're like desperate, starved animals pawing at one another, wanting to rip the other apart.

With lips still locked, I walk her backward, spinning her around and bending her over the front of the altar. I want to disrobe her, but I know how intricate a sister's habit is, and I can't wait that long. Sweeping the gold cross and candleholders to the floor, I clear the space I intend to defile in ways it's never seen before.

She stretches her arms overhead, gripping the far edge for support. Lifting her gown, I take a moment to appreciate her red underwear before I tear them off. "Spread your legs, Sister."

She does as I ordered, arching her back and angling her hips, offering me a gift too generous for words. Pulling down my pants, I place my hands on either side of her waist and align my cock with her sex. I don't have any protection, and I know she doesn't either.

But the moment I feel her heat, I don't care. I know she's ready, so looking up at the crucifix above us, I claim Sister Arabella as mine and mine alone.

I don't sink in slowly, allowing her time to adjust. In one

slick movement, I'm sheathed inside her heat, and I never want to leave.

"Oh, god!" she cries, her fingers clawing at the marble.

Her pleas feed my soul, and I start to move.

Anchoring her hips, I pump in and out of her, humming in ecstasy as I'd forgotten how good this feels. She stands on her toes, wanting to align us, and when she does, I bend my knees, changing the angle and plummeting in deep.

She turns her cheek, resting it against the marble, her body jarring upward with each thrust of my hips. Her sex grips me tight, milking my cock, and I know it won't be long until I come.

Spreading a cheek, I peer down at our connection—at the way our bodies unite and how we fit. Ella's pleasured whimpers are driving me crazy because that gratification is because of me. I haven't made someone moan that way in a long time.

My strokes are punishing, but the way she bounces back on my length, I know she likes it.

"Please, I want to come," she groans, grinding her ass against me. "It's been s-so long."

I understand why she's said this. The last time she was at the pinnacle of letting go, I denied her. But I'll never do that again.

After today, I know that staying away won't be possible. I vow to honor and protect her because she is the spark I've been missing. With her, everything seems more vibrant—flavors sweeter, colors brighter. I am lost to her, and if she turns me away, I don't think I'll survive it.

"Aleksei?" she begs, speeding up her movements and rolling her hips to milk her pleasure from my aching cock.

"Yes, красавица?" I taunt, enjoying her pleading.

When I speed up the momentum, her body grows lax as I dominate every inch of her. The noises spilling from her parted lips and the sounds created by our union are ones I want to hear from her every day.

"What does that mean?" she pants, slowly looking over her shoulder at me.

It's an endearment which can mean a lot of things, but to me, it means…

"Beautiful," I reply, slowing the drive of my thrusts. "Or baby."

Her entire body quivers around me, and her already flushed cheeks redden further.

"You can be really…sweet when you want to be."

With a smirk, I show her how sweet I can be when I reach around her hip and begin to play with her swollen clit. She continues to lock eyes with me, trembling and hot in my hand. I circle her bundle of nerves and begin to pick up the pace once more.

She rocks against me, taking me deep, and when I lean down to kiss her, she explodes around me. Her cries of passion vibrate through me as I don't let her lips go. I devour her with my fingers, my cock, my mouth.

I am everywhere, and I never want it to end.

She comes with a passioned whimper, her body writhing wildly. The warmth, the energy pulsating through her sucks me in, and the familiar carnality tackles me from behind.

Arching my head back, I peer into the heavens, and when the last tremor rocks her body, I pump my hips once, twice, and pull out, spilling my seed onto her ass with a sated roar. My orgasm is so fierce that I grip the altar, needing something to hold on to.

Once I'm done, I slide the altar cloth off to clean Ella.

My heart beats wildly, and I can barely catch my breath. I don't remember feeling this way before.

Once she's cleaned, I scrunch the material into a ball and drop it onto the floor. I tuck myself into my pants, my fingers shaking as I do up my zipper.

I was never one for conversation after sex, but I suddenly want to ask Ella if she's all right. She's slumped over the altar, panting. She arches her head backward, peering up at the crucifix above her.

"Yes, I'm afraid He saw our sins," I say, wanting to break the silence. If she regrets what we did, I don't know what I'll do.

She comes to a slow stand and turns around, casting her eyes downward.

"Hey," I say. Stepping forward, I gently place my finger under her chin, encouraging her to look at me.

A small smile touches her lips, which settles my nerves. "I'm sorry I ripped up your postcard. I shouldn't have done that. I was jealous," she confesses. "As I was with Renata. She follows you around like a lost puppy, washing your SUV and staring at you with stars in her eyes. I hate it."

Her jealousy means she cares; it means she feels this too.

"You have nothing to be jealous of, Ella. She has something

I need."

"And what's that?"

"She will lead me to my half-brother. And my mother."

"And when she does? What happens then?"

I suppose it's time she knows the whole truth. "And then I kill them both for betraying me. Have I said too much?"

Ella bites her lip. "Alek, don't think of me as perfect or fragile. I'm not."

"Neither am I," I reply.

I wait for her to share her sins, but she clams up. I can read the signs. She has done something monumental. Something she is ashamed of.

When she is ready, she will share what that is. But now, I feel she wants to deal with something else she is ashamed of. She has committed the ultimate sin—and I know she liked it, liked it a lot—so what does this mean for us?

Looking at the sad, torn-up postcard discarded on the carpet, I realize I don't feel guilty for what I've done. I thought I'd never find another woman who could capture my heart like Willow. But I was wrong.

Whenever I'm with Ella, Willow's memory still burns, just not as brightly as it once did. Willow will always be a part of me, but for so long, she didn't just own a part—she owned all of me. It's time I let her go.

Needing to do one last thing, I pick up the pieces of the postcard and put them in my pocket. Gently gripping the back of Ella's head, I draw her toward me and kiss her forehead. I then turn and leave.

She doesn't follow because she knows this isn't goodbye.

It's just the beginning.

Unlocking the door, I walk through the hallway, unsure of the time. Once again, I've been stuck in a time warp with Ella. It's dark out, and the corridor is quiet. I exit through the back door and make my way toward my SUV.

Willow's postcard has been in my glove compartment for days, and I haven't given much thought to it, which is astonishing, considering I was carrying the other around like it was my lifeline. Opening the door, I decide to approach this like ripping off a Band-Aid.

With a deep breath, I open the glove compartment and am prepared to use the interior light to read over the message. But that won't be happening because the postcard isn't there.

Confused, I retrace my steps because I'm certain I placed it in here. But as I rifle through the discarded receipts and fast food napkins, it's clear that it's no longer here.

So now, the question is…who took it and why?

CHAPTER NINE

"What do you think, Alek? Does the sign look okay here?" asks Sister Yali from the ladder.

I, however, am no help because I'm currently looking at something else.

Ella is feet away, setting the long dining table for tonight's birthday celebrations. Her flushed cheeks and stolen glances alert me to the fact she's aware of my gawking, but I don't care.

After being lost to her yesterday, I can't mask how much I want her.

However, no one can know of my desires because she's still in her full habit. So I focus on Sister Yali, who is peering down at me from the top of the ladder.

"A little to the left." I gesture with my hand for her to move it a smidge. She happily does as I ask.

The sisters are ecstatic to be doing this for Mother Superior. She is the head matriarch whether she wants to accept it or not. She is the glue that holds everything together, and although she'll hate every minute of tonight's surprise party, she'll be touched by the effort.

When Sister Yali turns to look at me with a smile, I don't have the heart to tell her it's even more crooked than before.

"Looks wonderful, Sister." She claps in excitement, causing the ladder to wobble. I race toward it to steady the legs.

Ella's soft giggles sound behind me, a punch to my very core.

It's a welcome distraction from the question plaguing me. Where is Willow's postcard? I asked Irina if she took it as she was in my car, but she stared me straight in the eyes and promised she didn't. I believe her.

That only leaves one other person. Renata.

She was alone in my car when I was talking to Pavel. She could have taken it then, but she was wearing a short summer dress, so she didn't have room to conceal it. It wasn't hidden in the Medovik box or the gift bag.

Renata left them down in the basement, and when I looked inside—not searching for the postcard but out of curiosity—I saw only the honey cake, and a candle, and an extravagant silver ballpoint pen. I don't know why she would take it anyway.

It's of no value to her.

So, I'm back to my original question…who took it and why?

My cell chimes, snapping me from this conundrum that seems to have no answer. When I see who the caller is, I don't know whether to be relieved or concerned.

"Hello, Santo." I walk out of the room, mindful of Ella's astute ear.

"Hello, dear friend. Do you have time to come over today?"

He's phrased it as a question, but we both know this isn't optional.

"Yes, of course. I can come now?"

"Excellent. I'll see you soon." And he hangs up.

I knew this was coming, but I just don't have time for this shit. I have enough of my own problems to deal with. However, I remind myself, by doing this, it'll help with solving some of those problems, especially now that I know the truth about Renata.

Sighing, I pocket my cell and wonder if I have time to down a few shots of scotch before I venture into the lion's den.

"Everything okay?"

Spinning, I see Ella poking her head out the doorway, looking down the hallway to ensure we're alone. When she sees that we are, she walks toward me and discreetly reaches for my hand.

We're playing with fire being open this way, but it appears she craves my touch as I do hers.

"All is well, sweet красавица."

But she doesn't buy it.

"Who was on the phone?"

"Just a friend. He asked me to come over." I run my thumb along the tops of her knuckles.

Her eyes flutter to half-mast. "I thought you didn't have any friends."

Her attention to detail should worry me, but it doesn't. It pleases me that she takes an interest in my life. "Come with me, Sister."

Her eyes widen, as she's unsure what I want, but when I loop my fingers through hers and drag her down the hallway and toward the empty art room, she catches up to speed. The moment we're inside, I close and lock the door, then slam her against it.

My mouth is on hers, kissing her fiercely. I want to eat her alive.

She fists my hair, whimpering into my mouth as her tongue lashes with mine. We are hungry for the other, and when I press my body into hers, the crucifix around her neck digs into my chest—a not so gentle reminder of what I'm doing, yet again.

I'm rock hard, an automatic response whenever we're coupled this way. I want her but without the habit and in my bed. Not a single bed unfit for vermin but a king-sized bed draped in silks and expensive cotton sheets.

I want to call a palace, our home, because I want her. I know what I'm asking, but for us to be together, she has to give up so much.

Our kisses grow sluggish before I pull away.

Rubbing my nose against hers, I inhale, taking her in. "Don't get me wrong, these covert rendezvous get me hard"— to prove my point, I lift her leg and hook it around my waist so she can feel just how much so—"but we can't continue sneaking around this way.

"Mother Superior is far from stupid. And doing this,

no matter how good it feels, and красавица, it feels utterly fantastic"—I circle my hips, hitting her center while she whimpers—"is disrespecting her in her own home."

She bites her bottom lip, rocking her body into mine. She wants more, so more she will receive.

Lifting her gown, it bunches between us, but it doesn't matter. I'll be able to find this pussy blind. When I feel she isn't wearing any underwear beneath her habit, I smirk, elated she was anticipating a tryst like this between us.

I sink two fingers into her sex, hissing when I slide in deep, thanks to her arousal providing the perfect lubrication. She presses her foot into my ass, begging I go faster.

"What are we going to do?" I present the question, needing to know her thoughts.

"I-I don't know," she gasps, closing her eyes tight, lost to this pleasure we're both feeling. But her response is a wake-up call I didn't want to hear.

She doesn't know? Does this mean she'll remain a sister, coming to me when she merely wants to get off?

It would be most men's dream for this to occur but not to me. I want her to choose me because I choose her. I want to see if this feeling is real outside these walls. Now, we're acting on lust, but once that is gone, will this feeling of being consumed whole still be there?

"You will remain here? Even after I'm gone?"

She slowly opens her eyes, expressing my fears with a single look alone.

She doesn't know. This feeling between us isn't enough for her to uproot her life and live it with me. She is conflicted, which means she's unsure if there even is an "us."

"Alek—"

I cut her off, not wanting to hear the pity in her voice. Then I kiss her wildly, pumping my fingers in and out of her sex, suddenly feeling like nothing but a tool, used solely for her pleasure.

I got lost in a fairy tale yet again. Lost to a version of my life where I deserved to be happy. But the ghosts of my past won't let me, and I suppose they're right.

She trembles in my hand, her body spasming when I circle her swollen bud with my thumb. Her orgasmic screams are muted by the hard press of my lips over hers. She comes wildly, kissing me like she cares...kissing me like I'm enough.

But I know when her high fades, she will go back to pretending, untroubled with the lies, and that's because I know now, I will never be enough for her. For anyone.

Once she grows lax, I remove my fingers and sever our kiss. I leave her panting as I lick the fingers that were inside her seconds ago. Her sweetness almost convinces me that she cares. Almost.

"You better go back out there. You wouldn't want anyone to notice you're missing." I don't overlook my sarcasm. I want her to know that I won't be used whenever she has an itch that needs to be scratched.

She reads the message loud and clear and steps to the side so I can exit. I'm disappointed it seems so easy for her to disengage. Unlocking the door, I don't look back as I walk down the hallway, attempting to catch my breath.

Ella robs me of air but not in a good way. In a way I need

it to survive, and that's dangerous. I need to breathe on my own because that's all I'm destined to be.

Renata comes out of the library up ahead. When she sees me, her face twists in anger and then fear. I don't blame her. I was prepared to kill her yesterday. There's no going back from there. We merely need one another, that's all. That's why we're being civil.

I give her a curt nod as I approach where she stands.

"Where are you going?" she asks, pressing a folder to her chest. I have no idea what's inside nor do I care.

"Out," I reply, not bothering to elaborate.

"Will you be back for the party?"

"I don't know."

"You have to be!" she almost shouts. But I don't have time for her theatrics.

"I don't have to do anything," I affirm sharply. "Besides, I'm not in the mood for a celebration."

"Don't be so selfish! You'll ruin everything."

Again, her theatrics are lost on me, but I humor her, nonetheless. "I hardly think my attendance will affect tonight's proceedings, малышка."

"Alek…" She grips my forearm, stopping me from walking away from her.

She knows better than to touch me, though, and smartly removes her hand.

"Mother Superior has been good to us. She loves you, and I think she'd be disappointed if you didn't come. But if you don't want to, then that's your choice."

Laying the guilt trip on me shouldn't work, but it does.

She's right. Mother Superior has been my savior time and time again. The least I can do is have a non-alcoholic glass of champagne with her.

"Fine. But I have to go right now."

She seems almost relieved I said yes, but I don't bother with deciphering why that is because Santo is waiting.

The roads are clear, and I make it to his house in record time. When I park my SUV and walk toward Santo's front door, I'm aching with the need to hurt someone. I can't shake this negativity away. It sticks to me like a second skin.

However, when Santo opens the door, brandy and cigar in hand, I need to rein in my anger because he cannot sense anything is amiss. A jumpy hitman is a careless, paranoid one, and Santo can't afford any blowback.

So I compose myself with a winner's smile, just as I've trained myself to. "I hope you saved some brandy for me," I quip lightly, wanting to settle the mood.

Santo laughs, and anyone looking in couldn't be reproached for thinking this was a casual visit between friends.

He opens the door wide and gestures for me to walk down the hallway toward his office. It's awfully quiet. I wonder where everyone is.

The moment I enter, I stand in front of his desk with my arms crossed behind my back. I wait for him to direct me. After all, this is his show.

"Brandy?" he asks, closing the door behind him.

"Please."

He walks to his desk and pours me a glass from the crystal

decanter. He passes it to me before waving for me to take a seat.

The moment I sit, he reaches into his desk drawer and retrieves a yellow folder. He takes a seat, sipping his drink. "My apologies this took longer than I anticipated," he says, tapping his cigar over the ashtray. "Discretion is everything."

"Of course." I nod, understanding the hidden message in his words.

"This folder has the power to divide my family, all for a pretty face," he reveals, and I suddenly realize this is a lot more personal than I thought. "This woman, this *bitch*, wormed her way into my family with an ulterior motive.

"She knew Frank was the weakest of this family. She played him, and he fell for her charms. They met when she was waitressing at some shithole. But he didn't care she was penniless. I told him. I told him to be careful and that women like her couldn't be trusted.

"But he didn't listen, and now, look where we are. Their meeting wasn't accidental. I'm sure of it."

Impassively, I listen to his story, as it's clear he needs to get this off his chest.

"But I was weak too. I shouldn't blame Frank because this is my fault as much as it is his," he confesses, revealing he isn't looking for her for revenge for his son but rather, himself.

"I'm merely a man, Aleksei. I fell under her spell, and I'm not proud of this fact. She made me believe she loved me, and that I should have my wife...taken care of so she could take her place. She called off the engagement because she said she wanted me. But I soon discovered it was my money that she really loved.

"She stole from this family, not only our riches but our dignity as well. She tricked Frank and me into believing what she felt for us was real. There is no greater threat than the beauty of a woman.

"Frank was merely a pawn for her to lure me into her web. And it worked. I fell for her, and I fell hard."

Nodding, I lean back in the leather seat and cross my ankle over my knee. "How much did she steal?"

Santo takes a moment, savoring his cigar. "One million dollars."

I maintain my poker face, but goddamn, no wonder he wants her found.

But the real reason isn't the money. To this family, that's merely pocket change. Santo knows this woman has leverage over him. She has the power to destroy his life because his family is everything to him.

This woman guards his dirty secrets, and if she were ever to tell Santo's wife, Mila, of their affair, it would be the end of the Macrillo family. His kids would side with their mother, seeing as their father fucked their youngest son's fiancée and allowed her to make off with a million dollars.

Whoever this woman is, I take my hat off to her. She conned one of the most powerful men in Russia. I almost feel bad hunting her down. But with her trade, I get my kingdom back.

What I don't understand is how a powerful man like Santo can't find her. Why does he think I'll have better luck than him?

"There is a reason I asked you to help me with my little... indiscretion," he states, reading my thoughts. "I know you can be trusted. But I also know you have ties with the orphanage."

Alarm bells begin to sound.

"Yes, I'm a benefactor," I calmly reply. This isn't a secret. Anyone who can read can look this up. But that's not what he means.

"Let's not play games, Aleksei. I know you're close to Mother Superior. I also know you're able to visit whenever you like."

"Yes, Mother Superior and I have a mutual respect. What does this have to do with who you're looking for?" I ask, unsure of what's going on.

Santo stubs out his cigar before sliding the folder across his desk and offering it to me. Resting my glass on the edge of the desk, I reach for the folder innocently, not realizing my entire world is about to be thrown into disarray.

"Because I believe she is hiding out there, pretending to be someone she's not," he divulges just as I open the folder and peer into the eyes of the devil.

There must be some mistake. I've surely gone insane, sick in lust and seeing her face wherever I look because there is no way this woman Santo is hunting, this woman who tricked him into falling in love with her, this woman who stole a million dollars from him is Ella.

But as I focus on those supple lips I've kissed and those hazel eyes I've been lost in since the first moment we met, it's her.

"I take your silence as you too have fallen under her spell.

But don't be fooled. She's a temptress. She uses people for her gain and then disposes of them when she's done," Santo says, but he has no idea why I feel as if I've just swallowed my tongue.

"Her name is Antonella Ricci. But she goes by the name Ella. She's from Chicago originally. She came to Europe hoping for an adventure, but when she ran out of money, she soon understood her naïve dreams landed her in trouble."

All I can hear on repeat is her name—Antonella Ricci.

"Call me Ella."

At least she didn't lie about one thing because everything else has been a blatant lie.

"Why do you think she's at the orphanage?" I ask, surprised I can string a sentence together.

"I can't be too sure as she never ventures outdoors."

"Sister Arabella behaved quite strangely moments ago when it was her turn to go into town to set up the soup kitchen for the destitute. She refused and was quite unhappy when I insisted she go."

Mother Superior's comment now makes sense. Her behavior had nothing to do with me and everything to do with the fact that straying outside the orphanage walls meant she was at risk of being found by Santo.

How stupid I've been.

"But my men found her car abandoned not too far from the orphanage, along with the dead body of one Sister Arabella Phillips buried in a shallow grave. Her car was sitting at the bottom of a cliff."

Bile rises as I clench the folder in my hands.

"I suspect the poor sister also fell victim to the venomous snake and paid with her life. Ella needed a new identity, and what a perfect ruse. No one would suspect her true colors dressed behind a habit."

All I can do is stare at the picture of the woman I thought I knew, realizing I don't know her at all.

"Are you all right, Aleksei? You look rather pale."

Composing myself, I nod, flipping through the rest of the information in the folder. Before me is the life story of the woman who played me for a fool.

"Have you seen her at the orphanage?" he asks, hopeful.

I shatter his dreams with a firm shake of my head.

I need to process this before I decide what to do. Throwing her to the wolves will mean her death. Yes, she lied, but the thought of harm coming to her...my heart constricts at the notion.

On the flip side, Antonella Ricci is a fucking liar. And a murderer.

"Now that you know why I asked you to do this, will you go to the orphanage and look around? I'm certain she is using Sister Arabella's identity, so she should be easy to find. I would do it, but I'm hardly welcome within those walls.

"Mother Superior won't think twice if you go and ask."

And he's right. That's why Ella has been safe thus far. She is somewhere Santo can't get to her, and I suspect she is merely biding her time until she sees an opportunity to leave.

An epiphany hits, and I realize that I'm that opportunity.

She needs protection and what better way to gain that protection than by fooling me into believing she has feelings for me. I was just a pawn—her get out of jail free card.

She guessed I'd see her as a challenge and her sisterhood a conquest for me to conquer. And I fell for her lies. She had no qualms about breaking her vows because she isn't a real sister. She murdered the real Arabella Phillips and stole her identity to save her own skin.

She knew about me, and just as she did with Santo, I have no doubt she studied me like a lab rat. The mystery of the missing paperwork from Mother Superior's desk is now solved. She was looking for a way out with someone who had money and power.

I may not be who I once was, but with a simple Google search, she would find the notoriety linked to my name.

"I'll make you a deal," Santo says coolly. "I'm so certain that she is there, but if she's not, I will still help you find your brother and help you work your way back to the top."

This confirms he knows her whereabouts. He just needs someone to retrieve her. I could lie and say that she's not, but sooner or later, he will storm the orphanage and destroy anyone who stands in his way.

The sisters, the children, and Mother Superior are all at risk with her being there. I don't have a choice.

"I'll be in touch shortly. Let me work on Mother Superior as I can't drag her from the orphanage, kicking and screaming." When he cocks his head to the side, I elaborate. "You want me to be discreet, correct?"

He nods in understanding.

"I will deliver her to you, just give me some time. We need to be smart about this."

He clearly doesn't know I'm currently residing at the orphanage, so this gives me an advantage. A small one but an advantage, nonetheless.

"Yes, you're right. I knew you were the right man for the job. This bitch's demise will be beneficial to us both, my friend."

Slamming the folder shut, I stand, hinting I'm done with this conversation. "I will call you with any developments."

If Santo senses my strange behavior, he doesn't address it. I have something he wants, and he's willing to overlook it because that's how badly he wants Ella.

"My wife and sons are away for a few days, so I'd like this settled before their return." His flippant approach about ending Ella's life has me wanting to jump over his desk and throttling him.

But I simply nod. "Of course."

A few days? That's all I have to decide what to do.

Needing to leave this instant, I bid Santo farewell and find my own way out.

The fresh air does nothing to calm this raging inferno inside me, but I keep my cool, knowing my movements are being watched as I step into my SUV and start the engine. Once I'm in drive, I cruise down the driveway, adjusting the radio until I find a station playing Beethoven.

My psyche is in sync with the intense orchestra, moments away from exploding into the jolted rhythm as I turn out of Santo's driveway and make a right onto the quiet street. For minutes, I drive on autopilot, attempting to process what I've just uncovered.

But as the powerful music crescendos, so does my need to hurt someone and hurt them really bad.

"I fell...in love when I shouldn't have."

"Because he was a very, very bad man."

Over and over, I hear Ella's words, feeling nothing but a fool now that I know who she's speaking about. Fell in love? With who precisely? Santo? Or his son?

Gripping the steering wheel, I clench my jaw as waves of anger overwhelm me. How could I have been so stupid? Both Renata and Ella fooled me. I thought I was breaking them, but in reality, both women were playing me at my own game.

The folder sits on the seat beside me, my stupidity staring back at me. All the information I need is within reach, and all I want to do is throw it out the window and forget I ever met with Santo. I don't want to believe him.

Taking a hard left, I pull over to the curb, ignoring the annoyed horn honks of whoever I just pissed off. Reaching for the folder, I rest it against the steering wheel and open it slowly. When I see Ella's picture, a sharp pain tugs at my heart.

She's in a red cocktail dress, smiling seductively at whoever is behind the camera. Her hair is pulled up into an elaborate bun, and her perfectly applied makeup gives her face a runway glow, but beneath all this, there is no doubt it's her.

With or without the jewels and makeup, she is a goddess, a goddess who played me for a fool. I trace my finger over her red lips, remembering how good they felt pressed to mine. But it was all lies.

Flipping through the rest of the information, I see Santo

has compiled everything on her—bank account statements, information on where she used to live, used to work, and the friends she went to college with.

It seems she was telling me the truth about her family. Her parents divorced when she was eight. Her father is estranged. And her mother remarried, creating a second, better family and forgetting about her first.

Twenty minutes later, I know everything there is to know about Antonella Ricci, but I only wish the information had come from her. That she'd trusted me enough to tell me the truth because what I'm forced to do could have been avoided.

But now, I can't trust her, and if you don't have trust, all you have is a warm body with a pretty face. There is no connection, no bond between us. She can be replaced.

With a sigh, I toss the folder onto the passenger seat and head for the orphanage.

I take the long way, wishing to prolong the inevitable. But there is no escaping what must be done. If she killed a sister, then she will be dealt with accordingly. I'm in no position to throw stones, but I'm really trying to be a different person. Someone like Ella, who is as morally corrupt as I am, will ruin any progress I've made.

Eventually, I will slip back into old patterns because it's so much easier being bad and not caring than it is to be good.

The orphanage looms ahead, but I drive through the back entrance and park my car. Rolling the folder, I clutch it tight in my palm and make my way toward the door. It's unlocked, which angers me. Now more than ever, we need to be on top of security.

My conscience screams at me that if I'm going to hand Ella over to Santo, then why should it matter? I tell my conscience to go to hell.

"Where have you been?" Sister Yali whispers in a panic, grabbing my wrist and pulling me through the door.

"I was just running some errands," I reply, tucking the rolled-up folder into my back pocket.

"You have to stall Mother Superior," she reveals in a rushed breath.

"Why?"

"Because we're still waiting on her cake, and she can't go into the dining hall. It'll ruin the surprise. She already senses something is going on with the sisters running around in a panic."

Stalling Mother Superior is the last thing I want to do as I know she will see straight through me, but saying no to Sister Yali would be like kicking a puppy.

So, I sigh. "Okay, fine. Where is she?"

Sister Yali claps happily. "Sister Margaret is holding her prisoner in the infirmary, claiming she has a migraine. But she'll only buy that story for so long."

The effort the sisters are going to have me walking down the hallway in surrender.

"Twenty minutes, tops," she calls out, and I just nod.

The moment I walk into the infirmary, Mother Superior looks at the door, hopeful someone will explain what is going on. That person isn't me. "Sister Margaret, if you're feeling okay, Sister Yali wants to see you."

Sister Margaret is lying on a bed with a damp white cloth

over her forehead. Mother Superior sits by her bedside with a crossword book in her lap.

Sister Margaret blows out a breath in relief. Her job here is done. However, she stays true to her part of patient and slowly sits. Removing the cloth from her forehead, she places it in the porcelain wash bowl on the bedside table and nods.

"Yes, I'm feeling better. Thank you, Mother Superior, for watching over me."

Mother Superior looks rather confused by the entire situation but smiles.

Sister Margaret stands and slowly walks toward the door. Her lips tip into a shy grin before she practically runs from the room.

I stand in the doorway with my hands in my pockets while Mother Superior stays seated. A silent hint she wants to know what's on my mind. I wish I could tell her, but I can't. I need to speak to Ella first before I figure out what I'm going to do.

"I suppose you're not going to tell me what's going on out there?" Mother Superior asks, placing the pen in the crossword book and closing it.

I laugh in response. "Whatever are you talking about?"

She shakes her head but smiles. "Come here, child," she says in Russian, which means I'm in trouble.

I do as she asks, sitting on the edge of the bed. The paperwork in my back pocket burns a hole through me, but I remain straight-faced.

"What's troubling you, Aleksei? Lately, you always look like you're carrying the weight of the world on your shoulders."

Running a hand through my hair, I reply, "It sometimes feels that way, but it will pass. Just as it always does."

She ponders over what I shared. "You grapple with your conscience, but in the end, you always do what's right. Look what you did with Willow."

This is the first time she's mentioned Willow. I never speak about her as it's not a time I wish to relive.

"She called me not long after she left. Did you know that?"

My mouth parts in surprise. "No, I did not."

"She asked how you were as she'd seen the renovations done to the orphanage online. I told her you were safe."

"Did she say anything else?" I ask, almost begging she says yes.

"I asked if she wanted me to pass a message to you. She said no."

I can't hide my disappointment.

"No matter, I want you to know that she cares for you, Alek. Maybe not in the way you want, but she gave you a second chance. I think it's time you did the same, don't you think?"

"Give Willow a second chance?" I ask, confused.

Mother Superior places her hand over my knee. "No, мой ребенок. Give yourself a second chance. You may not realize it, but you help many people in your own way. Willow, Irina, me, Renata, and the sisters. So many people see the good in your heart…one day, you will too."

Mother Superior has always been my biggest cheerleader. I wish I could believe her. Maybe one day, but that day is not today. The mention of Renata has me remembering her admission.

"I wanted to apologize for what Renata shared with you."

"What did she say?"

Clearing my throat as there is no easy way to say this to a woman of God, I explain, "She said she came to you, seeking advice on her, er, feelings…for me. I want you to know nothing happened. I would never…" *with her*, I silently add.

With Ella, however…

Mother Superior's expression confuses me because she appears as if she has no idea what I'm talking about. And that's because she doesn't. "She must have mistaken me for someone else. She never came to me to discuss such things."

Mother Superior may be getting on in age, but she is still as sharp minded as she was the day we first met. Renata's story is just that, but I don't understand why she'd lie.

Unless…we were talking about her being inside Mother's Superior's office. Did she deflect the comment to evade the truth?

"Mother Superior," Sister Yali chirps as the door bursts open. "Come with me please."

Mother Superior watches me closely as I attempt to decipher what's going on. I process everything Renata shared with me, trying to connect the dots to figure out why she'd lie.

"I will have no issues tying you up and taking you against your will," Sister Yali teases, but she doesn't realize what she's done.

"It didn't matter that the rope burns were so bad."

"My ankle was chained to that radiator. Sometimes my wrists."

Renata's story plays over and over, and I can't believe I

didn't pick up on the inconsistency sooner. Chained would imply a metal chain, yet rope burns would suggest rope. However, when I found her, there weren't any signs of rope burns. They were present *after* I tied her up.

If Serg bound her as she said he did and used her for his pleasure, then where is the proof? Apart from being filthy and scared, there weren't any signs she had been held captive the way she described it.

My stomach drops because this small discrepancy obliterates her entire story. I need to find her.

I jump up from the bed, ready to race from the room, but Sister Yali pushes her oversized glasses up the bridge of her nose, looking at me like she's prepared to make me a eunuch if I don't come to the party. Mother Superior is behind me, clearly worried she said something wrong.

With no other choice, I quash down my murderous rage and offer my arm to Mother Superior. "I will escort you. No restraints necessary."

Mother Superior loops her arm through mine, entertaining me and Sister Yali, but she senses something is amiss by my reaction. We follow Sister Yali down the hallway toward the dining hall where I assume all the sisters and the children wait quietly, ready to surprise their guest of honor.

Sister Yali looks over her shoulder at me, beaming brightly. I return the gesture, but on the inside, I'm far from smiling.

"Aleksei, what's wrong?" Mother Superior whispers.

"Nothing is wrong." I rub over the top of her hand, attempting to soothe her worries. "Just don't be angry with me."

She turns her cheek sharply, unsure what I mean. But she soon finds out when Sister Yali opens the doors to the dining hall, and everyone screams, "Surprise!"

Mother Superior places a hand on her chest over her heart while I chuckle, leading her forward.

The sisters swarm her, giving Mother Superior birthday hugs and kisses. It's quite wonderful to see. But as I scan the room, my sights are set on two people.

Renata stands with one of the sisters a few feet away, sipping what looks like punch. We lock eyes, and she appears happy to see me. At first. I wonder why. I'll deal with her later, though, because my senses are so in tune with Ella that it takes me all of two seconds to find her in a room full of people.

She's in the far corner, holding Irina's hand. The sight would usually warm my heart, but now, it merely breaks it further.

Now that I see her, really see her, I'm disgusted that she wears the stolen habit of the sister she buried in a shallow grave. I'm appalled she would use her beauty to trick any man into her bed. She uses people for her gain, and she had the gall to call me out when she'd done the same thing.

Her smile soon diminishes. She knows. She senses something is wrong, and because she is guilty, she will automatically think I've unearthed her dirty secret. This just proves her guilt.

She bends down to whisper something in Irina's ear. I find out what that is when Irina stands on her toes, seeking me out. When she sees me, she lets go of Ella's hand and runs through the crowd to me.

This buys Ella some time, but she won't escape. Not again.

Ella clutches the cross around her throat, sickening me further. She pushes through the masses, making a beeline for the side door. She rushes out of it, never looking back.

Irina throws herself in my arms as I crouch low. "Ski!" she shrieks, squealing when I pick her up and hug her tight. "Dress?"

Nodding, I kiss her warm forehead. "Yes, цветочек, your dress is very pretty. Just like you. May I ask you a question?"

She nods, placing small kisses all over my cheeks.

"Why did you call Renata a bad lady? And why fire? Did she hurt you?"

Irina stops kissing my cheeks and blows a raspberry. "Bad lady," she repeats in Russian. "Burn paper with picture."

"What do you mean burn paper with picture?" I ask, pulling back to look at her.

She uses both pointer fingers to draw a rectangle in the air, or rather, she draws the shape of a postcard.

Irina has never seen a postcard before; therefore, she refers to one as paper with a picture because essentially, that's what it is.

But when? There was no way she could have taken it when she was in the SUV. It was only one time. But then I realize, no, it wasn't.

"She follows you around like a lost puppy, washing your SUV…"

Ella's words come back to haunt me because Renata has been in my vehicle more than once.

"And you saw her do this?"

She nods.

"Did she see you?"

She nods once again.

My body vibrates in fear and rage. "Did she hurt you, Irina?"

So help me god, if she nods one final time, I will hurt Renata and hurt her good.

"No," she replies, her innocent eyes filling with tiny tears. "Ski mad with Irina?"

"Oh, цветочек, no. Ski is mad with himself. Don't cry. Shh." I use my thumb to wipe away a fallen tear. "I love you. You know this?"

She nods, sniffing and wiping her eyes. "Irina любит Ski."

I don't deserve her love, but I have it regardless. "I have to go find Sister Arabella. I'll be right back, okay?"

She nods and doesn't make a fuss, sensing the urgency to my tone.

Sister Yali runs toward me, the joy that she is, smiling broadly. "Thank you for everything. If it wasn't for you, this party would have been nothing more than a few boxes of pizza and some crisps."

Sister Margaret has told her of my contribution, but I don't want gratitude. However, there is something else. "Sister Yali, can you watch Irina? I need to do something."

Sister Yali nods, the concern clear on her face when I offer her Irina's hand. She holds on tight, which isn't like Irina. She usually shies away from such contact.

"Yes, of course. Is everything all right?"

"It will be. Thank you, Sister."

I stroke the apple of Irina's cheek before I chase after Ella. On the way out, I turn over my shoulder, focusing on Renata. She's seen the entire exchange, but instead of seeming concerned, she raises her glass in a salute.

Drink up, your time is coming.

As I run down the hall, my frantic footsteps echo my urgency to find Ella. She is no doubt packing, ready to flee because that's what the guilty do—they run to save their own skin.

I kick open her bedroom door and don't hesitate to storm over to her as she's hastily stuffing a bag full of clothes. Her face reflects her fear, and when she picks up the lamp, throwing it at my head and missing, that fear turns to pure terror.

She backs up, seeking a weapon or a way out. I grip her bicep and throw her up against the wall. She pummels her fists against my chest as I cage her in, desperately trying to escape my clutches, but she's not going anywhere.

"Let me go!" she snarls, eyeing me angrily.

I laugh in response. "You're not going anywhere. We need to talk."

"How dare you come in here uninvited?"

"You didn't mind when I came somewhere else, but I suppose that's just another day at the office for you, isn't that right…*Sister*?"

Her hand flies up, slapping me on the cheek.

Moving my jaw from side to side, I smirk, elated I'm getting under her skin because she has gotten under mine.

"Why are you packing?" I ask, gesturing with my head toward the bag on the bed.

"Because I can't be here any longer," she replies, purposely being evasive.

"Why not?" I question, and her anger, her fear is like a drug to me. I should hate her for what she's done, but I don't.

Her wickedness sings to mine. And now, it's time to uncover just how wicked Antonella Ricci really is.

"Does it have something to do with the fact that the habit you wear once belonged to the sister you buried in a shallow grave?" I ask coolly, waiting for her to deny it.

But she doesn't.

"H-how do you know?" she whispers, eyes filling with tears.

I almost feel sorry for her—almost—but she's conned me before.

"I know a lot of things about you. For starters,"—I lower my face to hers so we're inches apart—"I know your name… Antonella Ricci."

"Oh, god." She turns her cheek, squeezing her eyes shut.

"He won't help you."

"Let me explain." Her body vibrates, begging I listen to what she has to say.

"Go ahead."

"Let me go," she says, meeting my eyes once again.

"You're in no position to make demands. Talk." I place my hands on either side of her head, caging her in.

"I had to leave because I saw your face. I knew it was only a matter of time before you'd find out what I'd done. I should have left sooner, but I developed feel—"

But I cut her off, punching my fist against the wall. She

flinches as it's inches from her face. "Don't you dare play that card! Don't you dare!"

"It's true!" she cries, refusing to back down.

"If that were true, then why did it take me meeting that asshole Santo Macrillo for you to come clean now? If you had any...*feelings* for me, why did you lie to me?"

"It was never the right time."

Scoffing, I shake my head. "*Today* was the right time. When I asked you what we were going to do, you could have told me the truth then. Yet you've continued to lie to me when I have been nothing but honest from the very beginning."

Her regret over wanting me had nothing to do with God but rather, her wanting a bad man. It seems she has a type. And I fit the mold.

"I was scared," she states, her lower lip trembling.

"Scared of what exactly? What I've done in my lifetime is far worse than what you can ever imagine," I exclaim because my crimes precede hers. "But I still told you. I trusted you."

My comment wounds her, but I don't care.

"I think the truth is because you didn't want me to know what your true motives were.

"I think you didn't want me to know that you seduced both Frank and Santo Macrillo to work your way into a family with money. I think you wanted Santo's wife dead so you could be the head matriarch.

"When Santo saw through your bullshit, you ran scared, but not before stealing one million dollars from him."

I wait for a response, for her guilt to shine, but I don't get it.

"Get off! Get off! Get off!" she sobs, her body burning up beneath me.

Her hysteria isn't staged, and when she turns a sickly green, I release her and watch as she races to the small en suite and throws up in the sink. She grips the porcelain, her shoulders shuddering as she heaves uncontrollably.

This was not the response I anticipated.

When she's done being sick, she rinses out her mouth and splashes water on her pale cheeks. She stares at her reflection for a long while, and I wonder what she sees.

"If you really believe that, then you don't know me at all," she whispers, still staring into the mirror. "If I stole that money, then why am I here? Why aren't I a million miles away from here?"

When she turns to face me, and I see the genuine tears in her eyes, I suddenly realize she's right. But that doesn't explain what happened to the real Sister Arabella.

"That money was taken by Santo's mistress, not me, because regardless of what you believe, I was never his mistress. And I never stole any money from him. He wished I was his lover, and believe me, he tried, but after I turned him down one too many times, he snapped.

"He said he would have me killed. That I only loved Frank because of his money. But that wasn't true. I fell in love with Frank even before I knew who he was."

Her version of events differs quite drastically from Santo's, but I listen.

"I broke off the engagement because I found out Frank was unfaithful, just like his father. I was expected to turn a blind eye to his infidelities because the men of the Macrillo family could have as many girlfriends as they wanted, and us women were supposed to accept their adulterous ways.

"Mila knew Santo had many lovers, but as long as she was his first, and he continued to provide her with the comfortable lifestyle she led, she had no issues playing happy family.

"But when one of his mistresses stole from him, Santo knew he had to cover his ass. Mila was okay with the cheating, but the stealing was something far worse than her husband fucking someone other than her.

"Money is the only thing that family cares about. I just wish I'd known that sooner."

This is a lot to take in.

Ella has barely shared a thing about herself, and now, it's information overload.

The truth is, I don't know what to believe. The Macrillo family is very private about their family affairs. To the outside world, they're picture perfect, but behind closed doors, she seems to paint a completely different picture altogether.

"Santo wants me dead because he doesn't want anyone knowing he was trying to bed his youngest son's fiancée. It would tear them apart. I wouldn't tell anyone. I mean, who would believe me? But I'm a liability. As long as I'm alive, I have the power to ruin him."

If—and that's a big if—what she's saying is true, then I think she's gotten it all wrong.

Ella has done something no one has ever done to Santino Macrillo before. She bruised his ego by saying no, and to a man like him, that's far worse than death.

He wants her found not because she could ruin him, but because he wants her to pay for not loving him in return. I know this because I've experienced it firsthand.

"What happened to Sister Arabella?" I question, wishing she'd come out of the bathroom. But maybe she feels more comfortable this way.

"I knew Frank was playing squash, so I went to his house to gather my things. Santo was never home at that time of the evening," she recounts, wringing her hands in front of her. "He caught me leaving. He begged me not to leave, said that he loved me. When he realized nothing he could say would change my mind, he attacked me."

Tears spill down her cheeks, but she stubbornly wipes them away with the back of her hand.

"He pinned me to the floor, forcing himself onto me. I stopped fighting, and when he let his guard down, I broke a vase over his head. I only just got away, but not before he warned me. He said he would find me wherever I was and make me pay for dishonoring him and his family. I was scared because I know the things that family is capable of. I left in a panic. I didn't have enough money to fly back home. I knew I had to stay in Russia until I could come up with a plan.

"But I knew I had to stay hidden. If not, I'd be killed. I was terrified for my life."

And she's right. There was no way Santo would let her live.

"I was on my way to a motel. It was raining and dark; the visibility on the road was bad. I turned the corner, and that's when I saw Sister Arabella's mangled car. She had veered off the steep road, her flashing blinkers flickering in time with my frantic heart. I could see someone was in the car, so I stopped to help."

She closes her eyes, as if the memory is too painful to face.

"But when I opened the door, she was already dead. There was b-blood everywhere. I know it was wrong, but when I saw her crucifix hanging from her broken neck, and when I looked over her ID and saw how similar our names were, I wondered if maybe this was a sign. Her death didn't have to be in vain. She could help me.

"So I dragged her from her car, undressed her and replaced her clothes with mine, and then I…buried her. I used a tire iron to dig a shallow grave in my underwear because I couldn't get her habit any more dirty than it already was," she says robotically. "I said a prayer over her grave, thanking her for what she'd done for me.

"I took her belongings from her car, and then I put it into drive and sent it careening off the cliff's edge. I left my car, which was registered to Frank, knowing they would be looking for me. Sister Arabella was barely recognizable. Her face was all…smashed in," she reveals, placing a hand over her mouth.

"Which is why I dressed her in my clothes. I hoped if Santo's men found her, they'd think some Good Samaritan who didn't want any trouble found her and laid her to rest. By leaving my car and ID, my hope was that they'd think it was me in that grave and not Sister Arabella."

Sloppy work but she isn't accustomed to concealing a body. I suppose she did the best she could, considering the circumstances.

"She was already dead," she says, as if justifying what she did. "I needed a new identity, and I was offered it.

"I dressed in her spare habit, took her belongings, and walked to the orphanage. The sisters and Mother Superior were expecting me. Sister Arabella," she corrects. "And I knew I'd be safe.

"I washed the blood from her habit late at night, and just like that, Sister Arabella was gone. I'm not proud of what I did, but I did what I had to in order to survive."

She turns to face me now that her tale is complete, waiting for me to respond.

"Who was the bad man?" I question.

When she arches a brow, I clarify, "You said you fell in love with a bad man."

She appears wounded I need to ask because it reveals I doubt her story. "Frank, of course. At first, I didn't know what he did, but when I eventually found out, it was too late."

"So, you loved him?"

"Yes, very much," she replies sadly, and a sharp pain stabs at my heart. "But sometimes, love isn't enough. I could never be with someone who is unfaithful. I've seen firsthand what it can do to a family."

She speaks of her estranged family.

"You now know my dirty secrets, so now I want to know, why did you go see Santo?"

Walking slowly toward her, I come to a stop just before the doorway and brace my hands on either side of the frame. "Because Santo knows you're here."

She wavers, gripping the sink to stop from falling.

"And he's hired me to bring you back to him."

An eerie silence settles between us.

"What do you get for your troubles?" she whispers, unable to mask her sadness.

"My half-brother, my kingdom, foes becoming friends, and reclaiming my place back on top," I reply blankly.

"Oh, my god," she cries softly, now understanding what's at stake. "So by handing me over to Santo, you get your life back?"

Gripping the wood of the doorjamb, I nod. "Yes."

Her head bobbles numbly, biting her lip, eyes distant. "Oh."

There is no easy way to deliver such news, and I understand what hearing the truth does to her, but she needs to know this is happening because she lied. If she had told me the truth, we could have done something earlier, but now, I don't know what to do.

I give her to Santo; I get my life back. If I don't, no matter how civil Santo is behaving, he'll ensure we both pay with our lives. He knows she's here, so it's only a matter of time.

"What are you going to do?" she asks, holding back her tears.

Reaching into my back pocket, I present the folder. I don't need to explain what it is. "I—"

However, before I have a chance to deliver her fate, the room is eclipsed in total darkness. Not metaphorically but literally. That darkness is suddenly followed by a gut-curdling scream that turns my blood cold.

CHAPTER
TEN

Frantically reaching into my pocket, I retrieve my phone, and the moment I turn on the flashlight, a slash of silver slices through the air.

Sidestepping, I fend off Ella and the pair of scissors she's wielding like a sword. When she attempts to stab me in the stomach, I grip her forearm—hard. Her pained screams sound loudly, and when she drops the scissors to the floor, I yank her forward, pressing us chest to chest.

"Try that again, and I will whip you until your ass is raw!"

She spits in my face in response.

Furious, I cup her throat and walk her backward, slamming her against the wall. "You don't leave my side, we clear?"

I don't have time for this because when the generator kicks in and the emergency lights cover everything in a ghostly green glow, I know something is very wrong.

She gasps for air as my grip is tight but nods shakily.

Letting her go, I roughly clutch her wrist and drag her out the door. The hallway is shrouded in partial darkness as the lights are still not back on. I storm down the hallway with Ella in tow, but when I turn the corner and see a trail of black up ahead, my survival mode kicks in.

Running forward, I follow the trail of blood, which looks black thanks to the green lighting, but this is without a doubt blood because its source lies sprawled out ahead.

"Oh, my god," Ella cries when she sees the twisted body a few feet away.

It's a sister with her habit sprawled around her, but she is prone, so I can't see her face. No matter that I don't trust Ella, I let her go, not wanting her to see the fallen sister. I have a suspicion Santo is behind this attack. If that's the case, Ella isn't safe.

Her soft footsteps behind me reveal she is prepared for anything, but as I drop to a crouch and carefully pull back the head scarf, nothing can prepare either of us for what we're about to see because I was wrong…so fucking wrong.

"Hello, Brother."

A sharp pain in my side accompanies those words because the fallen isn't a sister—it's Serg.

Jumping up, I press my palm over my bleeding flank, thanks to the stab wound inflicted by my kin. Serg doesn't give me time to process that he's really here before he springs up and launches forward, intent on adding another stab wound to my torso.

But his eagerness and inexperience, a reflection of his

leadership, has me disarming him quickly when I kick the long blade from his hand. He wavers, which is all I need to leap forward and break his nose. The sound, as well as the blood coating my hand, awakens the bloodlust, and I dive on top of him, dropping us both to the floor.

He tries to fight me, but there is no way he's leaving here alive. I cradle his head in my palms and slam the back of his skull against the hard flooring. A pained *oomph* leaves him, music to my ears, so I do it again and again.

The habit does nothing to protect him as I continue my assault. I won't stop until he's dead. I don't need an explanation for how he got here; I just need him to stop breathing. That is, until I hear a voice that changes the course of everything forever.

The lights flicker back on, my eyes taking a second to adjust to the stimuli around me. In my hands, I hold my half-brother's bleeding head, but feet away where Irina stands is where my hands should be.

"Ski?" she asks, eyes wide when she sees me straddling someone in a habit, covered in blood.

Serg gurgles, a blood bubble popping from his busted lips. A smirk suddenly cracks at his mouth when he peers backward.

"It's okay," I assure her in Russian. But nothing will be okay because Ella's petrified screams reveal whose habit Serg stole. Whose blood paints the hallway's floor.

Peering ahead, I see a broken, bloody body, twisted at an unnatural angle, and a pair of oversized glasses is strewn feet away. Her white undergarments are now coated in thick red blood.

I return my focus back to Irina. I left her in the care of Sister Yali, but now that Sister Yali is dead, Irina is in the care of another.

Renata.

With Sister Yali cradled in her arms, Ella's confused glances bounce between Renata and me, not understanding what's going on.

"Why?" I ask Renata.

She clutches Irina's hand, and with the other, she holds a gun. Her white dress slathered in blood. "Because you should know by now that one will do anything for love. Get off him."

She waves the gun, gesturing for me to move.

Every muscle in my body is fighting against me, but I slowly do as she demands.

"What now, малышка?" I mock, hands raised in surrender.

Serg groans before using an elbow to prop him into a sitting position. He shuffles and rests his back against the wall. He looks dreadful, but not dreadful enough because he's still breathing.

"Oh, Brother," he taunts, removing the head scarf with bloody fingers. "She fooled you, and fooled you good."

"Stop referring to me as your brother," I coolly state. I need to approach this with a level head because I need to outsmart this дурак. "We may share the same whore of a mother, but our fathers are miles apart. Although, I suppose your father was quite close when I slit his throat."

Serg roars, thumping his fist on the floor.

"All this for a man you don't even remember. Trust me, I

knew him, and he's not worth the vendetta."

"Shut your fucking mouth!" Serg screams, bloodied spittle coating his chin. He looks like the crybaby he is.

"So what do you want?"

"I want you to pay for what you did to my father!" he bellows.

"Well, I'm right here"—I spread my arms out wide—"let Irina and Ella go, and you can have me."

"No!" Ella cries, drawing attention to herself.

Serg realizes she's here, and a grin spreads across his cheeks. "Ah, so this is the whore who was standing in the way?"

I'm about to drop to one knee and punch those vile words from his mouth when I realize what he just said.

"Yes, I've known where you've been this entire time," he confirms, throwing my stupidity at me.

"How?" I know Renata is the snitch, but how has he tracked her? How has she been able to keep in contact with him?

When Renata lifts her locket, I curse myself for not killing her when I had the chance. "He has always had eyes on me. It's amazing how small they make GPS devices."

So if Serg always knew where she was, why didn't he strike sooner?

"Why did you save me from being killed then?" I ask her, referring to those pups who killed an innocent woman.

"Because I sent those morons to scare you, not kill you, but that's what happens when you send in amateurs." Serg wheezes when he tries to move. "They watched your house, and when they saw you leave, they gave Ren a phone and instructed her of the plan.

"I told them I'd offer them a job if they did what I wanted. And they did that when they killed that old wench, forcing you to flee and come here. You're always thinking of others. It's your downfall."

Serg never intended for those two boys to live. They merely served a purpose, and when their job was done, Renata was ordered to take out the trash.

I keep my anger at bay. His plan worked because I suddenly realize what he's always been after.

The orphanage.

"Ren has been gathering all the information on this place. It's worth quite a bit of money," Serg says, whistling. "I knew you were closing in on me, so I had to think outside the box. Mother mentioned you've always had a soft spot for this place."

I grit my teeth at the mention of that woman.

"And anything that you hold dear, I will destroy. But thanks to Ren sending me photos of the finances of this place, I realized the orphanage could be very beneficial for me."

So Ella wasn't the one who stole the paperwork. It was Renata all along.

"You're off your A game because you were too smitten by the lovely sister over here."

Good, they don't know that Ella isn't who she says she is, which means she's safe—for now.

"I knew her resemblance to the lovely Willow would have you lowering your guard, and it worked like a charm."

Ella casts her eyes downward. She has no idea what happened between Renata and me, but it's safe to assume she's thinking the worst.

"But it seems you're a hard nut to crack," Serg says, disappointed. "It would have been far more entertaining if you'd fallen for her charms, only for her to break your heart like your sweet дорогая did."

I will not take the bait.

"How did you get in here?"

Renata smiles. "Did you really think I wanted to get that old wench a birthday present? I asked for the keys to the SUV because I know you have a master key to the place, the key which I got cut and hid inside the Medovik. I watched you punch in the code, and I memorized it.

"There was never a meeting, and you fell so easily for it. I was supposed to find the perfect opportunity to strike, and when I heard about this party, I just knew our stage was set.

"So I opened all the doors with the key I got cut, used the codes, and waited for my prince to come rescue me." She looks at Serg with stars in her eyes while I hold down my vomit.

"Your faith in me is embarrassing," she concludes with a giggle. "You thought you were breaking me, making me submit, but I was breaking you. I played you at your own game. I merely entertained you so you'd think you won.

"I was to collect everything I could about the orphanage and find out how loyal Mother Superior was to you. And I have discovered her loyalty is strong."

So this is what they wanted all along.

Find out everything they could about the orphanage,

about Mother Superior, and if she didn't comply with whatever their demands were, then they'd dispose of her.

I did this. I brought Renata here. I've allowed the lambs to be slaughtered.

"This is all very interesting, but I still have no idea what you want." I remain calm, attempting to devise a plan.

Serg smirks. And why shouldn't he? He outsmarted me, or rather, Renata did. "I want Mother Superior to sign the deed over to me. This place is worth a lot of money."

"No one will buy this place, you fool!" I exclaim, but I have completely misunderstood what he means.

"Oh, Aleksei, there you go, once again leading with your heart. The children, their innocent, young faces are what's worth a lot of money. I had a quick look around. They are sweetened peaches, ripe for the picking."

And just like that, time stands still.

"I'm sure you remember your dear yet sick and twisted friend, Oscar. Well, there are hundreds of men and women just like him, willing to pay top dollar for an hour or two to quench their…select tastes. And if they want to purchase one, then I suppose I'm doing the children a favor by finding their forever home."

I stare at him, simply horrified.

What he intends to do is unspeakable. He intends to turn this house of holiness into a house of hell because he's right; there are men and women out there—sick, vile animals who would exploit the children to cater to their perverted desires.

I should know. I've seen it firsthand within The Circle. There are many sick individuals out there who would pay ridiculous amounts of money to experience and witness things that would make one's blood run cold.

The most terrifying thing is that they're not monsters who lurk in the dark; they are respected in the community— doctors, lawyers, judges. They hide behind their veil of normality, masking their depravity because no one would suspect their true deviant form.

I shudder at the thought of the things they would do to these children.

"How could you do this?" I direct my attention to Renata. "He's planning on turning this place into a, a...brothel! Have you no heart?"

Serg clucks his tongue. "Get off your high horse. Not so long ago, I remember you laying down a hefty sum to purchase a virgin of your own."

Shame overcomes me because he's right.

Looking at Renata and seeing how Serg has brainwashed her, I come to understand this is my karma for Zoey because once upon a time, she looked at me the same way. I treated her worse than an animal, yet she would do anything for me, just as Renata would for Serg.

She lied to me, tricked me because she wanted to please her master.

"I know who the other benefactors are. It'll be business as usual. The do-gooders funding the depraved of Europe and beyond. It's rather genius. I intend to make this place renowned as there will be no rules. No one will suspect what's going on behind these Godly walls."

"They are children," I remind him appalled, but he knows.

"And so was I when you killed my father! Why should they have a family when I was robbed of mine? Every child who gets exploited and used for depraved acts will be on your head. You did this. You created me. I know how much this is going to hurt you, and that's far more satisfying than killing you. You can live with a lifetime of pain as have I."

"Mother Superior will never sign the deed over to you," I snarl, his words cutting deep because he's right. I created the monster in front of me.

"You will convince her. Ren has told me how much she adores you. I'd think with how loyal she is to you, you were fucking her while she was on her knees, praying for forgiveness," he crudely spits. "But it seems that's reserved for Sister Arabella."

Ella's cheeks redden.

Renata knew all along. She was sent to seduce me, but that didn't work, which is why Serg is here now. She knew she was running out of time.

"I will not help you," I growl, anger fueling the violence thrumming through me.

Serg snickers. "This isn't optional. You don't do what I say, I'll burn this place to the ground but not before I allow my men to have their fun with the sisters and children. Once they're done with them, everyone will be begging me to kill them…all except one."

Irina yelps when Renata grips her hair and yanks her head backward. "I suppose keeping one child alive does have its advantages. She'll be passed around like a turkey at Thanksgiving."

Unable to stop myself, I strike out and kick Serg in the jaw. His head connects with the wall with a thunderous thwack. It does nothing to soothe the murderous pulses within.

"Try that again and another sister will die," Renata warns, pointing the gun at Ella who yelps, eyes begging for me to help her.

Renata killed Sister Yali. She is far worse than I ever thought.

Serg spits out a mouthful of blood. "Aleksei, this will happen. You either do what I say, or I kill your beloved, slit Mother Superior's throat, and exploit your precious Irina. Oh, and I kill your beloved дорогая."

The walls close in on me.

"What did you say?" My body begins to vibrate in fury.

Serg cocks his head to the side, his expression changing before he bursts into riotous laughter. "Oh, this just makes everything so much better."

I wait with bated breath.

"You don't know, do you? You didn't read her postcard?"

Clenching my fists, I tip my face to the ceiling and steady my breathing. But no matter how many breaths I take, it'll never be enough.

"She is coming to visit. She and Saint. Shame, if you'd read the postcard you'd know when and where."

She is coming here? My heart beats faster for a mere fraction of time, but then it shatters once again when I realize what this means for her.

"Do what I say, and she'll remain unharmed. Don't give me what I want, then every single thing you care about will be taken away from you, and you'll have no one to blame but yourself."

Renata stole the postcard and burned it, ensuring I would never see it again.

Serg has everything that I care about in the palm of his hand, and I allowed it. This is all my fault. My karma has finally caught up to me. It's time I paid for the sins of my past.

Love is dangerous—more powerful than money and control—which is why I lock eyes with Serg and surrender.

"I do all this, and you promise their safety?" Even if he agrees, I'm putting my faith in a sociopath.

He grins in victory as he crosses over his heart. "Cross my heart, hope to…well, you know. You have one week to give me what I want. I understand it may take some convincing for Mother Superior to agree.

"Don't even think about going to the police. I own them. I own everyone," he smugly boasts. "You have no allies. They're all mine. You have no one."

He comes to a wobbly stand, using the wall as support while it takes every ounce of strength not to kill him.

He is wrong. I have Santo, but for that to work, I need to give him Ella. And when I look at her, she knows it too.

It would be simple. Trade Ella for the safety of so many. For the safety of Willow. She's coming back for me once again, oblivious to the trouble that faces her because of me. But Ella isn't a faceless name. She is a human being—one I have feelings for.

No matter what she's done, I can't hand her over to the wolves. But I can't let so many others die.

Ella flinches as Serg hobbles past, licking his lips deviously. Renata's eyes narrow.

"Come, sweet Ren. Olivia has missed you."

Serg's admission has me remembering Renata's tale about her friend being held hostage. Could it be true?

But when he runs the back of his hand down Renata's cheek, I recognize what this is. He has both under his spell. A harem of women who would do anything to please him, like I once did.

"It's been quite lonely without you. You know you're my number one girl, don't you?" He plays on her emotions, ensuring she feels "special" so she'll continue to do what he wants.

Renata nods, an obedient pet.

She deserves an Oscar for her performance because she had me fooled. But her likeness to Willow was the reason I was careless. I will live with that on my conscience for the rest of my life because whatever happens now, someone is bound to lose.

Irina looks at me, trusting I will save her, and I will. But what happens next, Serg is sure to have something up his sleeve to ensure I'll bow to his command.

"Just in case you get any ideas, we'll be taking collateral." When he bends down and tosses Irina over his shoulder, I race forward, heart in my throat. Her small legs flail wildly as she bursts into inconsolable tears.

"Take me! Take me!" I shout, slamming my hand against my chest over and over again. "I'll do what you want. Just leave Irina here."

Serg turns to me, his eyes void of emotion, and that's because he's dead inside. "Oh, I know you will. But the thought of you suffering, not knowing what I'm doing to your loved ones, that gives me far more pleasure than simply holding you captive.

"This is about breaking someone and having them do anything you command. This is about power, the power I have over you. If I wanted you dead, you'd be gone by now. But I intend to torture you for the rest of your life.

"And I can only hope that one day, when you've had enough, your death will be by your own hand. The greatest shame is a fallen leader ending their miserable existence because they're a failure. When they've failed everyone they loved."

Balling my fists, I swallow down my nausea because he just served me a dose of my own medicine. For countless years, I operated this way, and now, it's my turn to feel the pain I've inflicted on so many.

I deserve this, but the people I care about don't.

"Ski!" Irina sobs, her cries breaking me in ways I've never felt before.

Serg's knife is within reach. I'm quick. I'm also a perfect shot. I could injure him, but Renata reads me like a book when she storms over to Ella and presses the gun to her temple.

Ella yelps, raising her bloody hands in surrender. Sister Yali's head rests in her lap. So much destruction. So much death.

"We only need one hostage," she threatens with a smirk.

If I didn't want to detach her head from her shoulders, I'd

feel sorry for Renata. I know what happens to a person when they lose their soul and give it to another. All I can think of is Zoey on her knees, calling me мастер.

No wonder Saint hated me with every fiber of his being. Seeing this now, the hatred I feel is almost blinding. I wish this life lesson wasn't learned this way, but I now understand the pain, the damage I caused to so many.

Ella stares at me, surrendering, fearful for her life.

"I'm going to kill you, sweet Renata. Of this, I promise you. I know how you taste. And I know you liked it." I run a finger over my bottom lip, smearing it with my blood, just remembering I was stabbed.

She blinks once, taken aback by my threat. But I call her bluff. Serg won't allow any harm to come to those I care about until he gets what he wants.

They're all his pawns.

Serg growls, clearly upset I played with one of his toys. I'll use this to my advantage when the time comes.

He gestures it's time to leave as he too reads the seriousness of my threat, and although he has the upper hand, deep down, he knows if I ever get the opportunity, I'll deliver the same to him as I did his father.

"I will find you. I promise." I beseech Irina to forgive me. Loving me will be the reason for her demise. "Ski любит Irina."

I tell her I love her because I do, and her trembling reply has every part of me weeping tears I cannot cry.

"Irina любит S-Ski."

Serg doesn't allow me to say goodbye as he runs down

the hallway, Irina's terrified screams growing softer and softer until eventually, they stop. Renata removes the gun from Ella's temple, and we lock eyes for a second, but in that second, I promise her when we next meet, I will kill her.

She takes off after Serg like the good little lapdog she is.

A strangled sob leaves Ella as she slumps forward, resulting in Sister Yali sliding from her lap and onto the cold floor.

Her death is my fault. I asked her to tend to Irina while I looked for Ella. If only she hadn't, she'd still be alive.

I numbly walk over to Ella, offering her my bloody hand. She peers up at me with nothing but utter fear reflected in her eyes. But with a hesitant touch, she slips her own bloody hand in mine. She steps over Sister Yali with a small sniffle.

She was stabbed in the back. The pooling of blood reveals she died a slow, painful death. I can't offer her anything, to express how truly sorry I am, so I strip off my shirt and lay it over her body, wishing to conceal her dignity. It's the least I can do.

"You're hurt," Ella says, trying to look at the wound in my side. But I brush her hand away.

"I'm fine." The wound inflicted on my heart is far worse.

But when I hear a stunned gasp, followed by Mother Superior asking the Lord for protection, that wound becomes a gaping hole.

"Aleksei," she wheezes, and when I turn to face her, exposing Sister Yali's corpse, that turns into a smothered sob. "What happened? We must call an ambulance."

"She's dead," I numbly state. "Irina is gone."

"What?" The confusion on her face just highlights the fact that she will associate every birthday from here on out with this ghastly night. I just ruined every future birthday for her, which is why I need to leave.

"You're safe. I promise you. Just trust me. Okay?"

She looks over my shoulder at Sister Yali. She trusted me, too, and look what happened to her.

"Okay." She peers down at the wound in my side, gushing blood, and figures it out. This is my doing, and she does something that breaks both our hearts. "I...can't have you here, Aleksei. You're a risk to the children. Forgive me."

"There is nothing to forgive. You've been far kinder than anyone has ever been to me, and I will protect you and these children with my life."

I won't tell her of Serg's plans. I can't. She is safe as long as Serg thinks he's in control.

"Do not let anyone into the orphanage. It's locked down. Wait until you hear from me. Do not trust anyone."

When she opens her mouth, I grip her hand in mine. "Please, Mother Superior, just do as I say."

My blood now pollutes her clean, wholesome hand. "Okay."

I wish I could explain, but I don't have time right now. I need to work out what I'm going to do.

Mother Superior looks at Ella, and although she doesn't have all the pieces to the puzzle, she knows she's leaving too.

"I'll bring Irina back. I promise."

My empty promises mean nothing anymore.

"Go, I will take care of this."

I want to say so many things, but nothing will ever be enough. So I say the only thing I can. "I love you," I whisper in Russian.

In the entire time I've known Mother Superior, I've never seen her cry...until now. "And I love you."

I can't stay here a moment longer because her tears will be the death of me. With hands locked, I lead Ella down the hallway. She grabs her packed bag, and I stuff the folder Santo gave me into it. We then gather my belongings from the basement.

I wash the blood from my hands, place an adhesive bandage over the superficial stab wound, and slip into a clean shirt. Looking at Ella, I realize this is the last time I'll see her in her habit. Everything is about to change.

She watches as I smash out the bricks, collecting my hidden stash. This is how someone like me lives. Always in secret. Always needing a plan B.

With everything I need in hand, I dial the only person who can help me.

"Pavel, I need your help."

He doesn't ask questions and directs me to the only place I can be—his mother's house. It was here I was once offered sanctuary. It is here where my sins are buried.

I don't bid the sisters or the children farewell. It's better this way.

We toss our bags into the back of my SUV, and just like that, we slip into the night, leaving behind nothing but carnage and pain.

Larisa's house is about an hour away, so I turn the radio

on, needing to fill the silence. There are no words to explain what just happened because a few simple hours have changed everything I thought I knew.

Ella isn't who I thought she was. And Renata, she absolutely played me for a fool.

Serg left Zoya behind, but her time will come. The orphanage needs a face behind it with Mother Superior gone. No guesses whose face that will be.

He came here tonight, lifting his leg and marking his territory. This war has merely just begun, but I can't help but wonder how many casualties this warfare will see.

"What did you say to Mother Superior?" Ella whispers after minutes of silence, her eyes sealed shut. She's exhausted as she too doesn't know what tomorrow brings.

With eyes focused on the road, I numbly reply, "I told her that I loved her…and she said she loved me too."

I can only hope that love doesn't get her or so many others killed.

CHAPTER ELEVEN

Ella didn't say a word to me before she fell into a deep sleep, but honestly, I needed the silence. I needed time to think. I have no game plan because I don't have many options.

When I pull the SUV in front of Larisa's home, a cabin in the middle of nowhere, a sense of nostalgia overwhelms me. Switching off the engine, I take a moment to let it all sink in. It's impossible not to associate this place with memories of Willow, Zoey, with everyone I hurt.

Sighing, I gently touch Ella's arm as she's still asleep. Her eyes flicker for a moment, and I see it—hope that what she just experienced was a dream. But when she focuses on our remote surroundings, that hope is dashed.

She has no idea of Larisa's hatred for me, but she will soon find out because when the door opens and Larisa hobbles out, she does nothing to mask her annoyance that I'm once again using her home as a hideout.

Ella opens the door, and when Larisa sees her in a habit, she crosses herself. No doubt she is fearful for Ella to be in the presence of a monster.

Grabbing our things, I walk toward Larisa, who has her animals surrounding her on guard. A German shepherd bares its teeth when I walk up the front steps. Ella trails me.

"Hello, Larisa. Thank you for your hospitality."

She grunts in response, focusing on Ella.

"This is Antonella. But she prefers Ella." I speak in English, so Ella understands.

The fact I haven't used Ella's holy title hints at the fact she isn't a sister. Larisa has two sinners under her roof now. Nonetheless, she gestures for us to enter.

Turning to look at the barn, I can't help but feel like this is where I belong. It was good enough for Saint and Willow when they stayed here, and it's more than I deserve. But Larisa has granted me permission to stay inside her home, so I nod my gratitude as I walk into her sanctuary.

The place hasn't changed an iota, and images of Zoey sitting in the armchair, reading a magazine hit me hard. Now, she lies buried in a grave outside. As does Sara. We never found Ingrid because she selflessly strapped a bomb to herself and detonated it to save us all.

My feelings for Ingrid were real, contrary to my actions. I cared for her in my own way. She was so innocent and fragile, and to know how her life ended still makes me sick to my stomach.

Larisa points down the hallway. "One bedroom," she says in Russian.

There are three bedrooms here, but Larisa is a hoarder, so the other two are probably filled with her latest finds. Ella looks at me, waiting for me to translate, but I don't need to. When I walk down the hallway and enter the only open door, she understands.

The room is the same one I stayed in when I was last here. The white linens are freshly pressed, and even though it's small, the bedroom is homey. Ella, however, seems worried that we'll be roommates.

She doesn't say anything, but her pale complexion and the gnawing of her bottom lip reveals she is uncomfortable sharing a bed with me. She doesn't know if I'm friend or foe, but honestly, neither do I.

She places her bag on a wooden chair in the corner of the room and waits for me to speak.

"I'll sleep on the floor," I say, reaching for a pillow and tossing it onto the floor along with my bags. She watches as I open the cupboard and retrieve a gray blanket from the top shelf.

She's careful to keep her distance from me, which wounds me, but I soon realize I don't trust her either. She may run, which means I need to keep her from doing so. I won't take any pleasure in seeing her bound this way, but she is my get out of jail free card. She is the one bargaining chip I have.

"Can I take a shower?" she asks, the fear in her voice evident.

Nodding, I'm about to leave but decide to take my bag, the one with my money and weaponry with me. Ella reads this for what it is. Until we know what we are to one another, we're enemies.

The front door opens, and I hear Pavel greet his mother.

I leave Ella to gather her thoughts and make my way into the living room. When Pavel sees me, he shakes his head at my stupidity. Larisa leaves us alone.

He sits in the armchair, hinting he is listening, and I detail everything. From meeting with Santo and finding out about Ella, to Serg storming the orphanage with Renata in tow. When I tell him he has Irina and what he intends to do to her if I don't comply, Pavel cracks his knuckles.

Cruelty toward children is Pavel's breaking point. He knows how much she means to me.

But when I detail the last piece to the puzzle about Willow and Saint visiting, he sighs in frustration. "Why didn't you read it?" he asks, baffled.

"I don't know," I reply, any hope of him reading it before me being shot to hell. But I knew that he hadn't. It doesn't concern him; therefore, it's none of his business.

"Aleksei, this is bad."

Running a hand down my face, I nod. I know what he's going to say even before he speaks.

"You have to give Santo what he wants." His grim words are what I know makes sense, but every shred of my being fights against that notion.

"I know you don't want to, but if you don't, so many people will die. He will not only kill Willow, but he will ensure she suffers in ways that are unthinkable. He knows how much she means to you, so he will draw out her torture, knowing what it'll do to you."

Clenching my jaw tightly, I taste the sharp metallic sting of blood, but that pales in comparison to the stab wound which I crudely wrapped to stop the bleeding.

"So essentially, I have to choose? Who means more to me; Willow or Ella?"

Pavel shakes his head slowly. "No, my friend. You must choose between one life versus the lives of many."

And that is the truth.

I save one person, only to condemn the lives of so many innocents who never wanted to be involved in my mess. Ella knew who she was saying yes to when Frank proposed. She knew he was a bad man. She told me so herself.

But for her to pay for the mistake with her life doesn't seem fair. And for me to be her executioner seems more than hypocritical.

"Can we find Willow? You must know someone?" I beg, uncaring my desperation shows.

"I can try, but you know Saint. He will not make their arrival an easy one to detect. He will move heaven and earth to keep her safe. Your best option would be going to Santo," Pavel states the obvious.

"Pavel, he will kill her," I say, lowering my voice as these walls are thin.

He is unmoved. He merely sees Ella as a liar, regardless of her circumstances. But I can't condemn her to a death she doesn't deserve.

"That son of a bitch said I have one week, which means if he's telling me the truth, Willow and Saint will be here before then. We have one week to find them."

"And if we don't?" Pavel poses.

"We cannot fail," I reply with resolve.

"The lives of so many people are relying on you, Aleksei. What Serg proposes to do will succeed if we fail. The lives of those children and the children after them will forever be ruined because we didn't take the path we both know we should."

Lowering my eyes, I try to swallow past the guilt lodged in my chest. I may have washed the blood from my hands, but they'll forever be stained with what I've done.

"I understand, but she doesn't deserve that. There has to be another way."

"I'll try my best. I'll make some calls. In the meantime, you need to come to terms with the choice that you make. Just be sure it's the right one."

Pavel has no connection to Ella, so handing her over to Santo is the obvious choice. But my stomach twists in knots at the thought.

Pavel gestures to the bag at my feet. "Shall I put that in the safe?"

Unzipping the duffel, I retrieve my Glock and my knife and then slide the bag across to him. "Take some money and give it to your mother for her troubles."

Pavel nods, zipping the duffel back up.

Standing, I place the gun into the small of my back and the knife goes into my pocket. I need some fresh air.

Pavel looks at me, his surprise clear. I know why.

"She won't run," I assure him.

"And if she does?"

"I'll deal with it," I reply, angrily. His questions are reflective of my fears, and I need some time to process this before I decide what to do.

Pavel knows when to pull back, and now is that time.

Opening the front door, I inhale deeply when I walk down the stairs, welcoming the cool night air. I have no idea what time or day it is. What I witnessed at the orphanage feels like a lifetime ago. Thoughts of Irina wind me, and I hiss sharply, rubbing over my chest.

Opening my car, I retrieve the last cigar and my lighter from the glove compartment and walk to a place that crosses my mind at least once a day. My steps echo in the vast silence. No matter the time of day, it's always so quiet out here.

Some may say it's peaceful, but to me, it's just heartbreaking.

Lighting the cigar, I use the full moon as my beacon and head for the tree which stands out from the rest not just for its size, but because Sara and Zoey lay buried beneath it.

Memories of Saint laying his sister to rest still haunt me. He was the strongest man I ever knew, and to see him dig Zoey's grave, tears streaming down his cheeks, I couldn't help but feel indebted to him for the rest of my life.

I was the cause of her death. For all their deaths.

Once he said a prayer over her freshly dug grave, he turned to me and knocked me out cold. He never uttered a word to me; he simply gave me what I deserved and left. And that was the last time I ever saw him.

Willow had left, too, on a plane, safe passage back to America. I was pleased both could leave because they never wanted to be here. I forced their hands.

Sara was buried beside Zoey. Her grave dug by Max. He too left and never returned once Sara was given the send-off she deserved. I organized the angel marker for Ingrid because although I didn't have a body to bury, I still wanted a place to commemorate who she was.

Standing before their graves, I smoke my cigar, numb. Being here is a reminder that when we die, we are nothing but a memory to those who wish to keep it alive.

Pavel took care of the carnage that we left behind that night, but regardless of what they'd done, I ensured Oscar and Astra were put to rest in their family plots. They were the villains, but so was I. I would be a hypocrite if I thought of myself as anything but that.

Looking at Zoey's simple grave marker, I can't help but see her in Renata. Serg has copied every aspect of my life, and now that I'm on the outside, it disgusts me. At the time, I had no problem leaving Zoey on her knees as I had my way with two or three other women at a time while she watched, riddled with envy.

But she never complained. She knew her place.

This was another way for me to break someone who was already so broken.

"Hi."

Ella's voice reveals how hesitant she is. But she is here because we can't avoid the inevitable.

"Hi."

Her tentative footsteps sound behind me until she stands next to me. I continue smoking my cigar, eyes focused on the three markers in front of me. Ella's silence is uncomfortable.

She doesn't need a handbook. She knows these three women died because of me.

But I still want to honor them. And speaking their names is my way to do that.

"Zoey was such a spirited woman," I say with pride. "It was one of the many things I liked about her. All she wanted was to please me. And she did. Even when she claimed to hate me, I know she loved me. Our bond was unique.

"I know that won't make any sense to you, but I did care for Zoey...in my own way."

Ella is quiet, but it's only fair I share with her as she did with me.

"Sara was given to me to pay off her father's debt. He was a substance abuser, and when he racked up quite a debt, he offered me his daughter as payment."

"Why would you accept?" Ella asks, horrified.

"Because if he would offer her to me, he would offer her to anyone, and I knew I would treat her with a shred more compassion than anyone else would. In my world, it was a fair trade. However, I understand to most, it's seen as barbaric.

"Ingrid belonged to my friend Oscar," I explain, expelling the ghosts of my past. "I was enamored by her the first moment I saw her. I shouldn't have, but I acted on those impulses. I suppose a part of me wanted what I couldn't have.

"She was truly kind. Gentle, like a baby bird. But in the end, that baby bird emerged from the fire a phoenix. Her sacrifice saved us all. And the only way I can thank her is to lay this marker down, cementing her existence in this world."

Savoring my cigar, I blow the smoke into the wind as I

confess, "This is my personal graveyard of sins. I played a part in all their deaths. Although Renata sealed her fate tonight, I don't feel good about it.

"She was molded by my half-brother into what he wants. He preyed on her, just as I've done to these women."

"So Renata was working with him all along?"

Slowly turning my cheek, I look at Ella, completely struck by her beauty because she is out of her habit. She wears a green dress, her long hair damp, sitting in a high bun. Her face is void of makeup bar a pink gloss on her lips. Her feet are bare.

She is simply breathtaking.

Seeing her this way will take some getting used to. But the habit was her costume, not these casual clothes.

"Yes. I played right into her hands. I brought Mother Superior, the sisters, and Irina into my mess, and I need to figure out a way to get them out."

"And what about me?" she whispers, those poignant eyes begging for mercy.

Sighing, I turn back toward the graves. "What would you do if you were me?" I pose my situation to her, wishing her to understand the position I'm in.

"I would do everything in my power to save the people I love," she softly replies moments later. "And to do that, you need an alliance with someone as powerful as Santo."

She knows what this means for her, yet she doesn't back down.

"He will kill you, Ella," I state, my attention flicking among the three women I let down because my selfishness couldn't protect them. "But Serg, he will kill so many—"

"I know," she interrupts, her voice heavy.

"I don't want to do this. I have one week to come up with a plan. If not, well, you heard what Serg will do. If Willow is at risk—"

"You really love her, don't you?" she asks, shuffling her feet.

Without hesitation, I nod. "I really do. I don't love her the same way I once did, but my feelings for her will never disappear."

"And what about me? How do you feel…about me?" Her question almost takes flight in the wind with its softness.

But I heard her.

"I know you don't trust me because I lied to you, but do you believe me?"

Before the blackout, Ella had divulged the sins of her past. I listened, unsure what I believed, and the truth is, I still don't know. Her tale could have been spun to save her skin. Or it could be the truth finally setting her free.

Turning to her once again, I wish I could make this better for us all. But this isn't a scenario where we all win. One of us will lose.

"I don't know," I admit with regret. "I wish I could, but it would be foolish of me to trust you."

She conceals her sadness, her walls going up as she folds her arms across her chest. "I suppose the same applies to me then. I would be foolish to believe you won't give me to Santo."

With a smirk, I reach out and cup her cheek. She barely suppresses a shiver. "Yes, it would be very foolish of you to trust me."

With fire behind her eyes, she recoils from my touch and leaves me in a place where I belong to be alone.

I must be dreaming because when I wake, I could have sworn I heard the door closing on my SUV. It's still dark out, so I imagine I've only had a few minutes of sleep. Groaning, I reach for my cell and see that it's a little past three.

I'm about to roll over and attempt to go back to sleep, but when I hear a clicking, I realize I wasn't dreaming at all. Not looking at the bed because I know what's happening, I quickly put on pants but don't bother with a shirt or shoes as I sprint out of the bedroom. I'm out the front door in seconds.

The blood races through my veins as I see Ella sitting in my SUV, attempting to start it. When she sees me, her eyes widen, then she slams down the lock. She thumps her palm on the steering wheel when the engine continues to kick over, refusing to come to life.

Her scream echoes out here because it's just us.

I thought I was being paranoid when I removed the spark plugs, anticipating this happening. Just in case, I assured myself, but now that I see Ella trying to flee, I realize any faith she had in me is now gone.

"Get out of the car, Ella," I coolly order, standing in front of the hood.

The moon is full, so I can clearly see her hatred. In

response, she fruitlessly attempts to start the engine again. I admire her perseverance, but the longer she defies me, the angrier I become. I don't have a spare set of keys, so if she doesn't open the door, I'm going to have to force her out.

She watches as I search the yard for a rock big enough to smash the window. I couldn't care less about my car. So I walk to the passenger window, rock in hand and don't hesitate as I shatter the glass. Ella yelps and jerks away, avoiding the spray of tiny fragments.

Reaching into the empty window frame, I flip open the lock and yank open the door. Gripping the frame, I stare at Ella, my anger highlighting how much trouble she's in.

She backs up until she's trapped against the door, unable to move another inch.

"Scared little rabbit," I hum, leaning forward, still gripping the frame. "You didn't think I'd let you get away, did you?"

She licks her lip nervously.

"I wouldn't make it that easy for you. Get out."

"Screw you." Ella unlocks the door and flees from the car, running for the woods.

Sighing, I push off the frame and give chase. She has no idea where she's going, which makes this all the more fun.

"Come back here!" I demand, hot on her tail.

She takes a hard right, which leads to a steep cliff edge. If she continues running and doesn't pay attention to her surroundings, she'll fall of the unseen edge.

"Ella!" I call out. "Stop."

But she only runs faster.

My heart is suddenly in my throat at the possibility of

her being hurt, so the motivator of the chase soon turns from punishment to saving her life.

She is heading straight for the edge, which can't be seen thanks to the thick foliage and the night sky. Just as she's about to jump over a fallen branch, I tackle her from behind, sending us both to the ground. She thrashes wildly, attempting to break free, but I flip her over and pin her with my weight.

"Get off me!" she bellows, using her fist to pummel my bare chest.

"Stop fighting me! I just saved you from falling off the edge."

My words have her fight dying as she arches her head backward, attempting to see if I'm telling the truth.

"Save me?" she scoffs, returning her attention back to me. "I heard you talking. You'd do anything to save them. To save *her.*"

Tsking her, I grip her wrists and jerk her arms over her head. "Yes, I would. And you're making my decision easier by behaving this way."

"What way?" she asks, eyes narrowed, her chest rising and falling rapidly. "By trying to save my life? You'll never choose me over them, and that's okay. I understand. I'm only one person."

She stops flailing, her anger eclipsed by sadness.

"I've never been anyone's priority," she shares. "I'm there to merely fill in time until something better comes along. That's why I said yes when Frank proposed to me. I knew he was a bad man, but for the first time in my life, someone wanted to put me first.

"My parents moved on with their lives when they divorced, forgetting they had a daughter. I learned to fend for myself early on, but that doesn't mean I was okay with it. I had no other choice. Sink or swim, and I refused, I *refuse* to surrender."

Her words, her passion feed me, and the hunger I constantly feel for her consumes me whole.

"But meeting you changed everything I worked so hard to achieve. I tried to push you away when I said horrible things to you. I knew you were bad news, but I just didn't care. You made me...feel something I've never felt before. You made me feel wanted and not just in a physical way.

"When you look at me, it's like you feel whatever this is between us too," she confesses, turning her cheek, ashamed. "But it's stupid of me to think someone like you could feel that way about me."

"Someone like me?" I ask, her admission doing nothing to ease the racing of my heart. I grip her chin softly, coaxing her to look at me, and when she does, I fall deeper under her spell.

"Someone who can have anyone they want," she reveals. "You think you break people, but in reality, they're already yours the moment you meet. You're magnetic, and you don't even know it. You're a villain...who has a heart. And what woman doesn't want to try to fix a bad man?"

Her body grows slack beneath mine, but her heart gallops wildly.

"Why wouldn't I want you, красавица?" I question, her words touching me in a way I never thought possible.

Her eyes glisten with tears. "Because it doesn't make sense for you to want me," she whispers, professing her fears. "I'm nothing but a damn fool who always falls for the wrong man."

When she realizes what she just said, she bites her lip, but it's too late. Her honesty coupled with her uncertainties have me wanting to protect her, have me wanting to prove her wrong.

Before she has a chance to speak, I slam my mouth over hers, savoring her sweetness because I've become addicted to her taste. Her lips are slack, stunned by my actions, but within a second, they reciprocate, and we begin to kiss madly.

She bites me, threading her fingers through my hair, forcing me to kiss her harder. Ella likes rough play, a fact which pleases me immensely. I comply, devouring and owning her mouth because it's mine; *she* is mine, and that's why I haven't called Santo.

I can't deliver her to him because I protect what is mine. She may be a goddamned liar, but I want her all the more for it. I never was satisfied with the women in the past because they surrendered too easily. They were too eager to please.

I want a challenge. I want someone to drive me mad with their defiance. And that someone is Ella.

With frantic fingers, she unfastens my zipper and takes hold of my straining shaft. Groaning into her mouth, I pump my hips, desperate to bury myself inside her heat.

Reaching under her dress, I grip her underwear into my palm and tear them to shreds. She whimpers, her body trembling in need. As I sink two fingers into her wetness, her back arches off the ground.

"Fuck me," she pants from around my lips, her crudeness stoking the animal within.

I release her, practically ripping the dress off her as she props up on her knees, fumbling to get it over her head. Once she's bare, I reach around and unhook her lacy bra. Her nipples are erect, begging for me to take them into my mouth. And I do.

She bows her back, offering me everything, untroubled that she's kneeling on the ground. With a nipple in my mouth, I slip my fingers into her sex, working her body into a frenzy as her pussy grips me tight.

"Oh, Alek," she moans, bucking her hips.

When we were last this way, lies lay between us. But now that the veil has been lifted, I want her so much more.

Letting her nipple go, I kiss her longingly, unable to get enough, fast enough. I fist her long hair, angling her neck back as I continue to sink my fingers into her sex. She is so incredibly wet for me, and that fact pleases me greatly.

"I want you. Please," she pants from around my lips, yanking down my pants and pushing me onto my back.

I'm taken aback by her aggression, not because I don't like it, but because I like being controlled by her, which has never happened before. She doesn't give me time to adjust to this realization as she straddles me, gripping my cock in her hand.

I don't usually like the girl on top position, but with Ella, it feels different.

With eyes locked, she guides my length into her slowly, her mouth parting in surprise as I stretch her wide. When we last united this way, she was bent over an altar, so this is a lot more personal. Inch by inch, she takes me inside her, and all I can do is look between us, mesmerized by our coupling.

Gasping, she peers down also, trembling as she's taken my entirety into her body. She doesn't move. She places her quivering hands to my stomach, tracing over each bump in my abdominals. I allow her this because this is the first time we've been united with no barriers between us.

She continues to stroke over my stomach and chest while I fist the ground beneath me. She is driving me wild.

"I wanted you this way from the first moment I saw you," she confesses as she begins to rock slowly.

I slam my fist into the dirt because she feels so good.

"Did you want me?"

"Yes," I hum. Gripping her hips, I encourage her to move faster. But she doesn't.

Her movements are slow, taking me deep as she milks every inch of my length. I don't remember ever being this turned on before.

"Why?"

"Why did I want you?" I ask, wishing she'd stop torturing me and move.

"Yes." She palms her breasts and arches her back, looking like a goddess under the night sky.

"You were a challenge," I confess, grunting when she lifts her hips, only to slam back down on my cock.

She's mad, but she asked for the truth.

"Because I was dressed in a habit?" Her stilted rocking has me clenching my jaw because the torment is a heady punch between pleasure and pain.

"At first yes, but I soon realized something about you awakened me in ways I haven't felt in a very long while. Even wearing that habit, you defied me, and that intrigued me."

She begins to pick up the pace, anchoring her hands to my chest for balance.

"I couldn't read your motives," I confess, watching the way her breasts bounce and her stomach ripples. "And for someone who prides themselves on making that their livelihood, you just became more and more...special."

"I'm no one special," she replies, arching her neck, her long hair falling around her shoulders.

"Oh, Ella," I discord, reaching up and cupping her neck as I meet her thrust for thrust. "You have no idea just how special you are."

Moaning, she wraps her fingers around my wrist, squeezing tightly. She rocks against me, her slickness drawing me deep. Stones and sticks dig into me, but I don't care. Out here, naked in the wilderness, we've stripped back the bullshit and exposed ourselves; just how this act between two people can.

I tighten the hold on her neck, my go-to move because I like the control of feeling one's fluttering pulse beneath my fingers. With one squeeze, I could choke the life from her, but I don't feel that way with Ella. I rub my thumb along the column of her neck, coercing her head to tilt further back.

Her pert breasts jut forward, and the sight of her taking pleasure from me, riding me like she wants me and only me, constricts my heart, and I can't breathe.

She had every right to fight for her freedom tonight. It's

one of the many things I like about her. She isn't a quitter. She isn't afraid to back down, and when she cries out, clawing her fingernails over my chest with nothing but love and devotion, I know my choice is made.

It always has been.

I can't give her to Santo because she is mine. She always has been.

Seizing her hips, I lift her only to slam her back down. I hit a spot deep inside her, and she groans. "Squat over me."

She quickly does as I command, and the sight of her open to me this way is incredible. She begins to bounce on my cock, groaning when I grip her hips and encourage her movements—up and down, up and down. I'm hypnotized by the vision.

Her bare form is incredible. So are her moans as she milks my cock, taking her pleasure from me. Her hair falls around her breasts, so I sweep it over her shoulder, needing to see her unhindered.

A flush spreads over her.

"What's the matter, красавица?"

"I know I don't look like most women you're accustomed to being with," she confesses, startling me.

"And what are these apparent women supposed to look like?" I accentuate my question with a sharp pump of my hips.

Biting her lip, she rolls her body, sending me closer and closer to the edge. "Supermodels, I assume. Perfect," she adds.

Tsking her, I rub my thumb over her clitoris. "Does it feel like you're anything but perfect when I touch you?"

Groaning, she places her hand over mine, encouraging

me to speed up the rhythm. "N-No. I feel beautiful. Wanted."

"And that's because you are," I reply, sitting up and drawing her onto my lap into the lotus position. I do all this while still sheathed inside her.

She gazes into my eyes as she wraps her arms around me for support and begins to rock back and forth. This position is far more intimate than I'm accustomed to, but I like it. I brush the hair from her forehead, wanting to see her.

She leans forward, taking my mouth and claiming it because she owns it. She owns me.

Our kisses are languid, and I cup the back of her neck to angle her mouth so I can dominate and destroy her. I want her wild with pleasure when she comes.

She grinds against me, rubbing her needy center in just the right way. Our skin is slick, and feeling her glide against every part of me has me desperate to come.

"Never doubt my hunger for you because right now"—I reach down and begin to circle her clitoris again—"you're the only thing that can quench my thirst."

"Oh, god," she pants, bouncing wildly as I rub her center.

"And even then"—I bite her chin before working downward and sucking over her pulse—"I always want more."

My actions, along with my words are her trigger, and as she throws back her head, a sated cry leaves her. She shudders and comes so violently that I hold her waist and move her backward and forward speedily. She sucks me in so deep, I want to lounge in the afterglow with her.

The moment the final tremor rocks her body, I hastily lift her and spill my seed all over my stomach. A primeval grunt escapes me because it feels so damn good.

It takes what feels like minutes to catch my breath and for my heart to return to normal speed. Ella stays cradled in my lap with her arms looped around the back of my neck. Usually, I would not be interested in the absurd notion of cuddling.

But with Ella, I don't mind.

She cups my cheek and does what I can only explain as her looking deeply into my soul. I wonder what she sees.

With her thumb, she rubs over my beard, appearing lost in her thoughts. I guess she's questioning what happens now. Will I give Santo what he wants to save the people I love?

But what she doesn't know is that she's beginning to fall into that category too.

I've known her for such a short amount of time, but when you've lived the life that I have, you come to learn that time is precious.

Rubbing over my lips, she smiles. "Maybe one day we will make it to a bed?"

The hope in her voice has me desperate to find a solution because right now, I'm out of ideas and that seems so far out of reach.

CHAPTER TWELVE

"There is no other way," Pavel says bluntly, drinking his morning coffee calmly like he didn't just tell me that giving Ella to Santo is the only solution.

"I will not," I reply in an irritated whisper, not wanting to wake a sleeping Ella.

We ventured back inside after our outdoor tryst, and when I went to lie in my makeshift bed on the floor, Ella pulled back the covers, offering a place beside her. I accepted as staying away from her seems impossible, and although she fell into a deep slumber the moment I settled in beside her, I didn't sleep a wink.

When the sun rose, I left her sleeping soundly to take a shower and then went for a walk. The fresh morning air did nothing to clear my head, and when I returned and saw Pavel was awake, I'd hoped he'd been struck with an epiphany.

He hadn't.

"Well, then people will die," he replies in Russian. "And Irina will be pimped out to any sick asshole with enough money."

Groaning, I tug at my hair, frustrated. "Any news on Willow?"

"No."

Pavel's candor is something I usually like, but today, all I see is a roadblock.

Reaching for my cell, I decide to do the inevitable. "Hello, Santo."

Pavel lowers his coffee cup in interest, listening to what I intend to do.

"Hello, my friend," Santo warmly says, but nothing about this call is sociable.

"You're right. She's there."

Silence.

Us criminals are a paranoid bunch, so I don't give much away.

"I just need some time. We don't want any unwanted attention. Trust me." He said he wanted this done quickly, so I need to give him an excuse to give me some time to think this through.

"Of course," he says eagerly, his excitement clear.

"Leave it to me, okay?" I press, not wanting him to get any vigilante ideas. He needs to stay far away from the orphanage.

"The place is busy with tradesmen and press. They are starting renovations, and the journalists want to do an exposé," I explain, which is an utter lie. "You can't be seen anywhere near there."

"Yes, this is very true. Thank you for telling me," he says, appearing to believe my story.

This buys me some time as Santo will stay far away, knowing he could be seen. He can't be linked to the disappearance of a "sister," which is what he thinks will happen when I bring him Ella.

"I'll call with updates."

"I knew I could count on you. Bring her to me, and I will tell you what you want to know."

I clench my fist. "You know the coordinates of what I want?"

"Of course," he replies smugly, which means he knows where Irina is. "But sharing is caring. Talk soon. *Ciao*."

Slamming the phone onto the table, I inhale sharply, needing to calm down. I could end this all right now. But I know I can't.

I won't throw Ella to the wolves.

"You can only stall them for so long," Pavel states the obvious. "Do you have any idea what you'll do?"

"Not yet, but I shall think of something. In the meantime, I want to do everything we can to find Willow."

Pavel nods as he too wants to find her.

Willow has a way with people. Everyone who meets her seems to fall in love.

I think of the satisfaction I felt when I brought her piece of shit stepfather to her. That vile animal got what he deserved. To put his hands on her...I shudder at the thought because if I don't stop Serg, the children at the orphanage will be Willow.

Pavel digs into his pocket when his cell rings. When he

looks at the screen, he takes his piece of toast and is out the door.

Sighing, I reach for my cold coffee and stare into it, hoping the blackness will reveal a magical solution.

My lie will hold Santo off for a little while. It's Serg who I have to contend with. If he has hurt Irina…

Her cries haunt me because it's my fault she's in danger. I will never be able to make it up to her. No matter what I do, she will always associate me with that night. As will Mother Superior.

I let so many who trusted me down, all because I let my guard down.

I dial Mother Superior's cell, knowing we can speak freely this way with no worry of it being bugged by Serg.

"Hello, Aleksei." The fatigue in her voice is clear.

"Hello, Mother Superior. I would ask if everything is okay, but that would be a stupid question."

"Yes, it would be," she replies. Her response is clipped, so I don't waste time.

"No one has attempted to come onto the grounds?"

"No. We have done as you instructed. How long must this go on for?"

And that's the million-dollar question. "No longer than a week. I just need some time. Will you give it to me?"

"Yes, I shall. But what choice do I have? You've put the lives of all of us at risk. Where is Irina?"

She isn't trying to make me feel guilty. She merely speaks the truth.

"I don't know, but I will find her. I promise you. She

won't be hurt because my…half-brother, he is using her as collateral. As long as she's alive, he has the upper hand over me. He knows I'll do anything he asks."

"And what does he ask?" Mother Superior inquires.

"I cannot tell you that." Before she can argue, I add, "Because I'll never allow it. I will not worry you with such troubles."

"And what of Sister Arabella? The true sister."

Mother Superior has worked out that Ella wasn't who she said she was.

"She fell victim to an ill-fated event. I'm so very sorry." I don't know what happened to her body once Santo's men found it. I suspect they discarded it. To them it was merely evidence and not once a human being.

Mother Superior utters a prayer under her breath. "By the hand of the woman who wore her habit?"

"No, she hasn't hurt anyone. She is a victim in all of this. If anyone is to blame, blame me," I say, hating how the truth hurts Mother Superior.

"I do blame you, Aleksei," she replies honestly. "Who else am I to blame for laying Sister Yali to rest in the orphanage churchyard?

"She was twenty-five years old. A mere child."

A sob escapes her, kicking me straight in the heart.

"I understand you'll never grant me forgiveness, but let me make it right."

"How?" she asks as she realizes for me not to tell her of Serg's plans, they are most dire. "If what you say about your brother is true, then what can you give him that will make him surrender?"

And just like that, the epiphany I so desperately needed hits me.

It shouldn't surprise me that it occurred when speaking to Mother Superior. She has been my teacher for so long.

"I have the only thing he wants, and I intend to deliver. Please trust me. I'll never let you down ever again. Stay safe."

"Godspeed," she replies before hanging up. But he can't save me. He long ago turned his back on me when I turned mine on Him.

Placing my face into my palms, I exhale, pleased I've thought of a solution. However, if it fails...no, there is no room for error. I'll need Pavel's help because I can't do this alone.

"Is everything all right?" Ella's concerned voice sounds from behind me.

I need to pull it together because this plan will also save her. So, my mask slips into place as I remove my hands and turn over my shoulder to greet her.

Once again, I didn't prepare myself for her beauty. She wears a white summer dress as the sun shines brightly, giving us a false sense of security. But nonetheless, she looks beautiful. Her long hair is worn down, and a white ribbon contrasts with the dark brown strands it secures.

Her feet are bare, so I can see her toenails are painted a pale pink. Her signature fragrance lingers in the air.

She reflects such innocence, but I know what obscenity lies beneath that virtue.

"Yes, everything is fine," I reply when I can think straight.

She walks toward me, still apprehensive about how she should act. When she leans down to kiss my cheek, I turn it so her lips connect with mine. A startled yelp escapes her, but that soon transforms into a moan when I slip my tongue into her warm mouth.

Cupping the back of her neck, I deepen the kiss, angling her head so I have control. She allows me to dominate her, and wicked passion overwhelms me. It's only been a few hours since I last had her, but that's a few hours too long.

I've always had a ravenous appetite for sex, but with Ella, I'm always hungry for more. That spark, the one they speak about in sentimental literature? Well, I feel that with her. Whenever she's near, I feel complete. I feel worthy of her.

"Alek," she whimpers from around my lips, reluctantly pulling away.

She has more willpower than I do because I'm moments away from swiping this kitchen table clear and having my way with her on it.

However, a throat clearing sharply shrivels my impending erection.

Ella jerks away, horrified that Larisa caught us. Me? I'm used to the dirty stares.

She has every right to hate me. Zoey was like a daughter to her, and she saw the way I treated her. She looks at Ella with nothing but pity for she believes she's the next Zoey.

Ella straightens out her dress with a smile. "Hello. I'm sorry I didn't introduce myself last night. I'm…" Her pause is because this is the first time she'll use her real name.

"I'm Antonella Ricci. Thank you for allowing me to stay

in your home."

Larisa nods, but her attention is riveted on me. "Should I prepare a fourth grave?" she asks me in Russian.

I suppose I should be thankful she didn't address me in English for Ella to understand.

"I'll tend to the chickens," I reply, but she shakes her head.

"Already done. The cows need milking." Her lips twist into a grin, and the reason for that is because she expects me to milk them when I haven't the faintest idea how.

But I'll figure it out. "Of course. I'll do it now."

Ella looks between us, lost in translation. Standing, I reach for her hand and notice Larisa looking at our union. She appears surprised. I wonder why.

However, I can contemplate it when I'm attempting to milk these damn cows.

I lead Ella out the back door and toward the barn. "She doesn't like you much, does she?" she asks, picking up on the tension even though she didn't understand what was said.

"Larisa has every right to hate me," I reply, rubbing my thumb over the back of her knuckles. "She loved Zoey very much, and now the only time she gets to spend with her is when she visits her grave."

Ella is quiet, now understanding the hostility.

"So where are we going?" she asks, changing the subject.

"To milk cows."

She laughs, but when she realizes I'm not joking, she soon stops. "Do you know what you're doing?"

"Of course not," I reply, letting go of her hand to roll up the sleeves of my shirt. "But it can't be that hard."

I open the barn door and give Willow and Saint credit for lodging in here. It's what you expect a farm barn to look and smell like. There are a pair of rubber boots by the door, so I hand them to Ella.

She accepts with a small smirk. "This should be interesting."

Once she's put them on, I look around the barn for a milking machine, but of course there isn't one. It appears Larisa does this by hand. There are two cows. When they notice me standing by their stall, they moo, sensing the imposter that I am.

But I can do this.

I once ruled this city with an iron fist. Surely, I can milk two simple cows.

"Hi," I say to the black and white cow as I slowly step over the railing and into her pen. "I'll be gentle."

I wish to add, *I hope you'll return the favor*, but with Ella looking on, attempting to hide a smile behind her hand, I reach for the silver bucket and wooden stool, which is fit for an elf, and position them near the cow.

She instantly moos, backing away. If she weren't tied to a post, I'm certain she'd have run a mile. I have no idea how I'm supposed to sit on this minuscule object comfortably, but nonetheless, I squat over it and sit.

I feel ridiculous.

Placing the bucket under her udder, I grip her teat and gently pull down, expecting milk to flow like rain from the heavens, but all I get is an irritated moo from the cow.

"Well," I say, looking at the teat in my hand. "That was

very anticlimactic. I hope it was good for you."

Ella's magical laughter hints at the fact that I look as ridiculous as I feel. "Move out of the way before you hurt yourself."

"Yes, that's a good idea."

Rising from the stool, I watch as she climbs over the railing, suddenly looking at home. Tying her hair into a bun with the elastic around her wrist, she sits and gently pats the cow's side.

"Hey, girl. I'm Ella."

The cow moos and attempts to move away.

"Shh, shh, I know. I'm a stranger, and that's scary, but I won't hurt you. I promise," Ella coos, continuing to pat her. "If you want me to stop, you give me a sign, okay?"

And in utter fascination, I watch as the cow moves closer to Ella.

"Thatta girl," she praises, positioning the bucket, and when I hear a squirt bounce off the aluminum, I gasp.

She did it.

Ella milks the cow with skill, hinting she's done this before.

From over her shoulder, I say, "You know, you could have just done this from the beginning."

"I could have, but where's the fun in that?" she replies, giggling.

I should spank that glorious ass for her sassiness.

"I grew up on a farm in Illinois," she shares as she happily milks the cow. "Before my parents divorced, I would help my father tend to the animals every morning. It was my favorite thing to do. My childhood was a good one. I have some happy memories from it."

"How old were you when they divorced?" I ask, hoping not to bring up any bad memories.

"I was ten," she reveals. "After that, everything turned bad. My father left with our neighbor, whom he was having an affair with for years. It broke my mother. All she wanted was a happy family, which is why she remarried and made another family, forgetting about the one she had.

"I stayed with my aunt a lot. She saved me from becoming a statistic. But I always knew I'd outgrow Illinois, which is why I came here when I had enough money saved."

"To Russia?" I ask, intrigued by her tale. In a sense, we did everything backward. We skipped the "getting to know you" part because who I met is not the person she is.

"No," she replies, the milk hitting the bucket as background noise. "I went to France first. I always wanted to go to Paris. I worked to earn enough money to board somewhere cheap and then move onto the next place when I grew bored.

"I did this until I met Frank. He swept me off my feet."

Her admission has me clenching my jaw.

"I was waitressing in a small village in Italy. Talk of the town was that the infamous Francesco Macrillo had arrived. I had no idea who he was, but when he walked into that restaurant, I soon understood what the fuss was about.

"In the beginning, he was really sweet, and I fell for it. He promised me everything I never had. A family. We got engaged about six months after we met, and the moment he gave me that diamond, everything changed."

She is no longer milking the cow, lost in her thoughts. I don't speak, allowing her to purge the past because I fear she's not shared this tale with anyone.

"I wanted to stay in Italy, but Frank said he was needed back home. I knew he came from money, and that money wasn't necessarily legal, but he was so different from his brothers. Or so I thought.

"Our engagement party in Italy was small, which was what I wanted, but when we arrived in Russia, it was like that engagement wasn't good enough, and his mother insisted we throw a 'better' one," she says bitterly.

"I expected Frank to decline, but he didn't. He went along with everything his family said. Him being the youngest, he was expected to do as he was told. But I saw a side to him I didn't like. Those three boys competed with one another constantly, striving to be their parents' favorite.

"I felt like a stranger at my own engagement party. It was a lavish affair, and I hated every minute of it. I moved into Santo's home, which meant he saw anyone inside his house as his property. I didn't see the warning signs right away. I disregarded the sly touches or the inappropriate comments when no one was listening.

"He said he merely had an affection for me because I shared his lineage, being Italian.

"But when I realized what game he was playing, I couldn't tell Frank. He loved his father dearly. And I loved Frank. So I did what wasn't in my nature—I submitted. It killed me to stay quiet, but I just wanted to make the man I loved happy."

Scoffing, she wipes what I'm guessing are tears with the

back of her wrist. "You probably think I'm a stupid girl."

I want to reach out and comfort her, but I don't. "No, I do not."

I understand what it's like being involved in a world such as the Macrillo's. It was once my world too. The rules of society don't apply to us because in some ways, we're above the law. We have our own codes, and if those rules are ever betrayed, then one will pay with their life.

"We were together for two years," she reveals, which surprises me as I would have guessed much less. Maybe I'm naïve then to think what we share means more than a casual fling.

"But honestly, I only ever loved him for half of that time. In Italy, when we could be ourselves, well, what I thought was the real Frank, my love for him knew no bounds. But when we came here, the man I loved was left behind in Italy, and in his place was the cruel, unfaithful man I left."

My jealousy simmers for now.

"I could never tell him about Santo's advances. First, he wouldn't believe me, and then he'd have my head for spewing such lies about the man he desperately wants to please.

"Hiding that big secret put a massive strain on our relationship. I should have left months before I did, but I just didn't know how. I was stuck in a loveless relationship, doubting myself. I mean, would I find anyone who would love me? If my parents couldn't, the two people in the entire world who were supposed to, then what hope did I have?"

"This isn't your fault, Ella," I say, placing my hand on her shoulder. She leans into my touch.

"Yes, it is. I should have stopped it, but I was so desperate to live a fairy tale that I thought I was okay to turn a blind eye. But I wasn't. And then when Santo propositioned me, I knew I had to leave.

"Frank always promised I was the only one he loved, but I was merely another one of his possessions. Just another pretty thing.

"That night, I left with only the belongings I bought with my own money. I didn't want anything from that family. I just wanted to return to America and forget I was ever a part of the Macrillo family.

"But no one leaves that family. It's funny, so many are desperate to be me while I just wanted out."

Running my thumb along the column of her throat, I mull over everything she just shared. I once doubted her story, thinking that she was guilty of everything Santo accused her of, but hearing her tale…I believe her.

If she were to seduce Santo, then why leave? She could have had far more than one million dollars if she had played the Macrillo game. None of his story makes any sense, but hers does.

I just needed some time.

"I know I have been…difficult with you," she settles on. I would have used the word stubborn, but I allow her to continue. "But I promised myself no more. No more desperately seeking approval or love from anyone because I had to love myself.

"When I figured out how I was going to get myself out of the biggest mistake of my life, I was intent on change.

Happiness isn't found out there"—she turns over her shoulder to look at me and gently rubs my chest over my heart—"it's found in here."

The thing she speaks of, my heart kicks against her palm, responding to her touch like a lost ship seeking a lighthouse in the dark.

"Which is why I've made a decision."

All I can do is merely stare.

"I'll give Santo what he wants. You can deliver me to him, so the deal will go ahead, and he will help you catch Serg. Irina, the children, Mother Superior…Willow," she adds with sadness, "they'll all be safe. I won't fight you. It's time I paid my dues for all that I've done."

With her hand over my heart, she has given me the greatest gift—sacrificing herself for the people I love.

"We can go today. I'll just finish milking—"

But I won't allow her to utter another word.

Gripping her hand, I shake my head, lost to the feeling of her selflessness. "You're not going anywhere."

"But—" She attempts to argue, but silly girl, she should know by now that I always win.

"You're not going anywhere because you're mine."

She blinks once, her mouth parting in disbelief. "So you believe me? You believe I would never do the things Santo said? You believe I never hurt Sister Arabella?"

Her urgency is palpable, and I understand why. Ella and I are one and the same. Both seeking a family, a place to belong to. I never saw that…until now.

"Yes."

She leaps up, the stool falling over in her haste as she throws herself into my arms. My neck is wet from her tears when she buries herself in the crook.

"Thank you. That means everything to me," she cries, hugging me tight as I wrap my arms around her. "I've never had anyone do that for me before."

"Do what, красавица?"

"Put their faith in me."

My heart constricts. "Neither have I," I confess, a hidden message that she's done that for me.

For my entire life, I've been seen as the villain, and I have been. But behind every monster, there lies a complicated story, and Ella has always listened to mine.

I won't abandon her because she has never abandoned me.

"We're quite a pair," she half sobs in humor.

"That we are," I concur, kissing her temple.

I don't know what this means. In all of my years on this planet, I've never felt this connected to another human being. But what I do know is that I will protect her with my life because she is quickly becoming it.

"What are we going to do?" she asks, taking comfort in my embrace. These hands of mine have killed, but when they touch her, they only want to do good.

"I have a plan," I reveal.

She sniffs softly before pulling away to look up at me. Those inquisitive eyes know she won't like what I intend to do.

"I—"

But I never get to finish my sentence as words are robbed

of me and may be fleeced of me forevermore.

"Hi, Alek."

Every part of me demands I turn around, but no, I do not need to turn around to recognize that sweet voice. In the depths of hell, that voice could call to me, and I would welcome the burn. And all she's ever done is burn me.

But I love her, nonetheless.

I will always love Willow Shaw…my дорогая…who is standing right behind me.

CHAPTER THIRTEEN

I've dreamed of this moment more times than I care to admit. But now that it's happening—now that she's really here—I'm afraid.

I don't know what I'll see reflected in those beautiful blue eyes. I deserve hatred for all that I've done, but I don't think my heart can take it. However, I'm a masochist when I turn around slowly and see the woman who still holds my heart.

Willow Shaw stole my breath from the first moment I saw her, and now is no different. Her hair has grown longer from when I saw her last, and the atrocities she's seen, the atrocities I introduced to her have hardened her innocence, but she's still my дорогая. A fierce warrior with a benevolent heart.

Saint stands behind her—tall and brooding with the look of an angel but will happily rip out your soul. Those chartreuse-colored eyes focus intently on me—still wanting to maim me where I stand. When they lock on Ella however, they soften.

"Are you okay?" he asks her.

My hackles instantly rise, angered he would ask her that.

"Of course, I'm okay," Ella replies, confused. She doesn't understand why he'd think she was in harm's way with me. "Why wouldn't I be?"

But Saint has every right to think she's in danger.

"He thinks you're here against your will," I explain with a hostile smirk.

Saint doesn't appreciate my sarcasm. "Damn straight I do, Popov. History would prove that's the case."

"Saint," Willow coos, looking at him over her shoulder.

Always the peacemaker. Always showing compassion when she shouldn't.

When Ella hears his name, she realizes standing before her is Willow—the woman who turned me into the man I am today. She takes a step back, but I reach out behind me and clutch her wrist.

Turning to look at her, I smile. "No, красавица. You stay by my side."

Her insecurities are reflected on her face, but I shake my head, wishing her to know that this doesn't change anything between us. When she gently withdraws from my grip, though, I know she doesn't believe me.

When she looks at Willow, she sees the perfect woman—a supermodel, as she said in her words because Willow once was. But Willow is so much more than her looks. She made me see there is more to a person than their exterior. Once, that's all I cared for, but not now.

Besides, in my eyes, no matter what Ella thinks of herself, she's the whole package to me. Smart. Feisty. Sexy. She is everything I want. But as she casts her eyes downward, I realize she doesn't see what I do.

"We need to talk." Saint's sharp voice cuts through the tension we're all feeling.

"Yes, we do. Come, Ella."

But she shakes her head, still refusing to look at me. "No, it's okay. I'll finish milking the cows. Besides, you probably have a lot to catch up on."

Willow steps forward. "Hi, I'm Willow. And this is Saint. I wish we were meeting under different circumstances, but it's still nice to meet you."

Ella lifts her chin and nods a curt hello. "I know who you are," she gently replies. "I'm Ella."

Willow smiles, instantly welcoming Ella. She doesn't know of her circumstances, but this is who Willow is.

Saint, however, isn't interested in formalities. "As much as this place holds many fond memories for me, you being in here is polluting that. Let's go inside."

Willow's lips lift into a reminiscent smile. And why shouldn't they? It was in here she and Saint solidified their union. She didn't need to tell me. She no longer flushed a virgin's blush when she met the morning sunlight.

I was jealous at the time, but now, I just wish Ella would look at me.

However, she turns around and positions the seat so she can continue her milking.

I don't know what the right protocol is here. The old me

would force her up, demand she come with me, but that won't work with her. I don't want to force her. I want her to come of her own accord.

Running a hand through my hair, I exhale in frustration. But eventually, I climb over the railing and walk toward Willow and Saint.

My hands itch to touch her, to ensure she's really here, but the hard press of Saint's jaw reveals I will lose several fingers if I do. So I walk past them and out the door, heading for the house.

Pavel stands on the front porch, smoking. No wonder he left in such a hurry. He wanted to keep this a secret from me, knowing I would insist on coming, which would be dangerous to all.

"I suppose this is your doing?" I state to Pavel, who ignores my spite.

And who walks out the front door is the reason he doesn't bite back. "No, it was mine. Pavel only knew of this plan this morning when I called him."

"Max?" I stupidly ask because there is no question he's here. But I don't understand why.

"Hello, Aleksei. I would say it's nice to see you, but that would be a lie."

"Then why are you here?" I bark, riddled with questions. Clearly, no one wants to be here, so why are they?

"Because he wrote to me and told me of the mess you've made." It's Saint who answers, and I know sooner or later, our conversation will end with bloodied fists.

Larisa hobbles out the door, looking at everyone. It's like a family reunion. However, we're missing too many loved ones.

"I made food," she says, her attention focusing on Willow. She smiles when she sees her.

When she looks at me, that smile soon fades. "Where is the other one?" she asks in Russian. She clearly thinks I'm still in love with Willow to refer to Ella in that manner.

"*Ella* is milking the cows," I reply, attempting to conceal my anger as I won't disrespect her in her own home. "I asked her to come inside, but she refused."

Larisa shakes her head and raises her eyes to the heavens. "Typical of you to have other's doing your dirty work."

Pavel smirks, admiring the boldness his mother still has.

"Let's get this over with then, shall we?" I order, not interested in playing catch-up. I want to know why they're all here.

Larisa grunts in agreement and walks into the house. We all follow, and the tension's so thick, it's almost impossible to breathe. Delicious smells waft through the air, but eating is the last thing on my mind. Nonetheless, we follow Larisa into the kitchen where she finishes dishing up the food.

Leaning against the counter, I do my best not to look at Willow because she'll just distract me, but I'm so relieved she's here. She's safe and out of the hands of my half-brother.

"I wrote to Saint, informing him of Serg's plans."

"What plans?" I ask, angered when I hear that son of a bitch's name. "He has many."

"I couldn't care less what he does to you," Max continues, revealing that his anger for me still resonates strongly. "But when he began circling the orphanage, I knew he was up to no good."

"How do you know that?" I question, surprised.

"People talk, Alek. Just because they don't talk to you doesn't mean we don't know what's going on."

I straighten my spine, refusing to give in to my urge to stab him in the jugular.

"Saint gave me his number, which I was to call only when there was an emergency. When I uncovered Serg talking to some benefactors of the orphanage, I guessed he had plans to steal it from Mother Superior.

"I couldn't allow that to happen. Mother Superior was good to us. Good to…Sara." It seems this is the first time he's allowed himself to speak her name aloud.

"So, I called Saint. With no allies, you can't fight him alone. And although we want you dead, we all have a common denominator. And that's the orphanage. None of us want anything to happen to that place. Or Mother Superior," Max says.

"I called Pavel and told him Saint and Willow were coming, and that's when he informed me you would have known that if you'd read Willow's postcard."

Finally, I make eye contact with Willow. She stands by Saint, appearing regretful for her error. So it seems Saint wasn't aware of her sending it as he would have never approved of her giving out those details so freely.

But she did that to help me—once again.

"But it apparently fell into the wrong hands. Lucky for us, I was in contact with Saint and Pavel. Otherwise, God forbid what would have happened."

Max is right.

I trained Saint well—keep your friends close and your enemies even closer. He always had eyes on me, on Russia, as he knew he'd return one day.

Whether he likes it or not, we share a bond, and when he eyes me wickedly, it's evident that it's still a big not. But regardless, he'll do what's right. And that's help to save the orphanage.

"Serg only just came to me with this idea," I reveal, not understanding how Max knew of his plans before me.

"This has been in the pipeline for a long while. Your brother may be an indiscreet asshole, but he's smart."

Scoffing, I fold my arms across my chest. "Half-brother," I correct, "and smart? I wouldn't go as far as to call him that."

"He outsmarted you, didn't he?" Saint counters, arching a smug brow.

Ignoring his quip, I return my attention to Max. "So what do you propose we do? I'm assuming Pavel has informed you of what Serg wants? I'm assuming you know Serg wants me to force Mother Superior to sign the deed of the orphanage over to him so he can turn the place into a brothel."

Willow frowns while Saint clenches his fists by his side.

"And if I don't do what he wants, he'll exploit an innocent child he's holding hostage, a child who trusted me. And once that's done, he'll burn the orphanage with everyone still inside—but not before his men defile them all—to the ground. I assume you know all of this," I snarl, peering around the room, wishing every person to know how personal this is to me.

Yes, this is my fault, but not one second goes by that I don't blame myself.

"So next time, I'd think before you go around throwing the word smart and my half-brother into the same sentence."

No one dares speak.

"I understand I ruined your lives," I acknowledge. "For that, I can never apologize enough. But for this to work, we need to work together. Hate me, I don't care. But don't allow my past to stand in the way of saving innocent people who did nothing to deserve this.

"I can't do this alone. I need your help. Mother Superior, the sisters, the children—they all need your help. Once this is done, you can all go on your way and forget I ever existed."

"We can *never* forget you exist. Trust me, I've tried," Saint spits, leveling me with pure hatred.

And I intend to use that hate. "I want to speak to you in private."

Willow's eyes widen as she grips Saint's forearm. But he nods.

"Lead the way, Popov."

"I'm coming with you," Willow says, but Saint's anger soon simmers when he locks eyes with her.

"No, ангел, you stay here."

When her brow puckers, he gently smooths out the creases with his thumb. "I won't be long. Have something to eat. You must be hungry." Before she can protest, he presses a kiss to her forehead.

The exchange is filled with nothing but love.

That soon changes as Saint pushes past me and out the

back door.

Willow's worried look begs I don't hurt him. I'm hurt she'd think I would.

I follow Saint out the door, hopeful this doesn't end in a bloodbath. He continues trekking through the yard, away from prying ears as he's guessed what I want to discuss needs to be done in private. When we're far enough, he stops and spins around.

"You come here, but do you have a plan?" I question, unthreatened by his hulking stance.

"You're lucky we're here at all," he snarls.

"I'm thankful, but unless we have some sort of strategy, you being here is useless."

Saint is the only person I enjoy sparring with this way. He is intelligent and insightful, and when pushed in just the right way, he becomes a mastermind. It's how I crafted him into the ruthless man I still admire, regardless of our past.

"I didn't think so," I quip when he remains silent. "Listen to what I have to say, okay?"

Saint nods sharply.

"Irrespective of what you think, Ella is here of her own accord. I didn't force her in any way." I need Saint to know this. It somehow unburdens a small piece of my soul.

"She was pretending to be a sister at the orphanage to escape Santo Macrillo." I don't need to explain to Saint who Santo is. He is well aware of the power he holds.

"Santo wants her back. He knows she was at the orphanage, which is why he hired me to retrieve her."

"Son of a bitch," Saint utters under his breath. I don't

know if he's speaking of me or Santo.

"He doesn't know she's here. He still believes she's at the orphanage. If I do as he says, he will help me fight Serg. He will help rebuild my kingdom."

"If this is supposed to be working in your favor, it's not," Saint spits, eyeing me angrily.

"But I cannot do that to her," I reveal, rubbing the back of my neck, suddenly uncomfortable sharing this with the man who won the heart of the woman I wanted. "I have formed… an attachment to Ella. I simply can't give her over like some cow at market.

"But if I don't, then what becomes of Mother Superior? Serg was very clear in what he wanted. He doesn't want me dead. He wants me to suffer, and he will take that suffering in any form he can."

"So what's your plan?"

"We make him think he's won…and then we take him down," I reveal, watching Saint's defensive attitude relax slightly.

"How?"

"We make a deal with someone he trusts," I reply, hoping like hell this works. "We're not giving Serg what he wants, but rather, we're giving someone else what he wants."

"And what's that?" Saint asks, running his fingers over his growth in thought. How I've missed plotting with him.

"Me," I divulge, watching Saint catch up to speed. "Raul will have no qualms about making a deal with us, knowing the result will be my head at his feet.

"Serg trusts Raul, but all Raul wants is his revenge. We

use this to our advantage. We trade me for Serg. We ask Raul for extra manpower to help us so we're not outnumbered. Otherwise, it'll be a bloodbath. Serg may want me alive, but the rest of you are disposable.

"I wish I could do this alone and not endanger your lives, but I can't, and the moment I make my attack on Serg, his men will be on my ass. They'll either kill me, or they'll keep me prisoner. And I'd rather die than be that.

"I would have asked Pavel for some explosives, but I can't risk Irina. And besides, Serg will have me searched. After Ingrid, he's learned his lesson. We need the element of surprise on our side.

"We ask Raul to find out where Serg wants to meet, so we're able to have the upper hand. No surprises. I get Serg alone, where he dies by my hand, and my hand alone. When the deed is done, I will go willingly with Raul to pay my dues."

And there it is, my plan in a nutshell.

It came to me when speaking with Mother Superior.

"If what you say about your brother is true, then what can you give him which will make him surrender?"

It's not what I can give him, but rather, what I can give Raul to have him play by my rules.

I know men like Raul because I was one. They'd do anything for revenge. Righting the wrongs is the only thing that gives them peace. And killing me for killing his father, he'll do anything we want.

It's a simple trade, one Raul will agree to. He's been hunting me for so long, and now, he has me.

He has no loyalty to Serg. Serg is someone he does

business with, and that's all.

"He has to believe he's won. Otherwise, he'll hurt Irina. The little girl he's holding hostage," I explain. "He will only hand her over when he has the signed deed in his hand."

"And what makes you think Raul won't tell him this plan?" Saint questions, which is so like him—always thinking of every angle.

"Because my death means more to Raul than some stupid sibling rivalry. His loyalty to his father, to avenging him is the only thing he cares about. You should know how deep love and loyalty runs. Didn't you sacrifice everything for Zoey? Willow?"

Saint clenches his jaw when I speak his dead sister's name.

"Yes. You're right," he snarls, barely holding back his anger. "Raul will do anything to make you pay for what you did, but did you forget, *I* was the one forced to do your dirty work? *I* was the one who shot Chow. Not you."

"On my order," I state as this isn't his doing. He was merely the instrument behind my command. "I know how these men work, Saint."

"And you're certain he's still doing business with Serg?"

I nod confidently. "Yes, I know because Serg sent a spy, Renata, to infiltrate my life. She knew about Raul, information gained from firsthand experience. I have no doubt."

Saint ponders everything I've told him. "This will work. Max will know where Raul is. He may have kept to himself all this time, but that doesn't mean he wasn't watching."

Watching me suffer, he means. Max could have helped me, but he chose not to. I killed the woman he loved, and this was my karma for it.

"Yes, it'll work. We need all the manpower we can get. Up against Serg, we'll be outnumbered. But with Raul on our side, we can't lose. No matter what Serg offers Raul, it'll never be enough. I'm far more valuable to him than any sum of money. Or all the riches in the world.

"Serg won't want me dead. He's said so himself. He wants to make me suffer, and I can't think of anything worse than keeping me alive as he destroys the people I love. Therefore, Serg and Raul will not make a deal. One wants me dead. The other alive. There are no gray areas.

"Will you help me?" I ask, knowing what this means. "Willow or Ella cannot know of this plan."

I have no idea how I'll keep this from Ella. She is resilient and smart, and sooner or later, she will discover what I plan to do.

The veins in Saint's neck pulsate in rage because he knows if *either* Willow or Ella find out about what I intend to do, they'll try to stop me. No matter what I did to Willow, she will always try to save me. And it kills Saint inside.

"You're asking me to help deliver what you deserve?" he poses with a snicker. "You're asking me to rid scum from this earth, scum who had no problem exploiting my very existence to live?"

Willow.

"You're asking me to end your bloodline? Abso-fucking-lutely."

"Very good." I smile in response, pleased I can rely on him this one final time. "We'll inform Pavel and Max of the plans, and then I shall await Serg's call.

"Santo cannot know about Ella," I warn. "I'll arrange for Pavel to organize the documents for her to return home. I know I have no right to ask this of you, but will you ensure her safety when I'm gone?"

Saint doesn't know Ella, and rightfully, he should tell me to go to hell. But Ella is innocent, which is why Saint nods.

"You have my word."

"Excellent." I sigh in relief.

I can accept my death, knowing she will be safe.

This plan allows everyone to be unharmed and for the person responsible for it all—me—to be held accountable.

"Oh, there is something else."

Saint waits for me to continue.

"My mother and the woman who conspired with Serg, Renata, they too must pay for their crimes."

"Yes, your mother deserves everything she's got coming to her, but I won't condemn a woman who knows no better. Who is she?"

Swallowing down the hypocrisy I'm about to spew, I reply, "She is Serg's…plaything. A tool for him to do what he pleases. She's brainwashed, which is why she had no issues doing what he ordered."

Saint tips his face to the heavens, a bitter laughter leaving him. "Oh, so it seems you're closer related than you wish to be. I mean, didn't you do the same to my sister, the sister who lays buried under a tree because of you?"

He dares me to argue. But how can I?

"Yes, I did do that to Zoey."

There's no point apologizing because sometimes, sorry just isn't enough.

"At least you accept culpability. Yes, Zoey was far from being an angel. She was unhinged, but meeting you only fueled her demons within," he sneers, but it doesn't lessen his pain. He will always blame her death on himself. That's the type of man he is. "But that doesn't bring her back."

"No, it doesn't." His anguish affects me in ways it never has before. I am so terribly sorry for it all. I'm learning how to be human; it's just a shame these lessons are learned from the pain, the death of others.

I was never shown empathy as a child, and that continued into adulthood. Only now do I see how much destruction I've caused.

"Fine, I'll help you. But this woman, Renata, if she can be spared, she will be."

Clenching my jaw, I think of her cruelness toward Irina, toward Ella and a lifeless Sister Yali. "She is beyond redemption, Saint."

"So are you, but there is one person who never gave up on you," he replies bluntly, holding up his pointer finger. "If Willow had never shown you compassion, you'd be dead. So you have no right to tell me who can or cannot be saved."

"She shot and killed a sister. She plotted with Serg and has no qualms about allowing him to exploit innocent children to please the sick appetites of the dregs of society," I explain because there is no way I'll permit her to live.

"Get off your pedestal, Popov. You're no better," Saint argues with a scoff. "I did your bidding. You may be able to lie to yourself, but you can't lie to me."

"My friend, I know what I am. I'm the one who lives inside this head." I tap my temple. "But she must pay for what she's done."

"And what about your friend, Ella?" he asks, and the moment he says her name, the hostility between us becomes stifling. "For her to be messed up with Santo Macrillo means she's no angel, either. Would you order I condemn her too?"

Inhaling slowly, I feel every inch of my being vibrating in utter fury. "Watch your mouth, мальчик," I caution. "You have no idea what you're saying."

Saint bursts into jovial laughter. "Holy shit. You actually care for someone other than yourself. I never thought I'd see the day."

Tsking him, I pull the pin and toss the grenade. "You should know by now how much I care for your sweet ангел. And clearly, the feeling is still mutual for her to send that postcard, alerting me to her arrival. I guess some things don't change."

Saint's lips twist into a satisfied grin. He was just waiting, biding his time for this moment to come. This has been a long time coming…

We both launch at the other, both intent on ripping the other limb from limb. Saint punches me in the nose. I slam my fist into his chin. It's blow for blow. We circle one another, fists raised, blood dripping onto the ground, but neither of us will surrender.

Saint spits out a mouthful of blood while I wipe away the blood from my bleeding nose.

He has always been a worthy opponent, and if we weren't archenemies, I would call him my best friend. But that'll never happen. He kicks out, dropping me to one knee as he strikes me in the kneecap. With a roar, he knees under my chin, sending me onto my back.

He dives on top of me, pummeling my face with brutal fists. With each hit, I can feel his pain, his hatred toward me. These feelings bind us together, and no matter how much he hates me, he knows he'll never rid me from his world.

I allow him to punch me a couple more times before I strike him in the stomach, winding him. A split second is all I need to shove him off and switch positions so he's now under my brutal fists. I don't hold back as I punch him in the face, over and over again.

Saint is strong and flexible and uses his legs to toss me over his head. We both scramble to our feet, bloody and beaten, but neither of us will surrender.

"You've still got fight in you, old man," he mocks with a bloodied grin, thoroughly enjoying the violence.

"Don't forget, this *old man* taught you everything you know," I reply, returning his smirk.

"Shall we finish it then?"

"You and I, my friend, we'll never be finished. But you can try," I sarcastically taunt.

We charge for the other, punch for punch with no winner in sight. He tries to connect with my ribs, but I read his move and dodge his attack because I was the one who taught him his fighting style. I connect with his chin, and his head snaps back with a crack.

Anyone else, they'd be knocked out cold. But not Saint. He shakes his head, ready for more carnage. Just as he's about to deliver a sequence of punches, two shrill voices stop our advances.

"Saint!"

"Alek!"

Both our names are shouted at the same time, but by two different women.

Willow is behind Saint, hand over her mouth as she watches the bloodshed, horrified. Ella is behind me, so I can't see her. But as Saint looks over my head, a musing look etched on his bloody face, I guess she's as disturbed as Willow. I don't expect him to understand my feelings for Ella.

I don't understand them.

But what I do understand is that they're real.

"Stop it! Both of you," Willow orders while Saint shakes his head.

"Go back inside, ангел. This doesn't concern you."

Even I know he's about to receive an earful.

"Like hell this doesn't. If you're done whipping out your dicks, can we think of a way to work together to save the orphanage? Please."

I look at Saint through one eye—as the other is beginning to swell closed—and implore he doesn't tell her what we discussed.

He wipes his busted lip with the back of his hand, and with a sharp nod, confirming my secret is safe, he replies, "Only because you said please."

When he turns around to face his love, I turn to face

my…Ella. She wrings her hands in front of her, looking uncomfortable. She doesn't know where she fits in.

I understand this is a lot for her to take in. We all have history. Not pleasant history; but history, nonetheless.

We've just found our footing together, and now…I don't know what happens now. She opened up to me, only for my skeletons to come bursting out of the closet. I want to tell her it'll be all right.

But it won't be.

Saint draws Willow into his arms when she tries to fuss with his cuts. He looks at me over her head, a look of promise reflected in his eyes.

This is done. No one will surrender.

For now.

I'm sitting on the porch, rocking pensively in the old creaky chair, smoking a stolen cigar.

I have no idea of the time, but it's late. It's only me and the two orange cats who seem to be unable to sleep.

Once I got cleaned up, I informed Pavel and Max of my plans. As suspected, they didn't argue. They both knew it was the best plan we had. The only person who suffers is the one who has caused so much pain. It seems to have come full circle.

Max said he'd make a few calls to sniff out Raul. He and Pavel were in agreement that we had to let Serg "win" in order to overthrow him. I need the signed deed to be authentic, and for that to occur, I need to ask Mother Superior to trust me one last time.

I think about the night I offered myself to Oscar and Astra. I did it without any reservations because I knew it was the right thing to do. But it wasn't my time then.

I had so much more to do. I see that now. I may not have achieved all that I wanted—but I learned along the way.

I discovered true friendship with Pavel, Mother Superior, and the sisters who, regardless of what I'd done, stuck by me when they had every right to discard me as others had. I experienced an innocence in Irina which I've never seen before. I've never had someone look at me the way she does— with utter trust and utmost affection.

And then I met Ella.

After Willow, I had no interest in feeling that vulnerable ever again. But with Ella, it was almost an unstoppable force. She made me feel...period, something I never thought possible. She tore down my walls with her strength and sincerity. She accepted me for me.

I never saw her coming. She blindsided me—in the best possible way.

I came across such kindness, which had me believing I was worthy of it. Being surrounded by nothing but hatred and ugliness for so long, I was lost in the notion of maybe being forgiven for all that I've done.

But I'd need many lifetimes to repent for my sins.

And the person who walks out the front door is the main reason.

"Couldn't sleep either?" She's making light of the situation because she's uncomfortable. I don't think she'll ever stop.

"Sleep?" I mock, playing along. "That old friend evaded me long ago."

Willow pulls up a chair and sits beside me. "How's your face?"

I chuckle, taking a pull of my cigar. "I'll live."

There was a time when I would try to impress her, but not now. She's seen me at my worst. She can see through the bullshit. She always has.

"I know you and Saint have a plan, but of course, he won't tell me."

"And you think I will?" I amusingly accuse, turning to look at her.

She is such a magnificent being. My memory has done a poor job of remembering her. Maybe I went into self-preservation mode. I wish I could say I didn't still love her, but I do. I don't love her the same way I once did, but those feelings still have my heart beating faster and my mouth running dry.

"No, I don't think that at all," she replies, drawing her legs toward her chest and pulling the oversize T-shirt over her knees. "I was going to ask you to tell me."

"And risk being on the receiving end of your beloved's fists once again? I don't think so. This isn't your fight."

She scoffs, angered. "Don't do that. Don't treat me like I'm going to break."

"I never treated you that way, дорогая." It's out before I could stop myself.

The nickname causes her to flinch as I imagine she doesn't associate many fond memories with being called that name. "No, I suppose you haven't."

"Once upon a time, I may have been the one to tell you, but that time has come and gone," I state with a poignant smile.

She doesn't argue the point because she knows I'm right. For me to tell her would be a betrayal to Saint, and I've already done enough.

"So, who's Ella?" she casually asks, but I know she's querying whether Ella is here of her own free will.

The question reveals that no matter what I say or do, Willow will always see me as the man who bought her.

"She's in trouble," I share. When Willow looks like she's about to leap from her chair and strangle me, I chuckle. "Not with me. Well, some days…"

She clears her throat, not interested in my trip down memory lane.

"I need to get her back to America. She's in danger being here."

"How?"

"She fell in love with the wrong man," I reveal, smoking my cigar and staring into the darkness.

Willow is quiet, no doubt mulling over what I just shared.

"And why are you helping her?"

She is genuinely curious because the Aleksei she once knew wouldn't give a damn about someone like Ella. She would have been dispensable—merely a pretty face to warm my bed—but I'm no longer that man.

Yet I know Willow won't believe me. Only when I prove to her how I've changed will I gain her trust and respect. I won't be here to see it, but I can only hope her opinion of me will one day change. She will see the impact she had on me.

"I'm helping her because she doesn't deserve to be punished for falling in love." Meeting her expressive eyes, I profess, "One can't help who they fall in love with."

She wets her lips, averting her gaze as my comment is too close to home. And it was done with intent—for me, but also, for Ella…who is currently eavesdropping.

Even though I act calm, my senses are on high alert. They always are.

I always familiarize myself with sights, sounds, smells—everything that'll give me an advantage if the time presents itself; like right now.

There is a loose floorboard in the living room, two feet from the front door that creaks ever so softly when stood on. I heard it about a minute ago. The window to the left is slightly ajar, allowing the pleasant breeze in. It also allows Ella's mouthwatering fragrance out.

I know she uses the almost sheer curtain as coverage, giving her a false sense of protection that she remains undetected. And I allow her to think this when I give life to my plan, crushing her because I know she won't leave unless she's pushed.

Willow will eventually understand why Saint and I decided to keep our plan from her, but Ella will never allow it. Even if I ask her to stay, she will not. She has proven her stubbornness time and time again.

I can't allow another person I care for to get hurt, and just the thought of Ella being hurt has me realizing just how deep my feelings for her are. For someone who'd never experienced love, with Willow and Ella, I think I'm starting to learn.

I didn't know how to keep my plan from Ella, but now…I do.

"I understand this firsthand," I confess without regret.

"Alek—" Willow shakes her head.

"I will always love you, дорогая," I continue, refusing to let her speak. "You'll always be in my heart. You were the first woman I ever loved. I know I don't deserve your forgiveness, but I strive everyday to become a better man…for you."

And just like that, a gaping hole is punched through my heart when her fruity floral smell grows faint, before I hear those quiet footsteps trod over the loose floorboard as she returns to the bedroom.

My diversion worked. So why do I feel so hollow inside?

"I believe you're on your way to becoming a better man. And I think Ella has something to do with that." My дорогая has always been so smart.

She too has noticed the small changes in my demeanor. I'm sure she saw how I responded to Ella. She saw the way I held her hand. Willow knows Ella is more to me than…well, she is merely something more.

"Yes, you're right. Ella has seen something in me that I cannot see. I probably never will," I share now that Ella is gone.

"She's insecure, though," Willow says, resting her chin on her knees, looking my way.

"I know. She doesn't understand the relationship we have. I will always love you. But that love…I feel for Saint too. We are bonded in a way no one understands." I shake my head, hoping I don't sound like a fool.

But for the first time ever, Willow looks at me without complete hurt in her eyes. "I know what you mean," she whispers. "What you did…it was deplorable."

I hang my head in shame, but she's right.

"I left here, intent on never returning. When I went back to America, I just wanted to forget. But the harder I tried, the more difficult it became, and that was because I didn't want to forget.

"Yes, I'd never wish what I went through upon anyone, but in a way, if I never experienced such hardship, then I would have never fully appreciated the tranquility either. Meeting you brought me Saint. So if I had to endure that agony to meet the love of my life, then I would do it again in a heartbeat.

"Life is measured in extraordinary, unpredictable moments in time, and meeting Saint…meeting you, was the best and worst thing that ever happened to me…but I wouldn't take it back.

"So, even though I'll never forgive you completely, I still thank God that we met."

I stare speechless, unsure what to say. This benevolent woman robs me of air and breath time and time again.

"I'm strong, far more courageous than I thought myself to be, and that's thanks to you in a way. I wouldn't allow you to beat me. Each time you pushed, I pushed back twice as hard, uncovering my true self. The woman my father would be proud of. And meeting Saint…" She stares off in the distance, a smile tugging at her lips.

"I didn't know I was missing my other half until I met him. I don't just love him, Alek. He is a part of me. Every breath I take is for him. Every beat of my heart is for him."

Her confession stings but not as badly as it once would've.

"And the feeling is mutual, дорогая," I acknowledge as I want her to know I'm happy for her and Saint. I once wished she felt that way about me, but I don't anymore.

And that's because of Ella.

She has given me hope. Willow is my past…and Ella…she is my future. No matter how small of a time that future is, she showed me I can love again. She opened my heart, and if our circumstances were different, I believe she'd own it—wholly.

We just needed more time, but we don't have that luxury.

"I know," she replies, still smiling. "So, if something so pure, so…good can come out of such ugliness…then I can't hate you. Neither of us can. We found one another because of you."

I bring the cigar to my quivering lips, not wanting her to see how her words have touched me so.

"And if you can find someone, in ugliness and despair, then my advice is…don't let her go."

She knows Ella means more to me than I've let on. Women's intuition maybe? Whatever the reason, it makes what I need to do so much harder.

I need to hurt her. I need to hurt Ella…to save them.

They're both strong, stubborn, independent women who don't need a man to rescue them. Both have proven this.

Willow, when she fought for her freedom, regardless of her circumstance. And Ella, when she saw an opportunity to save herself, she took it.

They're fighters—far braver than any man I know.

Willow snaps me from my thoughts when she wipes the corner of her eye, wet with a stray tear. "Good night, Alek."

I look up at her when she stands. The oversized T-shirt belongs to Saint. I remember when she wore jewels and fancy dresses because I ordered her to. This look suits her.

"Sweet dreams."

She leaves me to my thoughts, sensing they're burdensome, and that I need time on my own to digest it all.

She's given me what I've chased since she left me— forgiveness.

With a smile, I inhale the nicotine, victorious.

Sacrificing yourself for the ones you love isn't for them— it's for oneself…because love is selfless, and knowing they'll be free…that's the biggest gift of all.

I get it now.

CHAPTER FOURTEEN

It's been two days, two torturous days that I've kept my distance from Ella.

My plan appears to have worked, and what she overheard the night on the porch between Willow and me was enough to keep her away.

She kept busy, tending to the animals with Larisa, while I worked with Pavel, organizing her safe passage out of Russia. Usually, her curious nature would have gotten the better of her and she'd ask what I was doing, but not now.

I've hurt her by playing on her insecurities. She knows what Willow means to me, so hearing me confess that I still love her has confused her about my feelings for her. But it's *because* of my feelings for her that I'm doing this.

Maybe in another lifetime, we'd work, but in this reality, we just don't. She deserves so much more than what I can offer her.

With a sigh, I punch in the new code on the keypad and watch as the gates to the orphanage open. I had to stick to my story in case Santo was watching and sent a flurry of workmen to work on the grounds. First on the agenda was changing every lock in this place and reprogramming the codes.

Serg has the master key and codes, and even though he needs this place, I didn't trust him not to storm it on a whim.

Even though she was kept in the dark, Mother Superior agreed to the plans. But when I park my car near the front entrance, not the back, I realize this will be the last time she ever has to trust me. Getting out of my SUV, I shield the sun from my eyes as I peer up, taking in the orphanage in all of its splendor.

It's come a long way since I first saw it, and I'm proud I played a part in its growth. I happily accept my fate, knowing I leave this legacy behind even though I'm merely a drop in the ocean. Mother Superior is the one who bleeds for this place.

But I guess in just a few days, I will too.

Pressing the doorbell, I wait for one of the sisters to come to the door. Good. They didn't just buzz me in. With the death of Sister Yali still fresh in their minds, I can imagine the fear of God has been instilled into them.

Sister Helena lets me in but doesn't greet me how she once would. I guess the orphanage is rife with rumors, and seeing as Ella, Renata, and I are gone, there's no guessing who is responsible for the sudden lockdown.

"Mother Superior is in her office." She doesn't escort me. I know the way.

Once she locks the door and arms the alarm, I walk

down the hallway, unbelieving of the heavy quietness in the air. Usually, I would be greeted with shrill cries of joy as the children play merrily with one another.

But now, a stagnant weight fills the once happy space.

My shoes echo loudly on the polished flooring. I wonder how long it took to scrub Sister Yali's blood clean?

Shaking my head, I focus on the task at hand and knock on Mother Superior's door. "Come in."

Opening the door, I see her sitting at her desk, reading over some paperwork. When she lifts her gaze and sees the healing bruising on my face, I can see the disappointment reflected in her eyes.

I try not to let it get to me and smile. "Good day, Mother Superior. Thank you for seeing me."

She nods, gesturing for me to sit. But as I close the door, I'd rather stand as my stab wound is still healing.

No matter how many times I've practiced this speech, there is no way to soften the blow. So I decide to put us both out of our misery quickly. "I need you to sign the orphanage deed over to me. Temporarily."

She remains stone-faced. It seems nothing I say can shock her anymore. "For you to ask this of me, I can only imagine what happens if I say no."

"I have no right to ask this of you, but I ask that you trust me this one final time."

She doesn't miss the finality of my sentence. "And what becomes of you once this is done? I can't imagine you benefit from this deal."

With a melancholy smile, I reply, "I benefit in more ways

than you'll ever know. This ensures Irina's safety. And yours. I made a promise to you to bring her back, and I meant it. This place will see no more evil because of me."

Mother Superior clutches the crucifix around her throat. "This place has seen far more good than evil by your hand, Aleksei." I wish I could believe her. "But if this must be done, then so be it. I shall have my lawyers draw up the paperwork immediately."

"Thank you." I nod in gratitude, as she's just saved this place once again.

"Aleksei, forgive me."

"Whatever for?" I ask, aghast.

"I should have never banished you from these walls. This place is your home."

"No," I gently disagree. "You did the right thing. My past has endangered this place for too long. I thank you for everything."

Her astute eyes narrow. "Thank me? This sounds like goodbye."

And that's because it is.

I have no intention of ever returning because once this is done, the wolves will come for their prize. But I can't let Mother Superior know this for she will try to change my mind.

I'm not afraid of dying. I'm far more afraid of living when my loved ones aren't.

Clearing my throat, I ensure my mask is strapped on tight. "You can't get rid of me that easily. Once this is done, I'll be back, and we can start on the rest of the renovations. I thought we could add an atrium in the west wing."

Mother Superior rises from her chair and walks toward me. I dare not move. "My child." She places her cool hand to my cheek. "Don't forget I know you better than you know yourself. If you must do this, then I will accept your choice.

"If children were God's wish for me, I often thought I'd like my son to be like you. You're courageous, loyal, but foremost, you're good. Thank you for whatever you plan to sacrifice for us."

I've never heard these words before as I was easily replaced by my own mother. So to hear them now, I barely hold it together.

Leaning forward, I kiss Mother Superior's forehead. "Ты единственная мама, которую я когда-либо знал."

My confession stuns her, and she softly folds herself into my arms—a mother's embrace. It seems fitting, seeing as I just told her she's the only mother I've ever known.

I don't just see her as a mentor, but she is also my mother in every sense of the word. She was there for me when my own flesh and blood wasn't. I'll never forget that, which is why I'll happily lay down my life for her and everything she loves.

Her sniffles are too much, so I gently break our embrace. I don't know how to say goodbye to the only person who has ever truly loved me. There are no words, so I simply caress her cheek with a smile, committing this moment to memory.

When I leave her office, a sense of liberation follows me out the door. Most would feel saddened this was the last time they were to walk these halls, but not me. Knowing Irina will take steps I cannot is enough. One might do a final sweep of the place that has been their home for so long, but for me, I could walk this place until I take my last breath, and it still wouldn't be enough.

So I simply nod in gratitude to Sister Margaret who opens the door for me and leave my sanctuary behind. This place will stand strong, and that gives me faith.

My cell chimes. Digging into my pocket, I see it's a text from Pavel.

> Passport organized. Transport too. Tomorrow. AM.

Inhaling in relief, I almost feel like this is a parting gift as I leave the orphanage for good. Ella is safe. She can leave here now.

> *Max?*

I type, asking if he's had any luck with Raul.

> Soon.

Raul isn't making it easy for us. But we've left a trail, and sooner or later, he'll take the bait.

> Deed?

> *Done.*

Pavel doesn't reply because he knew I wouldn't fail.

Getting into my SUV, I start the engine and don't look back as I leave the orphanage behind. With one job done, I decide to tick another off the list and dial Santo.

"Aleksei, I've been waiting for your call." He doesn't conceal his displeasure that it's taken me this long to call.

"It's all organized. You'll get her in three days," I state, not wishing to talk to this asshole longer than I need to.

His demeanor instantly changes. "My friend, this news pleases me so. How?"

"Just let me worry about that. However, I need more money. This has proven to be far more difficult than anticipated. I think another fifty thousand is fair. Half now. The rest on delivery."

I'm playing a dangerous game, but he won't say no. Two hundred thousand dollars is nothing to him.

"I've already given you more than enough."

"Really? How much is she worth to you?" I pose, gripping the steering wheel.

"You're right. No sum of money could ever amount to enough. I can wire it to you. Send me the details and I'll see to it immediately."

I shake my head at his greed because his stupidity has just cost him. "Excellent. Make whatever arrangements you need to. Three days from today." And I hang up.

Three days from today is when my fated meeting with my half-brother is to take place. Therefore, it seems fitting that I screw him and Santo over on the same day.

In three days' time, Ella will be long gone. Safe and sound, and seventy-five thousand dollars richer. The money will be split between her and Mother Superior. My final gift to them both.

Now, I just have to convince her to leave. She has no reason to stay. Pavel has her new life organized, just as he did with Willow and Saint. The new Antonella Ricci is within reach.

Classical music is my comfort as I drive to Larisa's home. I wish I could offer her something too, but Pavel and Max will benefit from my death. They'll fall in favor with Raul. With Serg gone, someone will have to fill his shoes.

I have no doubt that Pavel and Max have thought about it. But I won't be here to see what they decide.

Saint and Willow are training in the front yard. He trips her when her attention falters toward me. He offers his hand, which she accepts with a frown. In response, he draws her into his arms and kisses away her anger.

This doesn't bother me as much anymore. I suppose this is what moving on feels like.

I leave them to their canoodling and make my way into the house. Pavel gestures with his head toward the bedroom.

It's on.

My palms suddenly begin to sweat. I don't remember ever being this nervous before.

I don't bother knocking as I open the door to see Ella curled on the bed, reading a book. When she sees me, she continues to read.

Her detachment stings, but this is what I wanted.

"Pavel has your passport and new ID," I state, closing the

door and leaning against it. I don't trust myself as she shifts those long, supple legs.

"Your transportation has also been arranged. You leave tomorrow morning."

I'm expecting some sort of reaction, but I get nothing in response.

"Did you hear what I said?" I bark, frustrated at myself, not her.

She closes the book and rests her head in her palm, staring at me. "I heard you."

"And?" I prompt, not able to read her.

"And where am I supposed to go?"

"Back to America."

Ella blinks once, appearing wounded by my comment. I mistake her surprise for her being afraid.

"There's no need to be scared. Pavel organized this for Willow and—"

The moment I say Willow's name, an annoyed grunt leaves her, and she rises from the bed. "I'm not scared," she snaps, folding her arms across her chest.

She wears a dress, the low neckline exposing the tops of her luscious breasts. My mouth instantly waters, but I focus.

"Then why aren't you packing?"

"Because you don't speak to me for two days, and when you do, it's to tell me to leave," she replies, eyeing me angrily.

"You know why," I reason. "It's not safe for you here."

She laughs, but it's a sarcastic snicker. "Or don't you mean I'm not welcome here anymore?"

"What?" I admonish. Even though this is what I wanted,

it still hurts to hear her wounded this way because of me. "Of course, not."

"Will you come with me?" she asks, challenging me because she knows the answer.

"No." One simple word has never caused so much carnage.

"But you'll stay here with her?"

"Ella—"

But she is a woman scorned as she comes charging over, standing on her toes, attempting to put us at eye level. She has a few inches to go.

"No, don't Ella me," she snaps, her dark, fruity scent amplified with her anger. "You've had your fun, but now that she's back, I'm yesterday's news. Is that it?"

"You're being ridiculous," I snap, my anger mounting.

My plan has worked a little too well, which saddens me because it was so easy for her to believe I don't care about her. But that is the reason.

"Tell me you don't still love her then," she asks, her lower lip trembling in fury but also fear. "Tell me you don't still want her."

I don't reply.

She heard my confession. This would be the time for me to explain, but I don't. And my silence says it all.

Her fight deflates before me as tears sting her eyes. "Tell me you want *me* more than *her*," she begs in a whisper, breaking me in two.

At this moment, her pain has me desperately searching for another way. I can't hurt her this way, but if I die a martyr, she won't move on. For her to forget about me, she has to hate me. It's the only way she can live her life without the ghosts of what-ifs plaguing her every day.

I've never truly felt myself to be the villain…until now. "I cannot. I'm sorry."

She tongues her cheek, shaking her head. I've just rejected her, which is what I promised I'd never do.

I watch as she reaches for her bag and begins ripping her garments from the hangers. She is holding back her tears— my strong, stubborn girl.

"Okay, fine, you want me gone, then I'll go. But I'm not going back to America."

Her admission has heat burning up my neck. "You have to," I press, angered.

"I don't have to do anything," she argues, stuffing her bag with her belongings.

"Ella, goddammit! It's not safe for you here. Why can't you do what you're told for once?" I bellow, tugging at my hair in frustration.

"Why do you care?" she defies, pausing from cramming her bag full. "Tell me!"

My body vibrates in anger, frustration and…admiration. She won't give up, even if I appear to have done so.

She wants me to tell her that what I said, what I felt was real. That I don't want her to leave because I want a future with her. That I want to see where this will lead.

But I can't.

And it's because I want and feel all those things that I turn around and leave.

A thud crashes against the door, hinting Ella threw

something at it, probably wishing it was my head.

Sighing, I walk into the living room and collapse into the chair. Saint looks up from writing in a journal. Pavel pauses reading the paper.

"She won't go," I reveal, leaning my head back into the cushions.

"Did you really expect her to?" Saint says, shaking his head.

My mouth parts, as I have no idea what he means.

"Aleksei, for a smart man, you can sometimes be so dumb. That woman, God help her, is in love with you," he casually states like we're merely discussing the weather.

Pavel grins.

"In love?" I scoff, incredulous at his claim.

"Yes, you idiot. She won't leave here because she thinks there's still a chance for you two."

"No offense, but I don't want relationship advice from you."

"I don't care what you want. I'm doing this for Zoey," Saint snaps, closing his journal and setting it on his lap. "If you feel anything for her, you'll let her go."

"Just as you did with Willow?" I mock because he returned to her. In the end, they got their happily ever after.

"I tried, I fucking tried," he defends, "but being without her, I may as well have died with Zoey."

I give him the respect of keeping our eyes locked. It's the least I can do.

"I traveled the world without her, looking for something to make this"—he tugs at his T-shirt, over his heart—"pain go away. But it never did. It only got worse, and that's because her pain is mine. Mine is hers.

"So together, I shoulder her pain, and she shoulders mine."

Their love is sickening, but in a way, I'm envious that out of every single being in this world, they found that love with each other.

Does Ella feel that way about me?

"I've tried to make her leave."

Saint isn't convinced. "Try harder."

"How?" But there's no need for me to ask. I know.

As does Saint.

"I will fucking kill you before you get within three feet of her."

His threat isn't empty, but he's the one who suggested I try harder.

"Willow came to me, asking what our plans were with Serg."

Saint clenches his jaw. "I know. She told me."

"You know she won't stay away either, unless—"

Saint leaps up from the chair, fists balled by his side. "If you're proposing what I think you are, then you better come up with another plan, Popov."

"Do you want her to really hate me?" I ask, keeping a level head. "I do this, then I die a martyr, and my ghost will haunt your relationship for the rest of your lives. But if I show her that I haven't changed, that I'm still the Alek she once knew, then she will soon forget that she ever thought I had a heart."

"I won't lie to her," Saint says, lowering his voice so she

doesn't hear.

Raising my hands in surrender, I nod. "Very well. Tell her the truth whenever you deem fit, but now, let her hate me so she lets me go. So they both let me go. Or are you afraid she'll like it?"

Saint inhales deeply, not falling for the bait. "You overestimate yourself, старик."

"Well, let us see. If that's true, you'll have no problem with me seducing your beloved." My insides are thrilled with the challenge.

"Seducing? Rein it in, motherfucker. There will be no seducing."

"What do you propose then?"

Saint appears as though he's tasted something rotten as he replies, "I know how you work. You'll think of something. But mark my words, if you do anything that makes her feel uncomfortable, I'll fucking kill you with my bare hands."

"I have no doubt, мой друг."

Saint is wrestling with this agreement, but he knows I won't overstep any lines. And it won't take much for Willow to backtrack on our newfound friendship if I betray her.

The front door opens, and Max freezes when he realizes he's just walked into something. "Raul is in," he says, unsure if this is what we want to hear.

But it is.

"Very good," I affirm, a strange way to react to the news of my death. But it means I can begin to right the wrongs of the past. "You told him what needs to happen first?"

Max nods. "Yes, he understands. Irina is to go free. He

wants it to happen that night, though. No time to waste."

"Even better." This means there is less chance of Serg polluting the orphanage. He only has to believe he's won before we strike. It'll give me great pleasure to take it all from him.

"Once Serg gives us instructions on where this deal is to go down, we're to call Raul. He will let us know of any secret entries, and how many men Serg will have there so we can outnumber them with his own, etc…

"He will be our inside man, so we're not taken off guard like—"

He leaves the sentence unfinished, but we all know what he is referring to.

Like the night we were ambushed, and so many people lost their lives.

"What about Zoya?"

Max shrugs, but that won't do.

"He must ensure she is there. There is no way I'm leaving this earth knowing she still breathes."

"I'll see what I can do."

That is completely inadequate, but I don't press—for now—as I have other issues I need to deal with.

"This happens tonight," I say to Saint. "For this to be believable, you have to react how you would if you weren't privy to this plan."

"I would respond by stabbing you repeatedly," Saint replies blankly.

"What's going on?" Max asks, looking back and forth between us in confusion.

"You don't want to know," Pavel says, uninterested in the theatrics.

"Join the queue," I reply with a smirk.

It flickers for a mere moment, but I see it, and it validates what I've decided to do. Saint looks at me with what appears to be respect instead of contempt. Maybe one day, I'll gain his forgiveness too.

The dinner table is set for a family to feast, but we're anything but a family. The tension is so thick, it can be cut with a knife.

Saint glares at me over the table while Ella doesn't look at me at all. Willow has clued in to Saint's strange behavior, so she hasn't paid much attention to anything else.

Pavel and Max seem distracted too.

Once Pavel finishes his meal, he rises and takes his plate to the sink. He kisses his mother's cheek, thanking her for dinner, but he must return home to see his family. They would likely be sitting around the table if I weren't here because Pavel is smart.

He doesn't involve his family in his mess, unlike me.

Pushing my untouched plate aside, I reach for my scotch instead. I can't stop thinking about Irina. Has she been fed? Bathed? She must be so afraid.

Kicking back my chair, I stand, excusing myself because I can't sit here and eat when I don't know if Irina has. Or been given a glass of water.

It's only when I rise does Ella meet my eyes. I'm confronted with a mixture of anger, confusion, and hurt—emotions because of me. But once this night is through, all that'll be left is anger.

Saint is right. She isn't convinced because I haven't destroyed her completely. She still clings to a small shred of hope because she felt the same connection I did. She knows it was real. She hopes that I'll see that too.

If she leaves, however, then all hope between us is lost. She is a fighter. She doesn't give up, even when she should.

So I need to break her, to convince her that she'll never be enough. But if only she knew…she is more than enough. She is all I want and need, which is why I exit through the back door, needing to put some space between us.

Those hazel eyes will haunt me forever.

The night is warm, but it does nothing to thaw my chill. I continue walking, knowing my way in the dark as I reach the graves. With a frustrated groan, I tug at my hair.

So many people want to save me, which is ironic because I don't want to be saved. Doing this allows me to make amends for all the wrong I've done.

"Alek?" When I hear Willow call out to me, I realize my plan must be set into motion right now.

Ella clearly isn't interested in consoling me, and neither is Saint, which of course leaves Willow. She can't help but be good.

Looking at the grave markers for strength, I hope like hell this doesn't backfire. I can't fail. Ella's safety relies on me hurting her beyond repair.

"Is everything all right?"

"All is well, sweet дорогая. Go back and enjoy your dinner."

"I'm not hungry," she gently disputes.

The foliage rustles with her cautious footsteps. When she comes into view, she pauses, seeing where I'm standing. She and Saint have come out here no doubt, but no matter how many times I see these markers, I'll never accept what they represent either.

"What's wrong? And don't give me your bullshit."

Placing my hands into my pockets, I focus on Zoey's grave. "Very well. You want to know, so I shall tell you. I'm frustrated. Frustrated that my half-brother and mother are still breathing. Frustrated I have to play by their rules. Frustrated I live in a shack in the woods when I once resided in luxury. And I'm frustrated you don't love me as I love you."

Silence.

"But what is most frustrating is that you won't admit you have feelings for me. I'm pleased you've found happiness with Saint, but seeing you together…it never gets any easier," I confess, and thus far, these aren't lies.

With nothing but confidence, I turn to look at her. She's standing a few feet away, ensuring to keep enough distance between us, which is the perfect analogy for our entire relationship.

"I'm sorry I don't feel that way about you, Alek. I just don't."

"I don't buy it," I counter, shaking my head, and this is

where the deception will start.

I don't doubt her claims. I know she loves Saint and only Saint. That's how she loves—with her entire heart. But I can't let that show.

"I think if I were given a proper shot, I could win your heart."

She recoils, horrified. "I don't care what you think. That won't happen. Ever."

"Kiss me then and tell me you don't feel a thing."

"I don't need to kiss you to tell you that," she snaps, eyes narrowed. "Forget I even came out here."

"Ah, but alas, you did, so I can't forget. You can't help coming to my rescue, can you? Why is that?"

Her chest begins to rise and fall quickly. "I don't know," she honestly replies, her frustration coming through. "I should let you rot for all that you've done, but I just can't."

I walk toward her slowly, wishing I could pretend this wasn't real. "Because deep down, you have feelings for me, and you're ashamed. What does that make you, having feelings for the monster who bought you in a poker game?

"You may have yourself fooled, but I know you, дорогая. I always have. I know I can't offer you what I once could, but give me a chance. You never gave me a chance," I say, continuing my death march toward her.

"Alek, you are out of line," she warns, but she's scared, and I like it. It reminds me of a different time when she called me мастер.

"And I don't care." Before she can stop me, I swoop down, capture her cheeks in my palms, and kiss her.

The feel of her lips pressed against me brings back so many wonderful memories. She feels like home. Her smell, the softness of her lips, all of it—I want it back.

But this kiss isn't reciprocated—her kisses never were. They were always stolen, forced, and now is no different. For the first time ever, I wish I was kissing someone other than Willow.

Her lips are slack as she desperately tries to pull away.

I want to be lost in a fruity fragrance and held prisoner by those supple, warm lips. I want that lush body pressed up against mine as she holds my hair and pulls. I want that because she, *Ella*, wants me. She wants to kiss me, and that is the biggest turn-on above all.

My cheek stings—the cheek which Willow just slapped— reminding me that the person I'm kissing doesn't want me, and that's good.

"How dare you!" Willow seethes, wiping her lips with the back of her hand. "You haven't changed. I was so stupid to think that you had."

She turns on her heel, desperate to get away from me, which would usually wound me, but now, I simply smile. That was far too easy, which saddens me in a sense, but it's for the greater good.

Willow will tell Saint of what just occurred, and he will come looking for me, intent on ripping off my head. She'll stop him, though, and he'll back down on the proviso that she stays away from me.

I can still read those two like a book. I guess that's what happens when you've been around people who have seen you at your absolute worse. You begin to think like them.

This ensures Willow's safety as she won't be so inclined to come to my rescue now. Saint will probably insist she stay behind, and she'll respect his wishes because I'm the bastard who defiled her against her wishes.

And it also will hurt Ella enough that she will leave.

A kiss is most sacred, and once she learns I shared one with Willow, her insecurities will get the better of her and she will leave with her pride intact. She will hate me, but that's okay. As long as she's safe, I can go into this with no worries.

Saying a silent goodbye to the three women who will remain forever young, I wish I could say I'll see them soon. But I won't. The big pearly gates are locked.

I slowly walk toward the house as I want to give Saint some time. He has to make it believable, but I'm sure he'll have no problem achieving that when Willow tells him I threw in some tongue, for good measure, of course.

The kiss was lackluster, and I'm ashamed that's the last kiss she'll remember me by, but it was interesting to see how her kisses aren't the ones I crave anymore.

Raised voices catching the still night air confirm our plan has worked. No doubt, Ella has overheard what just transpired, and when the front door bursts open, my suspicions are confirmed. Ella charges down the front stairs, cursing under her breath.

She hasn't seen me yet, so I take a moment to examine her from head to toe.

Her blue dress dips low in the back, revealing she isn't wearing a bra. The hem is short, showcasing those tanned, shapely legs. My cock instantly stirs.

Her wavy hair is down and wild. Her feet are once again bare, and I don't know why, but I like it. Without a doubt, a pair of heels would look luscious on her perfect feet, but seeing her this way, she seems so unguarded, so innocent, which is what I find most appealing because I know she is not.

She comes to a sudden halt when she sees me.

Her hatred is more than clear, but when she charges over and slaps my cheek, she clears up any misgivings I may have. "You son of a bitch!"

Rubbing my cheek, I smirk. "I can't argue there."

"How could you do that? You don't give a flying fuck about anyone but yourself!"

Still rubbing my tender cheek which has been slapped twice in the span of twenty minutes, I repeat, "Again, I can't argue."

"Why would you kiss her when you know she's with Saint?" she inquires, desperate for answers.

I want to backtrack, to forget about this plan and think of another way, but there isn't another way out of this. The only way to make her leave is to push her away. To make her think I don't care.

"Because I want her to be with me," I state with no emotion or regret.

Ella's fury soon simmers, and she takes a step back, appalled by my words. "I was so fucking stupid," she says, shaking her head. "To actually think you cared about me. To actually think you'd pick me."

It takes all my willpower not to drop to my knees and beg

for forgiveness. She is so hurt, and I can barely stand it. So, I turn around and walk away.

However, she thinks I'm dismissing her. "Oh no, you don't."

She grips my elbow, forcing me to spin back around, and before I can say a word, she stands on her toes and slams her mouth over mine. I'm so taken aback by her actions that my lips fall slack, but they soon resuscitate back to life and take everything she gives.

She's angry, biting and pulling, and I take it because I know this is her taking back her independence. She feels a fool for ever being involved with me, and now, she wants me to know she doesn't care anymore. She will use me just as I have her.

The height difference just won't do, so I pick her up, groaning when she wraps her legs around me, positioning her warm sex over my aching cock. I cup the back of her neck, angling her head to dominate the kiss as I know it'll be our last.

And if this will be the last time I taste her, let it be something we'll never forget.

I charge through the yard, desperate to get her somewhere private. This coupling won't be loving or lengthy—it'll be unforgiving and raw.

The only place I can take her is the barn.

Kicking open the door with our lips still fighting for dominance, I slam her up against the wooden wall, relishing in the grunt that leaves her.

Her frantic fingers work at my buttons, but they grow

impatient and she tears my shirt open, the insolent buttons scattering all the over the barn floor. Her fingernails rake down my chest, a sated moan leaving her as she tugs at the curls near my navel which extend into my pants.

Using my weight to keep her pressed to the wall, I reach under her dress and rub over the front of her underwear. It pleases me that she's already wet. I need to be inside her because whenever we're locked this way, I can almost forget the dire future which awaits me.

Without regret, I tear her underwear off and unfasten the button on my pants. My zipper soon follows. With my pants around my ankles, I lift her and slam her onto my erection. She cries out, severing our kiss as she gulps in mouthfuls of air.

The way she nibbles on her lower lip does things to me it shouldn't, and I need to move. "Wrap your arms around me, красавица."

She does as I order, eyes locked with mine as I thrust into her, holding her hips and encouraging her to bounce against me. Our bodies move in unison, but they always have. I yank down a strap of her dress, freeing her pert breast.

Her nipple is erect; so pink, so perfect.

I lower my head, taking it into my mouth as I continue sinking into her heat. She throws back her head, squeezing her muscles tight, so tight that I almost come. But I rein it in. This is about Ella. This is about her taking back control.

She lifts her hips, then slams back down, taking me deep. She fists the hair at my nape, moaning when I suckle her entire breast into my mouth. I want to consume every hot inch of her. My hips pump hard, fast, and by the groans slipping past her parted mouth, she likes the aggression.

Her glorious peach-shaped ass bounces against me in the most delicious of ways. I wish I had more time with her. I'd punish that ass, and she'd like it because she isn't bashful in the bedroom. She gives as good as she gets, and that applies to all aspects of her life.

How I'll miss her.

The thought surprises me because it isn't until now that I've come to realize just how much I will miss her.

"I hate you," she cries out, locking her legs around my back to tighten the already vise-like grip between us.

"I know."

"This means nothing."

"Of course not."

But we're not fooling anyone.

"You're nothing but the past," she gasps, rocking against me fiercely.

This is what I wanted to hear, but it still doesn't alleviate the tightening in my chest.

"I won't even remember your name."

But the tears that well in her eyes tell me otherwise.

I can't stand it, so I kiss her, wishing I could erase the pain I've caused. However, knowing she will live a full life without me in it makes all of this worthwhile.

Her body vibrates around me, and the slapping of her flesh against mine is so primitive, I realize she is the first woman I've ever shown my true self to. She has accepted me, flaws and all, and some may even say, she loved me regardless.

I don't know what I feel for her. Love? Lust? Obsession? I don't know. I don't like labels because love comes in many shapes and forms. What I do know is that she's changed my life for the better, and if things were different, I think what we have could grow into something beyond love.

Love seems so basic a description for how I feel.

She bites my lip, her tongue sweeping it after the sting. She drives me crazy.

I devour her mouth as I own her body, and with two quick thrusts, hitting her deep, she shudders, coming with a satisfied moan. Her trembling grips my cock tight, so I lift her and frantically move her up and down my length until, with a strangled cry, I pull out and explode onto the outside of her bare pussy.

She's breathless with unstable legs, so I coax her to lock them around me. We're sticky, my arousal coupled with hers, but as she nuzzles into my neck and holds me close, it's clear there is no place we'd rather be for now—because come morning, she'll be gone.

CHAPTER FIFTEEN

I wake from a peaceful slumber, the most peaceful I've had in months, which is ironic because I know what the day brings. The floorboards creak as I slowly come into a sitting position. I don't need to look at the bed to know Ella is gone.

The room is empty without her.

Her scent lingers in the air, but it won't be long until it disappears, and all I'll be left with are memories of the woman who shook my world in ways I never anticipated.

Last night, she detangled herself from my arms and said nothing as she came back into the house. I gave her some time, and when I entered the bedroom, she had fallen asleep. I didn't want to wake her, so I took refuge on my makeshift bed on the floor.

I wanted to say so many things to her, like please don't go. I was wrong. But a world doesn't exist where she and I can be together. Santo won't stop looking for her, and I can't be the reason she stays here in Russia.

My phone rings, and when I see the caller is private, a sense of dread fills me.

"Hello."

"Hello, Brother."

His voice provokes so much violence in me that I need a moment to catch my breath. "Do not refer to me as that, please."

He chuckles in response. "Are we all ready for tomorrow?"

Gritting my teeth, I reply, "You'll get your deed. I want to talk to Irina."

"When will you realize you're not the one calling the shots anymore?"

"That will never happen," I affirm. "Put Irina on. Now."

Serg doesn't reply, and when I hear muffled voices in the background, I think he's going to comply. But then he does something which just has me wishing I could kill him a thousand different ways because once will never be enough.

"Hello, Aleksei."

Her voice is like a punch to my stomach, bringing forward memories I wish I could forget.

"I have nothing I wish to say to you...*Mother*." But of course, Zoya doesn't listen.

"How are you?"

I very rarely curse, as there are far more powerful words in the English and Russian language, but in this circumstance, I break my rule.

"How the fuck do you think I am? Your spawn is

blackmailing me and holding a little girl hostage to satisfy his sick and demented ways. Where is Irina?"

She clears her throat. Was she actually expecting a happy reunion? "I never wanted this."

"I couldn't care less what you want," I counter angrily.

"You forced his hand, Alek. You killed his"—sniff—"father. Boris was a good man. But you took him away from us."

And cue the tears.

I've heard this story one too many times, and as it was since I last heard it, I'm unmoved.

"My *father* was a good man. Boris was an asshole who deserved everything he got."

"You don't realize how much I suffered because of your actions." She ignores me, instead playing the blame game. "I was left a single mom, yet again."

"I'm sure you found some poor fool who fell for your sob story."

"I know I did wrong. I'm not perfect, but I tried—"

"You tried what?" I interrupt, not interested in hearing excuses. "You didn't try too hard to protect me from your beloved Boris. Nor did you try hard enough all these years to resemble anything of a mother figure.

"Instead, you nurtured a diabolical sociopath and showed more affection toward Astra than your own offspring. I have her necklace. Thank you for leaving that for me."

"She had nothing!" she cries, like that's supposed to warrant her actions. "You were always strong and independent. You didn't need me. You're the one who abandoned me."

"I've heard enough," I snap, uninterested in her melodramatics.

"No matter what you've done, I still don't want to see you hurt."

"That ship has sailed." I don't know why she feels the need to unburden her soul after so long. Then a thought occurs to me.

Renata.

Renata's hatred was the only real thing to her story. Could it be mother dearest is feeling like the third wheel? Is she afraid Renata will get to Serg, leaving her out in the cold? This deal makes Serg a very rich man. And money is the only thing that motivates Zoya.

Is she really trying to come to some sort of a truce? Does she believe I'm her fallback in case her castle comes crumbling to the ground?

If only she knew what I have planned for her.

"I miss you," she whispers, sickening me.

"Okay, that's more than enough," I say, irritated. "Put Irina on the phone."

"I've looked after her. You need not worry."

"That's *why* I'm worried," I dispute.

Thankfully, she gets the very blunt hint and ends this painful conversation. But all pain is amplified tenfold when Irina's frightened voice sounds over the phone.

"Ski?"

Taking a moment to compose myself, I steady my voice as she wants strength from me, to confirm that everything will be all right.

"Yes, Irina, it's Ski. Are you all right?"

All I can hear are her sniffles.

"I'm coming to get you," I promise her in Russian.

"When?"

And tomorrow suddenly feels like a lifetime.

"Today. I'm coming today. Okay, цветочек?"

"Okay," she whispers. "Irina scared."

"I know you're scared. Have they…hurt you?" I clench my fist against my thigh.

"Yes…scared of dark."

I suddenly can't breathe at the thought of her being hurt. What have they done to her? And dark? Have they locked her in the dark? This just confirms what I've always known—Zoya is full of lies.

"You've been so brave. I just need you to be brave for a little while longer. I'll see you soon." I try not to let my fear show.

"Brave for Ski," she says while I can't find the right words to articulate how much I love her.

"Happy?" Serg snaps, taking the phone from Irina.

"I want this done today. Now," I demand because this can't wait. Irina cannot spend another night in the dark. I won't allow it.

"Suits me just fine. I'm presuming you intercepted your дорогая, seeing as she wasn't where she said she was going to be."

I don't confirm or deny anything.

"That means you have help," he angrily says. "But if you don't want your precious Irina hurt, you'll come alone and unarmed. We clear? I'll know if you get any smart ideas. But you won't. That's your downfall. You care.

"When you were ruthless, you were untouchable. Now, you're nothing but a neutered puppy. Pathetic."

I'll show him who's pathetic when they're begging for their life at my feet.

"I'll text you details as soon as it's arranged."

"Make it quick," I snap, before hanging up with a growl.

Squeezing the cell in my hand, it splinters, threatening to crack under the force.

I know what I've just done, but I don't care. Mother Superior has emailed the deed. It's all I need.

Jumping up, I quickly get dressed and exit the bedroom, in search of Pavel. He's in the kitchen, helping Larisa put away some groceries. When he sees me, he understands the dire circumstance I've put myself in.

"I'm meeting with Serg today."

Pavel puts away the last can of tomatoes before addressing me. "Are you fucking mad?"

I shrug as it depends on who you ask.

"This isn't enough time, Alek. Raul can't pull this off in a matter of hours." He expresses my thoughts aloud, but I knew what I was getting myself into when I made this deal.

"If he can't, then I will accept the consequences. But I will not leave Irina there a second longer than I have to. She is scared. They've kept her in the dark. I can't allow her to suffer any longer because of me."

"You know what this means? With no backup, you'll have to go alone. We can't risk our lives. Not again," he adds, and I understand completely.

This has happened before. We were lucky to escape with our lives because others weren't.

Serg said he wants me to suffer, that he won't kill me, but that won't be an option once I come face-to-face with him. It'll be either him or me, and when I bait him with how I took pleasure basking in his father's blood, he'll snap.

The odds are against me, but it's a gamble I'm willing to take.

"I know. I would never ask that of you. But you must promise me, if something happens to me, you won't allow that monster to take the orphanage from Mother Superior."

"How am I to make such a promise?" Pavel questions, distraught.

"I don't know, but better that place burns to the ground than be subjected to the depravity Serg intends to inflict on them."

Pavel blew my house to the ground. He can manage this.

He nods once, displeased, but he will do what he must.

"This is worst-case scenario," I remind him. "Raul will make it happen. I'm sure of it. My head on a silver platter? He will move heaven and earth for that opportunity."

Pavel reaches into his pocket, retrieving his cell. "I'll make some calls."

He leaves the room, leaving me alone with Larisa who peers at me with a look on her face I can't quite place. She doesn't say anything, which has me wondering what she's thinking. She's not one to shy away from her thoughts, but now, she seems lost to them.

"What's up?" Saint walks into the kitchen, interrupting a weird moment I don't have time to decipher.

"I'm meeting Serg today. I have the deed. I won't wait, leaving Irina in his hands."

He nods, scratching over his tattooed chest. His tattoos are a part of him, reflecting his sins, but also, baring his integrity.

"Pavel is making a few calls. Raul may not be able to pull this off in time. So I'll go alone," I state bluntly.

Saint's fingers pause over the scroll across his chest. The inscription seems fitting.

Only God Can Judge Me.

"You do that, you'll die."

"I know. But that was going to happen regardless."

However, when Saint looks down at his bare feet, I realize we're not on the same page. We're not even reading from the same book.

"This self-sacrifice shit is fucking moronic."

"What's that supposed to mean?" I ask, genuinely confused.

"It means, I couldn't, in good faith, hand you over like a pig to slaughter." When I continue staring at him, lost in translation, he explains, annoyed. "I would have tried to get you out of there. But now, we're fucked."

Saint's nobility shouldn't surprise me, but it does. He would attempt to help me even after everything I've done. That shows what a good man he truly is.

"Thank you. I appreciate the sentiment. I honestly do. But I'll do what I must to get Irina back. Serg believes I won't fight, but he's wrong. The last thing I do will be to rob him of his final breath."

Saint nods, pleased with my choice of violence.

"However, Pavel knows what to do if I fail. Serg cannot take that orphanage. I know I don't deserve to ask this of you, but please ensure Mother Superior, the sisters, and the children are safe.

"He has leverage over me, and I know that makes me weak and pathetic, but I will do anything to get Irina back."

Saint folds his arms across his chest, eyeing me closely. "This could have been over with if you'd just handed Ella over to Santo. Her life for yours."

I clench my jaw, barely reining in my temper. "I would never do that to her. *Never*."

Saint's lips twist into a resemblance of a smile, which seems inappropriate as this isn't a time to be smiling. "Holy shit. I never thought I'd see the day."

"See what?" I question.

"See you being human."

I'm taken aback by his comment. But what he says next stuns me.

"I'll come with you. Regardless if Raul comes through or not."

"No, I will not permit it," I argue firmly, shaking my head.

"Well, guess what? I don't give a fuck what you permit," he replies with a carefree shrug of his broad shoulders.

This is unheard of. Two enemies, working together? I

believed he had no qualms about handing me over to Raul, but it appears I know nothing at all.

"This doesn't make us friends," he snaps, disgusted at the notion.

"Of course not," I scoff as that would be ridiculous. "How angry is she?"

Saint smirks. "She hates your fucking guts."

"Excellent. Our plan worked then. You do realize she'll hate yours too once she finds out what we did," I say with a smirk of my own.

"I know," he replies, already envisioning the wrath coming his way. "I'm gonna hit the shower."

Nodding, I'm about to go outside but am surprised when Larisa offers me a cup of coffee. Usually, I would expect her to throw it in my face, but not today.

Accepting with a cautious smile, I peer inside, wondering if she slipped in a fatal dose of arsenic. When she notices my hesitation, she laughs.

Another first.

I want to ask her what's going on because first with Saint and now Larisa, I'm confused why the people who hate me seem to not hate me as much.

"Your pain has made you wise," she says in Russian. I listen intently, mesmerized by what she'll say next. "But I still don't like you."

Unable to hold back a smile, I raise my coffee in salute. I'll take it.

I drink my coffee in silence, comforted by Larisa's words. I know I've changed, but that doesn't erase all the things I've done. I've hurt every person who's currently helping me. I don't fail to see the importance in that.

Pavel reenters, blowing out an exhale. "It's happening. Raul's in."

I now understand his relief. "I knew it," I express happily even though this cup of coffee will be the last morning coffee I'll ever have.

Going into this, I now know Raul will permit my revenge before he inflicts his own. An eye for an eye.

He might double-cross me, but I don't think he will because the stakes are too high. If he lets Serg know of my plans, he risks Serg ending me and not him. And when it comes to revenge, the need to see it out yourself is enough to have you bending in ways you normally wouldn't.

"Raul's going to make contact with Serg and find out where we're to meet. Raul said he's only willing to provide ten men. This makes me think Serg doesn't expect you to fight, therefore, security shouldn't be too tight."

"Ten men? That's more than I thought he'd offer. You can all stay here. I'll be fine on my own."

Pavel shakes his head. "We're coming. You want your revenge on Serg as much as we do. He is also to blame for the deaths of our friends. Of Sara. This is personal to Max as well. And the fact he wants to endanger Mother Superior; I want to see this asshole suffer. It'll give me great satisfaction."

Of course, this is personal to them. I won't deny their right to purge.

"You go in, act like it's business as usual, and then once Irina is safe, we're going to storm that motherfucker. Serg is so arrogant that he won't see us coming. He believes he has the upper hand because of your attachment to Irina.

"I also believe killing you isn't in the cards for him. Making you suffer is far more satisfying, and seeing as he's endured a lifetime of suffering because of what you did to his father, he sees this as the best form of payback."

Pavel is right. I'm glad we agree on this.

"And this arrogance is what will get him killed," I assure. "Zoya and Renata will follow the same fate."

"Killing your brother and his pet is one thing, but your mother—"

"She stopped being my mother a long time ago," I rebuke firmly. "She is merely a stranger who chose the wrong side. Don't ever question my hatred again."

I don't mean to snap, but thinking of her pathetic attempts to con me anger me fiercely.

Pavel grins. A rare occurrence for this man. "Your leadership still runs through those veins. If we're able to get you out alive, you do realize we'll just replace Serg with Raul and Santo. Raul will be out for blood because we double-crossed him. As will Santo when he realizes you've lied to him."

"I know, but let's just think about getting Irina out safely, and then I'll handle everything else accordingly."

The truth is, I plan on going with Serg. I'm sure he is prepared for any scenario. Although no one knows of my newfound understanding with Saint, Pavel, and Max, I'm sure Raul has his suspicions that they're not just doing this for the orphanage.

I thought they were, but now I see they're also doing it to save me, and it's because of this that I refuse to put them in danger. If they help me, they'll be looking over their shoulders for the rest of their lives. Pavel has a wife and kids. Saint, Willow, and Max have suffered enough by my hand.

I thought I wanted Serg dead so I could regain my kingdom, but the truth is, the thought of going back to who I once was isn't as appealing as I expected it to be. I know this is the coward's way out, but I'm just so exhausted.

The thought of having to build my empire again, the people I'll have to exploit to get there, I just don't want to be that person anymore.

"If anything were to happen to me, you know what to do with the money?"

Thanks to Santo, my bank account looks rather portly, but that money is to be divided between Mother Superior and the account Pavel set up for Ella.

"Who is she now?" I forgot to ask her who she'll become to escape me.

"Alexandra Bianco."

I nod with a smile, liking the similarities our names bear.

"You did a noble thing, Alek," Pavel says. "She's safe and will live a long life because of you."

I don't ask him if she boarded the plane okay. If there were any problems, he would have let me know. She's away from this hellhole, and that's all that matters.

Saint enters, and I can tell by the look on his face that something is about to happen. That something is Willow Shaw.

"I'm coming with you."

Saint shrugs when I arch a brow at him.

"It took me a while, but I figured it out. You'd do anything to save me, save Ella, and the only way to do that was to make us hate you."

She's too smart for her own good.

Willow's feelings aren't involved, but Ella's were. She didn't see her worth because I never fully showed her. Being vulnerable is something I've only ever done once before, and to go through that again…I can't. A once feared ruler, I was nothing but an inexperienced little boy when it came to love.

I decide then and there that when the time is right, I will ask something of Willow which only she can deliver.

"Saint?" I pose, but he looks as powerless as I feel.

"This isn't Saint's decision," she states, not appreciating me insinuating he had any hope of stopping her. "I won't fight. But who will keep Irina safe?"

She makes a good point, and Saint agrees with me, which is why he doesn't argue.

"Once she's returned to us, I'll drive her back here. Saint told me what you're going to do, and that'll mean you'll need Irina far away from those men. Nothing will stop Serg from using her again once he realizes he's been double-crossed.

"And I fear she won't leave there alive. He knows how much that'll hurt you, and he'll be desperate once Raul arrives."

She's sold me. I don't want her there, but we all know we can't stop Willow. If this is the compromise she offers, then I'll accept it.

The front door opens, and from the alcove in the kitchen

we see Max. He doesn't waste any time. "The deal is happening at Raul's house. Can you believe it?"

No, I honestly can't.

"Serg couldn't contain his excitement it seems, bragging how he had finally won. Raul convinced him the deal should happen at a safe location, in case you had backup, which Serg already knows. So he agreed when Raul suggested his home as a suitable meeting point.

"Raul said Serg will only have three men with him as Raul has offered his men as protection."

Saint curses under his breath. We both know what this means.

Any hopes he had of getting me out alive have just been dashed. We're playing by Raul's rules in his arena. We don't stand a chance, and he's done this to ensure we don't outsmart him as we've done to Serg.

"Excellent. What time?"

Saint exhales, turning his cheek to look anywhere but at me.

"Eight o'clock. Serg will text soon, thinking he has the advantage of you not knowing the location. Serg doesn't want you dead but has allowed Raul to have his fun with you for payment for his hospitality."

"You told him Zoya and Renata were also included in this transaction?"

Max nods. "He doesn't give a damn who you kill. As long as you suffer the same fate, it's free rein."

Willow pales, tugging at the crucifix at her throat. "No, Alek. If you go along with this plan, you die."

She's expressed what no one else is brave enough to say.

"It's a situation I've faced before, but this time, there is no lifeline. Promise me, all of you that when the time comes, you allow Raul his revenge. If not, he will hunt you and those you love and won't stop until you're all dead."

Pavel clenches his jaw. As does Saint. But the man who was the best right-hand man I could ever ask for is the first to end this once and for all.

"I promise."

Willow's eyes fill with tears. She most likely is reliving the past because she was faced with this decision once before. "I can't make that promise," she whispers, looking at Saint, shamefully.

But he simply reaches out and caresses her cheek. How can he scold her humanity?

Pavel and Max pledge as well.

"Very well. Then I shall await what's coming my way."

CHAPTER SIXTEEN

I used to take the simple act of securing a tie for granted. It was something I did almost daily, never fully appreciating the elegance of a fine suit and polished shoes. It was a part of me.

But now, looking at my reflection in the mirror, I wish I'd worn more suits, crisper shirts, different colored ties because these simple pleasures are ones I will no longer be privy to.

I drove into town, which I haven't done in a very long time, seeing as I was a fugitive, but now that my enemies know where I am, I got fitted for the finest suit. I also purchased a pair of Italian leather shoes. No expense spared. If I'm about to welcome death, I want it to be in my Sunday best.

Once my suit was zipped up in the garment bag, I went to the barber. I got a haircut and shave—straight razor of course. When I was shown my reflection, I was transported to a time when I was ruler of this town. But what I did next proved that

I'm no longer that man.

I've never been interested in tattoos, but when I walked past the tattoo studio, I knew before I left this plane, I had to get a tattoo in honor of my time on this earth.

A simple praying hands outline is now tattooed onto the back of my left arm. Even though I've forsaken my God long ago, it honors Mother Superior and Ella. The symbolism gives me the strength to face the inevitable.

I came back here, showered and dressed. My suit is a three-piece navy pinstripe. My black shoes are polished to perfection. The blue striped silk tie and matching pocket square complement the pressed white shirt wonderfully.

Slipping into my vest, I fasten the buttons calmly. Then I pat myself down and smile. I look good.

Serg sent word about an hour ago, unbeknownst that I was already aware of his plan. I replied with a simple:

`I'll be there.`

My hair is styled how I once wore it. I'm now clean-shaven. There is only one last thing I need.

Reaching for the gold ring, I slip it onto my pinkie finger with pride. Twirling it with my pointer and thumb, I realize the feeling that's roaring through me is excitement, not fear.

Although my life ends tonight, knowing Serg's does as well makes the sacrifice so much sweeter. Raul knows I wish to take my time with him because there is no way his death will be quick.

Oh yes, this is going to get messy.

Putting on my jacket, I tuck the envelope into my pocket, one which has Willow's name penned with care on the front. I've written a letter to Ella, and hope when the time is right, Willow will send it to her.

I can't leave this earth knowing she'll never know the truth. I want her to know she meant something to me and explain why I chose to do what I did. I'm not asking for forgiveness, merely wishing her to know that if things were different, I'd never have let her leave.

Adjusting my already straight tie, I take a deep breath, ready to face whatever comes my way. Taking one last look at the bedroom, I close the door and make my way down the hall. When I enter the living room, it looks like everyone standing around waiting is getting ready for a funeral.

I appreciate the sentiment, but there's no need for the somber mood. I'll march into death with a smile on my face.

"Let's go," I instruct, not wanting to draw this out.

Willow's eyes are cast downward, and a lifetime ago, I'd be pleased with her submission, but it's not necessary now.

This isn't her fault. She can't save me this time. No one can. I know Saint. He'll try, but with home ground advantage, Raul will win.

Larisa comes hobbling out of the kitchen, drying her arthritic hands on a dishcloth. She kisses Pavel's cheek, praying to Saint Christopher to keep him safe. I'm about to leave, but she stops me.

"Семь раз отмерь, один раз отрежь."

Larisa is a wise woman, and this proverb describes this situation perfectly.

Measure seven times, cut once. She is warning me to prepare accordingly before I do this because I only have one chance. If I walk out the door, there's no turning back.

But my mind is made up.

Nodding in gratitude, I reply in Russian. Not exactly poetic, but they're words I'm proud to leave as my legacy.

She appears stone-faced until a small smile, the first smile she's ever given me, spreads across her lips.

What I said is that the first pancake is always lumpy. I thought Larisa would like this proverb, seeing as she loves to cook. But the meaning behind it can be applied to me.

I failed miserably at my first attempt to be human, but that didn't stop me from trying to better myself. I never gave up, regardless of my first lumpy pancake. And that's thanks to the people standing in this room.

Putting my hands together, I nod in gratitude to Larisa. A kiss and hug are too personal, and we're not there yet. She nods back.

Without drawing out a long goodbye, I walk out the door, patting the black Labrador standing guard on the front porch. The lights on my SUV shine as I press the remote to unlock it. I've decided to leave the car to Mother Superior.

The sisters have some ancient van they drive when they need to go to town. At least they can ride in comfort now.

Taking off my jacket and placing it onto the back of my seat, I get into the car, expecting no passengers, but the door opens, and Willow jumps into the passenger seat. I look over my shoulder, expecting to see Saint, but it seems she's riding shotgun alone. I don't make a fuss as I begin our hour drive to Raul's.

She's quiet for a long while, content with Bach as our background music. She's in here to ambush me. I know how she works. She's going to try with everything she's got to change my mind. But my mind is made up.

"You look how I remember you," she says, breaking the silence.

"Ah, yes, but am I the same man?" I ask, keeping my eyes on the road.

"No, I don't think that you are. Ella left thinking you didn't have feelings for her, didn't she?"

"Yes."

Willow sighs, clearly unhappy with my decision. But Ella is stubborn, just as she is. The only reason Willow wasn't fooled is because she knows me. Ella and I were just at the beginning of something utterly beautiful…

"She's good for you, Alek. If—"

But I intercede. "Let's not talk of things we cannot change. What's done is done."

"What's done is that you're hours away from dying," she states, brushing some hair behind her ear.

"Death is merely a part of living. I've accepted my fate. You must too."

"You don't deserve it," she says in an almost whisper.

"Deserve what?"

She waits a moment before declaring, "To die. Not this way."

I'm touched because coming from her, that means a lot. If anyone should wish death upon me, it should be her. But even after everything I've done, she still doesn't want me dead. She didn't want me dead that fateful evening either and tried so hard to save me.

And she did. She *has*—time and time again.

"Someone like my ex-husband deserves that fate."

Oh, I'd forgotten about that inept asshole.

So cocky, so smug, but when he lost a game of poker and I ensured he wasn't leaving until he paid up, his cowardice shone. I'm a man of my word, and when you play a game, there is no backing out. You see it through.

I honestly didn't believe he'd deliver, and I would have taken great satisfaction in killing him. In hindsight, I should have. It would have saved Willow this entire ordeal.

But he delivered.

Willow was just an innocent pawn in our game.

"Whatever happened to that waste of space?" I ask, genuinely curious.

"I paid him a visit once my life resembled some sense of normalcy. I needed to ensure I was in the right frame of mind."

"To?" I prompt, risking a quick glance at her.

"To fuck up his life," she replies with a laugh. "You should have seen his face. Priceless. I took everything that mattered to him and forced him to disappear just as he did to me.

"I was happy with that outcome, but Saint wasn't."

No surprises there.

"Last I heard, he's a hermit, living in some remote part of Scotland. The villagers call him Pinocchio."

"Why?" I ask, thoroughly enjoying this story.

"Because after Saint…bit off his nose and broke every bone in his body, he now walks with a wooden limp. He went to the worst plastic surgeon in Hollywood and got a nose job, which, well, looks like Pinocchio."

I can't control my laughter, which has Willow joining in. It feels nice to laugh with her. What a gift she's left me with.

But she soon stops, and I know why. "Please don't do this, Alek. We'll think of something else."

"You can't fix it this time."

She sniffs because this remarkable woman is shedding tears for me. "Save your tears, дорогая. I'm okay."

I don't know why, but she doesn't press. The resolve in my voice maybe. Or maybe she knows that I speak the truth. There's no saving me this time.

As we ascend Raul's driveway, my stomach begins to churn for so many reasons. I just want Irina out of here before I can focus on anything else.

I park the car, looking at Willow who peers at the huge white mansion in front of us. I take this moment to examine her closely as it'll be the last time I witness her beauty—inside and out. She has changed me in the best possible way.

I wish I could offer her something more, but I can't. "Goodbye, дорогая." There isn't anything I can say that'll ever explain how much she means to me.

The moon allows me to see the moisture in her eyes, but

she quickly wipes it away with the back of her hand.

Opening the door, I reach for my jacket and put it on. Willow gets out also and walks to my side of the car.

"I don't know what to say," she whispers, her hair catching the breeze, allowing me to bask in her sweet scent one last time.

"Then let's say nothing at all." Opening my arms, I welcome her for one last embrace.

She's apprehensive, which is to be expected, but by the power of all that's mighty, she steps closer and wraps her arms around me with a small sigh.

At first, I leave my arms out wide, feeling undeserving of her offering, but when she snuggles closer, I surrender...to her...like I always have.

I hug her tight, and the way she fits in my arms shows me that no matter what happens, a part of her will always belong to me. And a part of me will always belong to her.

I've wasted so much time. I wish I had more of it, but I don't, so I cautiously reach into my pocket for the envelope and slip it into the pocket of Willow's jacket. I hope she doesn't find it right away.

Laying a kiss on the crest of her head, I gently pull away before I don't ever let her go.

She allows her tears to fall this time, and I appreciate each one. How lucky am I to have someone like Willow Shaw shed tears over me?

"Everything all right?" Saint wraps his arm low on Willow's waist, kissing her temple.

She nods, quickly brushing her tears away. "Yup. I'll wait

in the car."

She gives me one last look, and it's enough. I'm forgiven, completely. She's allowed me to unburden my sins with her clemency.

When she's in the car, Saint runs a hand through his long hair. He's frustrated, but I don't want him to be. "Raul will let us know when Irina is out of harm's way. We'll be in right after that."

Nodding, I button my jacket, ready to get this show on the road. "Are you sure we can trust him?" he asks one final time.

"When you had the opportunity to seek revenge on the man who sold Willow to me, did anything else matter?" I pose, circling back to what Willow revealed in the car.

Saint snarls, his eyes sparking to life under the moonlight. "No."

"Alas, my friend, there's your answer." Revenge will send a man blind to anything but it.

"Okay. See you soon," he says, satisfied.

I walk a few steps away but turn over my shoulder and smirk. "Pinocchio? Fucking...*A*?" I say with uncertainty because this is the first time I've used this strange phrase. But it's one Saint uses often, so I thought it was appropriate to use to show my approval on what he did.

And when he smirks in return, it seems he approves too.

Max and Pavel nod when I walk past them. There is no need to converse. We know what needs to be done. I walk up to the front door and press the doorbell. A beautiful woman in a red cheongsam dress opens it.

Chow was of Chinese descent, and his wife, Raul's mother, is Spanish. Raul has always favored his Chinese heritage more so because he is or *was* a daddy's boy.

The woman gestures I'm to enter as she rearms a very high-tech alarm system.

The foyer is impressive to say the least. Decked out in an oriental theme of reds and golds with dragon paintings on the walls, I would admire my surroundings if not for the fact the homeowner wants me dead.

I follow my escort, my awe at the decorations dissipating and giving way to this urgency to see Irina and get her out of here. We turn a corner, and when I enter a large dining hall, all time stands still. Serg stands a few feet away, arms behind his back, smiling happily.

Renata stands to his left. When she sees me, her slender throat bobs as she swallows. She's nervous. *Good*. She should be.

Three men stand in different corners of the room. Raul was right. Serg has underestimated me because he doesn't know what's in store for him.

Serg is under the impression I don't know who lives here. Since I've been an outsider for a long time, he assumes I don't know who the main game players are. How wrong he is.

Serg may be considered attractive to some. With dark hair and blue eyes, he clearly ticks all the boxes for Renata, but to me, all I see is a little snotty-nosed brat still suckling at his mother's teat. The suit he wears looks ridiculous. It's all white. He clearly missed the memo that he isn't Tony Montana.

However, I need to keep my cool.

One of his men frisks me, nodding when he doesn't find any weapons. "He's clean, boss. His friends are outside, but they're not coming in. This place is like a fort."

It seems rather unbelievable that I didn't bring my "friends." Serg already knows I intercepted Saint and Willow. If I were to leave them behind, he'd begin to question if I had plans of them storming the home later on because he saw what they did for me that night all those months ago.

"Where's Irina?" I demand, annoyed he's still breathing.

Serg clucks his tongue. "Where are your manners? Not even a hello?"

Refusing to entertain him, I remain quiet, which annoys him as I won't play his games.

"I didn't think you'd be so eager to hand your precious orphanage over to me. The buzz about the place is really incredible."

So help me God…

But I can't let him win.

"You're no fun," he whines, and I curl my lip, disgusted this idiot is the new "me."

Now that I see Renata again, I realize she was a poor substitute for Willow. She can only wish to be like her.

"Stop looking at my property," Serg spits, yanking Renata into his side. I can't help but see Zoey in her. I don't feel sorry for her, however. I feel sorry for Zoey and the way I treated her.

Zoey was smart enough to see me for the monster that I am. I doubt Renata will ever do the same with Serg.

If he wants to continue with these playground antics, I'll

show him.

Rubbing my thumb across my lower lip, I hum as if remembering a memory. "Your property tasted like warm honey."

Renata's cheeks redden in embarrassment. Serg's enraged. "Shut your mouth!" he sneers. "You haven't touched her."

"Ah, on the contrary," I refute with a smirk. "There isn't a part of her that I haven't touched."

"He's lying!" Renata cries, begging Serg to believe her.

But he won't.

He isn't angry because he cares for Renata, but rather, he is angry someone touched what he sees as nothing but chattel. Irony at its best as he is the one who ordered her to seduce me.

"That little strawberry-shaped birth mark on her right breast—" I bite my bottom lip, shaking my head. "Exquisite."

He is seething because for me to know such an intimate detail about Renata, I would have had to see her naked. With a sharp jerk of his head, one of his goons comes out of nowhere and sucker punches me in the stomach.

Buckling in half, I inhale steadily, catching my breath. I welcome the pain because it's confirmation that I'm getting to Serg.

Clutching my side, I slowly rise, smirking. If this is the best he can do, I'm sorely disappointed.

"Get on your knees and show me you're sorry," he orders Renata as he unzips his pants. She jumps to his command, dropping immediately in front of him.

Once his flaccid cock plops from his pants, I can't contain my laughter. "Oh, малышка, you're going to have to get closer than that," I mock, thoroughly amused.

Serg, however, isn't entertained by my small dick jokes and grips Renata by the back of her head, forcing his length down her throat.

We both gag.

With his hand on the back of Renata's head, he glares at me like he has something to prove. She steadies herself by clutching his upper thighs. The sight is disgusting, and only has me anticipating his death.

With a staged yawn, I look down at my Rolex. If he is trying to prove a point or assert his dominance, he has missed the mark—by miles. He forgets who I once was; who I associated myself with. Just like everything he's done with his life, this is an amateur move.

No matter how hard Renata works, it'll never be enough. He pushes her forehead with a frustrated grunt, sending her toppling backward. She wipes her lips sheepishly and remains on her knees as he hurriedly does up his fly. He then pats his thigh, where she slowly shuffles over, coming to a rest at his side like the good lapdog he's trained her to be.

Pushing away the memories which will forever haunt me of Zoey at my feet, I place my hands into my pockets, coolly. "Let's get this over with."

Serg's stunt backfired, which left him with his dick in hand—literally, so he nods, needing to reassert his power.

Retrieving my cell, I ask him, "What's your email?"

Mother Superior's lawyer organized the deed to be signed electronically in an encrypted document. I just need to email him the deed and give him the passcode, and Irina is free.

When he tells me what it is, I go to my email, realizing this starts now. Once I send this, there'll be no turning back. But that was never a question.

Without hesitation, I type in his address and press send. He reaches into his jacket pocket when his cell chimes.

He looks up once he's opened the email. "Passcode?"

With a smirk, I reply, "Иди на хуй."

A snigger sounds behind me from one of Serg's goons, but Serg clearly doesn't see the funny side. The password is fitting, it's *go fuck yourself.*

He scrolls through the document before typing in an address of his own. "Just sending it to my lawyer. I wouldn't want to sign my life away."

Joke's on him, though. His life is inching closer and closer to slipping away from him.

"He shouldn't take too long. While we wait, would you like a refreshment?"

"No, I don't want a refreshment," I reply bluntly.

"That's a shame," he says, shaking his head with a grin. "The owner of this lovely abode has some very fine Baijiu. You do know what Baijiu is, right? It's to China what vodka is to Russia."

I know where he is going with this, laying out clues like breadcrumbs, but I have to play along. Raul warned Max I was to be surprised; otherwise, Serg will clue in, and then the deal is off.

"Owner? Whose house is this?" I ask, faking surprise as I frantically look around the room for clues.

"You didn't think I'd actually invite you into my home,

did you?"

"I don't know. You're pretty damn stupid, so…" I reply with a shrug.

He doesn't appreciate my quip, nor does he like the fact I'm not trembling in his presence, which is why he claps once and smiles when his "surprise" enters the room.

Raul looks like Chinese royalty in his gold tang suit. The dragons embodied in the fabric look fierce; they look like they're about to eat me alive, which seems fitting because when I meet Raul's eyes, it's clear that's what he intends to do to me.

The similarities to his father are uncanny. His dark hair is slicked back, and he has the same Fu Manchu mustache Chow was notorious for. Both are, or were, proud of their heritage, so seeing Raul in this setting has me thankful I dressed up too. I wouldn't want to be sent to my death in rags.

I was renowned for being the Russian mafia boss with a taste for expensive, pretty things, so I'm glad I'll be remembered that way when I take my final breath as Raul will announce to his friends and foes that he was the one who ruined Aleksei Popov, not Serg.

Like all nostalgic killers, he'll take photos, maybe even a memento from my corpse to always remember the feeling of killing the man who ruined his life.

But now, I have to ensure Serg is convinced of our ruse first. "What are you doing here?" I ask, addressing Raul as he grins.

Raul is flanked by five of his men. False protection for Serg as those men are here for me, not him.

"Haven't you worked it out yet?" Serg speaks instead, unable to contain his excitement.

"Worked what out?" I snarl.

Serg taps his chin with his finger. "Oh, that this house belongs to Raul, not me. He kindly offered me his home. We have a lot in common—money, drugs, and losing our fathers because you killed them," he sneers, his sarcasm disappearing.

I remain calm because that's what would be expected of me if this were in fact a true ruse. "So what happens now?"

Raul laughs, but there is nothing pleasant to the sound. "You give him what he wants, and then he gives me what I want."

"And what do you want?" I question, turning to face him. Here's the moment of truth. Will he double-cross me?

He cracks his knuckles. "To deliver the same fate you gave my father."

I can't remember the last time I saw him, but I certainly don't recall him being this intimidating. For the first time since I made my decision, I'm a little anxious for what's headed my way.

"But don't worry, big brother," Serg pipes up sarcastically, oblivious to our plans. "I won't let him hurt you…too badly. You've still got a lifetime of suffering ahead of you."

It's the ultimate standoff between Raul and me. Serg is merely annoying static in the background. Raul seems to be playing along—for now.

Serg's phone rings, and I vaguely hear him talking. All I can focus on is Raul. He is staring at me, ensuring I'm aware of all the things he plans to do to me. I respect him for it.

"Excellent," Serg exclaims with a clap. "The deed is good. All I have to do is sign it, and that orphanage is mine."

Those words break my standoff with Raul, and I return my focus to Serg. I don't say a word. It's anticlimactic that way, and I like to see Serg stew.

"You do realize that once I sign it, everything you love will be destroyed, and Raul will probably have you wishing he'd kill you once he's done with you."

"Not everything," I oppose. "Sign it and give me Irina."

Renata has undoubtedly told him about my affection for Irina, so this won't come as a surprise to him. He sent Renata to work in his favor, but in reality, she's worked in mine.

Serg is oblivious to everything because he thinks he's outsmarted me this one final time.

With a few quick clicks, I hear the noise which indicates mail is sent. It's done.

I silently beg Mother Superior for forgiveness as this asshole is now the legal owner of the place she's put her heart and soul in for the last forty-plus years.

"It's done?" Raul asks as he too is eager for things to move along.

Serg nods with a victorious inhale. "Mother!" he calls out while I clench my fists.

A moment later, Zoya enters with Irina. When I see Irina, I feel sick to my stomach. She is dressed in a red dress with white stockings and black polished Mary Janes. Her face is slathered in makeup, and the white ribbon secured in her hair just sets off the costume which makes her look like a doll—a non-living thing that people can abuse and use without feeling guilty.

It's been over ten years since I last saw Zoya, and I thought that maybe I'd feel something when I saw her after all this time. But I don't.

All I see is the same selfish, weak woman who has her karma coming.

She is wearing a green pantsuit with a gold belt. High heels seem a little inappropriate because we're indoors, but it's just like her to show off her wealth wherever she is.

Irina runs to me, her tiny legs unable to keep up with her speed. "Ski," she cries, throwing herself into my arms when I crouch low to hug her. She smells of perfume, a scent belonging on a woman, not a child.

A feeling of utter completeness comes over me as I embrace her. It now feels like a part of me has returned. "Are you okay?" I ask, squeezing her tight.

"Irina 'kay. Home now?"

"Yes, цветочек. You're going home," I reply, elated it's finally time.

No matter how tight I hug her, it'll never be enough, so I gently pry her little fingers off my neck and level her with a stare. I need her to leave this place because I never want her to see what I'm about to do.

"My friend Willow is waiting to take you someplace safe. Okay?"

She violently shakes her head. "No! Ski."

"Shh, I know you're frightened, but I promise, Willow will look after you. She is an ангел."

Irina's eyes widen in awe.

"And an ahreл would never hurt you, right?"

She shakes her head.

"Good girl. I'm so proud of you for being so brave. Go now, I'll see you soon." Pressing a kiss to her forehead, I close my eyes, utmost sadness plaguing me as I realize this is the last time I'll ever see her, and at this moment, I wish I could live for her.

I wish to see her grow, be happy, and live the life she so deserves.

And by making the choice that I have, she'll be able to do all those things. I just won't be here to see it.

Reaching for my pocket square, I gently rub it across Irina's lips, rubbing the red lipstick away. I do the same to the bright blue eye shadow. She is to never wear this stuff again. Dressing her up this way, like a Christmas ham, reveals to me what Serg intends for every child at the orphanage.

Some individuals will like them to look their age—young innocents—while others will like them to be dolled up so when they subject them to their sick atrocities, they'll forget they're merely babies, pardoning them for abusing minors.

"Goodbye, Irina. Always remember…I love you."

Irina's eyes fill with tears. Can she hear the finality in my tone?

She reaches for the pocket square and tucks it into the pocket on her dress. The gesture touches me deeply. At least she'll have something to remember me by. "Irina loves Ski. Always."

Standing, I nod to Serg that this is done.

Raul steps forward. "I will bring her to your friend."

Is this a part of the plan?

Desperately, I attempt to read his face, hoping it'll help me interpret if he's telling the truth. But what choice do I have?

"I'm the only one who knows the codes to the alarms," he says, delivering the hint I needed.

For Saint, Max, and Pavel to come in, he has to let them in. I saw the security system on his door. No one is getting in unless he wants them to.

Nodding at Irina to trust me, she looks up at Raul and follows him out of the room. I never take my eyes off her, and when she's gone, I exhale in relief.

She's safe. I did what I promised her and Mother Superior I'd do. Now it's time I see to the rest.

"Did you like her outfit?" Serg asks, patting Renata's head.

"No, I did not like it," I spit, disgusted.

Looking at Zoya, I curl my lip. "How could you condone this? You're as sick as he is."

She wrings her hands in front of her, her gold bracelets jingling. "They're young. They won't remember."

I really wish I could say I'm surprised by her comment, but I'm not. This was her mentality toward me. But I did remember. I remembered every single thing.

"And you?" I look at Renata, whose eyes are downcast. "I saw the fight in you, yet you allow him to treat you like a dog. Do you think he loves you? He chose you because you looked like Willow. Nothing more.

"When something shinier comes along, you'll be disposed of. Trust me, I know," I share, speaking from experience.

She risks a glance my way, and I see it—a flicker of regret.

No matter that she was sent to seduce me, I know she isn't completely dead inside. She felt something, which makes having her pay for her sins not only hard but sad as well.

"He's right, dear," Zoya says, which has me returning my attention to her. What is she up to? "I know my son. He will grow bored."

"Mama! Enough!" Serg spits, not impressed with her meddling. But she's not done, not by a long shot.

"It's true, мой сын. I know you."

It seems the hatred between Renata and Zoya runs both ways. Both women want to be Serg's number one. Even though Renata is submissive with Serg, that doesn't mean she'll be with anyone else. I've seen this firsthand.

"You know nothing," Renata whispers under her breath, but we all heard it.

Serg looks down at her, stunned she'd speak when he didn't grant her permission, while Zoya smirks. I don't understand why that is.

"I told you," she says. "She's disobedient. How do you expect to control her? She isn't for you. You need a good Russian girl. She is nothing but an American."

Serg opens his mouth, but Renata jumps up, proving Zoya right because Zoey wouldn't dare break her orders until I commanded it. She's headstrong. I've seen it, and being a submissive takes a different kind of person.

Renata's feelings for Serg are real, but instead of being his submissive, she wants to rule alongside him; she wants to be his equal. I saw the pleasure she took in the bloodshed she caused at the orphanage. She isn't interested in being his lesser. She wants to be matriarch, and she's challenging Zoya for the job.

"Fuck you!" she cries, charging for Zoya. "This American is about to kick—"

But Renata never gets to finish her sentence, and I understand why Zoya was smirking. She knew how this would end. No one was going to threaten her position, the one she worked or, rather, killed for.

It happens so quickly that I don't believe my eyes. But the deafening boom is confirmation that Zoya reached into her pocket, pulled out a pistol, and shot Renata without hesitation.

The blast rockets Renata back three feet, where she lands on her back with a thud. It takes a second, but the front of her white dress begins to stain red. She appears in shock, her eyes wide as she looks around, attempting to gauge what just happened.

Serg blinks as he also appears stunned, but adrenaline soon takes over, and he runs to where a dying Renata lies. "No!" he cries, skidding on his knees as he cradles her against his chest.

Renata gasps for air, looking at her Prince Charming for help. But it's too late for her. Zoya's aim was a perfect bull's-eye straight through the chest.

"You're going to be okay," he says, rocking Renata awkwardly because there is no way to properly hold your dying lover.

"Why?" he screams at Zoya, who holds the pistol limply by her side.

"Because she was trying to take you away from me," she

replies with little emotion. "I won't lose another son. I won't be alone. Not again."

And there it is—the truth. She is afraid of being alone.

Renata was a threat to Zoya, and she needed to eliminate that threat. I meet Zoya's gaze, and for the first time in my life, I nod, showing respect for the same choice I would have made. It's survival of the fittest in this world.

Renata would have never made it.

But that doesn't mean she's off the hook. Her time is coming and soon, because one of Serg's men pulls out his gun and aims for Zoya. Promptly, I duck for cover as the room erupts into gunfire.

Serg's man acted about a minute too late, but it's the distraction I need because frantic footsteps come careening into the room with more gunfire exploding. I use the dining table as cover, peering under the legs of the chair to see what's going on.

A flurry of men are shooting, ducking for cover as Serg's men fire back. Their ammunition is impressive as I don't think Raul prepared for the Uzi one of Serg's men produces. They continue shooting at one another, unsure of what's going on.

I'm sure Raul instructed his men of the plans, but Zoya concealing a pistol and shooting Renata was not a part of the agreement. It's shoot first, ask questions later as she's just changed the course of everything.

All they heard was gunfire, and the reason for that single shot is running low to the ground to avoid being hit as she attempts to flee down the hallway.

But there is no way I'll allow that to happen.

"Alek!" I hear Saint call out.

"Don't let her get away!" I bellow to be heard above the deafening noise.

Renata's chest rises and falls sluggishly as she puts up a good fight. Her neck is twisted at an awkward angle, but her eyes are locked with mine. Tears trickle down her cheeks, and at this moment, I realize Saint was right. She deserved a chance for redemption.

But Serg has no reservations about propping her up and using her body as a shield when shots are fired his way. She vibrates uncontrollably as the bullets penetrate her body.

I scream in revulsion, disgusted with what I see.

Her long golden brown hair is stained a bright red. The life in her gone because she fell for Serg's lies.

He tosses her body aside as though she's nothing but trash, and like Zoya, he keeps low as he runs for a doorway at the back of the room. That's my cue to follow because he's not getting away.

With a deep breath, I spring up but keep low, hoping I don't get shot as I chase after Serg. Pavel and Max are using a large buffet as cover. "Zoya went down the hallway. Find her!"

They nod, and with a single look alone, we wish one another luck.

With adrenaline coursing through me, I kick open the door Serg exited out of to see it leads to the gardens. I follow in pursuit because I can see him up ahead. He has a good head start, but I'm fast.

Vicious barking sounds in the distance as Raul also has to ensure his prize doesn't get away. It won't be long until they're hot on my trail. Pushing with everything I've got, I use the anger inside me as fuel and chase him down. He veers left when a large greenhouse comes into view.

He is meters away, forcing me to move my legs faster. He turns over his shoulder, and when he sees I'm in hot pursuit, he realizes the time of reckoning has come. Just as he yanks open the door, I dive for him, sending us both careening to the floor of the greenhouse.

He thrashes madly, attempting to fight me off, but now that I have him, I'll never let go. We roll around on the paved path, wrestling for dominance, but when I grip the back of his head and slam his face into the concrete, the contest is over with quickly.

Snaring his hair, I yank him up and drag him toward an elaborate lattice flower wall. He twists, attempting to hit me, but I'm running on pure rage and dodge his attack. I need to restrain him, and as I frantically search my surroundings, my focus slips for a split second, which allows Serg to connect with my ribs.

A pained breath escapes me, and my fingers slip from Serg's sweaty hair. With a roar, he spins and punches me in the jaw. I stagger back a few feet and crash into ceramic potted plants, which is perfect.

Collecting a fistful of dirt, I toss it into his face as he comes charging for me, blinding him. I could have used one of the pots and smashed it over his head, but seeing his white suit soiled, literally, was too good to surpass.

He rubs his eyes, desperately attempting to see. I elbow him in the nose and grip the back of his collar, dragging him toward the flower wall. He screams, twisting and turning, but he's not going anywhere.

I visually search the work bench that is within reach, and when I see a jar of nails and a hammer, I realize I'll have to improvise. Shoving Serg against the wall, he flops forward, still unable to see, which works to my advantage as I lunge for the hammer.

With frantic fingers, I send the jar of nails toppling over, but I seize what I need. Just as Serg advances for me, I headbutt him, and when he bumps into the wall, I extend his arm to the lattice and nail his hand to the wood.

His screams are music to my soul.

He swings out with his free hand, which just won't do, so I punch him in the stomach, before almost yanking his other arm from its socket and repeating the same action to his other hand.

He attempts to break free, but the thick nails hold him tight. His guttural shrieks have me smiling.

The symbolism of him being crucified is not lost on me. I wish I had more time to admire the visual perfection, but the need to kill him is so overwhelming, I need to take a deep breath. I don't want to rush this, so I take a moment to calm down.

"долбоёб! блять!" Serg curses, his eyes flickering as he finally clears the dirt from them. When his vision clears, I wave with a grin.

"Sorry I dirtied your suit," I quip, laughing when he spits at my feet.

"My men will be here any moment," he exclaims, blood

dripping from the wounds to his palms as he wiggles.

Tsking him, I leisurely take off my jacket and fold it, placing it on the work bench. "Your men are dead. They couldn't fend off an old woman with a pocket pistol, so they don't stand a chance against grown men."

"I have an army at my disposal," he declares, arrogantly. "A hundred men are storming the house right now. Your friends are dead!"

I fake horror for a second, wanting to give him a false sense of hope, but that soon transforms into a husky chuckle. "That's your problem. You talk big, but you just can't deliver. You don't put in the hard work.

"You expect others to do it for you. I suppose some professionals may label it as younger child syndrome, but I label it as you being a stupid asshole."

Serg's bravado begins to diminish, feeding mine.

"I know you only brought three men because this was supposed to be an easy deal. But once again, you've underestimated my hatred for you.

"You didn't really think you'd win, did you?" I ask, cocking my head to the side.

"What are you talking about?"

"I'm talking about how I made a deal with Raul," I reveal, watching his bloody, dirty face twist in horror. "I'm talking about how Raul suggested his house, and you fell for it because again, it was the easy way out."

"You lie!" he screams, refusing to believe this ultimate betrayal. "He'd never do business with you. He hates you!"

"Yes, this is true, but I offered him something he couldn't resist."

"What?" Serg asks, blood dripping into his mouth from his broken nose as he gasps for air.

"Me," I reply coolly, rejoicing when I see the moment he realizes he's royally fucked.

"I don't believe you."

"I really don't care what you believe because you won't see morning once I'm through with you."

As Serg squirms, screaming obscenities, I search the greenhouse, smiling when I see a pair of garden shears along with other sharp tools.

Running my finger along the tools, I sing, "Eeny, meeny, miny, mo." When I stop on an aluminum hand weeder, I thump my fist over my heart twice because it's exactly what I wanted to use. I plan on starting small and working my way up.

Carefully removing it from the shelf, I flip it over and over, ensuring Serg can see the pointy tip. "Do you realize the mess you've made? This vendetta has ruined my life. You killed people I care for. You stole my life from me."

"You killed my father! You stopped me from living a normal life," he yells, eyes frenzied. That problem will be solved soon enough.

"If you think growing up with Zoya would ever be normal, you're even more delusional than I thought. She just shot your…Renata," I say, not knowing what to call her. "Why did you drag her into this? You clearly felt nothing for her because you just used her as a human shield."

"As if you felt anything for your subjects," he sneers.

"I did," I reveal, unashamed. "They were special to me in

their own way, and I showed them kindness the only way I knew how.

"You're here, crucified to a wall because you seek vengeance for a man who deserved everything he got. He wouldn't have fought for you. He would have used you. Boris was an animal, and I put him down and not once have I ever regretted my actions."

Serg's hollowed cries are most rewarding. "He was a good man!"

"Oh, Jesus Christ, between you and Zoya, you'd think he was moments away from being ordained. Your father was a cruel man. He was stupid enough to let a child take his life."

"Why? Why did you do it?"

We all want answers to the questions we desperately ask. But my response isn't going to put Serg's mind at ease.

"Because he deserved it." And he did.

He could have ruled with kindness, but instead, he helped nurture the monster budding inside me. I often wonder what would have happened if he had been kind. Would this darkness have eventually won regardless? I suppose I'll never know.

"Killing him was easy, and so will be killing you."

Serg doesn't deserve any further explanation. I'm not here to unburden his demons.

"What did you do to Irina? Why did she tell me she's scared of the dark?"

Serg laughs diabolically as it's his turn to torment me. "Because she asked me to turn off the lights when I sampled the goods. Try before you buy, right?"

His comment winds me up, and I clench the tool in my hand. Her painted face and revolting outfit flash before me, and I wheeze a strangled breath.

"Someone else had beaten me to it, though. Maybe you?"

Could it be true? Is this why she's so withdrawn? Could her past be so abhorrent, she has shut off from the world? Suddenly, I need to know. I need to know if it's true so I can find every motherfucker who hurt her and make them pay.

With an animalistic roar, I advance and thrust the weeder into his eye socket. The prongs pierce his eyeball, and with a wet twist, I yank hard. The optical nerve prohibits me from wrenching it completely from the socket, so it dangles over the lower lid, flopping like a fish out of water.

Serg is unable to vocalize his screams because the pain has robbed him of his voice.

"You've just made your death all the more painful." I refuse to believe him, but what if he's telling the truth?

If he speaks lies, then there is only one way to deal with such deception.

Lunging for the garden shears, I shove my fingers into his mouth, pull out his wriggling tongue, and hack through it with the shears. It drops to the floor with a slosh.

"That's your punishment for speaking such filth! You piece of shit." I stab him in the right pectoral with the shears.

Blood seeps through his red shirt and stains the lapel of his suit.

His muffled cries are everything I need, and no matter how many times I kill him, I'll never be satisfied. But what he said about Irina, he deserves to go to hell knowing that he's lost.

"That deed will be obsolete with you dead. All of this was for nothing. You lose. You die alone, and your memory will be forgotten. Your vengeance was for nothing. You got played. I win…again."

Holding my pinkie finger up toward his good eye so he can see my ring, I smirk. "Say hello to your father for me."

"See you in hell," he mumbles incoherently as he no longer has a tongue. He has figured out that for me to make a deal with the devil, only my soul in payment would do.

We both lose, but I only smile a winner's grin.

Unzipping his pants, I jar open the shears and slice off his vile cock. His muted screams do nothing to ease the anger inside me.

If what he said about Irina is true, this hideous appendage had harmed her beyond repair. And it would have had no qualms about ruining the lives of so many children he planned to exploit.

Bright red blood spurts from the wound, in rhythm with this frantic heartbeat. At this rate, he'll bleed out in minutes. But that seems too merciful.

With the flaccid muscle in my palm, I thrust my hand into his mouth and yank down on his bottom jaw. "Open wide."

He frantically tries to bite me and writhes hysterically, but I shove his cock into his mouth and force his jaw shut. When he refuses to swallow, I pinch his broken nose, staring him in the eye—an eye so much like mine.

Eventually, he gulps in mouthfuls of air because he can't breathe, where I then shove two fingers down his throat, forcing him to gag on his severed appendage. Elbowing him in the stomach, he inhales and chokes on his cock.

His throat bulges as it's blocking his airways, and I watch with a smile, wanting it to be my face he sees as he takes his last strangled breath.

What a way to die—death by choking…on one's own cock.

His face turns from red to purple, his breathing ragged as he struggles for air. His hot blood splashes all over me, and all I can think is, *what a shame, he's ruining my two-thousand-dollar suit.*

With a few jerky twitches, a noisy wheeze leaves him before he stops moving, and his chin flops forward. A strand of bloodied spittle splatters onto the ground. Gripping his hair, I yank his head backward, ensuring he's dead. Feeling for a pulse, I soon realize there isn't one.

My hands tremble as I drop the shears to the ground.

Stepping back, I examine the mess I've made—what a work of art.

Inhaling and exhaling, I wonder what the right protocol is. I just fed my half-brother his cock, and he choked on it. I do the only thing I can do.

I burst into maniacal laughter.

My sides hurt from how hard I'm laughing. I don't remember ever feeling this amused or…relieved. It's done. He can't hurt Mother Superior, the sisters, or the kids ever again.

"Holy fucking shit."

Turning over my shoulder, I see Saint enter the greenhouse, admiring my handiwork. He is bloody, but he appears fine, so the blood is someone else's.

He stands by me, and a pained *oomph* leaves him. "Where's his dick?"

"Down his throat," I reply as though we're discussing the weather. "He insinuated vile claims about Irina, so I decided to show him what I thought of them."

Saint nods casually. "Well, your brother was always a cocksucker."

"Half-brother," I correct, appreciating his sarcasm. "Zoya?"

When he doesn't reply, I know she's fled.

"Let's go. Max and Pavel have the car."

"Willow and Irina?"

"Safe," he assures while I sigh.

There is no way I can accept death knowing Zoya is free, and I need to know if Serg spoke the truth about Irina.

As I stare at Serg's crucified form, I take it as a sign from God—I need to find Ella and beg for forgiveness. I should have never let her go.

The deal is off.

Raul has probably fled anyway, seeing as our "plan" went to shit.

"Who shot first?" Saint asks as premature gunfire was not agreed upon.

"Zoya," I reply with regret. "She shot Renata because she was threatened by her."

"No wonder you're so fucked-up."

I don't argue.

With one final look at my handiwork, I smile as this is one of my finest kills because he deserved it. I don't know if he had a backup plan in regard to the orphanage, but I'll do everything in my power to find out.

Saint turns, and I follow, unbelieving I've been given a second chance. If Zoya hadn't intervened and messed up our plans, things would have turned out a lot differently. I suppose in some ways I should be thankful.

But as Saint suddenly freezes and curses, I realize there are no second chances for a man like me.

"I hope you weren't leaving," Raul mocks, and when I hear a snarl, I understand the hounds found me.

Saint backs up, his lips twisted in a scowl when Raul enters with a frothing Doberman by his side. I know Saint is armed. He may not have a gun, but he would have something to defend himself. And so does Raul.

"My issues aren't with you, Saint. Even though you were the one who shot my father, I know you were only following orders.

"So I'm offering you the chance to leave. Unharmed."

Saint shakes his head. "I'm not going anywhere without him."

This man's loyalty knows no bounds. I don't know what I ever did to deserve his allegiance, but I'll forever be thankful for it.

"Saint, go," I order, locking eyes with Raul.

"Yes, Saint, go. You didn't think I'd let your beloved out of my sight, did you?" And just like that, the game has changed.

"I have men following her, and she and Irina will remain safe. But I only have to make a phone call and that'll change."

"Motherfucker!" Saint curses, lunging forward.

Raul smirks, loosening the slack of the leash on his hound who leaps forward, snarling.

I won't allow this, not after we've fought so hard. "Saint, you promise me you'll find Zoya and do what I can't." When he hesitates, I press. "Promise me!"

"Fuck!" he bellows, fisting his hair in frustration as he too realizes there is no out this time. "I'm sorry, Aleksei."

I shake my head slowly. "You have nothing to be sorry for, мой брат. Keep them safe for me. With Irina—"

"I'll look after her. You have my word," Saint affirms.

He understood what I shared with him about why I cut off Serg's offensive member. If what Serg said is true, then I know he will find those who are responsible and make them pay.

"When the time is right, tell Ella that I—" But I don't know what to say.

However, Saint nods in understanding. "I'll tell her."

"Thank you, Saint. I'm truly sorry for everything I ever did to you. I know I'll never have your forgiveness, but please know, I wish I could have done so many things differently.

"You're the only true friend I've ever had."

Saint's jaw clenches, and I know even now, with all hope lost, he's still attempting to find a way to get me out of here.

"Go. Thank Pavel and Max for all that they've done."

"Alek—"

"Please, go. I can't save them, but you can. You always have."

Two men appear in the doorway, and Raul gestures for them to take Saint away.

"Hands off, asshole!" Saint warns, yanking his arm out of the man's hold as he attempts to drag him away.

We lock eyes, and all I can do is smile at the man who I am so proud to call my friend.

Before he turns and leaves, he does something that has the tears I thought I could never cry well to the surface. "Я прощаю тебя."

I forgive you.

And with that, he leaves, those parting words having me accepting death with a warm embrace.

He has just granted me forgiveness, something I don't deserve, but I'll accept it, nonetheless. Once he's gone, I look at Raul, not ashamed by the tears in my eyes.

"Let's do this then."

Raul grins. His revenge has come.

He hands the lead to the remaining man, indicating he won't need his mutt any longer. It's just us. The man takes the snarling beast away.

Raul takes a look at my handiwork and whistles. "Wow, what a colorful mess. I'm impressed with your creativity."

"Thank you."

Raul cracks his knuckles, appearing elated that his time has finally come. "Why did you kill my father? He spoke so highly of you. You were business partners for so long."

It seems to be the topic of discussion this evening. Why did I kill everyone's father?

If Raul is looking for answers, like Serg, he's sorely mistaken. "Your father didn't know loyalty, so he paid with his life."

And that's all I wish to share.

He appears disappointed as if he expected me to beg for my life and say I'm sorry. But I'm not. I take full responsibility for my actions and accept the consequences.

Raul tongues his cheek, clearly displeased with my reply. "As will you."

Like a stealthy ninja, he spins and kicks me in the face, catching me unaware. I stumble back two steps, cupping my bleeding, broken nose. He launches another attack, displaying his skills in martial arts with a series of high kicks and punches.

I don't stand a chance.

Dropping to my knees, he kicks me in the face, sending me careening onto my back with a thud. My vision blurs, and I groan as this pain is something else.

He yanks me up by the collar and drags me toward a bench where he tosses me onto it like I weigh nothing at all. He leaps on top of it, punching me over and over, not giving me a chance to fight back. But even if I could, I wouldn't.

A deal's a deal and knowing who I saved has me submitting. Flecks of my blood propel in the air as he breaks my jaw, my lip. But it's not enough.

Jerking me up, he presses us nose to nose. "Say you're sorry and I'll make your death quick."

I could do what he asks and make this immeasurable pain go away, but I'd be lying. So I whisper incoherent gibberish.

He leans in close to hear better, and when his ear is close enough to my lips, I pant, "Fuck you."

With a roar, he grips my head and smashes it onto the wooden bench. Nausea rises as he reaches for a small hand rake and slams it into my left thigh. He drags it downward toward my knee, severing material and my flesh.

This would be far more effective if he took off my pants, but that would be too easy. The pain I feel is unbearable, but I don't fight back. I bite down on my tongue, focusing on anything other than him taking turns flaying the skin from my thigh, then breaking bones in my body.

I go back to the best memory I have, and that was meeting Ella. She was so nervous, so perfect. Her laughter, her smile—I concentrate on that and will carry that into the afterlife with me.

My heart begins to slow, and breathing becomes a chore. The sound my lungs are making as they struggle for air has me shakily feeling my body to find a small hoe sticking out of my chest.

My vision is completely blackened, but as I welcome death, I see something I'd never thought I'd be worthy of—a bright light.

Is this the "bright light" people speak of? Am I welcomed into His kingdom, after all?

I don't deserve it, but I take it nevertheless because I now have hope I'll see Ella again. It's peaceful here, and for the first time in my life…I'm weightless, happy.

I've expired and am no more. Aleksei Popov is dead.

But that happiness is suddenly yanked out from under me, and the bright light becomes an ethereal haze as it whizzes farther and farther away until I'm sucked into a vortex of colors and explode into a million pieces.

I'm not breathing, and to survive, I need air to breathe.

But why would I need air…

"There you go," echoes a voice, a voice which forces me to swim my way through the fog and break the surface with a guttural intake of air because he should not be here.

My vision is blurred, but I coerce myself to concentrate and forget the pain. My sight goes in and out of focus like a camera lens attempting to center on a picture, but what I see, I wonder if my lens has been smashed beyond repair.

Raul lays in a crumpled heap on the floor. His rising chest reveals he's still alive—for now. But it's the man who stands by the bench with a grin who has my full attention.

It takes me three attempts, but I attempt to wheeze his name. "Santo?"

"Yes, my friend, I'm here. You took quite a beating."

My injuries can wait. "Why?" I manage to push out on an exhale.

"Oh, you're concussed and probably in shock. You've lost a lot of blood. Let me take you to the hospital."

When he attempts to help me sit up, I recoil violently, demanding answers.

He wipes his bloodied hands on a white handkerchief before he confirms my worst fears. "Because you delivered on your end of the deal. And so must I."

I haven't the faintest idea what he speaks of until the truth smacks me harder than Raul's punches ever could.

Ella isn't in America. She went to Santo and offered herself in exchange for my safety. She convinced him I delivered her as we originally planned, so now Santo is holding up his end. I realize she handed herself over a day early, thinking she was saving us all because she wasn't aware of our plans.

She did this. She sacrificed herself to save Irina, the orphanage, Mother Superior, me...because she loves me. She'd rather suffer the consequences than see me suffer. She thought this was an easy fix, but this was never an option.

However, by pushing her away, I made her believe that it was.

"You're back on top, Alek. I took a photo of what you did to Serg. No one will question your authority ever again. Are you ready to rule once again, my friend?"

I thought I was destined for heaven, but I should have known this life is hell.

"What of Ella?" I wheeze, coming to a half sitting position.

"She's had a change of heart," he replies with a sinister grin.

"What does that mean?"

"It means she belongs to the Macrillo family now."

Like hell she does.

With a newfound strength, I grasp the handle of the rake still imbedded in my thigh and yank it out with a wet squelching sound. Tossing it across the room, I inhale deeply before I grip the hoe in my chest and repeat the same action.

Santo stares wide-eyed. But I don't have time for his gawking.

Jerking him forward by his collar, I unthread his green silk cravat with shaky fingers and tie it over the wound in my leg. It's missed the femoral artery, so I won't bleed out.

"Handkerchief," I demand.

He passes it to me, no questions asked, and if I didn't

know better, I'd say he was scared. Good. He should be.

Reaching into my shirt, I press the handkerchief over the wound to my chest and secure it with my hand as I swing my legs and jump down from the bench.

The entire room spins, but that doesn't stop me from taking my first staggered steps, reborn. I know what awaits me on the other side, and it wasn't hell because in the words of William Shakespeare, *"Hell is empty and all the devils are here."*

I ignore Santo calling out to me and shove his men out of the way who gawk at me like I'm a walking miracle. And I suppose I am. I was dead, but here I am, resurrected and ready to live this life reborn.

My leg drags across the lawn as I step outside, the fresh air against my bloodied skin alleviating some of the pain and allowing me to focus.

Ella sacrificed herself for me even though she believed I didn't want her. But regardless, she wanted me to have my old life back. No one has ever done that for me before, and to know she believes I feel nothing for her—there's no way on earth I'll allow that.

She literally saved my life because if Santo hadn't intervened, Raul would have killed me. He did.

Reaching into my pocket, I retrieve my cell, and with great difficulty, I focus on the screen to call Saint.

"Popov?" he gasps, his surprise clear. "How are you still alive?"

But I don't have time for his questions. "Come...now."

"Okay, we're coming," he says on a rushed breath. "What

happens then?"

Stopping, I lift my face to the heavens and give thanks. He didn't give up on me. Neither did my queen. So, adjusting my crown—the devil's crown, that is—I reply, "We go get my girl."

The Devil's Crown-Part Two
Coming September 2020!

ACKNOWLEDGEMENTS

My author family: Elle Kennedy and Vi Keeland—I love you both very much.

My ever-supporting parents. You guys are the best. I am who I am because of you. I love you. RIP Papa. Gone but never forgotten. You're in my heart. Always.

My agent, Kimberly Brower from Brower Literary & Management. Thank you for your patience and thank you for being an amazing human being.

My editor, Jenny Sims. What can I say other than I LOVE YOU! Thank you for everything. You go above and beyond for me.

My proofreaders—Ellie—My Brother's Editor and Annie Bugeja.

Beta Reader—Lisa Edward. Love you.

My Russian Translator and lifesaver—Lana Kart, thank you!

Sommer Stein, you NAILED this cover! Thank you for being so patient and making the process so fun. I'm sorry for annoying you constantly.

Philippe Leblond—thanks for being my muse!

Ren Saliba—your photography is magic. Looking forward to working on more covers with you.

My publicist—Danielle Sanchez from Wildfire Marketing

Solutions. Thank you for all your help. Your messages brighten my day.

A special shout-out to: Bombay Sapphire Gin, Christina Lauren, Lili St. Germain, Willow Winters, K. Webster, Giana Darling, Callie Hart, Amo Jones, Cora Reilly, Aleatha Romig, Parker S. Huntington, S.M. Soto, K. Bromberg, Tijan (thanks for helping with the blurb), Kat T. Masen, Devney Perry, Tillie Cole, Cheri Grand Anderman, Lauren Rosa, Louise, Kimberly Whalen, Christine Estevez, Ben Ellis—Tall Story Designs, Nasha Lama, Natasha Tomic, Heyne, Random House, Kinneret Zmora, Hugo & Cie, Planeta, MxM Bookmark, Art Eternal, Carbaccio, Fischer, Sieben Verlag, Bookouture, Egmont Bulgaria, Brilliance Publishing, Audible, Hope Editions, Buzzfeed, BookBub, PopSugar, Aestas Book Blog, Hugues De Saint Vincent, Paris, New York, Sarah Sentz (you're my cover go-to queen!) Ria Alexander, Amy Jennings.

To the endless blogs that have supported me since day one—You guys rock my world.

My bookstagrammers—This book has allowed me to meet SO many of you. Your creativity astounds me. The effort you go to is just amazing. Thank you for the posts, the teasers, the support, the messages, the love, the EVERYTHING! I see what you do, and I am so, so thankful.

My ARC TEAM—You guys are THE BEST! Thanks for all the support.

My reader group—sending you all a big kiss.

My beautiful family—Daniel, Mum, Papa, Fran, Matt, Samantha, Amelia, Gayle, Peter, Luke, Leah, Jimmy, Jack, Shirley, Michael, Rob, Elisa, Evan, Alex, Francesca, and my aunties, uncles, and cousins—I am the luckiest person alive to know each and every one of you. You brighten up my world in ways I honestly cannot express.

Samantha and Amelia— I love you both so very much.

To my family in Holland and Italy, and abroad. Sending you guys much love and kisses.

Papa, Zio Nello, Zio Frank, Zia Rosetta, and Zia Giuseppina—you are in our hearts. Always.

My fur babies— mamma loves you so much! Buckwheat, you are my best buddy. Dacca, I will always protect you from the big bad Bellie. Mitch, refer to Dacca's comment. Jag, you're a wombat in disguise. Bellie, your singing voice is so beautiful. And Ninja, thanks for watching over me. To the newest addition, Wabbit; I love your apricot face.

To anyone I have missed, I'm sorry. It wasn't intentional!

Last but certainly not least, I want to thank YOU! Thank you for welcoming me into your hearts and homes. My readers are the BEST readers in this entire universe! Love you all!

ABOUT THE AUTHOR

Monica James spent her youth devouring the works of Anne Rice, William Shakespeare, and Emily Dickinson.

When she is not writing, Monica is busy running her own business, but she always finds a balance between the two. She enjoys writing honest, heartfelt, and turbulent stories, hoping to leave an imprint on her readers. She draws her inspiration from life.

She is a bestselling author in the U.S.A., Australia, Canada, France, Germany, Israel, and The U.K.

Monica James resides in Melbourne, Australia, with her wonderful family, and menagerie of animals. She is slightly obsessed with cats, chucks, and lip gloss, and secretly wishes she was a ninja on the weekends.

CONNECT WITH MONICA JAMES

Facebook: facebook.com/authormonicajames
Twitter: twitter.com/monicajames81
Goodreads: goodreads.com/MonicaJames
Instagram: instagram.com/authormonicajames
Website: authormonicajames.com
Pinterest: pinterest.com/monicajames81
BookBub: bookbub.com/authors/monica-james
Amazon: amzn.to/2EWZSyS
Join my Reader Group: bit.ly/2nUaRyi

Printed in Australia
AUHW010253110820
332053AU00015B/29